I0635177

Only Forever

by

Sophia Ryan

This is a work of fiction. Names, characters, places, and incidents are either the product of the author's imagination or are used fictitiously, and any resemblance to actual persons living or dead, business establishments, events, or locales, is entirely coincidental.

Only Forever

COPYRIGHT © 2016 by Sophia Ryan

All rights reserved. No part of this book may be used or reproduced in any manner whatsoever without written permission of the author or The Wild Rose Press, Inc. except in the case of brief quotations embodied in critical articles or reviews.

Contact Information: info@thewildrosepress.com

Cover Art by *Diana Carlile*

The Wild Rose Press, Inc.
PO Box 708
Adams Basin, NY 14410-0708

Visit us at www.thewilderroses.com

Publishing History
First Scarlet Rose Edition, 2016
Print ISBN 978-1-5092-0739-8
Digital ISBN 978-1-5092-0740-4

Published in the United States of America

Sometimes one lifetime isn't enough...

"Natasha thinks you're *her* hero."

"Why's that?"

"Because you're taking her to bed." Even she heard the jealousy in her tone.

He lifted his hand to the back of her head, let his fingers tangle in her hair. "Well, now, love. Isn't that what you wanted?" Dipping his head, he leaned a little closer, close enough for her to breathe in his exhalation as he spoke. "For me to fuck her?"

Up until that point, it had been mostly teasing between them. But when she felt his guttural "fuck" sink into her skin and lodge deep in her body, the mood shifted. At that moment, she was acutely, achingly aware that she didn't want him fucking Natasha. She didn't want him fucking any woman. Any woman but... No. She couldn't say it. Not even to herself.

"Do you want to?" she managed.

His eyes—lazy, hazy, and unwavering—gripped hers, holding her still. The intensity in their blue depths wouldn't let her look away or speak. She could barely breathe from the way he was looking at her. Time slowed, freezing them in place, mouths inches from each other.

"Breena." His whisper burned into her skin. "You're the only woman I want to fuck."

PRAISE FOR AUTHOR

Sophia Ryan

AND HER BOOKS

SIX DAYS OF YOU

"Think of the most bizarre example of mistaken identity and it won't even come close to the scenario that author Sophia Ryan has put together in *Six Days of You*. The author packs in plenty of surprises for the reader. The chemistry between the two characters is well developed with a nice bit of heat."

~*Rachel's Willful Thoughts, The Romance Reviews*

"I really like this book! Daryl and Lily find each other and then HOLY Hotness begins. And oh man if that was the best lovemaking. Seriously, I was like... Holy gees! Wow! And Wowsers! Then of course there is drama…"

~*Cyndi Garcia, Goodreads Reviewer*

DIRTY LITTLE SECRET

"A sweet romance of the first true love and the happy ending we are all looking for. The emotions are strong and vividly provided for the reader to experience and share."

~*Delane, Coffee Time Romance & More*

SHE LIKES IT IRISH

"*She Likes It Irish* is my new favorite read. I absolutely adored this book. The plot and story development will have you turning the pages just to see what happens next!"

~*Sarah Horwath, Fresh Review*

Dedication

Only Forever is dedicated to the awesome individuals
who played a part in breathing life into it.
My heartfelt thanks go to:
Gerry Twomey, my encyclopedia, who
introduced me to the world of archaeology, endured
with humor and grace my endless questions and off-
topic ravings, and reminded me that flawed reality
trumps perfect fantasy every time. Any archaeology
errors discovered are mine and mine alone.
Shelby and Kelly, my most enthusiastic cheerleaders,
my loving friends, who read and reread every iteration,
made helpful comments, asked leading questions, and
dried my tears and didn't visibly roll their eyes at the
plot and character drama that often straitjacketed me in
a padded cell of anguish.
My coach, SG, who kept me true and on track
with the relentless crack of her velvet whip.
Kristin Godfrey, my first reader,
whose excellent advice and keen insight
saved this book from taking a tragic turn.
Laura Colleran, my expert on Irish vocabulary,
who confirmed and corrected my word choices. Any
word errors or modifications are mine and mine alone.
My family and friends, whose gifts of love,
support, understanding, patience, and time allow
me to indulge in my passion.
Diana Carlile, my brilliant and brazen editor, who
fought for this book even though it meant breaking new
ground and old rules. You rock!

Love is composed
of a single soul inhabiting two bodies.
—Aristotle

Chapter One

The heater in the B&B's tiny honeymoon suite was cranked up to high, and Dominic Sullivan, even bare-assed naked, was roasting in the bed. He kicked the comforter and blanket off and yanked the sheet out from the bottom and sides of the mattress so he could stick his feet out and ward off a heat stroke as he lay spread-eagled, waiting for his wife to finish her shower.

Sabrina had been taking a lot of hot showers since they'd arrived in Ireland—three or four a day. She'd acclimate to the wet cold. Or wear more clothes. A pity, really. He liked her in the teeny tiny bikinis she'd worn in Maui during the first week of their honeymoon. He'd never had so much trouble controlling his libido. Not that he'd had much more luck controlling it while they were in California where they'd met or the few days they'd spent here in the land of his birth finishing out their honeymoon.

Desire for what they were going to do when she got out of the shower arched his hips against the crisp, white sheet. With an impatient groan, he slid his hand under the sheet, fisted the base of his rod, and stroked upward, his thumb and finger pinching the swollen head. Eyes closed, breath held in his lungs, he pictured Sabrina's tongue licking up his shaft, her mouth sucking his head, like she had when she woke him at dawn. His new wife was horny all the time. Horny for

1

him.

"Fuck this waiting," he said on a heavy exhale. "I want her now."

He was out of bed and headed to join her in the shower when his mobile rang. A quick glance told him it was his boss. Jack Ford hadn't been pleased about him missing nearly a month of work to get married in America and go on a honeymoon, and that was on top of being gone for four months to conduct the field school in L.A. where he'd met Sabrina.

Fortunately, he was too valuable to fire. They both knew it. And he had weeks of vacation saved up. He also knew Jack wouldn't ring unless it was urgent.

He picked up. "It's the sharp, flat end of the shovel that goes into the ground."

Jack chuckled. "Cocky SOB. I don't know why I—uh, hang on a sec." Dominic heard him cover the phone and call out, "Gabe, go drag McCanna's ass out of the pub. We need to get back. Dom, you still there?"

"Ian taken a liking to the local?" he asked with a chuckle. "I'm shocked."

"More like the gal who works there. Which leads me to why I'm calling. Sex games are over, Romeo. Time to get back to work."

As much as he was enjoying his and Sabrina's "sex games," as Jack put it, the possibility of a new dig intrigued him, and the urgency in Jack's faded Texas twang made it sound like a good one. "What's the job?"

"The road project on the outskirts of Anamcara turned up a human skull. Carbon dating estimates tenth century. Early scans indicate the whole area's a graveyard, with potentially four- to five-hundred HRs."

"Test trenches?"

"Bones in every one of 'em, four- to five-foot deep. We've been hired to extract and relocate. Government's giving us three months. I need my best people on it to meet schedule and budget."

"Meg running finds?"

"Yep."

"Is she okay? You know, about my marriage?"

"She took it hard but seems to have settled down."

Ian told him she hadn't taken the news of his marriage well, that she had knifed everything in his caravan when she'd found out. Her reaction had weighed heavy on his mind ever since.

They'd been lovers seven years ago, and although he'd hoped for more, she'd made it clear she wasn't interested in serious. So they'd kept their friends-with-benefits relationship in the years since very casual and very secret.

Why his getting married would cause such a violent reaction from her he didn't know. After all, at the heart, they were good friends. Surely, she'd be happy for him that he'd found his one. But, hell, if he could figure out women, he'd be a millionaire instead of a poor shovelbum.

"Sean back yet?" Sean O'Neill, one of his best friends, had been sent to America to run a field school in New Mexico and had fallen in love with Kristin. They'd been on their honeymoon when Dom left for California, so it had been a while since they'd seen each other.

"He and Kristin are already here at the site. She'll be working in finds with Meggan."

"Sabrina'll need a job, too."

"Already been approved. She'll work in media."

3

"Ian good with it?"

"Hell, he was all but drooling at the photography and videography experience on her resume. Question is, are *you* good with it?"

A surprising pang of jealousy jabbed him at the image in his head of Ian and Sabrina working alongside each other every day. He eyed the bathroom door. His wife was a beautiful, sexy, vivacious woman. The type of woman Ian couldn't resist. But their friendship, their brotherhood, was stronger than Ian's innate need to fuck every hot woman he came in contact with. The knowledge tempered the jealous pang. "I trust Ian with my life. I can trust him with my wife."

"If you say so. You know him best."

"They're so much alike, they'll either work brilliantly together or kill each other."

"You've, uh, warned her about him?"

"She knows enough."

"All right, then. See you and the wife tomorrow morning."

Dom heard the shower go off and felt an urgency to end the conversation, but he had one more thing to say. "I'll talk to Sabrina and ring you with our answer."

Jack made a noise that sounded like he was swallowing his tongue. "You're gonna *ask* the wife?"

"She and I make decisions together."

Jack scoffed. "Never thought I'd see the Holy Hell Trinity beaten to their knees with the pussy whip. First Sean, then you. The day Ian falls, I'll lay down nekkid in the dirt and wait for the good Lord to take me home cuz the end of the world is on us."

"Ian McCanna settle down?" Dom snorted dismissively. "We won't see that miracle in our lifetime."

"Yeah, you're right. Ring me in a couple hours to let me know when you'll be here." Jack hung up without another word.

Dom set his mobile down, his body strumming. About the job. About getting back to work in the field he loved. Shovels turning up the smells of rich earth, the sounds of trowels and brushes patiently scraping away the past's layers from long-buried secrets, the heat of the sun on his head and cramped back, the excitement of figuring out who had lived on the spot before him, and how they had lived, loved, died.

He'd missed it, being on an Irish dig, with his team. His friends. It was where he felt good. Capable. Purposeful. At home. It thrilled him. Every bit of it. Even the long hours, the almost constant layer of grit and sweat and sun on his body, the sometimes unfriendly and unpredictable weather. He belonged on a dig, with his hands in rich Irish soil, where God himself knelt to pray.

When HQ assigned him to run the field school in America, he had fought it, tried every tactic to get out of it, because he hated to travel outside his beloved *Eire*. But he had gone, and it had turned out to be the best thing he'd ever done. He came home a husband. With a wife.

Husband. Wife. Even after weeks of saying the words, thinking them, feeling them roll around in his heart, they still felt enormous, weighty, and as real and precious as the matching gold bands they wore to show the world they were one.

Joy surged through him like a kid at Christmas. Fuck. He had a *wife*! And she was everything he'd ever wanted—beautiful, smart, fun, loving, sexy. He groaned, remembering just how sexy.

"Wife, I'm starting without you," he called out.

"You do, husband, and I'll have to punish you," she called back.

The words brought a smile to his face. Her punishment was always more pleasure than pain. "Bring it on."

The door opened, and his wife stood naked in the doorway, pale gray afternoon light caressing the toned and tanned curves of her silky-smooth body, her rosy puckered nipples, her golden hair caught up in a clip.

"You think you can take a little punishment?" she said, her tone and grin as suggestive as the sparkle in her blue eyes.

His throat was suddenly so dry he could barely swallow the drool in his mouth. "I can."

"We'll see." She pulled the clip from her hair and shook her head. The long waves fell thick and loose about her shoulders and down her back.

His grin grew as she sauntered across the room toward the dresser, eyeing him as she did, her smile saying she was up to something new and fun and erotic. Again. As usual. As always.

She had schooled him in the ways of kinky sex. Nothing extreme, but even Ian the master would be impressed at his newfound skills. Not that he'd tell him. He was long past the age where he boasted about his sex life to Ian or asked him for sex tips.

Sabrina pulled open a drawer and extracted a small multicolored silk bag, then crossed to the bed with it, stopping at the foot of the mattress.

Desire simmered in her eyes as she grabbed the

edge of the sheet and inched it toward her. The brush of the sheet against his skin, against his cock, ramped up his desire. She pulled until the sheet was in a heap on the floor then put her bag on the bed.

"What are you—"

She put her finger to her mouth and shushed him. "No talking. You're being punished."

Her voice was stern and low but still managed to be teasing and sexy as hell. The sound of it plucked nerves in his body that were already zinging with lust.

She reached into the bag and pulled out a colorful scarf, a yard long and half a foot wide, with beads, gems, and sequins woven through it, tassels at the ends.

Dom's heart pounded just thinking about what it was for.

She gathered it up in one hand then, keeping hold of one end, tossed it toward him. It unfurled through the air, the end landing lightly on his head. He reached his hand up to brush it away.

"Leave it," she insisted.

His hand dropped back by his side.

Like she had done with the sheet, she drew the scarf toward her. The tassels tickled his face, his chest. The embedded artifacts scraped his nipple, his stomach. The silky material brushed over his already sensitive cock, and he felt the resulting chills all over his body.

She tugged it slowly down his thigh, his knee, his shin, his ankle. When it cleared his foot, she slid the scarf under his ankle and tied a knot there. Then she tied the ends of the scarf to the bedpost. Using a second scarf, she repeated the maneuver on his other leg, and before she finished, his swollen cock throbbed.

She sauntered toward his head with a third scarf.

To help her complete her mission, he flung his arms out on the bed. She tossed the scarf downward and dragged it up from his legs, across his crotch, up his chest, and down his arm to his hand, then slipped it under his wrist and tied a knot.

Her nipples were hard, rosy points, and God, he wanted to touch them, suck them, tease them with his tongue. His hand was so close to her breast he reached out to touch it. She jerked back as if she had anticipated the action.

"No touching. You're being punished," she said and pulled on the scarf to secure it to the bed post. With the same slow torturous pace, she secured his other arm with a fourth scarf.

Spread eagle by force, he pressed his hips up, showing Sabrina what she was doing to him, showing her his readiness. Her gaze traveled to his cock, and she licked her lips. His body jerked in response, his rod aching to feel the firm lick of that tongue, the softness of those lips, the brush of her hands, and the dewy heat of her pussy. The whole time she hadn't touched him with anything other than the scarves, and he was already out of his mind horny. Did she know what she was doing to him? The sexy smirk teasing her mouth told him she knew, all right, and was happy about it.

Practically panting, he yanked on the tethers, but they prevented him from reaching her. "I want to touch you."

The low, sexy sound of her laugh trilled over his skin. "What part of 'you're being punished' don't you understand?" She reached into her bag and pulled out a silky black blindfold. Slipping the blindfold over his head, she settled it into place over his eyes. Other than a thin rim of silver light around the edge of the material, he couldn't see a thing.

Dom felt her shift forward over his chest, felt her breath at his neck. "Maybe you need me to say it in Irish." She bit his ear. "Baby, get ready for your *pionós*." She climbed off the bed.

Her pronunciation was off and there were more fitting words she could have used, but he loved that she had tried. What he didn't love was that this situation he was in had triggered an overwhelming, almost painful feeling of vulnerability in him. That vulnerability made his entire body clench, trying to prepare for whatever was coming.

He felt the hungry weight of her gaze, felt her coming touch as a hot pulse running through him. Then the foot of mattress dipped slightly, and he felt her between his legs. He shivered as she crawled ever closer toward his crotch.

She ran her nails up the inside of his legs and lightly pulled his balls. His body jerked, his breath catching in his throat.

"I'm going to make you come. But I haven't decided how. Either with my hands." She trailed her fingers up the underside of his hard length and pinched his head. "Or my mouth." She licked her tongue up his cock from base to tip. "Or my pussy."

Whichever one she chose, his cock was so hard he'd likely erupt the second Sabrina did more than breathe on it. He was about to give his answer when her mouth came down on his cock.

"Ahh," he cried out, thrusting his hips off the mattress and his cockhead deeper into her mouth. She sucked him, licked him, stroked him, nipped him, then backed off. "No! Don't stop!"

A long, torturous time passed where the only thing touching his skin was the hot air blasting from the heater. Being this exposed and vulnerable made him feel anxious and achingly turned on.

His breath caught in his throat again when her fingers trailed lightly up his length, from his balls to his cockhead. As her hand left his tip, her other hand stroked upward from his balls. She gripped the base of his shaft and stroked upward, keeping her movements slow and deliberate. She had put some sort of oil on her hands, and the warm slick friction was heating him up and making the cum rise from his balls. He thrust himself toward her, trying to get her to go faster so he could reach his nirvana. As if she knew he was rushing her, she stopped.

Dom clenched his jaw to hold back the tormented moan wanting to erupt from his lips. He thrashed on the bed, trying to get loose so he could grab her, bury himself deep, and explode inside her, but she had tied him tight. Tighter than he initially thought.

She straddled him, holding onto his shoulders and grinding against him. He could feel the pulsing heat between her legs. Her ripe, swollen pussy was ready for him, and he needed to sink into her, balls deep.

"You didn't tell me what you want." Her voice was ragged and rough, and her desire scented the air, telling him he wasn't the only one affected by their sex play.

Knowing she wanted him as much as he wanted her ramped up his arousal. He was out of his mind with longing to thrust his tongue inside her, lick her clit, suck those wet pussylips, bring her pleasure, make her scream his name as she released into his mouth. Mmm.

He could almost taste her.

"I want *you*." His hips pushed up against her, again and again, showing her what he wanted.

"Tell me you want to fuck me."

Her words sent licking, hungry flames racing through his veins. Sabrina loved dirty talk during sex. He'd never been good at it, but he was learning, and the blindfold helped. "I want to fuck you, Sabrina. I want to fuck that sweet, wet pussy 'til you scream."

"Then do it." She rose up and settled the tip of his cock at her wet opening. He roared as she lowered herself onto him, her tight pussy gripping him on the long ride down. He wanted to let go and come right then but knew there was more pleasure in holding on. And he had never taken his pleasure before making sure she found hers first.

She rocked against him, her hands gripping his shoulders. The slap of flesh against flesh as she rode his dick enhanced the groans of their lovemaking, each stroke sending liquid fire through his veins. He yanked against his restraints, wanting to guide her, hold her, meld with her body, but he couldn't.

Her hips increased speed, her nails bit into his shoulders, her breath panted fast and hard on his face as she moaned. "Fuck me."

Dom thrust upward as best he could, bucking violently on the bed, giving her what she needed. And she took it all, her sounds revealing the pleasure she was getting from having him deep inside her.

Suddenly, his blindfold was ripped off and he was staring into her eyes, shiny pale blue ringed with dark blue, hazy and heavy with her arousal. They held tight to his as the first flutter of her orgasm teased his cock, then squeezed it hard, again and again, her groans increasing his upward thrusts to a frenzied pace.

The coiled tension in his belly broke free, and he shot into her, again and again, his growls of pleasure mingling with hers. The sounds and smells and sensations of their intimate joining flooded him with love and satisfaction, and he swore the room shook at the power of their release. His strokes slowed, then ceased altogether, and he collapsed on the mattress, sweaty and spent.

She dropped her damp forehead to his, her lungs gasping for breath like his, her heart pounding like his. She fused her mouth to his as her body quivered, and her lips devoured him, giving and taking. Then the kiss slowed, softened, and her hands cupped his face. He wanted to hold her in his arms, but he was still tied up.

"Sabrina," he whispered into her mouth. His mind groggy with sex, he couldn't find the words, English or Irish.

"You liked it?" she asked.

He pulled in another deep breath and let it go. "Yeah."

"How did it feel to be tied up?" she asked with a grin.

"Like you feel when the sheet's tucked in at the bottom."

The smile left her face. "Trapped and panicked?"

"Yeah."

She sat up, still connected to him, hurt flickering in her eyes. "Because you don't trust me? Trust that I wouldn't hurt you?"

"No, because I like to touch you when we make love. I like to see your face as I move inside you, as your body trembles beneath mine when you're coming. I like to know that what I'm doing is making you feel good. Bound and blind, I couldn't do any of that."

"And it had *nothing* to do with your not being in control of the situation?" she said with a wry grin, her eyes sleepy after her orgasm.

He grinned. Sabrina knew him so well. "Well…"

"That's what I thought." She kissed him. "You came out of it okay." She glanced at the headboard. "But the bed didn't."

Dom glanced up at the deep right slanting of the bed and laughed. "Yeah, I guess everything's okay, other than *you* breaking the bed, but I can't be sure until you untie me."

She laughed and climbed off him, moving to untie the scarves from the posts. "So the lesson is…"

"I can trust you, always, and I can give up control, some of the time, with no mal effects." He untied the scarves from his wrists as she crawled to untie his legs.

"You can trust me, Dominic. I'll never do anything that makes you regret sharing your life with me."

"I'll never regret it," he said, watching her untie the ankle scarf, her curvy ass pressed toward him, high enough that he could see his cum trickling out of her pussy. His flaccid cock twitched as she crawled to his other ankle, and he enjoyed the same view from the other side.

The second he was free, he sat up and pulled her into his arms. With her snuggled against him, her arm around him, fingers caressing his chest, his arms around her, he was complete.

"You're mine, Sabrina."

She smiled. "I'm yours."

"Only mine," he said.

"Yes."

That four line verbal bit, or a variation of it, had been their routine since the first time they'd made love at the field school. He knew she loved him, but hearing her say she was his and only his comforted him. Because the truth was, he still couldn't believe she was his.

Although they'd fallen hard and fast for each other, they were as different as night and day on most issues and wanted different things out of life. However, at the core they were the same, a perfect match—what he lacked she had, and vice versa—and he knew they'd run forever on love alone. The words they recited were a reminder to both of them that they belonged together because they wanted to, a promise to always stay that way.

As he caressed her head, her back, he wanted to shout out loud at the pure bliss flowing through him. Nobody deserved this much happiness, but he'd somehow managed it. Their bond, though new and delicate, was strong. He'd be with Sabrina for all of his days, this happy, this in love. He knew it.

Nothing could come between them, destroy what they had…ever.

Chapter Two

Sabrina had ridden with her window half-down since leaving the train station, hoping the bracing Irish air would slap her awake enough to be charming and social with her new team. Although she had been sad to end their honeymoon early, she was stoked about starting her first commercial dig, with her husband by her side. And she had relayed her excitement to him—in various positions—as they stayed up late the night before to pack. Then they were up early this morning to catch a series of trains to Anamcara, the rural dot on the map that would comprise their home and work lives for three months. She closed her eyes and smiled, her body still buzzing with satisfaction at the wonderful man in her life.

Her eyes popped open again at the cacophony of shouts up ahead, and she lowered the window all the way and stuck her head out, the wind whipping her hair back. Their SUV was still too far away from the turnoff to the site for her to see clearly what was going on, but she knew what it was. Teammate Rusty Cullen, who had picked them up from the station, had warned them about the protest raging at the dig site, and they had looked it up online the day Jack called.

The group calling itself *Chosaint*, a word Dominic said roughly translated to *protect*, had been protesting outside the dig site since the MacDougal Archaeology

Company, MAC for short, management team arrived almost a week ago to set up camp.

Chosaint was protesting the government's continued support of the road construction project through the strip of land even though ancient human remains had been unearthed, thus making it—in their words—a sacred site. They were also protesting that the MAC team, which had been called in to exhume the bones, would be relocating them in a nearby cemetery after they'd been analyzed to learn more about who the people were.

In the news piece, the group's leader, Ena Flanagan, had sworn they would do everything in their power to stop "the barbaric attacks" against the graves and those buried there. "Souls at this sacred site are crying out for resolution," she'd said. "We won't let them down."

The sharp crack of gunshot split the air, and Sabrina drew her head in. She pressed the button on the door panel, and the window slid up. The action muffled the sounds of the protest but didn't stop the thought banging around in her head that she, Dominic, and Rusty would need a miracle when their SUV drove into the chaos.

Rusty eased off the accelerator as they drew closer and let the SUV crawl through the crowd of fifty or so protestors blocking the road that led to the fenced-off and gated archaeological dig and camp sites.

She barely felt Dominic taking her hand in his, but when he squeezed it, she let her gaze leave the enraged faces behind the black tint of the window to find his. Dark eyebrows furrowed over his amber eyes, and a tight line narrowed his normally full lips.

"I won't let anything happen to you," he said.

"I'm not worried." She gave him a bit of a smile to prove her words. "I grew up in L.A. I've seen worse at Gucci's twenty-percent-off sale."

The sound of glass shattering yanked her attention to the windshield, which now looked like a spider's web on the driver's side. The windshield held together, but another well-placed rock could take it out, leaving them vulnerable to up-close-and-personal attacks. Maybe she'd spoken too soon.

Like a pack of hungry zombies, the protestors swarmed the SUV, slashing it with sharp shouts and curses. Some held signs with threatening messages and shook them at their windows, some going as far as banging them against the vehicle. Others shouted curses, using their fists as punctuation marks as the vehicle crawled past.

The sounds of the attack reverberated inside Sabrina, and her heart pounded in her throat. Adrenaline surged through her, putting her muscles on alert, preparing them for the call to fight or flee.

"Fuck." Rusty growled the obscenity. "They're gonna fucking kill us."

Her gaze darted to the teddy bear of a man white-knuckling his way through the war zone raging beyond the tinted windows. His cinnamon eyes in the rearview mirror were round and intense, his lips tight and pulled back over his teeth in concentration. Sweat trickled from his scalp beneath the curly russet Mohawk, down the sides of his ruddy face, and followed the dragon tattoo snaking down his neck into his T-shirt.

To his credit, he didn't hesitate, even when the protestors blatantly stepped in front of the vehicle to force a stop. If they succeeded in stopping them, it would be flipped. According to news reports, they'd done it two days ago to another MAC vehicle carrying their fellow archaeologists to the site. One had been sent to the hospital with internal injuries; another had emerged uninjured but so spooked he'd asked for an immediate transfer to another dig.

A half dozen MAC-paid armed guards stood sentry at the gate. At least a dozen more clashed with the more aggressive pockets of protestors, pushing them back from the road and the gate so the SUV could get through. As Rusty slowed for one of the guards to open it, a hand slapped the window on Sabrina's side, and she reared back in surprise.

A face peered in, nose pressed to the glass. Long, unruly, flaming red curls, stabbed here and there with blades of silver, framed a heart-shaped face that was stamped with a hard look, as if a smile would break it in two. The stormy gray of the eyes, masked somewhat behind the tinted windows, sparked with anger and with something deep, dark, and secret that made Sabrina's insides crawl.

It was the leader of the protestors herself. Ena. Irish for fire or passion. The grip of the woman's stare paralyzed her, and she felt violated, as if her insides were being strip-searched, those probing eyes digging for information. Sabrina wanted to look away, but she couldn't. The woman's tight lips moved, as if she were imparting something of great importance.

Suddenly, Ena's eyes rounded, and her mouth hung open in shock, as if she'd seen something inside Sabrina that stunned her. Seconds later, a guard grabbed her arms and pulled her away from the vehicle. The connection between them broke with an audible crackle, and Rusty gunned it through the gateway.

Sabrina gulped for air, realizing she'd been holding her breath for the moments she'd been trapped in the woman's gaze. The discomfort that had enveloped her faded the farther they got from the gate, but a ghostly after-feeling remained, as if the encounter had dug up and resurrected something ancient inside her that had been buried deep eons ago.

"There it is," Dominic said as they neared camp. "Home."

She forced herself to focus on his words. On the few tents and two dozen or so small travel trailers arranged like blocks across the wide green field ahead of them. On the people milling about here and there. On the present. Not on what had just happened.

"Home," she echoed and managed a small smile. For his benefit.

This foreign land did not yet feel like home to her. Ireland was wet and windy, cold and gray this time of year, a watercolor painting that had been left outside to brave the battering elements, and so unlike the purifying heat of the California sun she was used to. She hadn't been warm since they'd arrived.

The past felt alive here, like it had never moved on but stayed to jostle and chortle with the present over a pint or three. The constant presence of unseen entities dusted her senses with filmy cobwebs, making her skin crawl, and no amount of hot showers had been able to wash away the feeling or thaw the chill that seemed to go bone deep.

Her gaze took in their temporary home. The green carpet of richness that was the camp site swept gracefully down toward the distant river, stopping abruptly at the stark swath of dirt marking the dig site. The field had been stripped, gouged, and leveled with tooth bucket cranes and dozers in preparation for a road to go in. Somewhere in that sea of brown, a construction worker had dug up a tenth-century human skull.

As field supervisor, it was Dominic's job to lead his team to precision cut into that land, to unearth the remains of whatever ancient civilization lay there and bring its story back to life. Her job as media assistant was to preserve the site in video, photographs, and narrative, capturing everything dug up as well as the methods of doing so. Together the two of them—and the rest of the team—would add to the body of human knowledge.

Dominic took her hand in his. A relaxed smile replaced the tightness that had thinned his lips minutes before, as if being among his people had eased him, body and soul. It was clear he was glad to be back on a dig, back with the core team he'd worked with off and on since high school, back *home*. The man so disliked being out of Ireland it was a shock to her that he'd accepted the appointment to run the field school in California.

An even bigger shock was that at twenty-two she was married to him and working on a dig in Ireland. The sum of her practical knowledge of archeology consisted of participation in the archaeological field school Dominic had been in L.A. to run. The hosting university had hired her right out of college to photograph and videograph the dig for a recruiting video and brochure. She'd enjoyed the experience, despite the drawbacks of living in a tent, sleeping on the ground, showering communally and intermittently, having her skin baked into jerky, and wearing an ever-present layer of grit that burrowed into her skin and every imaginable crack. And she'd fallen in love with Dominic, hard and quick, almost instantly, like it had been planned by a higher power and they had no choice but to go along with it.

Whether by force or choice, she was happy. Ireland was lush and beautiful and mystical, and she was glad to be able to work with her husband on this new adventure, but she longed for the time when she could entice him to take a job where they could travel the world to work on various digs. MAC had itinerant positions, and she had already started planting the seed in his mind that it would be challenging and fun. But for now, she would enjoy being with him here for three months. And what newlyweds didn't hope for that kind of twenty-four/seven togetherness?

Rusty pulled the SUV to a stop near several other MAC vehicles, and Sabrina zipped her sweatshirt against the chill before climbing out. Dominic wore a short-sleeved T-shirt and so did Rusty, and neither seemed to feel the cold. She was wishing she hadn't packed away her coat.

She patted Rusty's shoulder. "Nice job getting us out of that mess."

The color in his face had returned and at her compliment went even redder. He grinned and stared at his feet. "Yeah, well, I was bricking it."

"We all were," Dominic said.

"Have the protestors gotten into camp?" she asked Rusty.

His eyes found hers, studied her. "You're safe here, Sabrina. We won't let anything hurt you." He patted her arm twice and nodded once, as if "that was that," then lumbered away, leaving her and Dominic to gather their belongings and make their way to their trailer.

"He means it, you know," Dominic said. "Everyone on our team will protect you."

She chuckled. "What have you told them about me that they're so sure I need protection?"

"It's not that. You're part of the team, and my wife." He said it as if it were obvious.

"And that's all that matters?"

He nodded. "We have each other's backs. All the time. No matter what."

"The Irish shovelbum's code?"

"Sorta," he said with a grin. "More of an extended family."

Hopefully not a family like hers.

They walked past the few tents toward a clearing with a small blackened pit set with firewood, where it looked like the team had already built a bonfire or two. A motley grouping of plastic, metal, and wooden chairs faced the pit, as if waiting patiently for the team to gather there to stare at the fire. And to tell wild Irish tales? Nearby, two large gas grills stood ready for weekly cookouts. Beyond that were the small trailers where the team lived.

Guys called out to Dominic here and there with a hello or welcome back as he explained to Sabrina about the setup, the team, and daily life as a commercial archaeologist. It was evident the team was keeping its distance to give them time to get settled in.

They headed down a row of trailers, and he

dropped his bags on the ground in front of one. "Welcome home, wife."

The sound of him calling her *wife* still sent her heart into a spin, and she'd had nearly a month to get used to it. Dropping her bags next to his, she wrapped her arms around him and kissed him. "It's perfect."

Apparently, he had arranged with headquarters to get the nicest trailer available so she'd be comfortable. Ian McCanna, one of Dominic's best friends—and her new boss—handled the delivery and setup for them.

"Hold that thought," he said. "It could be as fugly as a can inside. Ian's not much of a decorator. As long as there's a bed inside, he thinks it's home."

"I have to agree with him on that. Let's hope it's a strong one. The bed, I mean."

He chuckled. "I can see how you'd be worried about the strength of the bed after you broke the one at the—"

She slid a hand to his crotch and cupped his balls, squeezing gently. "Hey, I wasn't alone in that bed."

"No, you weren't." His eyes darted right and left to make sure no one was around to witness their PDA. "The mattress is brand new, Sabrina, the bed is strong."

"Let's test it." Untangling herself from him, she took a step toward the door. Shooting him a sexy look over her shoulder, enticing him to follow her, she headed up the steps. He hooked a finger in the belt loop of her jeans and pulled her back, lifting her up into his arms.

She laughed and wrapped her arms around his neck. "What are you doing?"

"Carrying my wife over the threshold of our new home."

Remembering the old lore of the threshold being fraught with danger, as well as Ena Flanagan's wicked stare earlier, she figured it wouldn't be a bad idea to cover all their bases when it came to warding off evil spirits in this place. "You worried evil spirits will attach themselves to me and bring bad luck to our marriage?"

"Nah, I don't believe in that hocus-pocus malarkey. I just like holding you in my arms."

He kissed her, and she drew him closer, slanting her head to better fit his mouth on hers, to better allow his tongue to possess hers.

"Let's take this inside." She reached out to open the door as he climbed the steps.

"'Bout time you got here, *skiver!*" a female voice called behind them.

One foot on the threshold, Dominic halted, his body tensing, as if he'd been zapped to the core by a bolt of lightning. His cheeks flushed, his eyes lit up, and his mouth softened into a smile. He backed down and turned, Sabrina still in his arms.

The tall, thin woman who had spoken was more striking than pretty and anything but ordinary. A high, tight ponytail barely contained the explosion of sunset red corkscrew curls that cascaded to mid back. While the severe style would be unkind to most women, it highlighted the creamy paleness of her freckle-dusted and well-formed face.

Sabrina didn't know whether the peachy stain on her cheeks was sunburn, anger, or passion. But the predatory grin stretched across her wide mouth and the bright, heavy-lidded eyes the color of roasted hazelnuts crawling all over Dominic meant she wanted him.

And Dominic's pounding heart against her ribs and

racing pulse at the base of his throat? His warm smile? His eyes locked with the redhead's? What did they say?

A jagged-toothed knife of uneasiness sawed her nerves. Dominic hadn't said anything about an ex being at the site, but it was clear by their reactions they had been lovers. This woman would be a problem. She felt it in her gut.

Her gaze left the ginger and collided with the man beside her. He looked like he belonged on the lens side of a Hollywood movie camera. An inch or two taller than Dominic's six feet, with wide shoulders and a lean, cut physique, he had an easy, terminally wild confidence about him that said he was serious about fun and pleasure and had the scars to prove it. Thick, short hair a rich dark chocolate was nearly black except for the threads of caramel and gold ribboned in by the sun.

But it was his eyes that arrested her breath. They were the same aquamarine as hers. That pale blue gaze, sparkling with appreciation, held hers as his full made-for-pleasure lips lifted in a flirty smile. This had to be Ian. Dominic's physical description of him had been accurate but lacking.

Dominic set her on her feet and headed toward the ginger. They almost flowed into each other's arms, like the action was old hat to them. The woman whispered, "Welcome home, Dom," to which he replied, also in a whisper, "Good to see you, Meggie." Their hug butted up against intimate before he eased back and turned to Ian, embracing him warmly, clearly happy to see him.

"How was the honeymoon?" Ian said as he pulled back. His sultry smooth lilt brought to mind sweet Irish honey simmering with a dram of smoky Irish whiskey over a low flame. She could almost taste it on her tongue, feel it doing a slow burn down her throat and settling hot between her legs.

"Fantastic." Dominic grinned and put his arm around her. "I highly recommend it."

Ian locked his gaze with hers again, his grin never leaving his face. It felt as if he had rifled through her head and was scanning her memories of the almost-unending sexcapades she and Dominic had enjoyed.

"And you brought me this lovely souvenir." Ian took her hand as he spoke and drew her toward him, his gaze darting back to Dominic for a split second before it was back on her, slowly caressing every inch of her suddenly flushed skin. "Thanks, mate. Just what I wanted."

A tolerant smile lit Dominic's face, and he pulled her back to him and enveloped her in a possessive hug. "This is Sabrina. My wife." His lips brushed her cheek. "Sabrina, this is—"

"Ian McCanna," she offered confidently.

Ian cocked one eyebrow, and his eyes sparkled. "And how would you be knowing that?"

"Dominic warned me—I mean, told me—all about you."

"Lies, all lies." He grinned, as if he were pleased Dominic had talked about him and that it hinted of his devilish and incorrigible nature.

"It was *mostly* good," she teased.

"Well then, it's definitely lies."

Unable to ignore the lure of his smile and charm any longer, she chuckled and stepped out of Dominic's arms. "Good to meet you, Ian." She extended her hand, because for some reason, she needed to touch him again. "Or should I say, boss?"

He stepped forward at the same time she did and took her hand. "Good to meet you, Sabrina." Then he surprised her by easing her into a full-frontal hug.

It started as a tingling just under the skin at her chest, an itch she couldn't scratch. The feeling sank deeper and spread like an infection through her veins. Then it swelled, morphed into something more, something she had never felt before, and her arms wrapped tighter around him, gripping him.

His heart beat a thunderous pace, and with a shock, she realized she felt it *inside* her chest, nestled against her thundering heart. She felt enveloped inside a wave of bliss with him, where there was nothing but exquisite sensation flowing through them and around them, filling their lungs and stealing their breath.

Pure euphoria exploded inside her, like the peak of an orgasm. Her fingers gripped his back, his hers. She exhaled, then inhaled sharp shuddering breaths, and he did the same.

One of them, maybe both, murmured, "Oh, God," as the feeling yanked them under. She bit his chest to stifle her cry of ecstasy.

For the first time since arriving in Ireland, she was warm. Too warm. Sizzling, in fact. A trickle of sweat rolled down her back, into the waistband of her jeans, between her ass cheeks.

Dominic was talking, but his words were muffled, like he was far away or she was under water. It didn't matter though. She didn't want to hear. She only wanted to feel, to drown in the tide of pleasure swallowing her. She was dizzy with the feel of Ian swirling inside her, like she'd had too much to drink.

But then, suddenly, as if her soul were being ripped

from his body, she was pulled away. It yanked the breath from her lungs, from his.

"Don't creep her out, mate," Dominic said, tucking her back against him. "She just got here."

It was evident Ian had felt something, too. She could see it in his eyes as they locked on hers. The smile was gone. The cocky confidence shaken off. Leaving him as open and raw as she was. He dragged a deep ragged breath into his lungs, and she did, too, realizing she'd been holding hers.

Away from Ian, the pounding pace of her heart was settling back to normal, but her breathing was still lacy, her body still shaky, her insides still humming with traces of euphoria that made her feel rubber-kneed drunk. All she wanted was to be back inside whatever had swooped around her and Ian, entwining them, filling all the grief-dug holes in her soul, making her whole, and it made her antsy that she couldn't be.

She swallowed hard, and Ian's throat bobbed as he did, too. With trembling fingers, she unzipped her jacket to cool the flames roasting her body. Ian wiped his brow with one shaking hand and stuffed his hands into his jeans pockets.

His tongue darted out to wet his parted lips, as if he would try to speak, but no words followed. She had forgotten how to speak, too. The thick silence stretched on and on, and they couldn't seem to break their gaze.

Dominic was her husband. She wanted no one else. Would never cheat on him. But there was no ignoring the sensations Ian's touch had stirred in her. With him, she had experienced the orgasmic flutters of her first full, soul-merging connection. The feeling made her both ecstatic and ashamed. Hopefully, no one but the two of them was aware of it.

Someone called Dominic's name, and he pulled her with him to a tall man with squirrely blond hair walking toward them, his arm around a petite woman with long brown hair. Dominic let Sabrina go and embraced the man just as heartily as he had Ian, accepting his welcome and congratulations. Clearly, this was the other longtime friend, Sean O'Neill. Sean didn't know it, but he was her new best friend. His timely appearance had broken the weird connection between her and Ian before things had taken a nasty turn.

"Let me introduce you to my wife, Sabrina," Dominic said when they'd eased back. He put his arm around her and tucked her close to his side. The pride in his voice when he said "wife" brought her the rest of the way out of whatever otherworldly lust dimension she'd slipped into while in Ian's arms.

"Ah, the third tip of the Holy Hell Trinity," Sabrina jumped in, relieved that her breath and her voice had returned. "Hi, Sean."

"Hi, Sabrina." Sean gave her a quick hug, then stepped back, his gaze flying to Dominic. "We need to have a talk, you and me, about just exactly what you've told your wife about the HHT before I let her talk to mine." He pronounced HHT as heat.

"I heard that," said the woman she supposed was his wife Kristin by the possessive way she slid her arms around his waist.

Sean's arm wrapped around her shoulder and held her close. "Darlin', this is Dom and Sabrina Sullivan."

Kristin stepped out of Sean's embrace and hugged Sabrina. "I'm so glad to have another American in the group." She pulled back. "Where are you from?"

"L.A.," Sabrina said. "You?"

"Albuquerque."

"So, is the meth problem really that bad?"

"As bad as the cocaine problem in L.A."

They laughed, and Kristin hugged Dominic. "Good to finally meet you. Sean's told me more than I ever needed to know about you and this Irish heartthrob." She bumped Ian when she said *heartthrob*, and he grabbed her, picked her up in his arms, and juggled her a couple of times, making her giggle.

Slivers of jealously shot through Sabrina's veins, and everything inside her wanted to yank Kristin out of his arms.

"The way I hear it, you begged for more," Ian said, smiling at Kristin. "Especially for stories about my sex life to, you know, spice up your bedroom activities."

Kristin laughed. "I have the real thing with Sean. Why would I need your fairy tales?"

"Ouch! And I thought Irish women had sharp tongues." Ian set her on her feet as everyone chuckled. "They've got nothing on you Yanks."

"Good thing you prefer women with bite." The words slid out of Sabrina's mouth, unplanned, unwelcome, and with more of a spicy spin than was appropriate. Dominic had never said anything of the sort about Ian, but somehow, she knew she was right.

Ian cocked one eyebrow and met her unflinching gaze with a grin. "Especially in bed." His voice was low, as if it were just for her. His gaze scanned her, head to toe, before finding her eyes again, the invisible caress making her stomach clench with desire.

Every thought in Sabrina's head converged into one primal thought—all the fun stuff that went on in

Ian's bed between him and a woman with bite. She swore she could read the same thoughts from him that seemed to be flowing to her in a wave of simmering heat.

"Thought you were coming in yesterday." Red broke the silence, allowing Sabrina to tear her gaze from Ian's, where it bumped into Dominic's. Guilt heated her face as his eyes danced between her and Ian, as if he'd noticed…something.

Shit! What the hell was the matter with her? Since stepping foot in this country a bit over a week ago, it felt like the person she knew herself to be was morphing into something she didn't recognize.

Dominic turned and acknowledged the gingernut's question. "We couldn't get a connecting train until this morning."

She cuffed him on the shoulder. "We were beginning to think living in America had turned you soft."

"I assure you, he's harder than ever," Sabrina said before Dominic could respond, and wrapped her arms around his waist. His face flushed red, and Ian didn't even try to contain a snicker as she continued. "Dominic told me all about Ian and Sean, but he never mentioned you."

A flicker of what looked like disappointment sparked in the woman's eyes seconds before Dominic cleared his throat. "Sabrina, this is Meggan O'Garra. Meg, Sabrina—my wife."

Sabrina noticed something in his voice, a cautiousness, a pause in his introduction, as if he wanted to make it perfectly clear who she was.

"Hello, Meg." Sabrina offered a polite smile with

her greeting, but taking in the woman's decidedly unfriendly gaze, she did not extend her hand. Meg didn't either. And a hug wasn't even a consideration.

"It's Meggan. Only Dom calls me Meg."

"Oh, yeah?" she said and turned to Dominic. "What did you do to earn that high honor?"

"That's personal," *Meggan* interjected and shot Sabrina an *I-fucked-him-first* look. The corners of her mouth lifted slightly into something that resembled a smile, but Sabrina sensed no warmth in it, no sincerity, only hatred, secrecy, and gloating.

"So, you're a photographer," Meggan said, abruptly changing the subject. "Any digging experience?"

"Yes. You?"

"I'm the finds supervisor, and I'm in the trenches with Dom."

Her meaning was clear, both to her and to Dominic, judging by how quickly his arm tightened around Sabrina, as if to show their solid bond.

"Interesting," Sabrina said. "In the U.S., finds supervisors are usually too busy processing the finds to be involved in daily digging." She didn't know shit about what was usual at U.S. digs. Dominic had said something similar at the field school, and she'd taken it for gospel.

"Yeah, right?" Kristin said. "I've discovered they do things differently here in Ireland."

"Here in Ireland we do things the *right* way." Meggan's emphasis on the word suggested she'd taken Kristin's and Sabrina's comments as an insult or a challenge.

Sabrina turned to face Dominic. "That's what my

husband keeps telling me." She went up on her toes and kissed him like she was starved for him. The full-on French was as much for Meggan as it was for him, to show her who had Dominic's heart, love, and attention, and who did not.

"I don't think I can stand three fucking months of this," Ian said, and Dominic pulled back from the kiss, as if he were embarrassed by his friends witnessing her passion.

"Three months of what?" Kristin asked.

"The two sets of lovebirds snogging every five seconds."

"You snog more than the four of us put together, so fuck up, *heartthrob*," Sean said, cuffing him on the shoulder.

Like a couple of twelve-year-olds, Sean and Ian did the mock sparing bit until Dominic cut in. "How long have those protestors been here?"

"Since Jack, Gabe, Meggan, and I arrived a week ago to set up," Ian said, still grinning from his row with Sean. "They were vocal, but relatively harmless. They've grown teeth and claws since their leader arrived yesterday."

"Ena Flanagan," Sabrina added. At Ian's nod, she continued. "Dominic and I read that she cursed the last dig she and her group protested. That four team members were injured and two in the government body that approved the dig died."

"She denied any involvement," Ian said. "Claimed it was spirits exacting revenge on those who desecrated the bones and the sacred site."

"Has she cursed us?" Sabrina asked him, remembering her encounter with Ena.

Dominic's arms tightened around her, as if he thought she needed comforting, when in truth, she was simply asking a question. Sparks of jealousy lit Ian's eyes, as if he wasn't happy about Dominic's arms around her. Sabrina pushed aside the thought for being completely ridiculous.

"She said she did," Ian said.

"Curses my arse," Meggan cut in. "The woman's no witch, just fecking *loopers*." She put her hand on Dominic's shoulder, left it there, and squeezed. "Jack wanted to see you when you came in, to catch you up."

"He didn't mean the minute you came in," Ian interjected. "He knows you need time to settle."

Meggan's face flushed as red as her hair, and her eyes shot arrows into Ian. "All key members but Dom have gone over the scope of work. He has to be ready to go in the morning."

"Dom's done this kind of work before," he countered. "I'm sure he'll pick things up pretty quickly." He patted Dominic's back. "Take my advice, mate. Settle in with your lovely wife first. Test the new bed." He winked at Sabrina, his gaze holding hers, and she couldn't hold back a soft grin.

"Meg's right," Dominic said. "I need to be prepared for tomorrow." Almost as an afterthought, he turned to Sabrina. "You don't mind if we see Jack first?"

Sabrina had hoped Dominic would take Ian's advice. But to do anything other than agree would make her seem churlish. He set their bags inside the trailer, and the six of them headed to the pit.

Jack was there with the rest of the team, eleven in all that would grow to more than double that when the interns—graduate and undergraduate archaeology students from various universities—showed up in a couple of weeks. They sat among the team, with Sean, Kristin, and Ian on one side, Sabrina, Dominic, and Meggan on the other.

As the briefing continued, the sun dipped behind the hill and night took the sky. In the light of the half moon, the protestors, right outside the gate, made their presence known. The faint light of their campfire appeared, and sounds of their chanting and drum beats from *bodrahns* rose on the smoke.

A chilly breeze swirled around Sabrina, and she scooted closer to Dominic, his arm going around her. The rest of the team must have felt the chill, too, because two of the guys got up and started the fire in the pit, and everyone better-angled their chairs to pull from the warmth. The flames flickered over the faces of her new team as they talked and laughed and shared wild stories of past digs.

Again and again, Sabrina felt Ian's gaze on her, like a tongue of heat and light licking over her in a random, erotic pattern. Whenever she looked his way, his eyes held hers for a moment, like he was trying to see inside her mind and listen to her thoughts, and then darted away. But his gaze always came back to her, and hers to him, as if they couldn't stop themselves. And each time it made her heart flutter, made her feel naked under his stare…as well as vulnerable, desirable, giddy, reckless, and—most of all—guilty as hell. An unseen force seemed to be pulling her to him, almost as if a rope was around her waist and he was tugging on it.

Otherwise, she was enjoying her first night with the team. They were a fun bunch, with a rough sense of humor and a strong sense of unity. From the stories they shared, she could tell that what Dominic had said about them was true. They counted on each other, enjoyed each other, had each other's backs in good times and bad.

What surprised her was the way they all, except Ian and Kristin, made the sign of the cross as Jack explained they would be finding a lot of bones before the dig concluded. Were they superstitious or religious or both? Whichever it was that prompted the ritual, she liked them and looked forward to making her spot among them. But at the moment, all she wanted was a shower, sex, and sleep, in that order. Maybe not even a shower.

She had stifled so many yawns her jaws hurt, and every time she and Dominic stood and tried to leave the circle, someone pulled him back with a question or a request that he tell a story from his work at a previous site or that she tell them about America.

Meggan was the worst offender of all, and Sabrina fumed at the woman's latest attempt to get Dominic to hang around and to rub their relationship in Sabrina's nose.

"Remember that *sheela* we found at that old church before you left?" she said to him.

He grinned and nodded.

Meggan's gaze darted to Sabrina. "*Sheela-na-gigs* are fertility figures," she said in a snarky, know-it-all tone before quickly continuing with her story. "Sure and it's the best piece anyone's found, but we didn't want to touch it—for obvious reasons." The lusty gaze sliding over Dominic suggested they had every reason to be concerned about pregnancy. His chuckle all but confirmed it.

At Meggan's insinuation and Dominic's almost confirming reaction, jealousy rose like a bellowing dragon in Sabrina's heart.

After the chuckles of the team faded, Meggan finished her story. "So we made Gabe bring it back. And now his wife's up the pole again. Feck! Dodged that one, right Dom."

"Why didn't you want to touch it?" Sabrina asked, her question severing the tail end of the team's laughter, everyone quieting to hear Meggan's response.

The snicker that came from Meggan's mouth suggested Sabrina was the stupidest person on the planet. "Did you miss the part about it being a *fertility* figure?" She spoke slowly, enunciating each word and then chuckling as she ran her gaze across her team, encouraging them to join in her laughter at Sabrina's expense. They grinned, but they didn't laugh.

"Are you saying you were worried about getting pregnant?" Sabrina said, cutting right to the point.

Meggan's grin sharpened. "Always a possibility when fertility figures are involved. Maybe you need me to define the word *fertility* for you?"

Sabrina burned with a desire to scratch the bitch's eyes out, but she was determined to keep it controlled for Dominic's sake. "The dominant prevailing theory today regarding *sheelas* is that the fertility aspects concerned cattle and crops, not humans. Since you're neither an ox nor a stalk of wheat, you had no cause for concern as far as pregnancy goes unless you were having unprotected sex with Dominic. Were you?"

Meggan's mouth hardened into a tight line at the thinly veiled challenge, and her eyes bore into Sabrina

37

with a ferocity that suggested she wanted to make her head explode.

Dominic squeezed her hand, and Sabrina mentally kicked herself for her *faux pas*. She was new to this group. An outsider. What had possessed her to challenge one of its members right out of the gate? One of its members who already didn't like her? A nasty case of good, old-fashioned jealousy, that's what.

The popping fire, the chants, and the drums amplified the itchy, uncomfortable silence that lay heavy over the team.

"Marrying an Irishman doesn't make you an expert on anything Irish." Meggan's words carried a bite, a challenge of their own.

"She's right, Meggan." Ian's smooth voice halted Sabrina's ill-advised retort and dissipated the tension. "I researched *sheela-na-gig* for a paper my final year at uni. Fertility of the land was everything to the early Irish because the survival of their king's reign—and therefore, their own survival—depended on it. Nothing symbolizes rich, lush land better than a woman's womb, the heart of fertility. The vulva is the gateway that guards that womb. *Sheelas* display the gateway to symbolize the importance of its job in protecting the womb, the fertility…the land."

The popping fire was the only sound for a few long seconds until… "Our priest said *sheelas* were a warning for us lads to keep our *willies* in our *cacks*," Rusty piped in, making everyone laugh. "No, truly," he added, making everyone laugh harder.

"My *mamó* has them all over her house," Angus added. "Says they protect her from *olc.*"

"In school, the nuns taught us that *sheelas* are

symbols of…what was it, Ian?" Sean said, staring across the fire at Ian with a grin. "Faith?"

"Nah, mate. You got it all wrong." A trouble-making grin lifted his lips as he met Sean's laughing eyes. "Clearly your mind was on something else when sweet Sister Brigid—God bless her," he made the sign of the cross over his chest, "explained how the vulva, and by extension the *sheela* showing her vulva, represents entry to the womb of Christianity and rebirth into the true faith."

The team chuckled in anticipation, like they'd heard this story before and couldn't wait for the punch line.

"How many times did you have to dip into that entry before the good sister pronounced you born into the true faith?" Angus asked him.

"Ah, Gussy, too many to count," Ian said.

"But not enough to have worked. Am I right there, Ian?"

Before Ian could respond, Rusty piped in. "Aye, that's because Father Michael caught you in the act and expelled you for deflowering the sweet sister."

The team cackled at the bawdy story, and Ian laughed unashamedly. "I keep telling ya mates. She deflowered me."

They laughed even harder.

Everyone but Sabrina, Kristin, and Meggan laughed at his story, at the salaciousness of it. All she felt was sadness and anger that he'd been taken advantage of, had his innocence stripped from him by someone who was supposed to protect him.

Desire to stand up for him, protect him, made her want to shout at all of them to shut the fuck up, then run to him, tug him into her arms, hug him tight, sooth the pain of the scars on his heart and soul that he tempered with sex and jokes. It would hardly be the impression she wanted to leave with the team of who she was, and she didn't want to embarrass Dominic, so she kept her solace to herself.

But Kristin, clearly prompted by a similar thought, leaned over and hugged him. That same angry, jealous fire raged through her at Kristin touching him and him smiling and patting her back saying, "Hey, love, no biggie."

"Nothing's sacred to you, is it, Ian," Meggan said, slashing through the laughter with her bitter tone and glare. "But what else can we expect, with your ma being a witch."

Ian's eyebrow rose at her comment, and he chuckled. "And snap goes the ginger."

At the low chuckles of the team, Meggan's gaze swung to Sabrina. "He's all charm and jokes, but you watch out. He'll put a spell on you, and you won't know it until it's too late."

"Are you speaking from experience, or are you just an expert on casting spells?" The words were out of her mouth before she could stop them. She had all but called her a witch. And by the speed with which Meggan shot to her feet, she'd noticed.

"Don't say I didn't warn you." She threw the stick in her hand into the fire like a spear, making the beast spark and roar, then she stormed from the pit toward the trailers.

In the ensuing silence of Meggan's warning and melodramatic exit, Sabrina's eyes tangled with Ian's. A spell? What she knew about spells could be scraped out from under her right pinky fingernail. But she'd bet her whole right hand she had nothing to fear from Ian.

If anything told her that, it was the little grin and head shake he gave her that seemed to apologize for Meggan's unfounded spewing of vitriol. It was the look in his sexy hooded eyes that said he would always protect her. But most of all, it was the wave of fluent familiarity pulsing between their bodies like an energy beam, linking them, like it had always been there, inside them, their first touch triggering it into the *On* position.

The sound of Dominic's voice and the feel of him squeezing her hand broke their gaze. She turned toward him. Blinked. "Sorry, babe, what?"

"I asked if you were ready for bed."

She smiled. "Past ready."

They stood and faced the team, and he put his arm around her. "All this talk of fertility and deflowering reminds me that I'm still on my honeymoon for another few hours," he said, getting a laugh. "We're off to bed."

Before Sabrina could say her goodnight, Jack got to his feet. "Dom, you wanted to go over the scope and schedule before you turned in."

"Yeah," Dominic said, then looked at Sabrina.

"I'll wait for you at home," she said.

"You sure?"

"Yeah, I'm blasted." She leaned in so only he could hear her. "But if you're not home soon, I will whip out the *pionós* again."

He grinned. "Want me to walk you home?"

Her arms slid all the way around him, pulling him into her. "If you do, I won't let you leave." She reached up to kiss him.

She was going for a long, slow kiss full of lip and tongue and desire and promise for much more pleasure. One that would steal the breath from her lungs, his lungs, and the team's lungs and make him say the hell with his business for the night. But she didn't get it. He pulled back after a brief kiss.

Public displays of affection, especially during work hours and with his team around, watching, made him uncomfortable. He said his behavior needed to be above reproach if the team was to respect and follow him without question, that it was up to him to set the example for expected behavior. The laid-back attitude at the California dig smoothed the edges of his rules over the course of four months and the honeymoon in Maui had destroyed them, but she could see he was back to his rigid Ireland ways.

She left his arms and forced a smile as she faced the team. "See you all in the morning."

As the team responded with a chorus of goodnights and see you in the mornings, she didn't mean to let her gaze dart to Ian. It just did. His eyes stared deep into her, caressing a secret place inside her that no one had ever touched before. She felt the sweet prick of his gaze on her body as she headed for home.

Only…in the dark, she didn't know where home was. Wasn't sure she'd be able to pick it out in the shadows filling the areas outside the fire's reach. Was it down the second row or the third? Was it blue and white? Or green and white? No way was she going back to the fire and admit she couldn't do something as simple as find their trailer. Dominic would think he'd married an idiot. So would the team. They'd pin her with a derogatory nickname depicting her lack of intelligence.

An icy uneasiness skated over her as darkness swallowed her, and she swore she'd give up her new bed for a few minutes with a flashlight. Seconds after the thought materialized, the bouncing beam from a flashlight gouged slashes in the ground ahead of her.

She glanced over her shoulder. Jogging toward her was the tall, dark-haired, blue-eyed, hot-as-sin heartthrob who had infiltrated her system like a fast-moving virus. A rush of tingling heat surged through her, settling full force in her pussy at the sight of the tight blue T-shirt clinging to hard, well-shaped muscles and low-slung faded jeans hugging long, strong legs and wantonly cupping the bulge challenging the strength of the zipper.

She had just met Ian, yet her body ached as if it knew him well and couldn't wait to have him again.

Shit! She hoped to God it was a spell. Spells could be broken. Fate was not as fragile. And this innate feeling of orgasmic déjà vu vibrating between her and Ian had Fate's fiery fingerprints all over it. Fate was unstoppable…or so she'd been told.

Please let it be a spell.

Chapter Three

"Thought you'd need some light." Ian stood in front of her, the flashlight pointing into the sky, the light sprinkling down on them, casting them in soft shadows. "Seeing how you're scared of the dark and all."

"How do you know that?" she asked, wondering whether Dominic had told him about her phobia.

"I read your mind." He tucked the end of the slim flashlight into the front of his jeans, the light beaming upward.

"Yeah, right," she said with a chuckle.

They fell into a leisurely, perfectly matched pace. Just being next to him swirled the heat inside her into tiny tornadoes, flushing her skin.

"Hey, thanks for having my back with the whole *sheela* thing," she said. "Unfortunately, I think you and I made an enemy tonight."

He muttered a curse she couldn't make out because it was spoken in Irish. "She was trying to make you jealous, so she deserved being called on it. But just so you know, she's right, too. Brides were often given a *sheela* on their wedding night to improve their chance of getting with child. Still are."

"Yeah, I know. I just wanted her to admit she wasn't having sex with Dominic."

"Dom wasn't having sex, protected or unprotected,

with her or any woman at that point. He was preparing for the field school in America and didn't want the distraction."

"Sounds like him." Despite their immediate attraction, she'd had to practically force herself on Dominic the first time they'd had sex because he was so intent on ensuring the field school ran perfectly and thought sex would be a distraction. "Thanks. You don't know what it means to me to hear that."

"No, I think I do."

She dug into her pocket and pulled out a pack of gum. "Gum?" She took out a piece and offered it to him.

"I'll half it with you," he said.

"Half?" She smiled at what she knew was coming.

He shrugged. "I always only want half."

"No way! Me, too." She broke the piece in half and held one out to him.

Giving her a raised eyebrow, he took the half she offered and the half in her hand and tucked them into her jeans pocket. The touch of his fingers so near her crotch triggered an involuntary Kegel that swept chills up her core.

"That's not how we do it here in Ireland, love," he said.

"Oh, well by all means, instruct me in proper gum-sharing protocol," she said, humor in her tone that matched his.

"Take another piece from the pack." His voice was low and sexy, like he was telling her to take off her shirt. When she had the piece in her hand and the pack back in her pocket, he continued. "Unwrap it part way." She did as he asked. "Now hold it out to me."

Eyes locked with his, she held out the gum. His hand wrapped around hers, holding it steady as he lowered his mouth to the offering, biting off his half. At the soft touch of his lips brushing her fingers, a trembling breath stuck in her throat.

The simple little move felt erotic and intimate, but no way was he being erotic and intimate with her. Likely she was reading more into it than he intended. He's a major flirt, Dominic had said, so it likely was nothing more than him being him. Nonetheless, she chuckled to scatter the desire swirling inside her.

"Oh, my God! That was a McCanna hack, wasn't it?" Trying to ignore her tingling fingertips where his lips had touched, she slid the other half of the stick into her mouth.

His eyebrow and his smile lifted higher. "A what?"

"A hack, a clever solution to a tricky problem. In your case, a way to get girls out of their panties."

Laughter danced in his eyes. "Are you feeling the need to take your panties off?"

Wow. She'd stepped right into that one. They needed a change of subject...and fast. "I'm stoked to be working with the media team," she said through a grin and started walking again. "How many of us are there?"

"That's called changing the subject," he said, falling in beside her.

"Aye, that it is, mate," she said in an exaggerated Irish accent.

"Stop trying to talk Irish, love. You're just sounding like a pirate."

She laughed at his teasing. "How many did you say?"

"Counting you and me?"

"Yeah."

Concentration gripped his face as he silently counted on his fingers the number of members on his team. He looked her straight in the eye. "Two."

"Two of us? For the entire site? We're going to be busy."

"Actually, Breena, *you're* going to be busy."

Breena. The nickname flowed from his mouth, as if he'd been calling her that forever, and the sound of it made her feel like a field of wildflowers was blooming in her heart. But then he called Kristin, Krissy, Angus, Gussy, Dominic, Dom, so maybe it was just his way of building a bridge to intimacy.

"What will you be doing while I'm doing all the work?" she asked.

"Supervising."

"So that's what they call napping in Ireland?"

"If I have a free moment during the day, I promise you I don't spend it napping."

"Oh? How do you spend it?"

A soft smile grew. "For now, we'll both be digging and shooting. As soon as the bones surface, we'll mostly be shooting. When the interns arrive, I'll leave you in charge at the dig and start editing the videos."

"That's called changing the subject," she said.

He laughed. "Aye, it is."

"I edited dozens of videos in school, so if you want me to—"

"I'll put you to work."

"I actually have a few new approaches I'm eager to try here."

"Oh, yeah?"

"Yeah. When I got the job shooting Dominic's

47

field school, one of my professors put me in touch with one of Britain's top experts on archaeology media."

"Twomey?" Ian asked.

"You know Gerry?" Her mouth curved into a smile remembering the media director working the Bamburgh Research Project who had been so helpful.

He nodded. "I shadowed him three summers ago to pick his brain before I took over the media component with MAC."

Somehow, it felt comforting to know she and Ian had both received advice—probably similar advice— from Gerry. They would work well together.

"And here I was all excited I could offer something brilliant enough to knock your boxers off." *Boxers? Shit! Socks! Why didn't I say socks?* Folding her hands together in front of her heart and ignoring his knowing grin, she bowed toward him. "*Jefe*, I bow to your awesomeness."

"Finally. Someone who recognizes my genius."

"I said awesomeness, not genius. There's a difference."

He put his arm around her shoulders and tucked her into his side. "It's all good, love."

Yeah. It was. But why was he touching her so much? Why was she letting him? As if he'd heard her thoughts, he let his arm drop away from her, but his hand brushed hers as they walked, and tiny sparks traveled up her arm and piled up in her cells every time it did.

"Now explain *jefe* to me," he said. "Is that like 'oh, great one?'"

"Nothing that majestic. It means boss."

"That Spanish?"

"Yes."

"Are you fluent?"

"I do okay."

"How about Irish?"

"Dominic's taught me a little." She couldn't stop a smile from appearing as she recalled the words he'd taught her, words that were best suited to bedroom activities.

"I'm guessing what he taught you has no place in polite conversation."

"What about you?" she said. "Do you speak Irish? Other than the colorful words?"

"Enough to impress the *wee dolls.*"

She chuckled at his affected brogue. "Oh, yeah? Impress me."

He stopped, gazed deep into her eyes, that sexy-as-sin grin still kissing his lips. "Are you sure, love? My Irish tongue has been known to melt the panties off the lasses. I don't want to make you uncomfortable your first night here."

Melting panties. So that's what was causing the inferno between her legs. "You forget I'm used to an Irish tongue. I can handle yours."

His eyebrow rose again, and his clever Irish tongue licked his grinning lips. Her face burned because holy shit that hadn't come out the way she'd imagined.

"You brave enough to test that theory?" he asked.

"Sure, why not. Bring it on."

He took her hands gently in his, linking their fingers, palms touching, tingling, and spoke in a soft, lilting voice words that had her heart flipping a few dozen times and her breath balling up somewhere between her throat and her lungs. She had grossly underestimated the appeal of his Irish tongue. Women's panties weren't the only things that melted at his lilt. Their bones melted, too. Like hers were doing.

She pulled her hands from his and used them to fan herself dramatically. "Okay. That was hot. What did you say?"

"I said..." He reached out and tucked her hair behind her ear and something wild and wicked zinged through her, threatening to sweep her legs completely out from under her. Her skin tingled where his fingers had brushed it. "Sorry I missed your wedding."

All those sweet words for such a short sentence? She swore she'd recognized the words *kiss* and *caress*. Had he told her the truth about what he'd said? It wasn't a conversation she was brave enough to have.

"Dominic was disappointed you and Sean couldn't be there," she said as they started walking again. "But he understood. We've talked about having a party after the dig's over. No way will you guys get out of going to that."

"Have you met his family?"

"Yeah, when we first got here. His dad was great, but his mom..." She shook her head. "She doesn't like me or that he married an American in a Las Vegas chapel instead of in the church. She treated me like I was the devil who had stolen her son's soul."

"Don't get the idea you're special. His mam's never liked any girl he brought home."

"It's clear I'm not what she had in mind for her only child."

"Probably not, but Dom doesn't give a fuck what anyone thinks about him, or you, or how you two live. Because he...loves you."

She heard something in Ian's pause he wasn't saying. "You're surprised he loves me."

"I am."

She stopped, so he did, too. "I hope you're going to explain that."

"Dom's the quintessential archaeologist. The job's all he's ever wanted. He swore he wasn't going to get married, have kids, do anything that would keep him from it."

Her chest tightened, and she swallowed back the stinging ache that rose up from her heart. "He said that?"

He nodded, his eyes on hers.

No wonder everyone seemed shocked and suspicious that Dominic had come home married. Had he had doubts? Did he have regrets? The idea that he might triggered her defenses.

"I didn't trick him into marrying me if that's what you're suggesting. I would have come here with him without being married to him, and I told him that. He's the one who insisted on marriage. I loved him and wanted to spend my life with him, so I said yes. I knew going into this relationship that his career is important to him, but I'm important to him, too. Everybody better get used to it, because I'm here to stay."

The moonlight kissed his smiling lips and laughing eyes. "Nice speech."

She grinned and cuffed him on the arm. "Shut up. Brat."

His hand wrapped around hers, their fingers linking, and they started walking again. For a second, she thought about pulling away, but she didn't. She didn't want to. It felt good, comforting, to have her hand warm in his.

"He never would have married you unless he was ready and willing to put you and the marriage first."

His words soothed her inner worry. "Yet he's still sitting around the fire with the team, talking shop, instead of carrying me over the threshold like he promised," she said lightly.

"Well, he's only human."

"What about you?" she asked, curious about the women in his life. Dominic's descriptions of him made it clear the man loved women and they him, and if he ever settled down, it would be a miracle.

"Aye, I'm human, although a few women I know would argue the point."

She bumped him with her shoulder. "I mean, is your job your priority or have you been successful at sharing your life with someone special?"

His eyes looked deep into hers, and his sexual prowess hit her full force in the chest. It radiated from him like sunshine and would draw women to him as fast and easy as the smell of chocolate.

As she looked closer, she saw something hidden in that heated blaze—an emptiness. No, not emptiness. A longing for something. Something lost. Or something he thought he'd never have. It scared her that she knew that about him, and she ripped her gaze from his in case he could see inside her, too, and see the same thing staring back.

"I *always* make time for someone special," he said.

"I'm guessing *Miss Special* doesn't wear the sash and crown for long?"

"We can't all be as lucky as Dom and Sean."

"Meaning?"

"They found their soulmates. The one person made just for them. It makes all the difference."

Soulmate. She thought back to what her nanny's psychic had told fourteen years ago—that her soulmate was Irish. She knew it was Dominic. Despite what her nanny had said in response. "How do you know I'm his soulmate?"

"He loves you. You love him. And love is a single soul inhabiting two bodies."

"Oh, my God," she teased. "You're quoting Aristotle? I'm a little impressed."

"Aristotle? Nah, I'm sure it was from a fortune cookie."

She chuckled.

"Ah, hell if I know, love," he said. "It's the only reason I can come up with to explain how it is Dom is married. Never thought I'd see the day. Sean, yeah. He's always been on the lookout for *the one*, so I knew when he found her, he'd go balls out to keep her."

She considered his words in silence as his hand left hers and settled at the small of her back before trailing up and down her spine. His touch—a stranger's touch—was no longer strange to her. It was warm and right, like a habit they'd shared forever. "What about you, heartthrob? If you're not the marrying kind, what kind are you?"

"What kind do you think I am?"

His low, rough voice slid inside her head, flowed into her chest, and squeezed her heart, making it pound. *The fucking kind.* As the thought zipped through her, a spark flashed in his eyes and he licked those sexy lips again. They looked so wet and tasty she wanted to lick them, too. Instead, she licked her own.

"I don't know."

"Yes, you do." He stopped, slid his hands down her arms to her hands, gripped them, and linked their fingers. "Don't hold back with me, Breena. Say what you're thinking."

She raised a brow. "What am I thinking?"

His half-mast gaze danced over hers, as if searching her mind for the answer. "That I'm the fucking kind."

She blinked a couple of times in surprise and had to remind herself to close her gaping mouth so her flip-flopping heart wouldn't jump out. *Oh, shit! How did he know what I was thinking? Was it just an obvious answer?*

A horde of tingles raced up and down her body, inside and out, making her pussy clench and her nipples poke out at him, whoring for attention, alerting her to the fact that their bodies had somehow, at some time, drawn closer and fused chest to thigh. His hardness was everywhere. And they were talking about fucking. This was so wrong. This was—

"Everybody thinks so," he said, interrupting her thought, his voice barely a whisper.

A trickle of some emotion she would not name caught in her throat as his gaze dropped to her lips and her gaze dropped to his. He was close. Too close. She was hot. Too hot. Her cheeks on fire. "Are they right?"

Eyes blazing with desire, he lowered his head to hers, his wet lips slightly parted, as if ready to fit over hers in a consuming, burning kiss that would show her how right "they" were. His breath on her lips parted them, making them tremble for his touch. Her breath joined his, the peppermint scent of their shared gum swirling together.

She pulled a shaky breath into her lungs to clear her head, but all she did was inhale him deeper into her until *he* was swirling inside her like before. He was filling her, all her empty, hurting spaces that had hidden from touch for years. It felt so fucking good. And so fucking scary.

She knew she should step back, away from him, from the lure of those lips, the touch of his eyes and hands, but she couldn't move, even to get her pulse under control. She closed her eyes. *Oh, God! Step away from him. Before you can't.*

Her eyes popped open when his hands and body left her. He had stepped back, breaking their connection, leaving her feeling empty, weak-kneed, and cold without his touch. All she wanted to do was yank him back into her body.

He grinned. "You're not ready to hear all my nasty secrets, sweet Breena."

For a second, she didn't understand what he meant, but then snatches of their conversation flitted back into consciousness.

"Who's holding back, now?" she said, hoping he didn't notice the tremble in her voice.

"For your own protection."

"Your little secrets don't scare me, McCanna. I've got plenty of my own." She tore her eyes from his and took a few steps onward, pulling a badly needed breath into her lungs. When she noticed he wasn't following her, she stopped and looked back, giving him a *why did you stop* look?

Silently answering the question she had silently asked, he nodded at the green and white trailer beside him. She glanced at it, took another, longer look. It was her and Dominic's trailer. One they'd passed at least twice before.

"Have we been going in circles?" she asked, walking back to him.

"Circles?" he asked, as if he had no idea what she meant.

"I'm sure I've seen this trailer a few times." His grin brought one to her mouth. "That's what I thought. Well, thanks for *eventually* walking me home."

"My pleasure. I left you and Dom a wedding gift inside. Irish tradition says it'll keep evil spirits away and remind the couple of their vows. And lucky for you, it'll help you always know where your home is."

So he'd known she had no idea where her trailer was. She wasn't going to ask how he'd known. "What is it?"

"You have to wait and open it with your husband."

"No, Ian, tell me." She grabbed his hands, needing his touch like a PMSing woman needed chocolate. "I hate surprises."

He linked their fingers, and the rush of it stopped her heart then eased it back to life.

"You really want to know?"

"Yes."

He shifted closer, and her breasts brushed his chest. His bulge—the flashlight? Or something else?—brushed her stomach. He leaned in, his mouth at her ear, and whispered, "Patience increases pleasure."

Shivers raced up and down her thighs at his nearness, his whisper, his words. He chuckled, and she reached up and pushed against his chest with her palms. "Fine, don't tell me," But she laughed with him as they faced each other in the moonlight.

"Fine, I won't." He stepped toward the trailer and opened the door. "Well, here you are, *Mrs*. Sullivan. Home. Safe and sound. And I didn't molest you once."

"Molest me?" she said lightly, joining him. "Where did that come from?"

"You said Dom warned you about me. I'm pointing out the fact that I didn't molest you so you know you're safe with me."

"When Dominic told me about your *special gifts* with women, he also made it insultingly clear that I'd be the last woman on earth you would 'molest' because you're his best friend and he trusts you with his life and everything in it."

A solemn look swept over his face. "Sean and Dom are my oldest, closest friends. I wouldn't risk those relationships for anything or anyone."

Their eyes connected across the dark stillness, and she knew he spoke the absolute truth. She could feel it. Despite the odd feelings zinging back and forth between the two of them, she had no need for worry where Ian was concerned. He was as loyal to Dominic as she was.

"I know." She laid her hands on his chest, over his heart, and his hands settled at her hips. The palms of her hands tingled, as if from a mild electric shock, but she left them in place and enjoyed the heat seeping into them and climbing up her arms to her chest. "I feel the same way. I love him, Ian."

"I know," he said.

"And despite your nasty secrets—I trust you."

He grinned. "I know." He took her hands from his chest and held them in his. "Sweet dreams, Breena," he whispered and kissed her palms, first one then the other, making her heart flutter. "I'm glad you're home."

Home? Yes. Right here with him, her hands in his, her heart beating in his, she felt at home for the first time ever. To shake the totally inappropriate feeling, she pulled her hands from his.

"Thanks for everything."

"You bet," he said. "See you in the morning."

She turned away from him, stepped up onto the first step…and stopped.

Staring into the open doorway at the blackness within sent a chill dragging up her spine, but she forced herself to take the second step. Heart trembling in her stomach, she stopped again, tried to take the next step, but couldn't. The bitter taste of fear oozed in her mouth as one of her secrets took center stage, and she backed down.

"Everything okay?" Ian's voice came from behind her.

She hadn't realized he was still there.

"Ian." She wanted to run into his arms to ease the fear that had crept over her, into her voice. Instead she cleared her throat to scatter it. "Do me a favor?"

He released an exaggerated sigh. "Another one?"

"Would you turn the light on for me? I don't know where the switch is."

He studied her. "Sure, love. I'll be your hero. If you tell me why you're afraid of the dark."

She sighed. "When I was a kid, I got trapped in the bowels of a haunted mansion," she said dramatically.

"Go on outta that."

"No, I'm serious. My family and I were visiting this renovated Revolutionary War mansion that was reputedly haunted. I had never seen a ghost and was determined to find one. I sneaked past a chain barrier and down a flight of steps. Deep in the tunnel my flashlight died, and I couldn't find my way back to the door. Being in the dark sends me right back to full-on panicville."

"How did you get out?"

She shrugged. "I don't know. I came to inside the house on a couch, my mom leaning over me."

"See any ghosts?"

She rarely shared this part of the story, but there was something in Ian's eyes, his face, that told her she could trust him with her nasty secrets, at least the relatively minor ones. "I've convinced myself that anything the eight-year-old me thought she saw and heard was nothing more than an overactive imagination."

"You saw a ghost."

"I saw a ghost."

The flashlight beam flickered and faded. Ian pulled it from the waistband of his jeans and smacked it against his hand to rattle the batteries. Instead of brightening, the light blinked out, leaving the two of them to stare at each other in the inky night, just enough light from the half-moon to reflect the surprise in their rounded eyes.

Zaps of fear snaked around her brain, tightening the skin at her skull and pushing her toward Ian where she grabbed a handful of his shirt at his stomach. "That wasn't weird."

"No, not at all." He rubbed the back of his neck, as if the conversation and the timing of the flashlight going out had made the hair there stand up.

She desperately wanted body to body contact yet was restraining every instinct telling her to wrap herself around Ian. "What would your mother, the witch, say about the timing of that flashlight going out?"

He stuffed the flashlight into his pocket, then rubbed his hands up and down her arms, trying to smooth away the chill bumps that had risen. "Well now, she's not really a witch, but she'd say, 'Better pay attention to signs, *agra*, while you're opening up graves and shaking out ghosts.' That's if I told her, which I'm not. If she knew I was about to disturb the graves of our ancestors, she'd string me up."

"Hmm. That would leave the media director job open for me."

"Yeah, but you couldn't live without me. Who'd share his torch with you? Who'd half gum with you? Who'd turn on the caravan light for you?"

"Rusty seemed pretty *hardy*. I bet he'd do it."

"Look at you trying to speak Irish."

"You making fun of me again, McCanna?" She dug her fingers into his sides, tickling him.

The quick jerk of his body told her she'd found the right spots. He grabbed her hands to keep her from tickling him again.

"Hate to break it to you, but the team will barely speak to you if Dom's not around. They won't want him to think something nasty's going on."

"It hasn't stopped you." She glanced at their linked fingers.

"Well, love, I'm more of what you call a rule *breaker* than a rule *follower*."

She grinned. "Yeah. This is my shocked face." She tried to pull away, but he held on.

"Takes one to know one." His gaze held hers.

"No comment."

Chuckling, he let her go and climbed the steps, stopping just inside the doorway. His hand brushed along the wall, searching for the switch, and soon a dim light gobbled the darkness. He turned to face her. With the light at his back, shadows hid his face, but she could feel his smile, his eyes.

"Want me to carry you over the threshold?" His voice was low with a hint of teasing.

In his arms was the last place she should be and just the place she wanted to be. "I'll walk, thanks." She ascended the first step.

His tall, muscular body filled the doorway, blocking her entrance, his raised forearms resting on the top of the frame. "It's bad luck, Breena. Spirits will attach to you and poison your marriage."

"They wouldn't dare." She ascended to the next step. Still, he didn't move.

He looked down at her, she up at him, and she felt his touch even though his hands never left the doorframe. Something made her raise her hands to his stomach to push on the rock-hard muscles. The palms of her hands tingled again.

"Move your ass, McCanna," she said through a grin.

Another step would put her body flush against his. Surely he'd move back then.

"You'll regret it," he said, almost in warning.

Whether he meant her refusal to let him carry her over the threshold or her decision to take the next step, her answer was the same.

"Regrets are just memories. Unlike the dark, they

don't scare me." She took that step.

Unfortunately, she had overestimated both his willingness to move back and the amount of room on that step.

One second she was tumbling backward off the steps, the next she was safe, Ian's arms tight around her, her body flush against his, her feet almost off the ground. The jolt rocked her to her core.

"*Hashkeh*," he whispered in her hair.

Her heart sped up. So did his. They beat in sync inside her chest. She couldn't breathe. No, she could breathe. She was breathing him. And by the way his chest rose and fell like sea swells during a storm, he was breathing her, too. It was like inhaling thick, warm fog. It was like they were tangled up together in that fog.

His arms and eyes tight on her, he backed into the room, leading her across the threshold and into the trailer. Still, he didn't let her go. Still, she didn't leave his arms. It was like she had been fitted to him, one puzzle piece to another, and glued in place. And it was perfection.

It was a struggle to think, much less to move away from him. But digging deep, she found the strength to step away, and it left her knees trembling and her body aching at the loss. With space between them and them not touching, she was finally able to breathe. Slowly, the haze receded from her lungs. They were out of their bubble, but that familiar force was drawing her back.

She tested a chuckle to scatter the feeling and the lingering heat. It sounded harsh and abrasive, but it did the trick and allowed her to speak. "You have my permission to say 'I told you so' if the ghosts attack me."

"Believe me, I will." His voice sounded as ragged as hers, and for some reason, it comforted her that whatever was happening, was happening to both of them.

He moved to one of the open windows, drew back the curtain, and stood there breathing in the air coming through, as if he, too, were starved for oxygen.

She opened the curtain on the opposite window and turned to face the slight breeze to let it cool her flushed skin.

"Ready for the tour?"

The sound of Ian's voice made her jump, and her head jerked toward him. He had left the window and now held out his arm to her in an exaggeratedly formal and elegant way, showing no effects of whatever had swooped them up. Was she losing her mind? Imagining things? It was feeling more and more like a spell.

But it didn't stop her from threading her hand through his arm and holding his forearm. "Tour away, my good man."

"We're in the foyer. Notice the lovely *faux* wood details of the door frame." He waved his hand dramatically along the top and sides of the door. "America's best."

"Hey!" She lightly elbow-jabbed him in the side for maligning her country.

Grinning, he continued. "The kitchen is straight ahead, complete with mini fridge, mini oven, and—"

"Mini sink?" she asked.

"Feck if Dom hasn't snagged himself a bloody genius."

"Yes, he has." She turned up her nose. "And she

shan't be concerning herself with kitchen duties, so move on."

"I surmised as much." He rolled his eyes dramatically.

"Brat." She was ready to tickle him again, but he grabbed her hands to stop her, as if he'd known her intention the second she had.

"What? You have the look about you, that's all."

"Oh? What look is that?"

He released her hands and put his hand over his heart and bowed low, his head at the level of her stomach. "Your royal highness."

She put her hands on his head and ruffled his hair, making it stand up. "Oh, I am soooo telling your mother." She enjoyed his deep chuckle as he stood upright. He didn't even try to smooth his hair back into place, confident nothing could detract from his good looks.

He took her hand in his and pointed to the near end of the trailer, toward a padded bench butting against the wall, a small table in front of it. "Your dining area-slash-office-slash-living-room-slash-guest-bedroom—"

"Ah, multipurpose space."

"Yeah, let's go with that." He led her the dozen steps to the far side of the trailer, just past the bed, and pulled open an accordion door. "Your throne, princess."

The "throne" included a toilet as well as a small sink and shower. The space could accommodate only one person at a time, but it was clean and—she tried the knobs and flushed the toilet—functional. "I'm pumped we have our own bathroom, even if it is a one-butter."

His eyebrow raised. "One butter?"

"One," she held up one finger. "Butt." She slapped

her butt. "A one-butt bathroom. A one-butter."

She saw when he finally got it, because he threw his head back and laughed, his arms roping around her waist. He eased her into his body, and she went readily, her hands settling on his chest, her palms absorbing the beats of his heart, the heat and electricity sparking inside him.

She laughed because he laughed. Because it felt good. Because the joy living inside them had found a way out and into each other. Because happiness was tying them together in that strange knot of pleasure she'd never felt with anyone but him.

"Ian, stop. It wasn't that funny."

"No, it wasn't," he agreed, still laughing. "Ah, Breena, love, you're *savage*."

Their laughter had nothing to do with her lame joke and everything to do with the magic filling their lungs as they breathed in the drug-kissed smoke of each other's essence. It had to do with them fitting together like two halves of a whole. It had to do with the desire weaving and mingling between them, braiding them together. It had to do with—

"Am I interrupting?"

Their heads spun toward the voice, and their laughter faded, hands fell from each other.

Dominic stood in the doorway, eyes beaded on them, arms crossed over his chest.

Chapter Four

"Yeah, you are interrupting," Ian said, a smile twitching at his lips. "I was about to show her the bed."

It happened too quickly to be sure, but for a fleeting moment, Dominic's eyes darkened and narrowed as they locked on Ian. She had seen the look too many times not to recognize the emotions behind it as anger and jealousy. But then his eyes were on her, and there was nothing but love and desire in them.

"Then I've arrived at the perfect time. Go away, Ian."

"You're kicking me out at the best part."

"I am."

Dominic stepped away from the door and into the multipurpose space to let his friend out, but Ian turned to face her and put his hand on her lower back. He leaned in and whispered, "Watch out for ghosts and spells and jealous witches with curly red hair." He kissed her cheek, then headed toward the door. "Glad you're back, mate," he said to Dominic, patting his back.

"Good to be back. See you in the morning."

Dominic shut the door when Ian left the trailer, then strode slowly toward her, stopping when there was still a river of space between them. "I thought you, of all people, would be immune to Ian's magic."

She raised an eyebrow in surprise. *Her of all*

people? What did that mean? But she had a more important question. "His magic?"

"Ian is a *dreeadore*, a magician. He has a way with making a woman forget she has a man."

And he was damn good at it. "Thanks for the warning. Now…who are you and what are you doing in my trailer?"

He growled, rushed forward, grabbed her in his arms, and dipped her backward, dropping quick kisses all over her neck, face, chest, mouth, making her giggle. "You like to make me crazy, don't you, woman."

"Are you crazy for me?"

He pulled her upright and kissed her forehead. "You know I am."

She met his gaze. "For the record, no one's magic works on me but yours."

His eyes stayed connected with hers for a long moment, and she could see that her response had pleased him. "You think you can work with him?"

They'd work well together, she and Ian. No doubt. She liked him. A lot. Despite their odd interaction she didn't yet understand. "Yes, but I don't want to talk about Ian or work right now."

"What *do* you want to talk about?"

"I don't want to talk at all. I want you to carry me across the threshold like you promised."

"Can't."

"Why not?"

"You already crossed it."

She *had* crossed it. With Ian. Sort of. "Not with you carrying me."

"Doesn't matter."

She felt like she'd lost something at that moment,

something important, something she desperately needed but could never get back. Disappointment flooded her stomach, making it clench. Hopefully, this moment wasn't one of those signs they needed to watch for. "I should've waited for you."

"I should've left with you to make sure our first night was perfect," he said.

Refusing to let their first night in their new home be anything but perfect, Sabrina left his arms. She kicked off her shoes and peeled off her sweatshirt and T-shirt, dropping them onto the floor. She unfastened her bra and let it join her shirt. Her breasts swelled as they bounded from the cups. She undid her jeans and pushed them and her panties off. She stood before him, wearing nothing but desire and love. "Let's make it perfect."

"Perfect," he whispered, his eyes flicking hot over her, the crotch of his jeans stretching tight.

That she excited him excited her. Sliding her hands up her stomach to her breasts, she cupped them, squeezed her nipples between her fingers, then ran one hand slowly back down her stomach and into the tiny puff of blonde curls at her pussy. Imagining it was Dominic's hands on her, her head fell back a little, desire making her eyes close to slits. Her finger dipped between her slick folds.

A groan slipped from his mouth. "Is your pussy wet?"

"Touch me and find out," she said.

He reached out and gripped her arms, pulling her to him. As his mouth claimed hers, his hand took her breast, moving over it like her hand had done. That hand then slid down between her legs to test her wetness. She held on to him, her hands at his shoulders, and shivered as his touch torched her body.

"I want you," he said between kisses.

"I'm yours."

"Only mine," he said.

"Yes."

She pulled his shirt off, and before it reached the floor, her hands were at the waistband of his jeans, wrenching down the tight zipper, flipping open the stud. He pushed his jeans down, and her hands were at his boxers, pulling them down, too. Finally, they were skin to skin, and he picked her up and laid her on their new bed, not taking time to pull back the comforter.

God, how she needed him. He covered her body with his, and she spread her legs wide, pulling his swollen cock to her swollen pussy.

His eyes tight on hers, he eased into her wetness, her tightness, giving her what she wanted, what she needed. He thrust his hips against her again and again, letting her feel every inch of him inside of her, sliding in and out, every touch of his head at the top of her channel driving her a little closer to the edge. She put her fingers to her clit and drew tight and fast circles around it, helping to bring on the climax she desperately needed, the one that had been building since...

The image of Ian's face flashed before her eyes and the crest broke. She let it take her away, her cry of pleasure spurring Dominic's growling climax that left him shuddering on top of her.

He stilled, dipping his forehead to hers. Their sweat mingled, their flush leveled out, their skin cooled. He took a deep breath and released it. "Ian's right.

You're savage."

Remembering her reaction to Ian's touch, his last words of warning, his face appearing to trigger her climax, she shivered as anxiety spiraled inside her, making her skin prickle as if danger surrounded them. Fear flared from some hidden corner of her soul and formed the plea *Dominic, take me away from this place. Away from Ian. Before it's too late*. But she swallowed it back, knowing it would hurt him, worry him, for her to say something like that.

"I hope that's a good thing," she said, the damning thought running up her spine, making her shiver, as if her body were trying to shake off the feeling.

"The best."

He kissed her mouth, softly, tenderly, and she felt his love, knew all would be right as long as he was beside her. Inside their trailer, wrapped in each other, she and Dominic, their marriage, were safe. He rolled off her but pulled her with him, into his arms.

A moment later, he nodded toward the wrapped and bowed box sitting on the floor against the wall. "What's that over there?"

"Ian's wedding gift to us. Let's open it."

"Now?"

"Yes, now." She scrambled out of his arms and over to the gift, brought it back to the bed, and sat with it between them.

He pulled off the bow. "There, I did my part."

"Try to curb your enthusiasm. You might strain something," she teased as she ripped the paper off, opened the box, and pulled back the tissue paper to see inside. Surprise and joy lifted her mouth into a smile. "No way."

"What is it?"

She held it up proudly.

"Wind chimes?" he asked, as if he thought it was a strange wedding gift.

"Wind *bells*." She shook it gently to hear the sound it made. The Irish-blue cascading copper bells were peaceful to her ears, sounding like a song instead of just ringing bells. "Don't you remember?" The confused look on his face said he didn't. "This was the one I wanted at that little shop in Dingle, but the only one they had was broken."

"Oh, yeah."

"Ian said it'll keep evil spirits away and help us to always know where home is. Let's put it up."

She started to climb out of bed, but he stopped her. He took the wind bells from her hands and put it back in the box, put the box on the floor, then rolled her beneath him on the bed.

"Not now." His mouth captured hers.

****

Ian hadn't planned to turn back to Breena's caravan. He hadn't planned to stand in the dark watching her strip for her husband. Hadn't planned to watch her cup her breasts, pinch her nipples, caress the wet spot between her legs. Hadn't planned to stay long enough to hear her cries when she found her pleasure. But he had done it all.

God, her breasts were luscious, like ripe, juicy fruit, with high points that begged a man to suck them deep into his mouth to nourish his soul. Feelings of familiarity and desire washed over him as he thought about tasting those breasts, about plunging his hard cock into her soft, wet folds, about feeling that sweet mouth on his. Like he'd done it all many times before.

He shook his head, trying to erase the random memories flitting through his brain about her. Memories that had to be false because there was no logical explanation for them when the two had never met before today.

Equally disturbing were the thoughts he was picking up from her. Thoughts that floated to him in broken whispers he couldn't fully hear or comprehend, but he knew were hers. As sure as he knew his own.

Something happened the moment he touched Sabrina Sullivan that exhumed strange, ancient ideas from deep in his brain. At the pit tonight, he couldn't stop ogling her like a horny teenager looking for his second fuck. She had been watching him with the same keen interest. The way they touched, laughed, teased. As impossible as it was, he knew—they wanted each other.

There also was no way in hell they'd ever do anything about it. He'd meant what he told her. Dom and Sean were his best friends, and he'd never do anything to risk those relationships. And he believed her when she said she loved her husband.

So why couldn't he stop touching her? Why didn't she stop him from touching her? Was it because they felt right and peaceful and balanced when they touched? Because touching allowed them to catch a full breath of air into their lungs? Because the full-body rush of pleasure it gave them made them feel so fucking good? Fuck, yeah. All the above.

Even now, his palms and fingertips tingled, itched, from wanting to touch her. He cracked his knuckles and opened and closed his hands to rid them of the inappropriate feeling of longing. But the feeling remained, strong and gripping, and seemed to be pushing him to go to her. His body was tight and edgy, his skin feeling an all-over itch that couldn't be scratched. His balls had climbed up inside him, and his cock stood as rigid and hard as a monolith in his jeans.

He drew a large, ragged breath, realizing he'd been holding them back as he'd watched her. If the grad students were here, he'd chat one up and take her back to her caravan for some fun. But they wouldn't arrive for a couple of weeks. And it was too late to go to the pub in town. He had no choice but to head across the way to his own caravan, fist his swollen cock, and jerk off to the image of his best friend's wife feeling herself up. And to the sound of her crying out *his* name in her head as she came.

As he turned, he bumped into Meggan when she stepped out of the darkness. Watching, too?

Sneering, she sidled up close to him and cupped his rod. "Is this for *her*?"

Her touch made his skin crawl, but he didn't want to step back and give her the satisfaction of knowing she affected him. He put his hand over hers and pressed it against his hardness.

"It's for you, Meggie. Give him a kiss."

She jerked her hand away. "Fuck you."

He grabbed her hips and jerked her against his hard-on. "That would work, too."

She shoved him away. "He'd kill you before he'd let you touch her. Or me." Knocking past him, she rushed to her caravan.

Yeah. Dom would. Shit. Apricunt was the last person he wanted to know he had a hard-on for his best friend's wife. Fortunately, he had dirt on her that would keep her mouth shut.

He headed home to the sweet tinkling of Breena's wind bells and the sexy sound of her thoughts swirling around him. He cleared his brain of his own thoughts and focused on her. Listened. She liked the gift, she liked him, and knowing it made his heart soar.

With a troubled mind and aching balls, he entered his blue and white caravan next door. And wondered how in the hell he had developed the gift of mind reading and why it only worked on a woman who could never be his.

Chapter Five

After a short post-breakfast meeting, the team headed to the dig site. In addition to her roll bag of excavation tools—trowel, brushes, small picks—and small cooler of bottled water, Sabrina was equipped with cameras, camera paraphernalia, and context sheets on a clipboard.

Because of the construction that had been going on prior to their arrival, the land had already been cleared of rocks and plant growth, and the team had mapped the site to identify the topography, the relative location of artifacts, bones, other features, and the best placement for excavation units.

With rope and stakes, Sabrina, Dominic, and Meggan set up a grid on their spot, a roughly three meter by three meter space labeled Trench 1. Other team members—including Ian, who also was equipped with similar camera gear—did the same on adjacent plots. The grids marked off square sections that would help them note the square in which objects were found.

She and Dominic dug in one area, Meggan a few feet away, all using pickaxes and shovels to clear away barriers to the lower stratum of the site. They filled wheelbarrows with soil that would later be sieved for any particles they'd missed visually. Every so often, she stopped to take a bit of video and camera shots of the digging to show the progress, then continued with digging.

A bit over two feet down, Dominic switched to his trowel and began to scrape the dirt from an area. Soon his gaze swung to hers, a grin spread across his face.

"This is it." He grabbed a handbroom and brushed dirt from a dot of bone that had just revealed itself. "First skeleton of the dig."

He stood and faced his spread-out team and called, *sheeohcon lat!* They called back, *slawnche!* The first phrase, meaning *peace be with you*, was uttered whenever someone uncovered his or her first skeleton to help usher any lost souls into their right place. Special props went to the person who uttered it first. It was said they'd have good luck for the rest of the dig. The second word, meaning *cheers* or *to your health,* was said to protect the person who found the skeleton from spirits wanting to hang around instead of going on into the beyond.

Sabrina left the video camera pointed at Dominic's hands to capture the moment the rounded dome of a skull materialized and grabbed her other camera.

"The light of day hasn't touched this person in hundreds of years," she said softly, almost to herself, feeling a little awestruck as she snapped pictures of the bones appearing out of the dirt they'd been buried in so long ago. The knowledge that this was once a person— with flesh, blood, organs, hopes, and dreams—hit her solidly in the chest, and she had to touch it to assure herself it was real. She reached out and caressed the patch of skull.

A zap of energy entered the tips of her fingers, rushed up her arm, and spread through her body. Her heart pounded a rapid-fire rate against her ribs. Her lungs tightened, and she couldn't seem to get enough air. Sweat beaded on her skull and trickled down her back, her chest, and her cold, clammy face. A squeezing pressure filled her head, making her dizzy, and she laid a hand at her forehead to steady herself. Hushed, unintelligible sounds whooshed in her ears, like multiple voices calling to her at once. She'd only felt this sensation once, and that was fourteen years ago, but she knew what it was.

Dizziness swirled through her, so she wasn't sure she could trust her eyes, but what she thought she saw paralyzed her. A man, as tall as Ian, with long, dark hair and icy blue eyes, dressed in warrior's garb of centuries ago, stood at the edge of their section, staring down at her, a scowl on his ruggedly handsome face. The man spoke to her in a rough but lilting language she didn't understand. He strode forward—floated, really—and laid his hand on her head.

Feeling the camera slipping from her hand, she tried to curl her fingers around it to hold on, but a curtain of black covered her eyes and she felt herself falling through a dark, cold tunnel.

Dominic's voice calling her name pulled her out of the dark. The pressure in her ears had been replaced with distant but real sounds—the swoosh of shovel to dirt, the scrape of metal to bone, the voices of the team, the tweeting birds, the bubbling river two hundred or so yards away.

She lay in the trench alongside the skeleton, Dominic crouched at her side, his arm around her back, cradling her head.

"Are you okay?" he asked.

A storm rumbled in her stomach and cold sweat

drenched her face, but she was back from wherever the ghost's touch had sent her.

"Yes." Fighting the desire to vomit, she tried to rise.

He helped her to a seated position, then dug into the cooler for a bottle of water, which he opened and pressed into her hands. Realizing her mouth was cotton dry, she guzzled the water, finishing the bottle.

The worried look he directed at her troubled her. "I'm okay," she insisted. "Really."

His hand cupped her face. "Maybe you need to get out of the sun for a while. Rest."

"It's not hot, and I'm not tired." The sensations that had flipped her upside down had faded. Other than an ache around her eyes and a queasy stomach, it was as if the incident had never happened.

He brushed back a strand of hair that had come loose from her ponytail. "Are you pregnant?"

The not-so-subtle twinkle that lit his eyes surprised her. They'd talked about having kids, of course, but had agreed to wait a few years, wanting time to enjoy each other. She also wanted them to travel. "Would you like that? If I were pregnant?"

His soft nod, his eyes closing half way told her he liked the idea of his baby growing inside her.

She leaned in and kissed his mouth, clinging for a few seconds. "Sorry to disappoint you, but there's no bun in this oven." *Thank God.*

"We'll have to keep trying then."

"Definitely. But unless you're willing to take me home to try right now, I need to get back to work before Ian fires me." She stood, and so did he.

"If you feel sick again—"

"Baby, I'm fine. I promise."

He still stared at her as if he didn't believe it, but moved back to the skull after she moved away to pick up her video camera. Ian's prized and expensive high definition video camera lay beside her in the dirt and had witnessed her disgrace.

"Shit. Ian's going to kill me," she muttered as she inspected the camera and brushed and blew the dust from it.

"What did you do?" Ian's voice coming over the earpiece she wore startled her.

"Nothing," she said quickly.

He chuckled. "I'm glad you're not pregnant, love. It's not easy to find someone with your qualifications."

Had he heard her thoughts from across the dig? No. The mic was in the on position. Her fall must have jiggled it on. "Get out of my ear," she said to his chuckling and shut it off.

Finding no damage to the camera, she went back to capturing Dominic's hands gently revealing the skeleton's hollowed features.

She angled the video camera to capture a longer shot of the excavation. After long, slow moments of careful work, the forehead and eye sockets came into view, followed by the nose hollow and the teeth. She grabbed the camera again.

"His teeth are relatively unworn," she said, snapping pictures from all angles. "And he still has his molars, so I'd guess he was in his early 20s when he died."

"Sure it's a man?" her teacher husband asked, picking away at the dirt with a dental tool. His sparkling eyes darted to hers, then back to his skull.

"Look at the size of those choppers." She and Dominic hadn't just fucked like wild rabbits on that university dig. He'd also taught her about archaeology, including that male skeletons tended to have larger teeth than the females. "And his brow, thick and pronounced? I'm convinced it's a man, but I won't know for sure until I see his pelvis."

"Or count his ribs," Dominic said with a chuckle.

"Funny, Sullivan. Remember, you're a scientist, not a creationist."

The jaw came into view. Angular and wide. "Five bucks says it's a man," she said.

"Your bucks are no good here in Ireland. What else do you have to wager?"

She zoomed back to capture Dominic and his skeleton in relation to their surroundings and snapped the shot. "You know what I've got."

Dominic looked her up and down. Smiled as if saying he did know. "Want to make it interesting?" He kept his voice low, for her ears only.

"Always."

"If you're right, we have sex tonight."

"With each other?" she teased.

He shot her a raised-eyebrows look.

"Don't get pissy," she said. "My scientist husband told me to always verify. And if I'm wrong?"

"Same deal."

Three voices from the trench Ian was working called out *sheeohcon lat!*

I need to go help Ian.

"Breena, I need you in T4." Ian's voice came through the earpiece as replies of *slawnche* rang out.

She pressed the mic button on her device. "I'll log

what I've got and head over."

She quickly noted what she had taken shots of on her clipboard, as well as location, time, and depth they'd been found, along with her belief that it was a male.

Dominic caught her to him as she was leaving. "Hey, be careful."

"Hey, no worrying." She dropped a kiss on his lips before leaving the trench to join Ian. "And I'll take that bet."

Ian shot the two skeletons at one end, and she shot the one on the opposite end, capturing information about the length, orientation, and position of each on the log as well as photo information and possible sex.

The cool of the morning was soon smothered by the thick humidity of the nearly straight overhead but clouded sun. More than once, Sabrina wiped the moisture from her face and from the camera's eyepiece with her T-shirt. It was an odd sensation being able to feel the air hugging her body like a wet sheet, feel it brush against her like cobwebs as she moved through it. It filled her head, too, making her thinking fuzzy, her body achy, and her mood irritable.

Or maybe her off mood had more to do with hearing Meggan's laugh and Dominic's answering laugh, drifting on the thick air again and again. Or the images in her viewfinder when she zoomed her camera in on T1, like now.

Dominic lay on the ground, arms and head in the trench, which was a good three feet deep, digging out his find, talking to Meggan, who was lying right by his side, digging as well, their shoulders touching, as if she belonged there, as if they were a team unto themselves.

Why wasn't the bitch working on her own skeleton?

Dominic pushed himself to his knees, and Meggan did, too. He dropped his hand on her shoulder, using it to support himself as he stood, making her fall forward. Laughing, she swung her arm around and smacked him on the legs. He laughed and turned away to grab his clipboard to log something he'd noticed. Laughed, again, at something she said. Rejoined her on the ground. Not as close as he was. But still too close for Sabrina's liking.

The team called out *sheeohcon lat* over the next few hours until every member of the digging team had unearthed a skeleton, keeping her and Ian hopping to capture footage and shots of each of the finds. Keeping her too busy to watch Dominic and Meggan but not too busy to ignore the jealously nagging her about them.

By lunch time, Dominic's skeleton was half free, and those in other trenches were in various stages of freedom. She captured it all, knowing Ian would sift through the images with her to give her a better idea what was good to shoot and what not to bother with.

****

"Good stuff." Ian scrolled through her downloaded photos on the computer monitor before the two of them broke for lunch.

Her stomach growled, telling Sabrina it needed something to play with before it began consuming her organs. When his growled, too, she pulled a stick of gum from her pocket, unwrapped it halfway, offered it to him. He lowered his mouth to her hand and took half.

"Not to brag," she said, taking the other half, "but some of my photos won awards back home. Of course, they weren't of skeletons, so I'm glad I did okay my first foray into HRs."

"Great composition. Clear, good exposure. Odd but effective angles." He grinned up at her. "Nice work, love. This afternoon, get a few more wide shots of the digging. Let's take a look at video."

He opened the first video from that morning. His eyes shot to hers after watching her crumple to the ground. He hit pause and turned to her, his eyes asking, *what happened?*

She shrugged to impart that it was no big deal. "I touched the skull and passed out."

"Has that ever happened before?"

"Uh…yeah." She raised one eyebrow.

He looked at her, waiting for an answer, then the answer flickered in his eyes. "The mansion."

She nodded.

"There was a skeleton, too?"

"Okay, look. I'll tell you, and then we don't talk about it again. I was stumbling around in the dark, more than a little freaked out. I tripped over something that I quickly realized was a skeleton. I was overcome with dizziness and felt like I was going to throw up or pass out, but I managed to crawl away from it. A ghost appeared, touched my head, like today, and I passed out. End of story."

"You saw a ghost today."

"Yes."

He nodded, his face tight, his blue eyes full of concern. The look they shared stretched over a long moment.

Ian, if you ask me if I'm okay I swear I'll smack you!

A little smile lifted his lips, as if in response to her thought. "Don't touch the bones, *Hashkeh*. Just film 'em. You're no good to me if you fall, crack your head open, and break my cameras."

She laughed. "Oh. Ian. Stop. Your concern is too touching."

"Make up your mind," he said, laughing.

"What do you mean, make up your mind? About what?"

He stood and took her hand. "Let's get lunch before all the cake's gone." He led them out the door and toward the mess tent.

Sabrina immediately searched the tent for Dominic. He sat at a table with Meggan, Sean, Kristin, Jack, and Gabe. She wanted to sit with him, but there wasn't enough room for her, much less her *and* Ian. And Ian wanted to discuss their afternoon schedule.

They set their trays at an open table nearby. "Be right back," she said and walked over to Dominic. She put her arms around him and kissed his cheek.

"Hey." He put his arm around her, raising his face for a quick kiss. "You're not eating?" he asked when he didn't see a tray in her hands.

"Yeah, I am." She nodded toward the table where Ian sat.

He eyed the table, then her. "You're not sitting with me?" The look on his face and the tone of his voice told her he was irritated.

She looked at the full table. "Where? On your lap?"

He looked around, too.

"Pull up a chair," Kristin offered and started to scoot.

"No, it's okay. It won't be comfortable for anyone being so squeezed in." She ran her fingers in Dominic's hair. "Come join Ian and me. It'll give you two a chance to catch up."

He caught her hand and held it. "We're in the middle of our planning meeting."

"After you're done," she said.

"If there's time."

"Okay."

His lack of desire to sit with her pissed her off. If he heard it in her voice, saw it in her face, he didn't show it, and he didn't stop her when she turned away to return to Ian. Not wanting to examine Dominic's attitude too closely, she sat across from Ian and focused on getting food down her tight throat.

She took a bite of her sandwich, then reached for her milk to open the carton. Where her cake had been when she got up to see Dominic now sat an empty plate. An empty red plate. Ian's plate. A blue plate—her plate—with a half-eaten piece of cake on it—her cake—sat in front of him, and he was shoveling it in.

"What the hell?" she asked.

"I thought you didn't want it," he said through a chocolate grin.

"Why would you think that?"

"You were kissing, not eating."

"Steal my cake again, McCanna, and you'll lose the hand you swiped it with." She gave him a little grin to know she was only half serious.

He laughed and held out the last bite to her on his fork.

She leaned in and ate it. "Delicious."

"Yes. Yes, it was," he said.

"You are such a brat. But I'll forgive you because I love the wind bells."

"You opened the gift."

"Yeah, last night." She reached across the table and put her hand on his. "It's wild that you chose that one. I found one exactly like it in a little shop in Dingle, but the only one they had left was broken, so I didn't get it. I was so disappointed."

He linked their fingers. "Did you put it up?"

"Not yet. I'm hoping Dominic will help me tonight."

"I'll help you after we eat," he said and released her hand when she pulled it back to continue eating.

Dominic came to their table, not to sit and talk, but to tell her he needed to get back to work. He kissed her, then headed to the door, leaving long ribbons of disappointment streaming through her. She had hoped to spend the last few minutes of the lunch hour with him in their trailer, clutched in a quickie.

Instead she spent them with Ian, hanging her wind bells.

****

Meggan's skeleton was coming along, and Dominic's was visible head to foot but not ready to be lifted. Sabrina snapped some shots of Meggan's then joined Dominic where he worked on the legs.

Rusty appeared at the lip of the trench. "Hey, Sabrina. Uh, do you mind if I take a gander at your trowel?"

"Uh, sure." She tossed it to him.

He inspected it. "Mine has a scratch on the handle like this." He turned it in his hands. "But yours doesn't have…" He tossed it back. "Thanks." He lumbered on to the next trench.

"Did he think I'd taken his trowel?"

Dominic shook his head. "He loses at least a dozen trowels per dig."

She sat at the feet scribbling notes about the shots, then picked up Dominic's log sheets and reviewed what he'd written about his find.

"He's one hundred eighty-five centimeters? That's as tall as you. Almost unheard of for that time in this area, isn't it?"

"Could be from a Viking line," he said. "They raided this area back then. Take a look at the left side of his head."

She put down his sheets, grabbed her camera, and walked around to that side. A large half-moon hole—and nearby it, a tiny one—marred the otherwise intact skull. She scanned the length of the skeleton, noting numerous slashes here and there. Four of his ribs were broken, indicating that the injury happened right before he died because they hadn't had time to heal. His left lower leg was broken in two from what had probably been a hard, direct blow.

"Judging by the slashes on his arm and leg"—she pointed to the marks—"and his broken ribs and leg, I'd say the blow to the head was likely from a sword. Didn't kill him outright but probably caused his brain to swell. Someone drilled that little hole to relieve the swelling."

He nodded. "That's my guess too."

She grabbed a measurement bar and set it alongside the body for more pictures, then sat again to take notes. A feeling of awe washed over her. "Incredible," she said, not realizing she'd said it aloud until Dominic spoke.

"What's that?"

"This man was brave. He fought a fierce enemy to protect someone or something he loved. Someone cared enough about him to try to save his life. But in the end, it hadn't been enough. Who wept and mourned for him? How did his death affect their lives?" She sat beside Dominic in the dirt. "I know if something like this happened to you, I'd want to jump into the grave with you. I wouldn't want to go on without you."

"I feel the same about you." His gaze shot to Meggan, then back to her, and he kissed her. "Are you glad you're here?"

When she had laid out plans for jobs after graduation, being on a dig wasn't even on the list. She'd had dreams of traveling the world as a photojournalist, capturing contemporary civilization's most awe-inspiring present moments, not confined to one place as a shovelbum digging up the past. She'd even turned down her dream job—an internship with a prestigious international magazine—to marry Dominic and come to Ireland.

It hurt to give it up, but being able to work alongside the man she loved as he worked in the field he loved was a gift. At least for now. She had hopes he'd eventually agree to join one of the MAC teams that worked digs all over the world so they could both have what they wanted. "I'm—"

"Dom, look at this," Meggan called out, interrupting her.

Without waiting for her to finish her statement, Dominic stood and rushed to Meggan's trench.

The two of them talked in hushed tones, heads bent

together, her pointing into the trench. She touched his arm as she spoke. He dropped down into the dirt, head first in her trench. Without a word he held up his hand and she handed him a small brush before dropping down next to him, right next to him, their bodies touching. It was like she could read his mind.

Well, son-of-a-bitch. Jealousy climbed Sabrina's spine like a *gruaimín* climbing a pole, and a heavy feeling lodged in her throat, making her jaws clench. She tried to focus on her shots, but her eyes kept drifting back to her husband as he lay next to *her*. She was tempted to march over to see what was so damn captivating. Maybe while she was there, she'd push Meggan into the trench, head first. Accidentally, of course.

"Camera," Meggan called out.

Chapter Six

Sabrina awoke with a start, sweat slicking her body, her breathing labored like she had been holding her breath under water. Dominic lay on his side, facing her, his arm over her, his hand cupping her breast. Feeling him solid and alive against her, she breathed easier. He was here. Everything was okay.

She closed her eyes, nudged deeper into his embrace and breathed in his scent, his warmth. The nightmare that he had been taken from her was just that...a bad dream.

Then the blood pumping through her veins turned cold, and goosebumps rose high on her skin, lifting the small hairs. She felt something in the room...a presence. Her eyes popped open, and she jerked upright. Her gaze darted around the dark room, but she didn't see or hear anything out of place.

In the shimmer of a moon beam, a man materialized at the foot of her bed, a familiar scowl on his face. Ice cold eyes, pale blue and narrowed, bored into hers. Dark hair, the color of the deepest shadows in the corners, hung loose past his wide shoulders to his mid back. Arms, rock solid and long, hung by his side. One hand held a sword, the other curled into a fist.

He spoke to her in an unfamiliar language, his voice low and chilling like the rustling of dry leaves on the frozen ground. When she didn't respond, he released a battle cry, raised his sword, and slammed it down on Dominic's head.

She screamed. Kicked. Flailed. Slapped at his hands grabbing her and holding her down. He called her name. At some moment, she realized it was Dominic's body covering hers, his voice trying to still her, calm her. The bedside lamp switched on.

"Sabrina, it's okay. Shhhhh. I'm here."

Her gaze darted around the room, looking for the intruder, but all she saw was Dominic hovering over her. Her hands flew to his head, touched his face. No gaping gash, no gushing blood.

"Oh, Dominic," she cried through ragged breaths and pulled him to her, wrapping her arms tight around his neck. "Thank God, you're okay."

"That was some dream," he said.

How did she tell him it hadn't been a dream, that it was the ghost of the man whose skeleton he had dug up? "A...a man was in here. He hit you. With his sword."

A pounding at the side of the trailer halted her explanation. "Everything okay in there?" Ian's voice drifted through the window. "I heard Breena screaming."

"Night terrors," Dominic called out.

"Scared the piss outta me," Ian grumbled.

"You and me both," Dominic muttered and held her tighter against his chest, stroking her hair.

She heard Ian say "night terrors" to whoever was outside questioning the reason for the blood-curdling scream. The interruption had given her time to catch her breath and gather her thoughts.

"He's the man you dug up today," she said to

Dominic.

"What?"

"Before I passed out, I saw a man at the top of the trench. He's the man I saw here by our bed. He's the man you dug up. I know it."

"You're telling me you saw a ghost."

Hearing the disbelief in his voice, she sighed. "Yes."

"You had too much sun, not enough fluids, too much physical activity, you got dizzy…it made you see—"

"See things that weren't there?" she scoffed.

"Baby, there's no other logical explanation."

"You want logic? It wasn't that hot, I was plenty hydrated, and I get more physical activity in a ten-minute run than I do in hours of snapping a few photos. I know what I saw. And what I saw was a ghost."

The lift of his brow, the twist of his mouth, the slight pulling away from her suggested he didn't believe her. His words confirmed it. "What do you expect me to say to that?"

"I expect you to say you believe me."

He brushed his knuckles lightly along her cheek. "Maybe you should stay in tomorrow. Rest."

She tensed, angry at his coddling, his patronizing, at his total disbelief of her story. "You did *not* just say that to me." She rolled out of his arms and faced away from him, wondering how it was possible that Ian, a virtual stranger, had believed her instantly, but her husband, the man who loved her, refused to.

"Babe…" He curled his body around hers and cupped her breast.

She pushed his hand away. "Leave me alone." It

was the first time she'd spurned his attention since they'd met four months ago.

"Okay." He rolled onto his back with a loud sigh and settled in. "But don't wake me up in a few minutes, wanting some lovin'."

"Don't worry. I won't."

She tried to go back to sleep but couldn't. It wasn't just the appearance of the ghost that disturbed her. She couldn't put her finger on anything in particular, but things felt different between her and Dominic in this ancient place. Off. Slightly disconnected. And it filled her with uneasiness. She thought about waking him up for sex to soothe her, but he needed sleep. So she lay in bed, staring out the window, wishing they'd never come to this place.

The sky was still a thin gray canvas just taking on the muted colors of daybreak when Sabrina gave up trying to sleep. She rose, washed, and dressed, and went to the mess tent for coffee, leaving Dominic in bed asleep. She didn't usually drink coffee, but lack of sleep had her feeling like a zombie. A zombie in need of caffeine.

Ian sat alone at one of the tables, sipping coffee, his first cup judging by the sleepy "Hey" he yawned at her. He wore running clothes and the fitted cap from her university that Dominic had bought in California and mailed to him. She had picked it out. It had a worn-in look to it, telling her that it was a favorite hat. It pleased her that he liked it.

"Hey," she responded and poured herself a cup, dosing it liberally with creamer to cut the bitterness. She plopped down across the table from him. "Just back from a run?"

"Yeah, and it kicked my ass," he said around another yawn. "Five o'clock came really early since *someone* woke me, screaming, at two forty-five a.m. and I couldn't get back to sleep."

"Your horny one-night stand?" she asked sweetly. His deadpan stare made her chuckle. "Yeah, sorry about that."

"The lame joke or waking me up?"

"Both," she said, grin in place.

"Wanna tell me what happened?'

Rusty joined them before she could begin." Hey, you guys seen Nessy?"

"Gone missing, has she?" Ian asked.

"Aye." He rubbed his hand in his hair, worry lines scrunching his forehead. "I'm sure I had her here last night."

"Sean put some tools away last night," he said. "Check the tool tent."

"I'll do that." He hurried away with a hopeful grin on his face.

"He named his trowel Nessy?" she asked. "As in loch ness?"

He nodded.

"No wonder it keeps disappearing."

"You're full of the jokes this morning, aren't you? Back to last night."

She told him everything, then stared into her now-empty coffee cup. "Go ahead and say it." She lifted her hands. "You think I'm crazy, too."

He looked around to make sure no one was listening, then leaned in toward her. "I was eight. I had been in bed, asleep for hours, when I heard my *daideó*—"

94

"I don't know that word," she said.

"Grandpa. I woke up when I heard him call my name. He was sitting on the edge of my bed. I tried to sit up and go to him, but I couldn't move, couldn't speak. He told me to be a good lad, handfast with the woman in blue, and—do you know handfast?"

"Isn't that where the hands of the bride and groom are tied together."

"Basically, yes. But to him, it meant marry, connect with, love forever."

"Who is this woman in blue?" she asked.

"I have no idea," he said with a grin. "But I'm staying away from anyone who even remotely fits the description."

She smiled. "What happened next?"

"He told me he loved me, then sang the song he'd sung to me since I was a babe until I fell asleep. The next morning I jumped out of bed and ran to the kitchen to see him. Deeda, Sean, and his sister Shannon were at the table eating breakfast."

Dominic had told her that Sean's mom's name was Deirdre, but Ian could never say it when he was young. It always came out Deeda. Soon everyone called her that.

"'Where's my *daideó*?' I asked. They looked at me like I was daft. I told them what happened. Deeda hugged me, said it was just a dream to tell me he was thinking of me. I was arguing with her about it when the phone rang. It was *mamó*, uh, my grandma, telling us he had died during the night."

Chills ran up Sabrina's arms and down her back. Without a thought, she grabbed Ian's hand across the table, and he gripped it. Tears stung her nose, but she didn't let them go. "He came to say goodbye."

Ian nodded. "And that's why I believe you."

"I get why your *daideó* came to you—he loved you—but why did that man come to me?" She released his hand and lifted her cup to her mouth. Remembering it was empty, she set it back down. He slid his cup to her. She took it and sipped. The coffee was so sweet it hurt her teeth, but she sipped again, hoping the sugar rush would spike her energy levels. She kept her hands around the cup for something to hold on to other than Ian's hand.

"Because you wouldn't let me carry you over the threshold." One corner of his mouth tipped in a grin. "Told you so."

His comment pulled a smile from her, and she shook her head. "You've been dying to say that, haven't you?"

"I have."

She chuckled. "You're such a brat."

"Did your ghost say anything?" he asked, getting back to the subject.

"Yeah, he was quite vocal. Problem was, I didn't understand a word. It sounded like…I don't know, Old Irish, maybe Old English? I'm not a linguist."

"Do you remember any specific words?" He took his cup from her hand, his fingers brushing hers, and sipped.

"I was paying more attention to the sword in his hand than the words he was shouting, but he did repeat one word a lot…something that sounded like *sun-a-car*." She covered a yawn. "I couldn't make out much else."

"I know that word," he said, yawning in sympathy.

"It's Irish. Means something like soulmate." He removed his hat and rubbed his hands on his face and into his hair. "But it doesn't tell us what he wants."

She had reached for his cup again, her fingers on his, when Dominic headed their way, a plate full of food in his hands. She pulled her hand away.

"What who wants?" He sat beside her.

Ian and Sabrina stared at each other, then at him. "The ghost," she said.

Dominic looked at Ian. "You told her your *daideó* story, didn't you?"

Ian set his cap back on his head, the bill pulled low to his eyes. "What if I did?"

"Don't be putting those ideas in her head. It was a dream. That's all." He dug into his food.

"She saw a ghost."

"Ian…" Dominic said around a bite of food and shook his head.

"Just because you've never seen one doesn't mean we haven't."

"If she said she saw a *fae*, you'd believe that, too, would you?"

Ian shifted back in his chair, and his gaze narrowed at Dominic, as if he were insulted. "For damn sure I wouldn't be dismissing her as *loopers*."

Dominic shot forward in his chair, faced off with his best friend, his volume rising with every word. "I never said she was crazy, and I never dismissed her."

"You just don't believe her."

Dominic's eyes narrowed, too, and his teeth clenched, working his jaw. "Mind your own business, McCanna."

Ian stood, leaned over, and placed his palms flat in

the middle of the table, staring into Dominic's eyes. "Don't fucking tell me what my business is, Sullivan."

Dominic's fork clanged to his plate, and he shot to his feet, fists at his sides. Ian stood upright, facing him, his fists at the ready, too.

Sabrina jumped up. "Stop it! Both of you."

Surprise, anger, and a little fear pushed the words out of her mouth fast and furious. Dominic had described his friendship with Ian as being as close as brothers, saying they rarely argued, had never in all the years they'd know each other fought each other. At the moment, they both seemed anything but friends and clearly consumed by a voracious need to do each other bodily harm.

"Ian, where do you want me today?" she asked.

Ian kept his eyes locked on Dominic's, ignoring her.

She walked around the table to him and settled her hand at his chest. "Ian."

Her soft touch, soft voice, severed his gaze from Dominic's and found hers. As if seeing her face for the first time, he blinked away the anger making his eyes burn.

"What?" The word left his mouth like a breath.

"Where do you want me to start today?"

He swallowed. "T8." Gone was the tension in his voice and his body. "Get stills and vignettes of digging, get whoever the trench supervisor is to give us an updated PTC, and leave your takes a little long so there's some editing wiggle room."

She nodded, then her eyes left his, flicked over Dominic's, and turned to leave.

"Aren't you eating?" Dominic asked her.

"The smell of bull testosterone in the morning kills my appetite," she said and headed to T8, just as Sean, Kristin, and Meggan joined them.

"What's all the yelling about?" Sean asked.

Ian jumped in with a quick response filled with humor. "Breena called Dom a dickwad."

"She was talking about you, arsewipe," Dominic responded, in a not so humorous tone.

All the way to T8, she cussed herself for not grabbing something to eat before storming off, but no way was she going back. She stopped by Ian's office trailer to grab cameras and gear, and her tool roll, then headed to the trench.

She set the cameras aside but within reach and, kneeling by the closest skeleton, began gently loosening the dirt from one of the feet with her pick, careful not to touch the bone with her hands. Last thing she needed was a trailer full of ghosts attacking her. Now and then, she stopped, took a few photos as the exposed areas grew, and noted them on the log sheets.

Meggan jumped into the trench beside her a few minutes later, pulled her tools from her backpack, and started scratching at the other foot. Shit. Meggan was the last person she wanted to see. But if she was here, at least she wasn't with Dominic.

"Heard you saw a *puca*," Meggan said after a few minutes of silence, her eyes on her work.

Sabrina wasn't totally sure what a *puca* was, but considering recent events, she could pretty accurately guess. "Where'd you hear that?" Only Dominic and Ian knew about the ghost, so she could answer that question, too.

"Dom and Ian. They're arguing. About you. They

never argued about anything til you showed up."

Shit. They're still arguing?

At Sabrina's silence, Meggan sat back on her haunches and stared at her. "If you ask me, you're making it up to get attention." She was obviously trying to bait her. "Or you're mental."

"I didn't ask you, so keep your opinions to yourself."

"Make me."

The small, sharp pick in her hand, Sabrina rose to her feet before she even knew why she was rising and stepped toward Meggan.

Red shot upright and took a few steps back, stepped on her backpack, and fell on her ass. "*Olc!*" Her eyes narrowed, and she scrambled to her feet, brushing dirt and embedded rocks from her palms. "Seeing a *puca* at a dig site is bad luck. It'll bring trouble to all of us."

"Meg." Dominic's stern voice came from behind them.

Red joined him where he stood at the lip of the trench. "You know I'm right."

While Meggan was tattling, Sabrina dropped down and continued her work on the feet.

"Leave it alone," Dominic warned Meggan. "Sabrina, can I talk to you?"

"Yes." She kept her head down, her hands busy.

"Over here. Please." His voice was flat.

He was her husband, but as one of the field supervisors, the other being Sean, he was also one of her bosses. She stood and slowly joined him, boldly returning Meggan's evil glare. "Better watch out," she said, her voice low and serious to make her point. "I'll send the *puca* to your trailer."

Meggan's freckled face paled, and her mouth pinched into a pucker, leaving Sabrina to immediately want to retract her threat. It didn't help anything and would only feed into her claim that she was *olc*, evil, and had cursed the site because of what she'd seen.

"On to digging with ya." Dominic's voice was soft and soothing to Meggan, as if he were consoling a frightened child.

Meggan shoved her tools into her backpack, grabbed it, and rushed away to her trench with a barely muffled, "Bitch."

Dominic stepped into the trench with Sabrina. "You don't like her much, do you?"

"Is that what you came here for? To ask me how I like Meggan?"

He took her hand. "I came to apologize."

"For?"

"For dismissing your feelings last night. Upsetting you at breakfast. I'm sorry."

"You should be."

"I am. Truly." He held out a paper bag.

She took it, looked inside, and smiled. A plastic-wrapped peanut butter sandwich nestled next to a banana and a carton of milk. Her stomach rumbled, as if it could see the contents and knew it was on its way down. "You're sorry, but do you believe me?"

His rigid stance—feet planted and arms crossed over his chest—gave her his answer even before he opened his mouth. "I've never seen a ghost, and I won't believe they exist unless I do, but it's also unlike you to pass out or wake up screaming in terror or make up things. So, yes, I believe something happened. I just don't know what. Yet."

Not the most glowing endorsement of her sanity, but better than before. "Baby, I don't know either, but I do know I need you with me on this."

He slid his arms around her waist, and her arms went around him. It felt so good.

"I'm with you, Sabrina. Always. No matter what." He kissed her head.

"Thank you for breakfast," she said into his chest.

"You're welcome." He held her a few seconds longer before releasing her. "Come see me in T1 today. I'm lifting your ghost's bones."

He turned to leave, but she grabbed his arm, stopping him. Letting his little ghost jab go, she asked an important question. "Is she right? Is it bad luck?"

"Some of the team believes it is. But I don't, so don't worry about it." He cupped her cheek, rubbing his thumb across her lips. "Love you."

She covered his hand with hers and turned her head to plant a kiss in his palm. "Love you, too." She wanted to ask him to hold her again, kiss away her fears, but instead she watched him go.

As she sat at the foot of the skeleton, knees to her chin, she scarfed down her breakfast, vowing to check the MAC website tonight to see what other digs were needing a field supervisor and a media person. She was beginning to think Meggan was right. This dig was cursed.

Chapter Seven

After two weeks of watching her ghostly warrior run his sword through her husband, the unrelenting nightly haunts became almost old hat to Sabrina. She no longer awoke screaming, and she wasn't afraid, but she was always restless, never getting a full night's sleep.

It didn't help that the ghost talked incessantly, right in her ear, like a mosquito buzzing in the dark. Even though she didn't understand his words—except *sonuachar*, which he said constantly—two things were crystal clear. He despised Dominic, and he desperately needed her to do something. And she could feel his frustration, sadness, and even anger that she remained clueless about what that action was, despite his determined efforts. She didn't know much about her warrior, but she knew he wasn't going to let up until she had done what he asked.

As tenacious as he was in death, she could only imagine the force he had been in life. It was surprising to her that human characteristics like tenacity, ferocity, gentleness, and humor remained in a soul after death of the body. Even more surprising was how quickly she'd become accustomed to his presence, found comfort in it even, like a steady-burning night light to a frightened child...like a night-time version of Ian.

The ghostly appearances were cake compared to the bevy of practical jokes they had stirred up. Team members found things in their beds, from rocks and sticks to bones and dead birds. Others awakened to a blood-like substance slashed on the doors of their trailers, as if suggesting they had been marked for something sinister. And everyone had been on the receiving end of strange pranks involving their personal possessions, like things going missing or being destroyed, or sheets and blankets on the beds being shredded.

For some odd reason, which didn't go unnoticed by the team, Sabrina and Ian had been spared the pranks. As the newcomer, an outsider, and the one who hung out with a ghost, the finger of blame was pointed directly at her.

To Sabrina's mind, the pranks were not of the supernatural variety but someone using her ghost to stir up trouble and cast dispersions on her. It could be the protestors getting in, piggybacking off the camp drama, trying to derail the project. She hated to think it was someone from the team, but it was a possibility. Her money was on the latter and on Meggan as the culprit.

But when more serious things began to happen, she knew it couldn't be just Meggan. Equipment, like the washing tub that had been working fine one day was broken the next and work had to stop for a trip into town to get parts to fix it. Several trenches, which held skeletons that were nearly ready to lift out, were filled in the following morning, causing extra work. Bones that had been washed, dried, labeled, and bagged one day were the next day out of the bags and partially assembled on the finds office floor. Food was missing, which not only meant added cost, but added time to drive into town and fighting through the protestors' line to replace it.

Everyone was spooked, irritated, on edge, and looking for someone to blame, sure that finding the culprit would end the trouble. Everyone that is except Dominic, who said he didn't believe in that stuff, and Ian, who never seemed to let things bother him. There was only one thing Ian seemed to worry about.

"There better still be cake," he said as he and Sabrina headed to the mess tent for lunch a little late after uploading their morning photos onto the hard drive to free up their memory cards for the afternoon shift.

"It's a good thing you run every day," she teased.

"I don't see you saying no to cake."

"Why do you think I run with you every morning?"

"You love my company."

"Yeah, that's it." She laughed and he opened the door for her.

As they stepped through, all talk inside the tent ceased and every eye turned to stare at them. The team looked at her like she'd sprouted a second head and started spewing fire from both mouths. Some of them made the sign of the cross over their hearts.

She glanced around for Dominic, but he wasn't there. More and more, he wasn't coming in to lunch, choosing to stay in the trench a little longer, or discuss the morning's findings with Gabe, who was grooming him for his assistant site director position. Meggan usually stayed in the trench with him, but because she was in the tent, Sabrina knew he was probably with Gabe or Jack. Sean and Kristin, also absent, were likely rocking their trailer.

She turned to Ian, who was watching the crowd,

brow raised. Putting his hand on her back, he guided her to the food line. She handed him a tray and got one for herself. He stayed close behind her as they helped themselves to food, including the perennial cake.

"The table in the back," he said, motioning to it.

The silence unsettled her as she negotiated the sea of disapproving looks to reach the table. Ian sat with his back to the tent wall, a seat that allowed him a clear view of every person in the space. She sat adjacent to him, her back to the other tent wall. Trying to ignore the eyes on her, she bit into her sandwich, chewed slowly, and swallowed. Barely.

Ian had eaten his cake first, as he always did, as if nothing unusual were happening in the tent. He leaned toward her. "The cake's terrible today. I better take yours to save you from the horror of it."

She didn't respond with her typical "touch my cake and you'll lose that hand" remark. Instead, she put her sandwich down and stood, facing the room. "You all look eager to tell me something," she said firmly but calmly, meeting each of her teammates' eyes.

"You brought bad luck into camp." It was Angus who finally spoke.

"How so?" she asked him.

He turned his eyes to Meggan.

"You have an evil spirit attached to you," she answered for him. "And that brings bad luck to everybody."

Sabrina shot Meggan an accusatory glare. "The ghost is not related to the trouble going on in camp. He only bothers me, and he's not evil." Okay, so her ghost shot her mean looks. And his ghostly clamoring kept her awake most of the night. And he repeatedly slashed and stabbed Dominic. But he wasn't evil.

Meggan's lip curled. "You need to leave before one of us gets killed. Do you want Dom's death—or Ian's—on your conscience?"

She felt Ian behind her, his hand sitting protectively at the curve of her waist. His touch and his presence gave her legs to face her accusers.

"Wow, Meggan, that's a little dramatic, even for you," she said.

"Mock if you will, but I've seen it with me own eyes. This is Ireland, not America. Things happen here that outsiders can never understand."

"Bullshit," Ian said. "This has nothing to do with mystical, magical Ireland. This is Meggan being *cheesed off* that Dom married Breena. What better way to get revenge than to pull pranks and get you all to blame her just because she saw a ghost."

That explained a lot. From day one she felt Meggan hated her and wanted Dominic. Turning the team against her might get her to leave...or get Dominic to leave her.

"Yeah, that, but it's not Red's fault Sabrina sees a *puca*. And a *puca* at a site is bad luck. You know that yourself, Ian." Angus's gaze shifted to Sabrina. "Sorry, Sabrina, but she's right. If you stay here, bad things will keep happening until someone ends up hurt or dead." He crossed himself again, and several others followed suit.

Ian held her steady against him, as if he could feel her internal shaking and was there to calm her, to show a united front.

"Funny how none of you had any problems with Breena until Meggan started her blathering. If you want someone to blame for what's going on here, blame the person who's causing the trouble." He stared hard at Meggan. Kept his eyes on her. And soon the team's gazes shifted to her as well. Meggan's eyes darted back and forth, from Ian to the team, showing her panic.

"Dom will never leave Breena," Ian continued, speaking directly to Meggan. "If she goes, he goes. You might keep that in mind before executing your next prank." He faced the others. "You all might keep it in mind, too. Dom's gone above and beyond for each one of you, on a personal as well as professional basis."

Heads nodded.

"Rusty, who donated two weeks of vacation to you when your mam was in hospital so you could go home and take care of your family?"

Rusty dropped his head. "Dom."

"Gussy, who bailed you out when you got that DUI?"

"You did."

"The time before that."

"Dom."

"Shane, who loaned you money so you could take that certification workshop last summer?"

"Dom."

Ian turned to Meggan. "And you. Have you forgotten why you still have a job with this team?"

Red's cheeks flamed, and she glared at him for bringing up an obviously tender topic.

"Is this how you thank him? By tormenting his wife, the woman he loves? Trying to run her off for something that's not her fault? That's shit."

Sabrina stared at the contrite faces of the team. No one spoke.

"Let's get out of here," he said to Sabrina, contempt in his voice. "I've lost my appetite." He took her hand and led her through the gaps between tables to the exit. He pushed the door open for her, letting her walk through, then stopped and turned back to deliver a parting shot. "Betraying his wife is the same as betraying him."

Once away from the tent, he grabbed her hand and ran toward the vehicles.

"Where are we going?" she asked when they got to his jeep.

He grinned. "Into town for a burger. I'm starving. But no way in hell am I going back in there."

"No, of course not," she said when they'd climbed in and buckled up. "You wouldn't want to disturb the layer of pathos you just poured on."

"A little thick, was it?"

She laughed, her gaze tied to his, and shook her head. "You're my hero, Ian McCanna."

"Fuckin' A, love." He laughed with her as he fired up the engine and headed toward the gate. He called Jack to let him know the two of them were going into town for supplies.

"I have a confession," he said once they were on the road.

"Let me guess. We don't really need supplies," she teased.

He grinned. "Okay, two confessions."

"What's the second?"

"I've never been anyone's hero before. So don't expect too much."

A dark subtitle ran beneath his teasing tone, a warning that he was used to disappointing people.

Emotion swelled inside her, and the message flowing in it was that he'd never disappoint her.

"I've never had a hero before, so I have few expectations." She cupped her hand around his where it rested on his thigh and squeezed. "But so far, you've exceeded them all."

Linking their fingers like he'd linked their eyes, he brought her hand to his mouth and kissed it, then set their joined hands back on his thigh, not letting go until they approached town and he needed his hand to shift gears. In the cafe, he sat next to her in the booth, and they laughed and teased while they ate.

She'd been so happy to get away from the site for even a short time, she didn't realize until later that night that the protestors hadn't done one thing to stop them, coming or going. Just stared at them. With an odd look of…awe…on their faces.

****

Ian's heavy-handed guilt-trip had the intended effect. The site remained prank-free for several days. The team was friendly and respectful but still watched her with a cautious eye, as if they were on the lookout for any signs of toil and trouble bubbling around her.

Sabrina had just finished noting the morning's filming work on her log when she heard Rusty shout, "Fire!"

Thick smoke billowed into the air from the camp site. The acrid smell of it filled her nose. How they'd all missed it before then, she didn't know. Everyone jumped out of the trenches and sprinted toward it. The mess tent was in flames. Their food, eating supplies, tables and chairs, refrigerators, generator—everything was in that tent.

Dominic was suddenly right behind her and caught her to him. "Stay back!" He ran toward where Ian and Sean were spraying the fire with extinguishers. Never one to just sit and wait for help, she ran to join her team.

The water resources at the site included bottled drinking water and separate tanks of water for showering and for kitchen cleaning. The tank for the mess tent, which was up on a wooden platform at the back of the tent, was too close to the flames to dip into and be of use.

Even if they used every last drop of their water supply, they had to put out the fire. If it spread through the entire site they would lose everything. The team quickly formed a line from the showers to the mess tent, using buckets and bowls and everything big enough to hold water and dumped it onto the flames. Sabrina took up a spot toward the front with Kristin. Not because she was brave, but because it was the best spot to keep an eye on Dominic. And Ian. The extinguishers soon ran out, and Dominic, Ian, and Sean joined the brigade at the front of the line.

Dominic got in front of her. "I told you to stay back."

She ignored his comment and passed him a bucket of water. "I saw this movie where the hero used a vehicle to push a water tank over, putting out the fire. What if we tried that?"

"If we nick it at the right spot so it falls right, it might work." He left to tell Jack.

Minutes later, Jack pulled the SUV behind the tent and gently bumped the platform. The rocking water tank finally tipped over toward the tent. The tank cover popped off, and water poured out, dousing the fire. The bucket brigade took care of the few remaining flames.

Jack got out and headed their way, a scowl on his face. "The tires on all the vehicles are flat. The front right on that one," he nodded toward the old SUV, "is nearly flat. One of the protestors was stabbing it. He and three other little shits ran toward the fence and hopped over when they saw me coming."

"I think we found our vandals," Kristin said.

"Breaking our equipment and stealing our food didn't get rid of us, so they tried a stronger tactic. We're low on water, out of food, and our vehicles are out of commission," Jack said, shaking his head. "They hit us where it would hurt most. We're stuck here like pioneers waiting for the Calvary to arrive."

"Did they get the spare tires?" Sabrina asked.

The vandals had either overlooked the spares or hadn't had time to damage them. Since all the SUVs took the same tires, Rusty and Shane were able to get one SUV running. Dominic, Jack, and Gabe went into town for the supplies they needed in the short-term until the company could bring in the rest in a larger truck. Sean and Ian directed the cleanup efforts.

Dominic was on her mind as she, along with the rest of the team, shoveled piles of burned and indistinguishable mush into her bucket, then carried it to the trash bin to dump. An uneasiness had settled into her bones in the aftermath of the ghost's appearance, and she'd felt a distance growing between her and Dominic that made her needy for his attention. It was like she was constantly grasping to hold on to him before he slipped away. She wished he was here now, beside her, arms around her, giving her the comfort she needed. But his job left little time for coddling. She was forced to get through it on her own. At least she had…

She noticed Ian across the way. He was taking pictures of the damage and working with Sean to organize the search through the remains to note which items were salvageable and which needed to be replaced so they could call it in to Jack. Thinking she could help him with the photographing, she set aside her shovel and bucket and walked toward him. He looked up, his gaze finding hers before she was half way there. He instantly walked toward her.

"Need help?" she asked.

He put his arm around her waist, squeezed her close, and she did the same to him. That was their way, now—to hug when they greeted each other, like they were reconnecting after a long separation. She wasn't even sure when it had happened, or how. It just was. And she really needed it today.

"Sure. You take photos, and I'll go take a nap," he said, a teasing smile on his lips.

"Thought you didn't do naps."

"That was before all this madness hit and stole my sleep."

"I know what you mean." Their gazes tangled, and it was all suddenly too much. The ghost. The lack of sleep. The accusations from the team. Meggan's constant desire for Dominic and hatred of her. The fire. The vandalism. That Dominic was gone when she needed him here. Her unwelcome and guilt-inducing feelings for Ian. It all rushed over her. She averted her eyes so he couldn't see them water. "Well, I'll let you get back to work."

He grabbed her hand to stop her from leaving.

"You okay, love?"

"I'm fine," the lie stuttered out.

"No, you're not." He dropped his clipboard to the ground and set the camera on it. "C'mere," he whispered, his arms going all the way around her and pulling her flush against him.

Her hands rose to settle on his heart, and she dipped her head there to hide the emotions and tears on her face. The smoky smell of the fire clung to his shirt along with his sunshine smell, and she breathed him in, drawing his comforting scent and heat into her body. "I'm sorry. I don't even know why I'm crying." Maybe she was just PMSing. Maybe she just needed her hero's arms around her like this.

"There now, love. You got a lot coming at you at once, I know, but it'll be all right," he whispered into her hair. "Your hero's here to help you through it."

How was it possible that he always knew exactly what she was thinking and what she needed to hear without her having to say a word? "Thank God," she whimpered before she realized how desperate it sounded.

"You don't waste time, do ya?" Meggan's sharp voice acted like a pry bar to separate them. She stood in front of them, an evil grin on her face like she'd caught them in the act of some gross infidelity and couldn't wait to tattle. "Dom's been gone, what, a thirty at the most? New record for you two to start going at it." She smirked at Ian. "Obviously your spell is working."

"Make yourself useful." Ian picked up the clipboard and thrust it into her hands. "Everyone else is."

"Since when is putting the moves on your best

friend's wife useful? To anyone but you that is." She walked away, clipboard in hand, and joined Sean.

"She does not like me one bit," Sabrina said when Meggan was out of earshot.

"She doesn't like anyone." He dug his fingers into the front pocket of her jeans and pulled out the pack of gum she always kept there for them.

"Except Dominic," she said. "She wants him."

"No shit." He unwrapped a piece and held it out to her.

She bit off half. "What happened between them?"

He took the other half and worked the pack back into her pocket. "Ask Dom." He picked up his camera and stepped away from her, but she grabbed his T-shirt and pulled him back.

"I'm asking you."

He eyed her, as if he weren't sure he should be the one to share the story. "You can't tell Dom."

"Doesn't he already know?"

"Not all of it. Promise me."

"Of course. I promise."

He took her hand and led her several feet away from the team so they wouldn't be overheard. "They hooked up at a field school Sean, Dom, and I were helping Jack run the summer before we started uni. They were…tight…from day one."

They *had* slept together. Shit. Why hadn't Dominic told her?

"This is the part he doesn't know. I caught her fucking some guy in the mess tent. She begged me not to tell Dom. I gave her a choice—tell him what she'd done or break up with him. If she did neither, I'd tell him. She broke up with him."

"Did it hurt him? That she broke up?"

"Yeah, more than he let on and more than I thought it would since he'd said that once the dig was over he'd have broken up with her anyway."

"Strange that she ended up on this team with you guys."

"It's stranger than that, love. Every summer dig and internship Dom, Sean, and I were on after that, she was there…not as a participant, but as paid help, like us. She got a job with MAC about the same time we did, assigned to our team."

"Shit. Who did she have to sleep with to get that level of special treatment?" She'd been half joking, but by the way Ian's eyes flickered, she knew someone had paved the way for Meggan. "Who?"

He shook his head.

"Why are you protecting her?" It pissed her off that he'd protect Meggan.

"I'm not protecting her."

"So you're protecting someone else." Her eyes went wide. "The guy you caught her with." And wider. "Someone who's here now."

Ian said nothing, his poker face not giving away anything, but his eyes stayed on hers, intense and steady.

The only person on the team high enough to pull those kinds of strings back then was Jack, maybe Gabe. Oh, shit. She felt sick to her stomach thinking about either one of them having sex with the then-teenage Meggan. That was just wrong. "What else?"

"Dom would work with her after that, was friendly, but as far as I know, he didn't ask her back to his bed. She stopped openly trying to get him because she knew

I'd tell him, but I know she still wants him."

From what she'd seen of her behavior, she *was* still after him despite the fact that he was married and off the market. "How did she react to the news that he got married?"

He blew out a breath. "She knifed everything in his caravan—mattress, blankets, pillows, clothes. Which is why you needed a new caravan."

She scrunched her mouth in hurt and confusion. He'd told her it was because he wanted a nicer trailer for her. "Why is someone that unstable on the team?"

He shrugged. "She's good at her job. Jack was ready to reassign her so she wouldn't cause trouble, but Dom told him it wasn't necessary."

Everything Ian said explained a lot—why Meggan hated her, why she and Ian didn't get along. She probably blamed both of them for stealing her chance at happily-ever-after with Dominic. Her mind filled with images of how troublesome Meggan could be. How far she might go to win Dominic back. But why had he fought so hard to keep her around?

"They work well together, and he didn't want her to lose her job," Ian said, as if she'd asked her question aloud.

At first it was creepy that he seemed to be able to read her thoughts, but now it was comforting. He got her, understood her.

"Either that or he still loves her and can't let her go," she said. The reality of that possibility hit her firmly in the chest, making her heart thump in her throat.

"Nah. He loves you. He married you."

His words eased her a little. "I know, but—Ian,

who's that going into our office?"

He spun around in time to see the door close. "No one's allowed in there."

Together they sprinted toward the trailer, heard a crash seconds before he yanked open the door, her right behind him. Two men stood in the middle of the room. They'd knocked over the tall cabinet, the contents—log books, DVDs, boxes of batteries, memory cards, T-shirts, hats, a blanket, tools—scattered across the floor. The cabinet had barely missed the desks with the computers and monitors.

"What the fuck?" Ian shouted.

One of the guys picked up and threw a tower of DVDs at his head and tried to dash past him. Ian dodged the projectile, then rushed the guy and punched him in the jaw. The guy fell against the wall and crumpled to the floor. At the same time, the other guy lunged at Sabrina.

In one quick motion, she rotated her body, raised her knee, and struck out with her heel, catching him hard in the stomach. A deep "oomph" erupted from his mouth as he tumbled backward a few steps. He gripped his stomach and fell to the floor, then rolled to his side in a ball, moaning.

"What the hell was that?" Ian asked, a grin dancing on his face as he stared at her.

"I took a couple of years of self-defense classes. Guess I haven't forgotten it all."

He shook his head. "Hand me those zip ties from the drawer, Rambo."

They bound the intruders' hands and hauled them into the campsite, seating them near the fire pit. He and Sean were still interrogating them and getting nowhere an hour later when Dominic, Jack, and Gabe returned from town with supplies.

"Call the *garda*," Jack told Gabe, who pulled out his phone. "Have them get these little shits off my dig site."

"You don't need to make that call." A loud, clear voice shot across the silence, capturing all eyes. A woman with long, flaming red hair walked into the circle.

Jack slowly approached Ena Flanagan, leader of the group antagonizing them. "These your guys?" He cocked a thumb over his shoulder at the two sitting by the pit.

"They are part of *Chosaint*, yes," Ena said.

"Hope your little club has deep pockets, 'cause these boys are going to need legal help."

"What have they done?"

"Assault, vandalism, trespassing—that's just for starters."

"Mr. Ford, as leaders of our individual 'little club,' this matter is between you and me. May I offer a mutually beneficial compromise?"

Jack wiped his hand down his mustache and scratched his strawberry-blond scruff, a sign Sabrina had learned meant he was troubled. She'd bet most of his worry had to do with the fact that Ena was on his turf and she knew his name. "What do you have in mind?"

"*Chosaint* will vacate this area. We will not protest. We will not block the road. We will not come into your camp or work site again, for as long as your team is here."

"What'll it cost us?"

119

Ena nodded toward her two men. "They leave with me."

Jack stared at her a moment, looked at his team, then back at her. "How do I know you're not lying your ass off?"

"You don't. But I'm not."

After more beard scratching, Jack straightened to his full five feet eight inches. "If I see even one of you in my camp again, I'll prosecute to the full extent of the law."

"Agreed, but there's one final condition."

"Shit, I knew it." Jack shook his head and started to walk away but came to an abrupt halt when she caught his arm. He jerked away like he'd been shocked.

She held up her hands to show she meant no threat. "I wish only to speak with Sabrina."

Chapter Eight

Dominic and Ian, who were on either side of Sabrina, drew closer to her.

Ian put his arm around her waist.

Dominic stepped in front of her. "Hell, no."

She put her hand on Dominic's back. "If my talking to her will get them out of here and keep us safe, I want to do it." She met Ian's eyes, silently telling him she'd be fine, then slipped out of his embrace, around Dominic, and walked to where Ena stood next to Jack.

Without a word, the woman turned and walked toward the dig site, Sabrina at her side.

"Not without me," Dominic said, and he and Ian both stepped forward.

Ena stopped, her face cold and hard as she glared at him. "Not you, Dominic Sullivan."

Sabrina felt energy crackling around the woman. "Dominic." She held out a hand to stop him from coming any closer. "I'll be okay." She turned back to Ena, looking her straight in the eyes. "She won't hurt me."

The two continued on. Without warning, Ena stopped and turned back. "Ian McCanna." She pointed at him. "Join us."

Sabrina scanned the faces of her team. Suspicion blazed in their eyes as they stared at her, then at Ian, and lastly at Dominic as he turned a hard look on Ian. In his jealous eyes flickered the question, why you? But then he put his hand on Ian's shoulder. "Keep her safe."

Ian nodded. "Count on it." He jogged to catch up with them. Taking his promise seriously, he inserted himself between them and took Sabrina's hand in his, as if to remind her he was in it with her.

At the edge of T1, where Dominic had unearthed the skeleton of the man who now haunted Sabrina, Ena stopped and faced her. "Tell me of your *sprid*."

Sabrina wasn't sure she wanted to give this woman any information. Who knew what she'd do with it.

"We feel the presence attached to you," Ena said when Sabrina kept silent. "I see him. Tall, warrior's body. Long, dark hair. Eyes as blue as glacial ice. He speaks to you, yes?"

"Yes, but I don't know what he's saying."

"He's asking you to find his soulmate—his *sonuachar*—and set her free."

Soulmate. So Ian had been right. "Where is she?"

Ena turned her silver eyes toward the sea of trenches. "Out there."

"What does this have to do with us?" Ian asked.

"I will take my people and leave this place if you two give your word to find his *sonuachar*. Free her. So the lovers can reunite."

"Why us?" Sabrina asked.

"He has chosen you."

"How will we know we've found her?"

"He will tell you."

"Is he also going to tell us where to dig?" Ian asked, not even trying to hide his sarcasm.

Ena bristled. "I expected more from you, Ian

McCanna, than mockery."

"I'm not mocking," he said, his tone more respectful. "I'm serious. There are hundreds of skeletons out here. What if we can't find her? What if she's not even here?"

"She is here, or the *sprid* would not be," Ena said. "And he will stay attached to Sabrina until she finds his other half. He will not give up. That is the way of soulmates."

Sabrina wasn't sure she believed the witch, but she wasn't willing to take the chance that she was right. Her eyes slid to Ian's. She wanted to ask him what to do. He was the experienced digger and would have a better idea whether it was possible.

Ian's blue eyes revealed no answers, but they calmed her and gave her courage to give Ena her answer. "If I do this, I have your word that you and your people will leave and not vandalize our camp or dig site or harm our team?"

Unblinking, Ena stared deep into her eyes. "You have my word."

The woman's word meant nothing to Sabrina, but if there was even a slim chance to keep everyone safe, how could she not do what Ena asked? It was only her time and effort. Ian would help her. Dominic would, too.

Ian gripped her shoulders, turned her to him, drew his hands down her arms, and caught her hands. "*Hashkeh*, there's no way to know where she is or what to do if we find her."

His continued use of the word 'we' and 'us' tugged at her heart.

"Help her, Ian," Ena said. "You're the only one

123

who can. You two must come together to succeed. To change your life."

"*Hashkeh*, you don't have to—" Sabrina started, her voice unable to go above a whisper. She had used his word for her. She didn't know what it meant, but it felt right, as if the emotions embedded in its hushed syllables bound the two of them into a strong and unstoppable force.

"I'm in this with you. All the way," he whispered back.

She wanted to kiss him. Instead, she put her hands on his heart and nodded her thanks.

"Do we have an agreement?" Ena said, shattering their connection.

They turned toward her. "What's in it for you?" Ian asked. "Why do you care whether they're reunited?"

"Their souls were marked for each other but separated in the manner of their death or burial or both, which doomed them to an eternity apart. Reuniting them is...the right thing to do." She reached out her hands, one to Sabrina, the other to Ian. "Do we have an agreement?"

They looked at each other, then at Ena. "Yes," they said in unison and reached out to take a hand.

The witch grabbed their wrists, pressing the pointed nail of one thumb into her vein and the other into Ian's in the same place. It felt to Sabrina like she'd been injected with some paralyzing substance. She couldn't move, and she was sure if Ian could move, he would have.

Ena's eyes were closed, and strange words, garbled together into a long string of monotonic whispers, flowed from her lips. Heat circled her and Ian, and a pale blue light rose from them like smoke from a genie's bottle, enveloping them. A thick, blue blood-like substance oozed over their wrists. Ena brought their wrists together, pressed them tight against each other, and Sabrina felt a tingling, burning sensation where they touched.

She released them suddenly, so suddenly they stumbled, crumbling to their knees, gulping for air, and breathing hard, as if they'd run a mile at full speed. Ian put his arms around Sabrina and struggled to his feet with her, holding her against him. She was glad for his support. It felt as if all the energy had been syphoned from her body.

Ena's eyes popped opened, and she grabbed their wrists again. An eternity symbol branded their wrists, glowing with the same blue that had surrounded their bodies. The glow quickly dissipated, but the color—a ghostly pale blue—remained. Her wrist throbbed like a living thing lived inside the twisted symbol. One look at Ian told her his did, too.

"Yeeesss!" Ena tossed her head back in euphoria and cackled. "I knew it. I felt it." Her focused stare felt like a needle prick. "You are *bunaidh*."

"Originals," Ian whispered, his voice thin.

Sabrina looked at him, then at Ena. "What does that mean?"

"You and Ian share one soul. Two halves of a whole. True *sonuachar*. Like the soul you will reunite at this sacred place. Your *sprid* isn't just telling you about his *sonuachar*. He is telling you about yours."

A sick feeling rushed through her body, as if her heart were pumping toxins through her veins instead of blood. "What have you done?"

Ena's gray eyes gleamed like steel, and a freakish grin lifted her lips away from her teeth. "I did nothing. I only reveal the truth of what is, give an explanation for the hunger that rages between you. Your passion for each other will burn forever."

"I'm married to Dominic. I love Dominic. He's my passion, my soulmate. Not Ian."

"That union has served its purpose and is dying. You feel it. The threads binding you loosening, unknotting, allowing the distance between you to grow. He is meant for another."

Dread and fury surged, making her insides burn. "Undo this spell you've placed on us." The demand growled from her throat.

"The connection between you and Ian is stronger than any spell. It began eons ago, at the time you were first separated. I can no more unknot your ties than I can stop the sun from rising in the morning sky."

"No," Sabrina shouted and rushed at her, wanting to force her to take it back, reverse whatever she'd put into motion. Ian held her back, his arms around her, pulling her back.

Dominic must have heard or seen her distress, because he suddenly appeared at her side, pulling her out of Ian's arms and into his. She lunged into him, hugging him tight.

"What did you do?" he shouted at Ena over Sabrina's shoulder.

Everyone else would only hear the fury in his voice. Sabrina also heard the fear, felt it in his tense body. He was right to be afraid. She was. And it made her tremble in his arms.

"I showed her the truth."

"About what?"

"That is for her to say. Or not." Ena left them and walked toward the fire pit.

Ian followed, Sabrina beside him, wrapped in Dominic's arms.

"Release my brothers so we can leave this place," Ena said to Jack when she drew even with him.

"Is Sabrina okay?" Jack asked Ian.

Ian looked at her, his eyes narrowed, his mouth tight. In that look was evidence that he knew she was anything but okay after the witch's pronouncement. His low *yeah* was about preventing her from having to explain a *no*.

Jack stared at Ena, long and hard, then approached the two men. "Get up." They struggled to their feet. "Boys," Jack said to Dominic, Ian, and Sean. "Let's escort our guests out."

Sean put a protective arm around Kristin and kept her close as they escorted Ena and her men to the gate. Sabrina wouldn't leave Dominic, so she joined them, too. With his knife Jack sliced the ties biding their hands, and the protestors climbed over the gate.

"What did she say to you?" Dominic asked Sabrina as they headed back to camp.

Her eyes darted to Ian, who was watching her. "She told me what the ghost wants."

"What does it want?"

"For Ian and me to find his soulmate. He'll stay with me until we do."

"Why you and Ian?" Suspicion gripped his voice and steeled his eyes.

The lie and the truth wrestled in her mind. A lie was bad, but in this case the truth was worse. How could she tell her husband she and Ian had been chosen because they were soulmates, originals, destined to be together? Not only would it hurt him, it would also cause mistrust between them, and between him and Ian.

"Because Ian and I are…the only ones who can see him," she said finally, her eyes flying to Ian, silently begging him to lie for her.

Dominic's gaze cut to Ian. "You never mentioned it."

"If you didn't believe your wife, you sure as fuck wouldn't have believed me."

All she wanted was to go home and lie in her husband's arms for a few minutes, let his kisses and love work the whole nasty business out of her head. But his tight stance, mouth, and fists at Ian's comment told her he wouldn't let it go until he had all the answers to his questions.

"Where is she? This soulmate?" he grilled Sabrina.

"Fuck, Dom, take her home," Ian growled, showing his irritation at the interrogation. "Can't you see she's not up to answering a bunch of questions?"

"Don't tell me how to take care of my wife," Dominic snapped and stepped toward Ian.

She got in front of him and put her hands on his chest. "Baby, I want to go home. And I really need you with me."

His gaze cut to Jack, as if asking permission. As management, Dominic would be needed to right the wrongs that had happened today. He couldn't do his job if he was coddling his wife. She understood that. But right now she needed him more than the project did.

"Go take care of your wife," Jack said. "Sean, take over for Dom til he gets back. Ian, you're with me. I want to know exactly what that witch said to you and Sabrina."

Jack stormed away to his office, expecting Ian to follow. Instead, Ian watched Dominic lead her away. She felt the weight of his eyes all the way home, felt the soothing heat of his touch, felt his desire to be the one comforting her. It's what she wanted, too.

She loved Dominic. There was no room in her heart to love anyone else to that extent. Especially his best friend. What Ena said wasn't true. Couldn't be true. It was a spell, or a way to cause one last bit of trouble before she and *Chosaint* cleared out. *If* they cleared out.

The witch's prophecy would not come true, she vowed as she took her husband into her body. *I will not let it happen.*

The next morning, there was no trace of *Chosaint*.

That night, after dinner, she and Ian kept their word, too, and began digging for the *sonuachar*.

****

Dom checked the clock for the third time. He had completed the rest of the report and was waiting on Meg's finds data, but she was now four minutes late to their meeting. If it were anyone else, he wouldn't be worried. But Meg? You could set your watch by her promptness. Five minutes late. Something was wrong. He rang her mobile, but when it went to voice mail, he left the office and headed to her caravan.

His first knock went unanswered. After his third, he opened the door and walked in. The shower was running. He moved deeper into the space. He was about to call out her name when he heard moaning. Had she fallen in the shower? Was she hurt?

His heart pounding, he rushed into the bathroom, doing a hard stop just inside the doorway. Meg's naked body was clearly visible through the transparent shower curtain, one hand buried in her pussy, one on her *diddie*, pinching her nipple. She fucked her hips forward and back, head back, eyes closed, calling *his* name, begging *him* to fuck her. The moans he'd taken for injury had been the sound of an orgasm blooming.

He knew he should back away and leave her to this intimate, private moment. But he couldn't tear his eyes from the vision of her self-pleasuring. Her pussy juice scented the steamy air, and he inhaled deeply, licked his lips and could almost taste her.

His body responded like it always had when her scent and taste infiltrated him. His breathing rough, his pulse racing, his hand instinctively dropped to the front of his jeans and cupped his cock that was straining the faded denim. He rubbed hard over the aching flesh.

For a moment, he pictured himself stepping into the shower with her, dropping to his knees and moving her fingers away, wrapping her leg around his shoulder, and letting his tongue take over, giving her the release she needed, taking the release he needed. He'd done it before. Many times. And it had been delicious for both of them.

As he watched her fuck herself, her hand movements increased speed, and her other hand squeezed her little *diddie* relentlessly, again and again, like he always had. The orgasm hit her hard, ripping a long, loud moan from her throat, and she came to the sound of his name groaning from her lips.

Feeling like a pervert—and worse, a cheater—he stumbled out of the bathroom, out of the caravan, back to the office. He fought the urge to rip open his jeans, pull out his swollen cock, and jerk off into the trashcan to the image burned on his retinas. It would only take a few hard strokes. But he didn't deserve to come after what he'd done. To Meg. To Sabrina.

Shit. What kind of fuck was he? He sat his arse down in his chair and tried to get back into the report, starting with double-checking his figures, but the image of Meg's figure writhing in pleasure while fantasizing about his cock plunging inside her pussy would not fade.

Meg arrived minutes later, but he kept his eyes firmly on the computer monitor. He did not want her to look into his guilty eyes.

"Hey, mate," she said, her voice calm and silky after her orgasm, and sat in the chair next to him.

"Hey." He cleared his throat to smooth the roughness in his voice. "Do you have the data?"

"Of course. That's why I'm here." She rolled her chair close to his and opened a folder.

Her skin smelled like soap and a hint of cum, and the scent was doing crazy things to his body. In a purely protective move, he shifted his chair away from her, putting a good half meter between them.

"Something wrong?" she asked.

"No."

"You moved away from me like I stink."

"No."

"You *cheezed* at something?"

Hell, yeah, he was. Himself. "Just ready to get this report finished."

"Sorry I was a little late," she said. "I was pretty *manky* and wanted to shower before coming. You wouldn't have wanted to be in the same room with me earlier."

"No problem, but let's get to it. I promised to help Sabrina dig tonight."

She scoffed loudly at his comment, and his gaze cut to her. Her face was fresh and rosy from her shower, from her orgasm, her mouth full and wet, her eyes bright.

The enticing picture she made annoyed him, slanting his eyebrows into a scowl. "You have a problem with me wanting to help my wife?" he said, his tone harsher than he'd intended.

"You work all day in the trenches, part of the evening on paperwork, and she wants you to work later into the night digging up her ghost's soulmate." She rolled her eyes. "But, hey, if her selfishness doesn't bother you, why should it bother me?"

"My job and my relationship with Sabrina is none of your business."

Overhead, thunder boomed, shaking the caravan, and lightning lit up the small space, showing the passion flaring high in her cheeks, turning them red. The rain beat the roof like a hail of bullets, echoing the noise in his head at the conversation, at…at…at every fucking thing going on at this site.

"When someone is hurting and disrespecting the people I care about, I make it my business," she said, her tone matching the fire in her eyes. "I learned that from you."

She was right. He'd do the same thing. Her concern was coming from a good place. That knowledge tempered his harshness.

"You don't even know Sabrina," he said. "Where

is this hatred of her coming from?" When she didn't respond, he leaned forward, elbows on his knees, fingers linked between his legs, his eyes on hers. "Tell me. We've always been straight with each other."

Her chin lifted slightly and she stiffened her spine, but her sad eyes showed her real feelings. "You hurt me, Dom."

"Because I married Sabrina?"

"Yes."

He sat upright. "You and I were good friends who had sex now and then because it was...easy. We weren't more than that, partly because you said you didn't want serious. So you don't get to say I betrayed you, because I didn't."

"Bollocks! You betrayed me, the team, and yourself by marrying a woman whose only contribution is giving you a happy cock."

"I married Sabrina because I love her."

"Why? Why do you love her?"

"She's everything I've ever wanted in a wife, in a partner. She makes me happy. She makes me want to be better than I am."

"You mean she wants to change you into something you're not." Before he could answer, she continued. "I'm the best partner you've ever had." She jabbed a finger at her chest. "In the trenches and in your bed. And you never wanted a wife until you went to America. This is about ego."

"What does that mean?"

"You just couldn't resist bringing home the quintessential big-boobed, blonde, blue-eyed American bombshell to show off to all the guys, specifically Ian, your idol. *Jaysus*, I thought you were smarter than that."

The ugly snort of derision she ended her sentence with pissed him off. So did her comment about his idolizing Ian. "You don't know what the fuck you're talking about."

"I know she has absolutely no ability or willingness to understand the things that are important in your life. She's all about getting what she wants. And what she wants is Ian. *That's* what I know. *That's* what you'd know, too, if you were thinking with the right head."

Meg had always been able to zero in on his hidden fears, draw them out into the light, and talk him through them until they dissolved or he had a plan for eliminating them. But his marriage, his wife, was one thing he would not let her comment on, because it was clear she was not interested in helping keep it solid.

He stood. "Leave your data on the desk and go," he said through gritted teeth. "Before we both say something we regret."

She jumped to her feet and slapped the folder with the data onto his desk. Then she lunged toward him, grabbed his head, and kissed him hard on the mouth, her tongue stabbing between his lips, past his teeth, and finding his tongue. The minty taste and heat of her in his mouth flashed him back to the image of her in the shower, calling his name as she came around her working fingers. He tasted her deep before he came to his senses.

He pushed her away, harder than he'd meant to, and she landed back in her chair. He stumbled back a few steps, too, away from her. Their fiery gazes mingled in the fireworks popping in the air between them and in the rain popping against the tin roof. Her chest was rising and falling as deeply as his was, and her nipples were as hard and erect as his cock.

"Go," he growled. "If you can't respect my wife and the boundaries of my marriage, I *will* end what's left of our friendship."

She stood. "You still want me, Dom. Or you wouldn't have stayed to watch me fuck myself in the shower." She turned and stormed out the door, into the slashing rain, leaving him sick with disgust over his behavior.

He collapsed into his chair, dragging his hands over his face and into his hair, his stomach roiling, his body cold at what he'd done. He loved Sabrina with all his heart and soul and was glad he'd married her. But Meg was still alive in his system, like a virus that came back to life at unexpected times to pull and scratch at him.

Goddammit! He should have let Jack transfer her. It would've been better for all of them. From now on, he'd be with Meg only as much as he absolutely had to for work.

He grabbed her folder, opened it, and began transferring her numbers to the main report. He'd entered four numbers when he did something he'd never done before. He saved and closed the unfinished report, then left it to go help his wife, which is where he should have been all along.

****

Sabrina glanced heavenward as thunder rumbled through the thick soup of darkening sky, then snapped pictures of their first skeleton—a female—from all angles. She had touched the bit of skull that was showing and felt nothing, no odd sensations like when she'd touched the warrior skeleton. And her ghost hadn't appeared. Not that that was the test for *sonuachar*, but it was the only thing she had to go on.

"Let's put her to bed," Ian called out. He'd heard the thunder, too.

Snapping a final photo, she put away the camera in its case as Ian gathered the tools. She'd asked Dominic to join them digging, and he'd said he would after doing the weekly report, but he'd never showed. Had he simply underestimated the time the task would take, or had something, someone, else snagged his attention? The idea rolled around in her head like spiked balls as the wind spit raindrops at them, and she focused on the work at hand.

Ian climbed out of the trench with the tools, and she handed him the camera and the lantern. Setting the lantern down, he put the camera in his backpack, then reached out to her. She took his hands, and he pulled her out.

He zipped his backpack closed over the cameras, and she put their tool-rolls in hers. Together they positioned the tarp over the trench, securing it with weights and boulders at the edges so the rain wouldn't destroy their work. Then he slung his backpack over his shoulder and picked up the shovels.

She did the same to her pack and picked up the lantern. He grabbed her hand and together they sprinted toward the media office through the raging rain and wind.

They burst through the door and slammed it closed on the storm. The light from the lantern sufficiently illuminated the room, so they left the overhead light off.

Ian set the shovels inside the tall metal cabinet and his backpack on the floor.

Sabrina put her pack next to his, the lantern on the table. Pulling the clip from her hair, she flipped her head upside down, wrung some of the water from her hair, then flipped it back. Shivering, she peered into the cabinet, which held an assortment of clothing and a plethora of tools and supplies. "Any towels in here?"

"Nope. But if you want to get out of those wet clothes..." He eyed the shirt clinging to her breasts, then grabbed a shirt from the cabinet and tossed it to her. "Here. Just your size."

She caught it, held it up. Two large white shamrocks dominated the breast area, and a suggestive message blazed beneath them. Everything about the Kelly green belly shirt, from the size and cut to the message, said that it had belonged to one of his many women.

Her eyebrow lifted as she read aloud. "Kiss my lucky charms, and I'll kiss your lucky leprechaun."

He laughed at whatever look crossed her face.

"Did you follow the instructions?"

"I'm not a kiss-and-tell kind of guy."

"You don't need to be. That grin says it all." Chuckling, she tossed the shirt back to him. "Thanks, I'll pass."

Just as he threw it into the cabinet, lightning lit up the space like a camera flash, and thunder boomed around them, shaking the trailer and rattling the windows.

They both jumped. "Shit!" they said in unison.

"That was close." She rushed to the window. "Good thing we came in when we did."

The wind howled like a banshee while sheets of rain slashed the ground and electricity raced across the sky in jagged bolts. Making a run for camp would be foolish. For safety's sake, they were stuck here for a while.

She felt Ian standing close behind her, a thin layer of energy, like static electricity, dancing between their bodies, making things rise—hair, skin, nipples, desire. Her gaze settled on their reflection in the window. He was looking at her, not at the weather raging outside, as if he were listening to her body, her thoughts.

"We're stuck here for a while," he repeated her thought, his breath sliding across the goosebumps on her skin.

Turning to face him, she realized she should have made a run for home, no matter the risk. Being trapped with him here was a thousand times more dangerous than dodging lightning bolts. Water slicked from him, off his hair and cheeks, down his neck into the wet and clinging T-shirt outlining every muscle in his arms, chest, and stomach.

She had the overwhelming desire to strip him naked and run her tongue over every wet inch. Her body tingled head to toe at the thought of it, and her nipples puckered to steel points. A moan rolled in her throat, but she swallowed it.

He pushed her wet hair off her face, and she shivered.

He ran his hands down, then up her arms in a slow caress, and she shivered.

His hot breath caressed her face, and she shivered.

"You're shivering," he said.

She was. So hard her teeth chattered. But it wasn't

just her cold, wet clothes hugging her cold, wet skin causing it. Or her wet hair hanging in dripping ropes. It was also Ian. His closeness. His eyes. His body. His heat. His voice. His scent. There wasn't a place on her that didn't feel him.

"I can fix that." He left her side, went to the cabinet, and dug inside.

"I'm not wearing that shirt," she called out as she followed, making him chuckle.

He pulled out a blanket and twirled it around his back, looking like a kid pretending to be a caped superhero. Lifting his eyebrow and grinning, he joined her again, holding open the blanket to welcome her inside.

"Never fear. My superhero cape and I will warm you up."

She had no business warming up in his arms, pressed against his hard, wet body, but with her body shivering, goosebumps riding goosebumps, blood in her veins turning to slush, she considered his invitation.

"A real hero would give the damsel the cape," she said through chattering teeth.

He shook his head, his eyes shining with devilry. "Maybe that's how it's done in America. But here in Ireland, a real hero rescues the beautiful damsel and lets her show her appreciation in various and pleasurable ways."

"How lucky for the hero." She giggled at his silly attempt at heroism and fought to resist the desire to step forward and answer the pull of his body.

When she didn't step closer, he did—slowly—and wrapped his arms and the blanket fully around her, holding it closed at her back, enveloping her in his arms and his heat. He shifted her closer until their bodies fit perfectly against each other, and she let her palms flatten on his chest with a stifled sigh. Her doubts about being in his arms dissolved the instant she was there, breathing him in, feeling his body warm against hers, feeling his heart beating next to hers.

He surprised her by guiding them in a slow, easy dance. They shuffled together, barely moving, wrapped up in the blanket and in each other, warming themselves. His essence swirled around her, through her, smoothing out her goosebumps and thawing her deep chill.

Out of the corner of her eye, she saw her ghost appear, sword in hand. But for once he wasn't frowning or raging. He was nodding, smiling, and speaking in soft tones as if saying, this is right. Feeling the same way herself, she sighed, closed her eyes, and eased deeper into Ian, resting her ear on his chest to hear and feel the comforting thud of his pulse, his lungs pulling in air, his emotions swirling like spun candy in her head.

This is good, Ian, so good. Better than a hot bath. Better than anything.

"Better?" he asked.

"Much," she murmured and let her arms slide all the way around him.

The light from the lantern dimmed, flickered, then sputtered out, plunging them into near darkness. She grabbed fists full of his wet shirt as her eyes popped open. A lightning bolt lit up the room, showing her ghost by the lantern, a proud grin on his face, taking credit for the outage. She glared at him. "You did that on purpose."

Ian chuckled, thinking she'd been talking to him. "Love, my hands never left your body."

To cover her slip, she found Ian's eyes. "What is it with you and failing flashlights?"

He grinned and pulled her tighter. "If you're scared, there's a wee torch in my pocket."

"A *wee* torch? I wondered what that was."

"Smartass. Just get it."

"No way. You get it."

"I'd have to let go of the blanket, and if I do, all the heat will escape, and you'll start shivering again."

"Fine." She let go of him and slid one hand into his pocket, the wet denim making the maneuver challenging. "It's not there."

"Go deeper."

She pushed her hand all the way in and felt something hard that wasn't a torch.

"Mmm, love, that feels grand. A little to your right."

"Ian!" She yanked her hand out and pinched one rigid nipple. "Jerk!" She chuckled.

He laughed an "ouch!" and held her tight to him so she couldn't leave the blanket. "Just messing with you, love. The torch is in the other pocket."

"Sure it is."

"Seriously."

"If you're lying to me, I'll make you regret it."

"Regrets are just memories. I'm not afraid of them. Or your threats."

She grinned at his throwing her own words back at her. "Brat."

Repeating the maneuver in the other pocket, her fingers touched a small, hard, metallic phallic object she prayed was his *wee torch*. She wrapped her hand around it and pulled it from his pocket. A press to the button shot a slim beam from the end, illuminating the blanket with a diffused night-light effect that calmed her fears.

"Say it," he said, an *I-told-you-so* grin on his face.

"Say what?"

"Say, 'Ian, you're my hero.'"

Her arms went back around him. "What have you done today that's so heroic?"

He began their slow dance again, every brush of his thighs, his pelvis, his stomach, his chest against hers building a need to snuggle closer into him.

"My blanket...uh, cape...and I are keeping you from freezing, and my wee torch is keeping you from freaking. That's pretty heroic."

"You'll need more than that to deserve hero status."

"I let you put your hands in my pants."

"First of all, my hands were in your *pockets*. And second, it was a bit self-serving and, therefore, not heroic."

"All right. How about this?" He flung off the blanket, and his arm tightened like a steel band around her waist, yanking her body into his. She felt a long, hard, thick object pressing into her that definitely wasn't another *wee torch* in his pocket. His other hand slid to her head and threaded his fingers in the wet mass of her hair, gripping and tilting her head back, making her scalp tingle, locking her eyes with his. His hungry gaze devoured her face, her mouth, before moving back to her eyes.

"It's against my nature to ignore an opportunity to

make love to the beautiful woman in my arms who's looking at me like she's as eager to get naked with me as I am with her. But I'm playing nice because of who you are. And that's as fucking heroic as I can get."

Chapter Nine

Ian's touch, his words, his meaning vibrated inside her, as if she had absorbed every bit of the electricity zapping through the air. Yes, he was being honorable, if not outright heroic, by ignoring the voice inside him that demanded he touch her. Kiss her. Take her.

The same voice was demanding she do the same to him.

Trying to be heroic herself, she released her hold on him and eased out of his arms, out of their bubble, out of trouble. He didn't hold on. Because of that, she gave him what he asked for. "Ian, you're my hero."

Another crack of thunder busted overhead, almost in anger at their parting. They stared across the distance at each other, hearts racing, breaths shallow, eyes locked, desire crackling between them like the lightning crackling outside, their bodies tense and trembling from wanting to fly to each other but holding back with every ounce of strength and decency they possessed.

Nearly cracking from the tension between them, she was a breath away from launching herself back into his arms and letting her body have its way with his when he rushed to her, closing the gap between them. One hand dove into her hair at the back of her neck, the other around her waist, and he drew her in, against his hardness, for what she knew would be an ovary-popping, womb-shredding, orgasm-triggering kiss.

"Breena," he sighed and lowered his head.

The door banged opened, and the raging storm poured in loud and wet. Ian released her immediately and backed off, grabbing the blanket and tossing it into the cabinet as she swung the flashlight beam toward the door. A drenched Dominic had stepped into the trailer and stood just in the doorway. Her ghost surged toward him like a comet, slid through him, sword first, and out the door, making it bang closed behind him.

Dominic flipped the overhead light on. "Why are the lights off?"

"The lantern was on," Sabrina said, squinting against the flood of light. "It just went out."

Dominic eyed the lantern on the table, then the two of them.

Still under the spell of Ian's magic, it was a stiff walk across the floor to Dominic, but she made it and hugged him tight to dissuade the suspicion in his face, in his voice.

He drew her into his arms, his mouth landing where Ian's was headed seconds before, giving her the kiss she had craved.

And more.

The sizzling hot kiss was usually reserved only for the privacy of their bed. And that rigid phallus stabbing hard into her stomach was no flashlight. Her husband was turned on and didn't seem to be shy about showing it. Had he seen her in Ian's arms and was protecting his territory, reminding them both that she was taken? No. That wasn't his way. What, or who, had put him in this mood?

"You're soaking wet," he whispered when he pulled back. "Ian, any towels in your press?"

"No."

The anger in Ian's tone mirrored the emotion in his eyes when her gaze found his.

"You still keep a blanket in there?" Dominic asked.

Ian's eyes flitted to hers, then away. "Yeah."

"Toss it to me for Sabrina."

"No, it's okay," she said. "I'll change when I get home."

"You ready to head up then?"

"As soon as we put the tools away." She walked over to their backpacks and grabbed Ian's. Before she could unzip it and take out the cameras, Ian tried to take it from her, but she held on.

"I got it," they said together.

"Head home with Dom," he said.

The fire and desire that had infused his body and voice seconds earlier had morphed into guilt and anger. The emotions were clear in his eyes, almost rolled along her skin like a shimmering heat wave.

"Ian—"

"Breena. Go." He whispered the words like they pained him, and his expression said volumes more than the two words expressed.

Dominic walked over, grabbed her hand, and tugged. "C'mon, let's go before we're stuck here all night." Irritation threaded his voice, spurring irritation in Ian's eyes.

She released her hold on the backpack and grabbed hers. "See you in the morning."

"Five sharp." For their run.

Realizing she still held his *wee torch* in her hand, she stared at it, held it out to him, their eyes locked as they relived the memories attached to it.

"Keep it," he said. "To help you see your way home."

See her way home? To her trailer or to Dominic? She didn't know which he meant, but she was glad to have his flashlight to light her way through the storm. By the time she and Dominic reached home, her bells calling to her, she was also glad Dominic had showed up when he had. The storm had worsened, which might have prevented her from going home at all, which might have meant spending the night with Ian. And that would have been dangerous. Disastrous. Delicious.

The rain had rinsed the sticky layer of dirt and sweat the day had covered her with, but she was dying for a real shower. Once inside the trailer, though, after they'd kicked off their boots and socks, Dominic hooked her around the waist and drew her against him, his cock jutting against her ass.

"I've had a hard-on for you all day," he growled against her neck, sucked her earlobe, making her heart tremble.

"Oh, yeah? Was it when I slipped in the mud in T139 or when I fell on my ass climbing out of T127?"

He ground against her. "Before that, this morning, when you bent over, snapping pictures of the brooch in T119 and your shorts tightened against this sweet little arse. I wanted to come up behind you, like this," he pressed himself harder against her and wiggled, "yank your shorts down, and fuck you right there in front of everyone until you screamed my name."

Her pussy constricted at his arousing words and at feeling his hands at the waistband of her shorts. He undid them, and his hand slipped inside to tease the topic of conversation. Her head dropped back on his chest as his finger played in the wetness—the wetness Ian had started.

"Thanks for controlling yourself. I can't imagine Jack approving of something like that. It would set a precedent he'd never be able to reverse."

He chuckled into her flesh and ground against her again, his hand in front, his cock in back. "I want your pussy, Sabrina."

The heat of his words licked across her already sizzling skin, sending a fiery rush through her. "She's all yours, after my shower." She pulled out of his arms, but he roped her back in.

"No." He bit her neck. "Now." He pushed her shorts to the floor, then her panties. He pulled off her shirt, made quick work of her bra, and soon his hands were on her wet breasts, squeezing them, teasing the cold nipples already standing painfully rigid at attention.

"Dominic, I'm filthy." A husky laugh sounded in her throat. "And I smell."

"You smell like you need to be fucked," he murmured against her stickiness.

Did she ever. A primal moan of pure need growled up from her throat. "You're nasty." She turned, pulled his face to hers, and kissed him deep, tasting dirt and salt and rain from her neck on his lips.

His tongue took her mouth, her tongue, and devoured her until she was moaning and ready to beg for his touch. The feel of his hands on her breasts, cupping, tweaking, kneading made her forget they were sweaty and dirty. All she wanted was his mouth on her, his hands on her, his cock inside her.

He had yanked off his T-shirt when he'd come in,

dropping the wet mess on the floor, so the only thing between him and her hands were his pants. Hands shaking, she pulled at the snap and yanked down the zipper, then shoved them down. His boxers were right behind. The musky smell of him whiffed up, but strangely it fed her desire rather than deterred it.

He cupped her breasts and leaned down to lick her nipples. "And you're fucking delicious." He sucked them, making the points so hard she felt like they'd come off in his mouth.

"I need to touch you, too." She reached for his cock, but he dodged her touch. "Don't torture me."

"Torture? No, this is loving you."

"Do it faster."

"I don't like to rush making love to you."

"Try."

"Patience increases pleasure."

A wave of goosebumps shivered over her skin at hearing the very words Ian had whispered in her ear the night they'd met and he'd walked her home. Dammit. She didn't want Ian in her head. Didn't want to be patient. Didn't want to wait for pleasure. She wanted it now. With Dominic. Her husband. The man she loved.

Trying another tactic, she tried to go to her knees and take him in her mouth, but he wouldn't have it. He lifted her in his arms and wrapped her legs around him, tucking his stiff cock between her thighs. He sat on their bed and settled her onto his lap, arms around each other, his cock up her stomach, pressing into her pussy. Their scents mingled, making them one. It seemed so raw, so dirty, to be so intimate without being clean, and she couldn't believe how turned on she was.

His lips and the feel of his heat at her center made

her frantic with desire. She ran her fingers through his wet hair and tightened her grip when his lips trailed from her mouth to her neck and lower to worship her breasts again. He tweaked each nipple with his tongue before drawing them one at a time into his mouth, sucking the hard tips.

"Do you like fucking dirty, Sabrina?"

Her eyes closed, she moaned her answer.

"Tell me." He ceased his attention to her breasts.

"Don't stop. Please!"

"Say it."

"God, yes, I like fucking dirty," she moaned.

His hands continued with their actions. "What do you want me to do?"

"Fuck me."

He thrust his hips against her, his cock riding against her clit, and she gasped.

"Now?" he asked.

"Yes."

"Then ride my cock."

She quickly positioned herself on his hard cock and slid down onto him, groaning her pleasure at being so filled. Gripping his hips with her legs so she could raise and lower herself, she began to post up and down on him. He held her hips, not letting her move.

"Please." She rolled against him. "Make me come."

"Don't I always make you come?"

"Yes." The word whimpered from her mouth.

He kissed her again, his mouth wet and open and hot, at her breasts, her chest, her neck, her face, her eyes, her mouth. He sucked her tongue. He licked her. He kissed her thoroughly. All the while he rocked against her, slowly, just enough movement to make her feel him inside her but not enough to get her to the top on the express. The drag from the small movement tweaked her clit in a teasing graze that drove her insane, and she rolled her hips back and forth, leaning forward to increase the pressure there, at that tiny ball of light and color and nerves. She squeezed her core around his cock deep inside her, doing her part to get them off.

"Look at me," he said, his voice low but urgent.

She met his gaze, and a little thrill rushed through her, touching every part of her body before erupting in a bright heat at her center where they were joined.

"Do you feel me inside you?"

"Yes," she moaned in pleasure.

"That's my love filling you." He thrust into her a little bolder, letting her move a little, too. "You feel it?"

She nodded. "I want to hold you this tight inside me forever. Never let you go."

"Never let me go."

He began moving faster, thrusting into her, and she rode his movements, matched his rhythm, keeping her eyes on his even as she felt them lose focus. He was breathing hard, his eyes glazed over as they held hers. Her breath was coming in short bursts, too. His words, his movements, the feel of his hard thighs beneath hers, the feel of his chest rubbing against her nipples, her pussy clenching his thick cock were taking her to release. A few more thrusts and she'd be there.

As if he knew what she needed, he turned them quickly, her on her back on the bed, still connected to each other, and thrust, all the way in. He pulled out and plunged in again, out, then all in again. He kissed her deeply, his tongue fucking her with sharp thrusts. The rhythm of his cock and his tongue pushed her to the edge.

"Come for me, baby," he growled.

At his command, the ache inside her exploded into tiny sherds. She gripped his shoulders and her knees went wide, her feet locked around his waist, her pussy squeezing his cock, her whole body spasming.

"Ah, fuck. Ahh!" Dominic groaned into her mouth as he shot his cum into her again and again.

Soon his movements stilled, but his body shook as he dipped his forehead to hers, as if his orgasm had ripped everything from him.

Trying to catch her breath, she cupped his head with her hand. "Wow!"

His breathing was hard and irregular, but he brushed his lips here and there across her face. "Yeah."

"I've never heard you talk like that without me dragging it out of you."

He raised his head to look into her eyes, his face red, as if he was embarrassed how he'd taken her. Instead of answering, he rolled off her but kept her in his arms.

She kissed his lips softly. "Baby, I loved it."

"We didn't make love last night, and I've wanted you all day. Then when I went into Ian's office, saw your shirt plastered to your body, I...." He chuckled. "I almost took you bent over his worktable."

Tingles raced up her back at the thought of him taking her hard and fast from behind, spanking her ass pink as Ian watched...or joined in. "I would have liked that." She rubbed herself against him, a second orgasm waiting in the wings. "Why didn't you?"

"Ian would have wanted to join us. Or offer advice

on how I could do it better."

"Baby, you don't need advice."

He smiled proudly. "There was a time I eagerly accepted Ian's sex advice."

"What's the worst piece of advice he gave you?"

He thought a minute, grinning as he found the one he wanted. "A man needs to know when to caress a woman's face and make love to her, and when to pull her hair and fuck her."

Shivers applauded all over her body. "Sounds like something he'd say. But why was it bad advice?"

"He gave Sean and me lessons on how to know when to fuck and when to make love and even gave us tips on how to talk dirty. But the first time I tried it dirty, I blew it. Big time. The girl I was with…well, I misread her signals. She started crying. I quickly apologized, but it ruined the night. I felt so bad I didn't try it again. Until you."

Her heart drew up tight in her chest at hearing more evidence that she wasn't really his type. "We don't have to do it rough and dirty if you don't like it."

"But you like it."

"Sometimes. But—"

"I love you, Sabrina." He stared so deep into her eyes she could see the love he had for her. "I want to do what makes you happy because I want us to be together for the rest of our lives. I can learn to be what you want, what you need."

Tears trickled from the outer corners of her eyes at his declaration. She cupped his face. "Baby, you already are what I want, what I need. You're the man I love. My husband."

"You're mine, Sabrina," he whispered and kissed

the tears away.

"I'm yours."

"Only mine."

"Yes." The small but powerful pause between his response and hers wasn't just because her ghost chose that moment to pop in or because he hovered in the corner over them or because he glared at her and shook his head like an angry lion. It was also because she hesitated to lie to her husband. She had been only his. Then she'd touched Ian, touched her soul in him, and now she belonged to him, too.

Before she could analyze the possible repercussions of that truth, Dominic's mouth was on hers again, and soon his cock was back inside her, hitting the spot that released her second orgasm.

Sex with Dominic was rarely wild, rough, dirty, exciting, adventurous. But it was always deep, loving, and satisfying. It was…enough. She loved him, and he loved her, and she would not let anything break that love. To make sure, she would not get that close to Ian again. She would resist him to her last breath. And for damn sure, she wouldn't listen to a ghost that seemed to be telling her she was with the wrong man.

Chapter Ten

The team gathered at the pub in Anamcara to celebrate Kristin's and Ian's birthdays, which were within a day of each other. They had taken over three pushed-together tables, and all were working on a drink of some kind. In the corner, a small band played traditional Irish songs as well as some more familiar contemporary pop.

Sabrina sat next to Dominic, her attention not on the team banter, but on the scarred dance floor where Ian was teaching Kristin an Irish *céilí*. The aggravation spearing her body like thorns was more than just envy that she wasn't out there dancing. It was white-hot insane jealousy that another woman was with him, in his arms, making him laugh, getting to feel his arms around her, getting to have her arms around him.

"Dominic, I can't stand it," she said finally. "You have to dance with me."

Laughter burst from the table, with a few derogatory exclamations like "Dom dancing?" and "Want to lose some toes?"

"The only reason I married an Irishman was so he could teach me the traditional Irish dances," she joked.

"Then you married the wrong Irishman, lass," Gabe said.

Dominic laughed good-naturedly. "They're right. I'm hopeless when it comes to dancing, Irish or any other kind."

155

"You've danced with me before."

He smiled, as if he were remembering the times they'd danced. "No, I held you in my arms and shuffled my feet. That's not dancing."

"You never heard me complain."

"No, I didn't."

"If you want to be twirled in proper style, Ian's who you want." Angus nodded toward Ian and Kristin, who at that moment left the dance floor, smiles on their flushed faces, eyes shining, like they'd had the time of their lives.

Oh, hell no! Ian was not who she wanted to dance with. A week later, and she was still reeling from that night in the media trailer. They had never spoken of it, and they made an unspoken but conscious effort to stay out of each other's arms for all but short hugs of greeting, even though what they wanted was to be back there, snuggled tight, close, naked, and they wanted that kiss that was denied them.

Ian took Kristin back to her chair next to Sean, who pulled her into his lap and accepted her kiss. Ian sat in his own chair between Kristin and Sabrina.

"Don't settle in, mate," Angus said. "Sabrina's looking to have a lesson, too."

Sabrina's eyes slid to Ian's just as his slid to hers. She couldn't hold back her smile or a heart flutter at seeing his confident and sexy grin.

"Dom, I'm taking your wife," he said as he held out his hand to her.

She looked at Dominic. He smiled to show he didn't mind. She kissed him, then took Ian's hand. Linking their fingers, he stood, helped her to her feet, and led her to the dance floor, twirling her a couple of times on the way there. He requested a specific song from the band, then took her in his arms, showed her the steps, and talked her through them.

After a lot of laughing and more than a few missteps where she bumped into him, banged her head on his chin, and crushed his feet, she got the hang of it, and soon they were heating up the floor in sync like life-long partners. Once she had relaxed, it was almost as if she could hear his cues before she felt them.

The band played several trad songs, giving her time to practice the steps. When it switched to a slow, bluesy tune, Ian led her in a different kind of dance, one that kept their bodies plastered together, his thigh between her legs, their hips and chests pressed together. He dipped her, rotated their connected bodies in a slow circular motion, slowly twirled her, his hands never leaving her body.

Their movements felt less like dancing and more like foreplay. Desire had replaced blood in her veins, and if it were Dominic dancing with her, she'd have already dragged him to the bathroom or to the backseat of the SUV to satisfy the lust flaming inside her.

"Ready?" Ian whispered against her mouth, his sexy voice turning her insides into oozy marshmallow sauce.

She didn't know what he intended, but with him she was always ready for anything. "Ready."

Grinning, he tightened his hold on her. "Hold on."

She didn't even get out an okay before he whirled them around the floor.

"Oh, God, Ian, don't let me go," she said through her laughter.

His gaze held hers as they spun. "I'll never let you

go, love." His smile reached all the way to his shining eyes, his promise all the way to his soul.

****

"Would you look at that," Meggan said, elbowing Rusty.

"What?" Rusty asked.

She nodded toward where Ian and Sabrina danced, their joined bodies bathed in a blue spotlight. "Good thing Dom's not the jealous type."

"Feck, yeah." He grinned. "Hey, Dom, Ian's getting pretty cozy with your wife out there. I'd be worried if I were you."

All eyes swung toward the couple, watched them spin and laugh, their movements perfectly in sync, not a sliver of light showing between their bodies. Their gazes locked tight.

The table grew silent.

"If that was my wife he was *lurching* with like that, he'd be bleeding," Gabe said thickly, the words and tone a sledgehammer shattering the silence into sharp sherds.

Kristin rose from Sean's lap and slid her fingers into his hair. "Either dance with me like that or take me to the SUV."

Grinning, he stood, took her hand, and led her toward the door.

Meggan smiled. The love spell she'd paid Ena to put on Ian and Sabrina was working even better than she'd hoped it would. By the time the dig was over, Ian and Sabrina would be gone, and Dom would be hers again.

****

Their feet barely shuffled on the floor to the

melodic strains of the slow love song, but Ian's heart was racing...right alongside hers. Maybe it was because of the spin they'd come out of moments before. Maybe it was because they were still gripping each other so tightly, their bodies fused together. Maybe it was the invisible bubble surrounding them and fusing them together. Maybe it was something else. But no way was it Ena's prophecy coming true. It couldn't be.

A weak voice inside her appealed to her good sense. *Let Ian go. Go back to the table. To Dominic.* But she felt so good in Ian's arms, she couldn't make herself leave.

"I'm impressed," she said, her voice low to hide how breathless she was. "I'm guessing your mom pulled you, kicking and screaming, to dance lessons."

"I did extra work for Deeda for months in exchange for her paying for dance lessons when I was twelve."

"Why would a twelve-year-old boy willingly take dance lessons?"

"So I could hold the girls in my arms at the school dances without getting wacked with Sister Agnes' ruler for being 'ungentlemanly.'"

She chuckled. "That makes perfect sense."

Ask him. Stop the bullshit chit-chat and just ask him what you've wanted to ask him since Ena cursed them.

"How long did you live with Sean and his family?" *Chickenshit.*

"About ten years."

"Why?"

He shook his head. "Don't hold back, love."

"What? What do you mean?"

"I know Dom told you the whole sordid story. Ask me the question you really want to ask."

She licked her lips, her mouth suddenly as dry as the bones they'd unearthed. "Do you believe Ena? That we're soulmates?" Her voice came out in a whisper, not because she had intended it, but as if she were unable to speak any louder. As if hushed tones were required when discussing something as sacred as a soulmate connection.

"I don't know." His low response caressed her lips. "I only know that *something's* happening between us, something that feels beyond my ability to control." His hand moved up into her hair and caressed her. "Like right now. My head's telling me to take you back to the table, to your husband, to my best friend, but every instinct inside me is telling me to hold on to you, that you're mine."

His tone was edgy, as if the war raging inside him angered him. She slid one hand to his head, into his hair, too, keeping the other arm around his neck.

"I feel the same way, and it scares me, Ian. I love Dominic. Vowed to spend my life with him. And I want that. But when I'm with you, I feel—"

"—like you're where you really belong." His breath brushed against her hair.

"Yes. And—"

"—happier than you've ever been." His lips brushed the words at her temple and kissed them in.

Her breath shivered inside her body as the circle of heat and pleasure tightened around them. "Yes."

His hand caressed the swath of bare skin on her back her dress didn't cover, his touch so heating her skin she was certain an imprint of his palm, his fingertips, would remain forever.

"And whole," they said at the same time, their gazes locked. The fire in his eyes sent her into a meltdown, and if he hadn't been holding on to her to tightly, she'd have collapsed to the floor. His breath was as labored as hers, and her body heated and tingled with need.

This wasn't the first time it appeared that he'd read her mind. It wasn't the first time they'd stood together in each other's arms, connected in their bubble, breathing each other, and felt as if they were alone in the world. It wasn't the first time she'd felt fiery sensations from his body rippling into hers. And somehow she knew it wouldn't be the last.

She tucked into him, resting her head on his chest, and let the rise and fall of his breathing rock her, soothe her. "Right this minute, what does it feel like to you? Our connection."

He answered immediately, as if he'd analyzed it a million times. "It feels like the world around us has disappeared, and it's just you and me inside a bubble of pleasure I never want to leave."

Yes. That was it. There was more she wanted to ask, but she wasn't ready to say it aloud. So she looked deep into his eyes and sent him her thoughts. *Can you read my mind, Ian? Do you know that I want you with an almost uncontrollable passion? Do you feel the same about me?*

The blacks of his eyes dilated, his heartbeat under her hand sped up, and heat pulsed from his body to hers. "Breena—"

"Mind if I take my wife back?"

Dominic stood behind Ian, his hand on his

shoulder, ripping a hole in their bubble, halting Ian's response. But it was like her body and Ian's had fused together. It was that hard to move away from him. The look he gave her told her he didn't want to let go, and she was sure hers said the same thing.

He didn't speak, just slowly released her. Pain, like thousands of pinpricks, slid into the spaces where only pleasure had been seconds before. Sounds of music and people, the acrid smell of beer- and whiskey-scented body sweat, the movement of life around them suddenly burst into focus, when only a moment ago, wrapped in Ian's arms, it had all been muted, far away, irrelevant.

He'd only had a few sips of his beer before they'd taken the dance floor, but his gait was unsteady as he made his way back to the table, as if he'd imbibed more than his fair share. She felt pretty weak-kneed herself. They were drunk on each other.

Then Dominic's arms were around her, his body severing her gaze from Ian's retreating figure. Forcing back the lingering out-of-control and achy feelings coursing through her, she fought through the fog to give her attention to her husband. She put her arms around him, eased closer, and tried to connect with his body, with his soul.

"About time you came to dance with me," she said, giving him a small smile.

"Couldn't let Ian have all the fun."

She ignored the little dig in his tone. "He's a hell of a dancer. But there's something I want that only you can help me with."

"What's that?"

"A kiss."

A kiss fixed everything. All the fairy tales said so. His kiss would bring her back to her life. Bring her back to him. Would make her world right again. Would clear her head and body of the spell that being with Ian had cast on her.

After a brief—and puzzling—hesitation, Dominic lowered his head and pressed a kiss to her lips. When he would have pulled back, she held his head close to deepen the kiss. She toyed with his tongue, fed on his lips, tried to pull his essence inside her and push out Ian's.

She broke the kiss and caught his eyes. "Bathroom or backseat?"

****

Ian reached his chair seconds before his legs gave out. Leaving Breena's arms had ripped the energy from him, leaving him as weak as a newborn. He needed a stiff drink, but that would only lower his inhibitions, make matters worse, so he'd make do with the nearly full pint he'd left before he went to dance. He took a long swallow.

"If you'd danced any closer to Sabrina, she'd have gone up the pole," Rusty snickered, elbowing Angus, who joined in.

Pure rage slammed through Ian's body, and he was breaths from coming up out of his chair and over the table and popping Rusty in the mouth for saying something that disrespectful about Breena. Instead, he tossed the rest of his beer in the man's face and banged the glass down on the table. The amber liquid also hit Meggan and Gussy, who were on either side of Rusty.

As if having a beer thrown in his face was an everyday occurrence, Rusty didn't even flinch. He wiped the brew from his eyes with his fingers and let his tongue lick it from his mouth. "Feck, Ian, why'd you go and waste a perfectly good beer?"

Everyone laughed, except Meggan, who was furiously wiping the beer off her scowling face and off her shirt. Finally seeing the humor, Ian shook his head, grinned, and the rage ebbed. He called over the waitress.

"Bring the lad a pint on me, would ya, lass," he said to Lena when she arrived, and nodded toward Rusty. "And a towel."

"Anybody else need something?" she asked.

Everyone else signaled they were fine, and she left to fill the order.

"Where's Sean?" Ian asked no one in particular.

Gussy grinned. "Your dirty dancing moves with Sabrina got Kristin all hot and bothered. She dragged him to the SUV."

The statement set off another round of bawdy chuckling that didn't pull Ian in. As his mates talked and laughed, he tried to join in, but he couldn't keep his eyes off the dance floor where Breena danced with Dom.

He could still feel her body against his, like a lingering warmth. He had been close to kissing her when Dom had shown up. The last thing he'd wanted to do was let her go. Especially after discovering that whatever connection was binding them closer every day, she absolutely felt, too. That she wanted him as much as he wanted her. With an almost uncontrollable passion, she had said—thought.

The feel of her hands on him. The feel of her body against his. The smell of her skin. Her hair. Her desire.

He'd do anything to experience it again. He was one bad decision away from walking back to the dance floor and taking her away from Dom, even if he had to kick his ass to get her.

Cold gripped his body. Fuck! What the hell was wrong with him? He wasn't going to fight his best friend. Especially over the man's own wife. Shit. He needed a distraction before he got his fucking ass justifiably kicked.

"Here's your pint," Lena said as she leaned over him to set the beer in front of Rusty, pressing her ample breasts into him. "And a towel." She tossed Rusty the towel, then turned to Ian. "That be all for ya?" she asked him, her double D's almost in his mouth.

He heard the offer in her voice, saw it in her eyes and in the nipples that hardened against her blouse. He'd been with her when he'd first arrived at the dig. She was too loud and coarse for his taste, and she scratched the hell out of his back with her nails, but she liked to fuck fast and hard and, like him, was only in it for the sex.

His expanding cock tightened the front of his jeans. She could be the distraction he needed to get Dom's wife off his mind. Temporarily, at least.

His eyes left her tits and found her eyes. "What else you got, lass?"

"Some tasty stuff in the back. Be glad to give you a sample during my break."

"Be glad to try it."

She winked and hurried back to the bar to pick up another order.

Ian knew by the grins on the faces around the table they'd all heard their close and low exchange and knew exactly what he planned to sample.

"God, is there nothing you won't shag?" Meggan said.

Ian glared at her, in no mood to hide his disdain or control his frustration. "Apricunts."

Embarrassment flickered in her eyes before she could mask it with anger and disgust, and his stomach clenched in shame. He immediately regretted saying out loud the private nickname he'd given the redhead back at that first summer dig. He didn't like her or she him, but she didn't deserve being shamed like that in front of the team. Before he could apologize, she jumped up from her chair, her eyes shooting daggers at him.

"You're a disgusting manwhore," she said and stormed from the table.

"Apricunt?" Shane repeated. "Mate, that's fucking brilliant."

Everyone except Ian, Jack, and Gabe roared with laughter, the word bandied about several times, like each of them wanted a chance to taste it rolling along their tongue.

"That's enough," Jack said sharply, scattering the laughter. "She's your teammate and a woman, and she deserves more respect than that."

Several pairs of eyes dropped to the table, but the grins stayed in place.

"And the next one of you I hear using that word is off the team. Understand?"

The threat wiped the grins from their faces and brought out the quick nods.

"Ian?" Jack prompted when he didn't respond.

"Yeah," he said shortly.

Minutes later, Lena gave him the look, and he

stood.

"Eh-oh," Gussy said. "Take this with ya." He tossed Ian a condom, and the team snickered.

Ian caught it. "You knick this off a fucking leprechaun, Gussy?" He tossed it back. "I've got me own." He grabbed his crotch and grinned. "And they're man-sized."

Peels of ribald laughter danced behind him as he headed for the back. He tried to keep his eyes off the dance floor but couldn't. Breena was leading Dom out the door.

He strolled into the *jacks*, confident that Lena would've cleared out anyone who was in there. He locked the door as she yanked off her shirt and launched herself at him, her mouth smashing against his, her hands going right for his zipper. He backed her up against the wall and placed his hands there, bracketing her head. In no time at all, she had his jeans undone and his cock out.

"*Johnny*," she growled.

"Pocket," he said, lowering his head to her breasts to suck one long nipple into his mouth as she dug into his pocket. Her skin smelled and tasted like sweat and beer. Breena smelled like sun-warmed flowers and tasted like sweet cherries. His mouth sucked hard as she ripped open the wrapper with her teeth and rolled the condom onto his stiff cock.

"I only got ten minutes, so fuck me fast," she said.

Hands on her ass, he lifted her up so she could wrap her legs around his waist. She guided him into her wet and willing pussy, and the groaning began. All hers. He usually started slow, built the pleasure layer upon layer, talking dirty, driving the girl crazy, making her beg for his cock, but Lena's fingers and heels digging into his back like spurs told him she didn't need the extras. He pounded away, hard and fast.

Minutes later, she growled so loud at her climax he was sure somebody would burst through the door any second, checking to see who was being murdered. He pumped unyieldingly now, scratching for his own release. A blue flash lit up behind his eyelids, and he saw Breena's face in his mind, tasted her kisses on his mouth, felt her body bucking beneath his, and felt her coming pussy grip his cock. When he exploded, his eyes squeezed tight, it was inside her sweetness.

"Ahh, fuck," he whispered as cum filled the condom. "Breena."

"Breena?" Lena lowered her legs to the floor and pushed him away from her.

His cock still twitched, shooting its last streams of cum, and he tugged himself to finish off while she adjusted her clothes.

"You could at least get the name right. It's Lena."

Ian nodded, the blur of his climax, the blur of Breena's face still wrapped around him. "Lena. That's what I said."

"No, you said Breena." She yanked her shirt on.

He backed away and pulled off the condom, throwing it into the trashcan.

She stared at his spent rod. "If you weren't so good with your *willy*, I'd be twisting off your *clackers* and shoving them up your arse."

She stepped closer and dropped to her knees. Holding his hips tight with her hands, she sucked his wet cock into her mouth, let her tongue lap the clinging drops of cum, then rose, kissed his mouth, her tongue going deep so he could taste himself. "But you are that good, so I don't care what name you call out when you fuck, as long as it's me you're fucking." With one final tug of her short skirt and tight shirt, she unlocked the door and rushed out.

Not bothering to relock it, Ian moved to the sink to wash off his cum and her saliva. These *manky* hookups didn't feel right anymore, were unnecessary now that he'd found the one he'd been looking for all his life. Now that he'd found Bree—

The squeak of a stall door opening behind him pulled his eyes to the mirror. Meggan came out, the smirk on her face telling him she had heard and seen everything.

Holy fuck.

He turned to face her. Time froze while he waited to find out what she was going to do with the information she'd overheard. She didn't speak, either, just watched him tuck himself into his boxers, zip and button his jeans, and buckle his belt.

Then her eyes rose to his. "You said Dom will never leave Sabrina. The opposite is also true. Sabrina will never leave Dom, no matter what kind of spell is on her. You and I will end up broken and bleeding at the end of this one."

She was right, of course, but knowing the outcome wouldn't stop either of them from going after what they wanted, foolishly holding out hope that a twist of fate would intervene on their behalf. The truth was in her eyes, and he felt it in his soul. United in the twisted moment together, they stared at each other in shock that they were feeling sorry for the other.

She blinked first. "Since it's your birthday, I'll

keep mum about what I heard." She headed to the door.

"Meg," he said, and she stopped and turned back. "Sorry for what I said at the table."

She flushed, lifting her chin slightly. "Apricunt?" She spoke the word slowly, as if incanting the word would render it powerless over her emotions.

He nodded.

"Just so you know, I prefer *frotch—fire crotch* if you're not into the whole brevity thing."

Surprise and humor lifted Ian's eyebrow, then the corner of his mouth, and he chuckled softly, shaking his head.

Shooting him a sassy smirk, she continued on through the door.

Ian washed his hands and face and rinsed his mouth for a long time before heading back to the table.

Except the few minutes in Breena's arms, worst birthday ever.

****

Sabrina straddled Dominic's hips, grinding her pussy against the bulge in his jeans, and she kissed him hard and deep, sliding her lips over his, sucking his top lip into her mouth, then the bottom, her tongue conquering his mouth, his tongue. Her arms wound around his neck, her hands in his hair, pulling his head closer to her, pressing her mouth closer to his. He thrust his hands up her dress, pushing it high up around her waist, and cupped her almost-bare ass.

"I want your cock in me," she said, desperation in her tone and in her movements as her hands flew to his jeans. In seconds, they were undone, his cock out and rock hard. She rose up over him and, yanking aside her thong, lowered herself onto him, engulfing his erection.

"Oh, fuck! Yes! Fuck me."

He cupped her ass tight to hold her on him, and he jerked his hips up, the hard length of him stabbing inside her hungry channel, and she met his thrusts, sliding up and down and forward and back, bouncing on him, scratching for her release.

She moved a hand between her legs, and the tips of her fingers circled her clit. She increased the pace, and she rode him faster, harder.

Her breathing sped up, her breasts falling and rising like she was out of air and grasping for even the tiniest breath that would save her life. But still she devoured his mouth, moaned high little sounds in her throat that expressed her level of need. Oh, God, she was there! She just needed a little more… something…to push her over the edge.

She was about to ask him to spank her ass when a sudden blue flash lit up behind her eyelids, and an image of Ian's face burst into view. The kisses she tasted on her mouth were his, the hands digging into her ass were his, the hips thrusting against her hard and fast were his, the long, rigid cock buried deep inside her was his. The ecstasy of him inside her, surrounding her, triggered her orgasm and ripped a loud, long cry of pleasure from her throat.

A deep guttural noise exploded from his mouth as he released, too, growling fuck, growling her name, growling his pleasure. Seconds later, they collapsed into each other, trembling, hearts racing, lungs fighting to catch breaths in the thick, steamy, sex-filled air they had created. For a few precious moments, they were the only two people in the world, kissing, caressing, as connected as a man and a woman could be.

As the rush receded, so did the image and presence of Ian. And when her husband's face came into view, shame burned a quick trail up her spine and burrowed inside her until she was nauseated with it. Sure, everybody fantasizes during sex, but what she did felt wrong. And what made her prickle with anxiety and confusion was that it was more than a fantasy. It was a memory. A memory buried deep in her flesh that burst to the surface at the moment of orgasm. She was still shaking from it.

"You're mine, Sabrina," Dominic whispered between kisses, bringing her back to him. Breaking protocol, he didn't wait for her to respond before he tacked on, "Only mine."

A warning? A reminder?

She pulled back and let her eyes tangle with his. Brushed back his sweaty locks of hair. Tenderly kissed his damp forehead, his eyes, his mouth. She loved this man, wouldn't hurt him for the world. Because of that, she would fight like hell to keep Ian out of her head, especially during sex, and to keep away from him as much as possible so their connection couldn't take over.

"*Is tú mo ghrá,*" she responded. And it was the truth. He was her love. Just not her only love.

Chapter Eleven

The arrival of the student interns—twelve in all—had turned the camp site into a chaotic place teeming with laughter, loud music, and hormones. With more people in camp, it was harder to find a place to sit around the fire at night and it took longer to get through the meal line, the shower line, and to wash clothes at the only local laundromat, or launderette as it was called in Ireland. It also added to the core team's workload, necessitating longer hours on the job to get it all done.

Each intern would get a turn at various jobs at the site, from digging and sifting to washing and bagging. Sabrina and Ian would also get some help in the trenches shooting video and stills.

"How many are we getting?" Sabrina asked Ian as they sat at their computers, trying to make a dent in editing the videos they'd already shot.

"Two," he said.

"That's it?"

"Meggan got most of them. She's up to her knickers in bones."

Sabrina kept to herself her catty remark that Meggan would be further along if she spent more time in finds with Kristin than in the trenches with Dominic.

"Especially since Kristin switched to analysis," he added.

173

Oh. "Do our two have photography skills?"

"Other than selfies?" He grinned at her groan. "Seem eager to learn, though."

"With the extra help, maybe we can actually take a day off," she said.

He snorted. "Don't count on it, love. Any day you're not in trenches, I need you here."

When Dominic had started working his day off, she worked hers helping Ian with the editing, and it had somehow become part of the regular schedule. Not that she minded. She loved her job, and getting to spend more time with Ian was just frosting on the cake.

She pushed back from the desk and stood. "How do you guys do it?" She dropped to the floor in downward dog, dipped up into upward dog, then back to downward.

He had pushed back from his computer to watch her. "You're going to have to be more specific, love."

"Work all the time. I haven't done yoga in a week. I'm stiff, clogged—spiritually speaking—and my Qi is hiding in a dark corner of my soul." She stood and went into forward bend, letting the weight of her arms and head stretch the knots from her back.

"You need chocolate." She heard him open his desk drawer where he kept her favorite candy—bite-sized dark chocolate chucks wrapped around an almond.

"What I need is a massage." She moved upright. "But I'll take chocolate."

He tossed her a tiny, foil-wrapped square. "Here. Take a break. Go yoga yourself. Then come back to me, ready to tie yourself to that computer."

She smiled. He always knew what she needed. She

unwrapped the chocolate and popped it into her mouth. "Do it with me."

He cocked one eyebrow. "*It* being?" His look made it clear what he thought *it* was.

"Really?" she said, raising her eyebrow, too.

He grinned.

Instead of inviting that conversation, she skipped over it. "Yoga would do you good. I can see from here how tense you are."

"I'm not tense. I'm…" He yawned noisily and stretched, pulling the soft expanse of T-shirt tight across his wide chest. "Tired." He rubbed his eyes and turned back to the monitor.

Stifling a sympathy yawn, she went to him, dropped her hands to his shoulders and squeezed. "Nope, you're tense." So tense, his muscles felt like bunched ropes of steel. "I'm sorry."

"Not your fault I'm tired or tense."

"Actually, it is. You work all day, then dig most of the night because of me." She dug into his flesh with her fingers as she talked, working her way through the tight knots, down his back, then back up.

Even through the thin layer of his T-shirt, the feel of his hard, warm body under her fingertips created a tingling sensation that stimulated and energized her soul deep, had it reaching out for more, almost as if it wanted to enter his body.

His head dropped forward, and his eyes closed. "Mmm, love. Keep that up and all's forgiven."

"Feel good?" she asked even though she knew the answer.

"Aye, it's grand. But you should stop."

"Why?"

He slowly swiveled to face her, and she dropped her hands from him. He shifted to the edge of his chair, slid his hands up her thighs and settled them at her hips. As he eased her forward, trapping her legs between his, her hands rose and settled on his shoulders. She could smell him, his heat, his unique scent that always seemed to cast a spell over her and make her heart flutter.

His fingers slid around and fanned her ass cheeks, digging in and pulling her even closer. They then slid up the back of her shirt, slowly, making her skin tingle at his touch. His face was so close to her breasts his breath teased her nipples to attention. "Turn around, love. I'm gonna do you."

"Ian!" barked a voice at the door.

Startled, Sabrina jumped and spun to face Jack's glare.

"Sabrina, excuse yourself while I talk to your boss."

****

Ian watched Breena, red-faced, rush out of the office, then let his eyes slide to Jack, who stood stiffly by the door, his eyes smoking angry.

"What the hell's going on in here?" the older man demanded.

"We're editing videos."

"Funny, 'cause from here it looked like she was giving you a goddamned massage and you were about to return the favor."

"What do you want, Jack? I'm too busy for a lecture." He kept his voice low and calm, refusing to be shamed or bullied into feeling bad about anything he and Breena did.

"I don't even remember what the fuck I came in here for. But you need to quit that shit. She belongs to Dom."

Ian swiveled his chair to face his monitor. "You don't need to remind me of that."

Jack stormed over and spun the chair back around, making Ian face him. "Somebody sure as hell does."

Ian surged to his feet, anger tensing his body into a mountain that towered above Jack, silently asking his boss whether he thought he was man enough to be the one to do it. "Make your point."

"I can't get through this project without you, Sean, and Dom, and I won't have you and Dom at each other's throats over *his* wife. It'll jeopardize the project and my job."

"We're not at each other's throats over anything."

"It's only a matter of time. The entire team is jawing about the way you and Sabrina act together. The way you're always gawking at each other, pawing at each other, running off to God-knows-where together in that jeep of yours. The only reason Dom hasn't already kicked your ass is because you're his best friend. He *trusts* you...and his wife. Don't abuse that trust."

"Breena and I are friends, teammates. Dom knows it. Everybody else needs to mind their own fucking business."

"I'm not going to argue with you. Knock it off."

"And if we don't?" Ian's quick retort snapped out in a low, defiant tone.

Jack's face tightened into a red scowl so deep it looked painful. He pointed a finger at Ian's face. "If you two can't keep your fucking hands off each other, I'll move her to finds with Red. And if that's not far enough away to keep you two apart, I'll remove her from this project. I'll lose Dom as an employee before I let his marriage—his life—be destroyed by an affair." He turned away without waiting for a response and shoved open the door, stormed out, then slammed it closed.

Anger surging through him, Ian flung his chair across the room, where it slammed into the door. His head roaring with fury, he fought to calm the uncustomary flare of temper. To help, he slowly crossed the floor and set the chair upright, then rolled it back to his computer, sat, and tried to refocus his attention on the video he'd been editing before Breena's touch wiped out every thought but the one of her.

A moment later, though, he clicked into a different video, fast forwarded it to a certain spot, paused it, and zoomed in.

He had caught her just becoming aware of his camera trained on her. Her blue eyes, lids half-lowered in a sultry look that stared deep into him, hooked him, made his insides feel like an earthquake had moved in. Her mouth parted slightly, the first blush of a grin kissing the corners. That little strip of hair that forever fought her ponytail holder swooped across her brow, one eye, and—oh, God—that mouth. Full lips a tempting tint of pinkish red he could almost taste. Like cherries or candy. They were ripe. Sweet. Ready to be devoured. And he was hungry.

His tongue darted out to lick his lips, and he hit play, his mouth turning up in a smile when she laughed and said his name, called him a brat for recording her, then spontaneously went with it, assuming a few sexy poses…just for him.

Show over, she laughed self-consciously and rushed toward him, saying his name again, one hand over the lens, the other on his arm, her breasts a whisper of a space from his chest. He swore he could feel her hard nipples brushing his skin through their shirts. He had almost put his hand to one full breast, wanting so badly to weigh it in his palm, cup it, squeeze it, roll her nipple between his fingers, bite it through her thin shirt. But if he did, he wouldn't stop there. Doing the right thing, he had pulled back and shut off the camera.

The recording ended there. He rewound it to his favorite pose, paused it, and absorbed the image he wanted to wallpaper his caravan with.

She had pulled the rubber band from her hair. Had flung all that silken gold forward then back, shook her head. Her bare arms were up, bent at the elbows and placed behind her head, her hands pushing up the back of her thick hair. The pose thrust her breasts out, and her high, taut nipples poked hard against her cami. And because her arms were lifted, her shirt rode up, exposing her tanned, toned stomach and sexy-as-fuck belly button that was deep enough to lap shots from.

But the thing that stabbed a blade of need hilt-deep into him was the look on her face, the unmistakable *let's fuck* she directed straight at him. He'd seen that look in her eyes more times than he could count, heard it in the thoughts she couldn't silence, and each time it hit him in the balls, stealing his breath, scrambling his brain until he could no longer tell right from wrong.

The now-familiar ache settled heavy in his groin, turning his cock into a pulsing steel rod, ready to throw off sparks. His mouth had gone bone dry. The sound of his own heavy breathing brought him out of the trance he'd fallen into, where it was just the two of them. In a place where she was his woman, and he was her man. A place where her body belonged to him—to love, to please, to pleasure, to worship, to fuck in wild abandonment.

He swallowed, gripped his cock to shift it to a more comfortable position. But the only comfortable position for a cock this hard was deep inside a wet pussy. No. Only in hers.

Fuck! Jack was right. Breena belonged to Dom. His best friend. He needed to quit lusting after her, quit touching her, quit thinking about her all the damn time.

He could easier sprout angel's wings.

The woman was embedded in his DNA. Had been from the moment he touched her skin, held her body against his, inhaled her scent. Maybe her essence had been there all along and had been waiting for her touch to awaken it and bring it to life. Maybe there was a spell on them. Maybe they were soulmates. Whatever the cause, there didn't seem to be an off switch for what he was feeling.

He launched himself out of his chair and dropped to the floor on fingertips and toes and did pushups until his muscles burned and felt like they would rip from the bone. Then he collapsed onto the floor on his back, his heart pounding, his lungs pushing out all but the thought of another breath, blood thundering in his skull instead of his cock.

When the red receded and he had found a little clarity, he rolled to his feet and sat in his chair, clicked back to the first video, and continued with his edits. But the image of her face, the feel of her touch, the sound of her voice remained. Breena was alive in him now, connected at the soul, forming an unbreakable bond. Nothing would change that fact. Not even staying away from her.

****

Sabrina fumed. Her husband stood in the trench next to his ex-lover, smiling, taking the offered bottle of water from her hand, drinking deeply before handing it back, so she too could drink from it. He knelt down, next to the skeleton, and she joined him, looking up into his face like he was God and she his most devout disciple.

Dominic had said he was helping Gabe with reports today, his day off. Why in the hell was he in the trench with Meggan? Why wasn't she in finds, washing, labeling, and bagging all the bones the team had already dug up? Why wasn't she training all her new interns?

Sabrina was on her way to get answers to those questions when Jack stormed toward their trench and climbed in. Even from this distance, she made out his pointed words to Meggan. "Quit your fucking around and get your ass to finds and do your job."

Even before Meggan had climbed out of the trench, Jack had turned to Dominic, yelling that the team was "moving too goddamned slow" and how he'd better "step it up" or he'd "fire the whole sorry-ass bunch."

Dominic tried to talk calmly to him, but Jack wasn't having it.

"Just do it, Sullivan! Or I'll give your fucking job to O'Neill." Cussing a blue streak, he stormed off toward his next victim. Dominic stormed off toward camp.

What had set their volatile boss off this time? Had it really been Meggan and Dominic? Or her and Ian? Her money was on the latter.

Oh, God. What had possessed her to massage Ian's back? Problem was, she'd acted solely on impulse, like she always did with him, that constantly burning need to touch him taking over. She needed to stop giving in to her impulses before something more disastrous than Jack's wrath resulted.

What she needed was to get away from this place with Dominic to reconnect. It had been so long since they'd been alone or even together for a significant amount of time. He worked his days off, planning and conducting training sessions for the students, helping Gabe and Jack with special projects for management, preparing reports and presentations. She was more and more being relegated to the peripherals of his life, and she didn't like it one bit.

Unfortunately, he didn't seem to notice, or worse, didn't seem to care. And with Jack demanding he work harder, her conscientious husband would be even less willing to take time out for her. Fuck. Just fuck. *We're getting out of here for a few days if I have to kidnap him.*

She went back to the office to finish at least one video before lunch. Ian was strangely quiet. Off. So much so that when she asked him, "What bug crawled up Jack's ass?" he didn't laugh or grin. He simply shrugged.

As the minutes ticked by, his mood crawled over into her, affecting hers. So much so that when they went to lunch, she had little appetite.

They got their food and sat at a small table in the

far back. Her eyes zeroed in on Dominic, sitting at his usual table with his usual bunch, and it pissed her off. She always went to say hi to him. He never came to her. He never asked her to sit with them, and he never sat with her. If she didn't go to him, she suspected he wouldn't even look around for her.

She picked up her fork but couldn't force herself to eat the food she'd selected.

"No appetizer today?" Ian asked.

"Appetizer?" In confusion, she looked at her plate, then at him.

He pointed his fork at Dominic's table. "Kisses for hubby."

"I'm conducting an experiment," she said.

"Hypothesis?"

"If I don't go over to him, he won't notice I'm here."

"Sure he will."

"Wanna bet?"

"Name the stakes."

"If you're right, and he comes to see me or in some way shows that he's noticed me, you get my cake for a week. If he doesn't—"

"You're not getting my cake."

"If I ate your cake and mine, I'd have to run three times a day."

He grinned. "So, what do you get if I'm wrong?"

"If you're wrong, then you can still have my cake because I'll be too depressed to eat it and you'll have to listen me bitch and moan for at least a week."

"Deal."

"And you can't call out his name, bump his chair, throw something at him, burp, fart, sneeze, or cough loudly, laugh, or do anything to catch his attention or that of those he's with."

He chuckled as if it made him happy she knew him well enough to know his tricks. "You're good at the fine print."

She chuckled because he was back to his old self. "My mother's a lawyer."

"Of course. Deal," he said, and they clinked forks to seal it.

Minutes later, the whole bunch stood and filed out. Dominic didn't come by to say hello. He didn't come by to kiss her. He didn't wave. He never even looked around for her. Meggan, however, shot Sabrina a smug look, then slid closer to Dominic as they walked out together, her hands at his back.

Sabrina set her fork down before she threw it at them. "Told you so."

Ian scooted his chair away from the table, turned it, and dragged hers around to face him. He trapped her legs between his, his hands on her thighs, and he leaned in, looking her square in the face. "We don't hold back with each other, right?"

"Right."

"Okay. Don't be a pussy."

She shot him a dirty look. "What?"

"If you want a seat at that fucking table, you march your sweet little ass over there and insist they make room for you."

"You're missing the point. I want him to want me to sit at that table. I want him to insist they make room for me. I want him to never even consider that I'd sit anywhere other than with him. Or I want him to sit with us. He doesn't want to sit with me. And *that's* the problem."

"Have you told him that?"

"Well, no, not in so many words, but—"

"Talk to him before you move into that dark place in your head. He doesn't realize what he's doing and for damn sure doesn't know how you feel."

"I'm his wife. He should at the very least look around to see if I'm at lunch. I swear, I could be having sex with you on the table and he wouldn't notice."

He scoffed. "The way you scream? He'd notice."

"I do not scream."

"Oh. My mistake." Eyes shining, he leaned in. "It must be Dom, then, who's screaming, 'Spank my ass! Harder!'"

Face burning, her hands rose to his chest and shoved him. "Shut up!" She laughed. "You're such a brat."

He laughed and grabbed her hands. "Just messing with you." He linked their fingers. "Ask for what you want and give him a chance to do it for you. We men... we're not mind readers."

Her eyes danced over him. "I don't know, McCanna...I think *you* are."

"Well, I'm special. Me mam tells me so every day."

His affected brogue made her chuckle. "If it wouldn't give you a swelled head, I'd tell you your *mam* was right. But I know you." She released his hands and started to straighten her chair, but he stopped her, hands on her thighs again.

"Tell me anyway," he said.

Smiling, she slid her cake in front of him.

He laughed. "Good enough."

"You're management," she said as he dug into her cake. "Why aren't you in the planning meetings?"

"I like to spend my break in more pleasurable pursuits."

"Yeah, right. You spend your breaks with me."

"It doesn't get much more pleasurable than eating a beautiful woman's delicious cake." His tongue snaked out and licked the frosting off the corner of his grin.

Her cheeks burned at his words and at the naked desire sparkling in his eyes. Chills swirled across her hot flesh, but she didn't take her eyes off him, couldn't wipe the grin off her face, couldn't stop the pussy trickle wetting her panties. "I wouldn't know."

He forked the last bite of cake and held it to her mouth, brushed the tip of it to her lips, teasing her. She opened her mouth. His fork slid in, but before her lips closed on it, he pulled it back. Grinned.

"Brat." she said.

He chuckled and held out the fork again. She kept her mouth closed, raised her eyebrow, and shook her head.

He shifted closer. "Trust me, love," he whispered and teased it to her lips again.

She opened her mouth. He slid the fork in. She closed her lips on it. He slowly pulled out the empty fork, leaving the tasty sweetness behind.

"Delicious," she said.

He wiped a dab of frosting from her lip with the tip of his finger and put it in his mouth. "Delicious."

Shivers danced along her heated skin and lowered her eyelids halfway as she wondered what it would have felt like had he used his tongue instead of his finger.

He grinned as the thought swirled in her head.

She didn't know whether he really could read her mind, but just in case, she needed to learn to hide her thoughts better. And she needed to tell Dominic what she wanted because he, for sure, couldn't read her mind.

****

"Is there a reason you always sit with Jack, Gabe, Sean, Kristin, and Meggan at lunch?" Sabrina asked Dominic that night after sex. She'd cut off early from digging with Ian to spend more time with Dominic.

"We've always used that time to plan the afternoon schedule. Why?"

"I thought maybe *we* could have lunch together," she said.

"Sure, it'll be tight, but we can pull up another chair."

"No, I mean just you and me. Alone. Once a week and on our day off." She'd decided that was what she wanted most.

"Oh."

"You don't want to have lunch with me?"

"No, I do. But as I said, that time's not just lunch, it's our management meeting."

"Ian's management. He doesn't go."

"He used to…until you got here."

Oh. "If Ian can skip them all, surely you can skip a few."

He shook his head. "Sabrina, I'm being groomed for the assistant site director position, which will eventually lead to the director position. I have to show I'm serious about work, committed."

Her shoulders dropped. "Congratulations." She got

out of bed and headed to the bathroom. "You've mastered it."

"Are you seriously mad?" he called out, sounding irritated himself.

Was she mad or just disappointed? Mad or sad? Mad or discouraged? All the above.

"Sabrina?"

She flushed the toilet, washed her hands, rinsed her mouth, and climbed back into bed.

"I want to spend more time with you." She took his hand in hers. "We get a few minutes in the morning and a few minutes at night. That's not enough. I miss you."

"Give up digging for ghosts with Ian, and we'll have more time together."

His snide comment didn't surprise her, but it did sting. She let go of his hand. "Never mind. Sorry I brought it up." She lay down and rolled onto her side away from him.

A beat or two passed before he spoke. "I'll talk to Jack about skipping a meeting."

She rolled over to face him. "I know your work is important to you. But our marriage is important, too, and we need to treat it like it is by giving it the attention it deserves."

"Would tomorrow work for you?"

She smiled, then hugged him to her and kissed him. "Tomorrow would be awesome."

"Sabrina, I've never had to split my focus at work before, and I guess I'm not very good at it yet. But our marriage *is* important to me. It's part of the reason I'm working so hard to get ahead. So I can give you more than..." he glanced around the trailer, "this. I want to give you a house, a car, nice things, everything you want and deserve."

"Baby, I grew up with things, all the things I wanted. I don't want more things. I want you, your time, your love."

"You have it, Sabrina. Always." He kissed her. "Don't give up on me. I've never been a husband before."

"I won't." She kissed him again to show him she meant it. "One more thing... When your meetings are over, would you take a second to come say hi to me? Give me a kiss?"

"I do that."

"No. I always come to you."

He thought for a moment. "Were you at lunch today?"

"Yes."

"I didn't see you."

"You didn't look. You just walked out, chatting with Meggan."

Realization that he hadn't looked, hadn't talked to her, and how that made her feel showed in his face. He kissed her forehead. "Baby, you're always in my heart, and I think about you a million times a day, even if I don't show it."

"Less thinking, Sullivan. More showing."

He rolled on top of her. "How about I show you right now?"

It used to be uncomfortable having sex while her ghost watched and complained, but she was long past it. If he was going to hang around, he'd have to get used to it. She wasn't leaving her husband.

She spread her legs for Dominic and guided him into her body.

****

A short time later, they awoke to angry shouts coming from outside. A glance out their window showed the fire still burning and the team gathered around two guys facing off. Even without hearing the angry threats they slung at each other, their threatening stances said the two were ready to rumble.

"Dustin and Marcus fighting again," Dominic said.

Sabrina plopped back down onto the bed and yawned. "Their hormones are going to destroy this place."

The sound of glass breaking and more shouting sent Dominic on higher alert. "Or each other." He started to leave the bed.

"No." Sabrina wrapped her arms around his hips. "Ian and Sean are probably out there. Let them deal with it."

"Sean and Kristin went to bed right after dinner, so he's not out there."

She'd never known any couple who had as much sex as those two. She sometimes heard them in the morning before breakfast, saw them head to their trailer after the lunch meeting, and before dinner, and she'd heard them going at it at night. She envied them.

"And Ian's busy tonight," Dominic said.

Busy? Doing what? She focused her thoughts on Ian and zeroed in on his emotions. She felt heat, pleasure, and the sensation of sex rising from him. A plume of fire-hot jealousy filled her from head to toe.

"Any chance Dustin and Marcus will figure things out on their own?" she asked.

"Not before they kill each other."

She sighed. "Let's go break it up." She let him go

and started to get out of bed to get dressed.

"No, I got this." He leaned over her, trapping her against the mattress. "Why don't you stay in bed and think about what you want me to do to you when I get back." He kissed her, then rolled out of bed, grabbed his boxers, and pulled them on.

"You might need help."

"I'll knock a few heads, send them all to bed, and be back before my side of the bed gets cold."

He was pulling on his boots when Meggan banged on the door, calling his name. "You need to get out here," she said when he'd opened the door. "Marcus is threatening Dustin with a trowel, and Dustin's waving around a broken bottle. They're both twisted and—"

Not even taking time to tie his boots or put on a shirt or say goodbye, he left the trailer, Meggan at his side. Meggan. Dominic's perfect dig partner. The kind of wife he needed. The one he wanted beside him as he knocked heads or unearthed finds or wrote reports or ate or anything else he did on a dig. So said the green-eyed demonic monsters howling in her head.

Or maybe that was just her ghost in her ear, annoyed as usual at something she was or wasn't doing. By the angry digging motions he was making, she surmised he was pissed because she wasn't digging for his *sonuachar* with Ian.

"Can't you leave me alone for one fucking night?" she growled, then covered her face with her pillow when he kept talking and gesturing.

****

Dom and Meg ran to where the two men faced off. Ian and Sean got there at the same time, both wearing nothing but boxers and boots.

"Thought you two were busy tonight?" Dom asked them.

"She'll wait." They both said and laughed.

They eyed the two hooligans, both second-year undergrad students. Ian crossed his arms over his chest, shot a look at Sean. "They look a little overheated, don't you think?"

"I do," Sean said.

Ian and Sean grabbed the large bucket of water the cook used to wash up dinner dishes—and that the team used to douse the fire at the end of the night—and tossed the contents onto both of the men. The fire sizzled, and the two sparring partners staggered back in shock and surprise, dropping their weapons, coughing and sputtering, hands going to their faces to wipe away the slimy water.

The team gathered around the fire quieted, too, no one saying a word, just staring at the ground or at the wet, gray smoke rising from the pit where the fire had burned moments before.

"All of you, go to your caravans." Dom's low but firm growl invited no argument, and people slowly moved away.

"Except you two," Sean tacked on, pointing at the two instigators.

The rivals shot a darted glance at each other and stayed put, carefully keeping their eyes averted from the infamous Holy Hell Trinity.

Ian waited until everyone was gone to speak, then started with Marcus. "What's this about?"

Marcus gripped his hands into fists, his gaze digging holes into the ground.

"Dustin?" Sean's prompt got nothing from him but

a tight mouth.

"You two better get this straightened out and fast," Dom said. "If it happens again, your arses are out of here, you won't get credit for the semester, and I'll make it my personal mission to let every prof in the department know what you're about. You'll not be approved to attend any other field school or internship."

That got their attention, and two sets of glassy eyes snapped up to him.

"Aye, which means you won't graduate. At least not in archaeology. Got it?"

They both nodded.

"Off to bed," Ian said.

They wandered off to their caravans looking a little like their world had just been tilted.

"Elsa's fucking both of them," Meg said. "Playing them against each other."

Ian spoke low to Sean and Dom in Irish. The two laughed.

Dom patted Ian on the back. "Go. Your date won't wait all night."

"Yeah, she will. I left her tied to the bed."

Dom and Sean chuckled again. Meg scoffed.

Ian cocked his head and grinned at her. "What was that, nutmeg? You want to join us?"

"Hump off, Ian."

He laughed and headed back to join his *date* in *her* caravan; Sean headed the other way, to his own caravan.

For as long as Dom had known him, Ian had never brought a woman to his caravan. When he once asked him why, Ian had said that the woman he allows in will be the one who stays forever. So far, none had been invited in.

"G'night," Dom said to both of them.

Ian raised his hand in response, Sean called out "night," and both kept going, eager to be on their way. Dom was eager to be on his way home, too, and would be as soon as he'd cleaned up the mess.

He gathered up the broken bottle and the pieces of glass he could see and threw them away. He also picked up the trowel—Nessy. Together he and Meg kicked dirt over the few flames that had survived the flood. Job done, they found themselves standing alone together in the still, moonlit night.

"Thanks for your help," he said finally.

"Hey, you know I always got your back," she said, softly cuffing his arm with her fist.

The truth of her statement hit him like a rock between the eyes. Despite their argument a few weeks back, which stemmed more from his guilt than her actions, the truth was he could count on her to be beside him whenever anything happened at their digs. She was a good friend. Right up there with Sean and Ian.

He wondered every day how had he gotten so damn lucky. He had everything he'd ever wanted— great friends and coworkers, a job that fed his mind and soul, a wife who made him glad to be alive. He was living the life he'd always dreamed of. He was happy, in spite of that kernel of uneasiness embedded in his gut that told him he could lose it all in a heartbeat.

"That Nessy?" Meg asked, nodding toward the trowel in his hand.

"Yeah." He glanced at it with a grin. "I thought I'd put it on his steps tonight so he won't waste an hour looking for it in the morning."

They laughed softly together, and she held out her hand. "I'll do it."

"You sure?"

"I'm sure." As she took Nessy from his hand, her fingers lingered on his.

The touch of her hand and her eyes sent a flush across his body and a prickling feeling of awareness swirling in his chest. He pulled his hand away.

"What did Ian say?" she asked. "When he spoke in Irish?"

He grinned. "Oh, that's no fit for the ears of a sweet lass like yourself."

She grinned at his exaggerated brogue. "Knowing Ian, it had to do with sex. C'mon, tell me. I'm not some silly little girl who'll faint at hearing a nasty word. I've worked with you foul-mouthed thugs for years. I've heard it all."

He looked at the twenty-four-year-old woman he'd known since she was seventeen, moonlight softening her features, and thought a *girl* was exactly what she looked like, with her freckle-dusted face, wild red hair curling down her back, breasts no bigger than a wild pear, and long, filly legs. An innocent. But he knew for a fact she wasn't.

He repeated Ian's sentence in a whisper.

"It's the translation I'll be needing," she whispered back, moonlight caressing the smile on her lips.

"Pussy and whiskey are the most powerful things in the world. They change a strong man into a weak fool after a single taste."

The look in her eyes changed, and her smile vanished. "Has it changed you?"

"You know I don't drink whiskey anymore." He'd

only needed his stomach pumped once to learn that whiskey—all the hard stuff, really—wasn't his friend.

"I wasn't talking about whiskey." Her voice had lowered to a seductive pitch.

He knew what she was asking, but he wasn't having a conversation about pussy with her.

Yes, he'd do anything for Sabrina. Would do anything to be with her and to bury himself deep inside her. Nothing made him happier than when he brought her pleasure. Had that obsession made him a weak fool? How would he act if he lost her? Or if he had to fight another man for her love? Probably like Marcus and Dustin. Worse. He'd kill any man who tried to take her from him. Or die trying.

He wouldn't go so far as to admit that his obsessive love made him a fool, but he would admit, to himself, that it was distracting him from his work. He pictured Sabrina in their bed, waiting for him, naked and horny. Constantly horny. Just thinking about her and what he was going to do to her when he got back made his cock tent the front of his boxers, a place where it had spent most of its time since she came into his life.

Meg's gaze dropped to his crotch, and her tongue darted out to lick her full pink lips, as if she could taste him there. When her gaze rose to his, there was no doubt what she wanted. He smelled her heat, her hunger. The power of it stroked his cock to an even harder state.

"Dom…" His name melted from her mouth, the mouth that had been a source of great pleasure to him over the years. She stepped closer, her hands reaching out, fingers trailing down his bare chest, over his stomach, and heading south. In the wake of her light touch, his nipples puckered, his abs clenched, and his cock hardened to full length. "Do you miss us?"

His mouth was so dry he wasn't sure he could speak, but he opened his mouth to try. "G'night, Meg."

He turned and hurried home, hoping she wouldn't try to stop him. Hoping he wouldn't have to embarrass them both by shutting her down if she tried to do more than touch.

Chapter Twelve

"I can't sit with you at lunch today," Sabrina told Ian the next morning as they were getting home from their run.

"What? Too good to eat with me now that you beat me home?"

That morning, for the first time in the month they'd been running together, she'd beat him home, and she was feeling proud of herself even though she had a nasty suspicion he had let her win. But it didn't matter. Even when she lost she won. Every time they ran, he pushed her, challenged her, and as a result, she was faster, her technique and endurance had improved, and she'd never felt stronger and more in tune with her body…and his.

The best thing about their running together was that it gave them a chance to reconnect after they separated at night. Like all their daily habits—running, sleeping, showering, eating, breathing—their daily syncing was a necessity.

"I'm sitting with my husband. Just the two of us."

"So, you took my advice."

"Go ahead and say I told you so," she said, keeping the grin in place. "I know you're dying to."

"I don't need to say it as long as you know it." He wrapped one arm around her neck and rubbed his other hand on her head to mess up her hair.

She ducked away, laughing. Pulling off her ponytail holder, she smoothed her hair but left it loose. He looped his arm back around her shoulders and drew her close.

"Good for you, love," he said into the top of her sweaty head as her arms wound around his waist. They stayed wrapped around each other until they got in sight of the camp.

Only, when lunch time came, Dominic wasn't there.

Neither was Meggan.

Josette, the intern Ian had been with the night before, sidled up to him right as he and Sabrina walked in.

Sabrina left him and walked over to where Jack, Gabe, Sean, and Kristin sat at their table. "Hey, guys, where's Dominic?"

Jack spoke. "I sent him and Red into town to pick up a couple of government suits who came in for a tour. They'll be back in an hour or so."

Her stomach clenched in disappointment. Dominic had forgotten their plans. Had forgotten her. Or he'd blown her off.

"You need help with something?" Sean asked her.

"No. Thanks."

She left the table, eyes flying to Ian, but he was occupied with Josette. She left the tent and rushed to her trailer to pound Dominic's pillow, the constantly nagging question about whether she was the right kind of wife for him gouging trenches in her chest.

Ian called her name as she reached the trailer, but she ignored him and went inside, slamming the door. Seconds later, he walked in, filling the space with his essence, as if he'd flipped on a flood light. "Where's Dom?"

She lay in bed on her side, facing the wall. "With Meggan, in town."

"*Hashkeh—*"

"Ian, go back to Josette."

Somehow knowing that what she really meant was *hold me*, he ignored her jealous snark and lay next to her, inched his body closer until it fit perfectly around hers. He slid his arm under her head and draped his other arm around her waist.

Snuggling her head against his arm, she grabbed his hand around her waist and held it.

"I've asked and begged him to spend more time with me. It's always no, and it's always because of work. The one time I'm able to guilt him into it, he blows me off. He doesn't want to spend time with me. He wants to work. I get that now. And it breaks my heart, Ian."

"If you two worked different places, you'd never see each other during the day, and the idea of having lunch together wouldn't even be an issue."

"It's not just that he can't have lunch with me or spend time with me during the day, it's that he broke his promise, that he didn't respect me enough to let me know he couldn't make it. I can't keep saying, 'I understand' when he comes up with reasons not to spend time with me. I can't keep begging for his attention. I'll never be the kind of wife who accepts that he puts work before me, our marriage, our family. Our life has to be about more than just work."

"Love. Look at me." He helped her roll over to face him. He settled his hand at her hip and slid one leg over hers as her hands went to his chest and curled into his shirt. "I've known him practically my whole life. He's always taken his responsibilities seriously, and he doesn't mix work and pleasure. Hell, I don't even think he knows how. Accept that about him, or you'll have no peace in your marriage."

"So our relationship isn't a responsibility he needs to take seriously?"

"That's not what I said."

When she didn't respond, he continued. "Does he show you his love when you *are* together? Do you feel it?"

His voice had gone to a whisper that kissed her face. Hers took on the same tone. "Yes."

"Do you still love him?"

"Yes."

"Then let go the idea of spending every free moment with him. The key to dealing with him on a dig is to work when it's time to work, play when it's time to play, and in your case, remember that you mean everything to him, even if he doesn't always show it the way you want him to. If he didn't make it to lunch today, there's a damn good reason for it, because Dominic Sullivan keeps his promises, especially to the people he loves. And darlin', he loves you."

Their gazes locked for a long moment. "How do you do that?" she asked softly, in awe of the peace trickling through her.

"Do what?"

"Know just what to say to make me feel better and believe everything will be all right."

"Mind reading," he said, tapping his head. "It's my super power."

"God, I hope not." *Or else you'd know how much I want to kiss you.* The second the thought formed in her mind, his eyes dropped to her mouth, and his tongue slid out to wet his full lips. The air between them thickened and heated with static. A fluttering began low in her stomach as she breathed him in.

A loud gurgle sounded between them, making her laugh, making him grin, shattering the mood.

"Please tell me you're better and in the mood to eat," he said. "My stomach's about to eat my liver. And I fucking hate liver."

"Can't you just read my mind and find out?"

"Too...hungry," he moaned. "Powers...weak."

"Yeah, I'm hungry," she said. "Let's go. Before all the cake's gone, and I have to dry your tears."

He dropped a kiss on her forehead then untangled his body from hers, stood, and pulled her up off the bed. She headed toward the door, but he drew her to him and hugged her. She hugged him back, happiness and other, wilder, emotions racing through her.

"What would I do without you?" she whispered into his chest, forcing herself not to rub her crotch against the erection filling his jeans.

"I was thinking the same thing about you, love," he whispered into her hair, and she felt him press in slightly.

A moment later, after managing to ease out of each other's arms, they headed back to the mess tent, his arm draped over her shoulders, his banter teasing her mood back over to the happy side of the scale. And he ate with her, not with Josette. What would she do without him? She didn't want to find out.

****

As Dom toured the clients around the trench where Sabrina was working, she didn't talk to him or look his way, a sure sign she was mad. And he knew it was because he'd missed their lunch.

While the clients were listening to Meg describe the finds they'd brought up in that trench, he slipped away to talk to her. "Baby, Jack sprang it on me the second before I needed to leave to pick up the clients. I didn't have time to tell you I couldn't make it to lunch, and I didn't have my mobile with me."

"Did Meggan have her phone?"

"Probably." Meg always had it. "Yeah."

"You could have used it to call me, or you could have asked someone to let me know before you left."

"You're right. I should have. Sorry." Truth, he'd been so focused on work, he hadn't given a thought to their lunch until it was too late. He would have to do better if he wanted to keep Sabrina happy. He would do better. "I'll make it up to you. Tomorrow we'll—"

"Tomorrow you'll eat with your group so you can discuss your work, and I'll eat with Ian so we can discuss ours." She moved around him to shoot the other skeleton.

He followed her. "Sabrina, I said I'm sorry. Truly. Give me another—"

"Dominic, I'm fine," she interrupted. "Truly. But I have work to do. Talk to you tonight."

He watched her leave the trench and climb into Rusty's across the way. Watched her kneel to shoot some close-ups. Watched Ian join her, crouch down beside her, his hand rubbing up and down her back before settling on the back of her head and tugging her

203

ponytail. Watched her answering smile after he leaned in and whispered in her ear. Watched them laugh, their eyes locked. Watched them scroll through photos on her camera, bent heads together. Watched her grab his leg—he her waist—when she almost fell as she stood. Watched her stand, grab his outstretched hand, and pull hard to help him up. Watched them walk away together toward the media office, his hand low at her back, their bodies close, their steps perfectly in sync.

Their touching was becoming habit. So was their being together all the time, for more than just work. Well, fuck. He'd have to do a lot better.

****

"Erin still happy with her rugby guy?" Sabrina asked Ian.

They'd been digging for an hour and had kept up a lively, eclectic conversation to pass the time. After weeks of night digging, none of the skeletons were the *sonuachar* that would release them from their mission. As far as they knew. She still wasn't sure how they'd be able to know when *she* presented herself. Her ghost always appeared while they were digging, but only to check in, show his approval that they were working on it, before popping out again. She also noticed that he never came into the trench, but stayed on the lip.

Ian smiled. "They broke up."

"Don't sound so heartbroken, there, big brother," she said teasing him.

"He wasn't right for her."

"Says you."

"Says Erin. She's the one who dumped him."

Sabrina stopped in mid-dig to stare at him. In their previous conversations on the subject, he'd bemoaned the fact that his sister Erin was in crazy in love with—in Ian's words—the loser rugger. For her to suddenly dump the so-called love of her life was odd.

"And you had nothing to do with it."

He grinned. "You wound me, love, thinking I'm the kind of man who would sabotage his baby sister's love life."

"Did you?" she asked.

"The loser wisely decided he preferred to be unattached."

She laughed. "I used to wish for a big brother, but now I think I'm lucky to have dodged the meddling that comes along with it."

"Meddling? No, love. In Ireland it's called watching out for our own. We'd rather go through torture ourselves than to see someone we love hurt. And because of that, we'll do anything to protect them."

Sabrina had never experienced that level of protection until Dominic. Until Ian. The two of them, standing on either side of her, figuratively and literally, made her feel protected, buffered from the punches of the world. It felt wonderful.

"You're a good brother, Ian. And a good friend."

"But?"

She shook her head. "No buts."

"A compliment? Breena, you should sit down. You're obviously feeling loopy."

She tsked. "You act like I never say anything nice about you."

"You don't. Not out loud, at least." His eyes held her in place. He lifted an eyebrow.

It wasn't the first time he'd intimated that he could read her mind, and she hadn't completely believed he could, despite the many times he'd proved it. It was time she found out for sure. "Can you read my mind, Ian? Tell me the truth."

"I can hear your thoughts."

Oh, shit. Her face flushed at the memory of what most of her thoughts about him had been about. About wanting to kiss him, touch him, try out the package behind his tight zipper.

"What am I thinking now?" she asked.

He walked toward her, took her hands in his, linked their fingers, and held her gaze. Her gut said to pull away, not let him in, but she couldn't. She had to know for sure. She stilled, opened herself to the idea of him being inside her head. As he gripped her hands, she felt him in her brain, like a feather tickling her.

"You want to kiss me."

Der.

"And touch me."

Yeah.

He grinned. "Try out my package."

Well, shit. He'd even used her words. Okay. He could read her mind. But he wasn't the only one with a gift. She could read his mind, too, in a way. His thoughts came over as sensations, emotions, and the main one slamming into her was desire. He wanted the same things she did.

She pulled her hands from his and shoved him lightly in the chest as she backed away. "I retract my compliment." She picked up a dirt clod and threw it at him. "You're a brat."

He laughed and dodged the clod. "Why am I a brat?"

"You shouldn't be eavesdropping on my thoughts."

"You shouldn't be having nasty thoughts about my love muscle."

"Love muscle?" Giggling, she picked up another clod, a bigger one.

"Sure you want to play this game, love?" There was a gleam in his eyes, and a wicked little smile curved his mouth.

"I'm sure." She drew her hand back like she was going to throw it.

"I'm warning ya—" He moved toward her just as she hurled it, and it struck him on his swollen love muscle.

The shocked look on his face made her snigger with laughter.

"Think that's funny, do ya?"

"Aye. I do," she said, mimicking his accent.

He picked up a clod the size of a softball, weighed it in his hand, eyeing her as if he were carefully choosing his target. A rush of excitement filled her chest when he advanced toward her, the intense look on his face suggesting he was out for revenge.

"Ian, no." With a giggle, she tried to climb out of the trench, but he snaked out a hand and grabbed her arm, making her fall into him. He caught her around her waist and pulled her close. She immediately swatted the clod in his hand and part of it crumbled off, falling on his shirt and hers. He raised the clod up over her head. She grabbed his arm, trying to pull it down so she could grab the clod, but he was too strong.

"You want it?" He brought it close to her hand.

"Yes," she said, laughing, swatting at it just as he pulled it out of reach. "Give it to me." She grabbed at it again, and he laughed again when she failed.

She jumped up on him, wrapping her legs around his waist, one arm around his neck, the other reaching for the clod. The sudden imbalance knocked him down, and he fell, pulling her along with him, holding her tight so she fell on him and not on the hard ground.

They grunted when they landed, her squarely on top of him, chest to chest, pelvis to pelvis, thigh to thigh. He quickly wrapped a leg around her legs and rolled her over onto her back, him on top of her. His arms were around her back, holding her close and supporting her head.

Her hands were at his chest. Her legs were open and bent at the knees, his body fitting perfectly between them. She couldn't ignore the feel of his cock hardening at her crotch or how his hips pressed against her, like he was sinking into her. She couldn't ignore the yearning suddenly coursing through her, urging her to lock her legs around his waist and bring him as close as they could be.

Her chest rose and fell with his, their hearts pounding as one. Her lungs worked overtime to send oxygen to her brain so she could think straight, but it wasn't working. She was breathing him in. Just him. No air. Like smoke from a burning drug, he swirled inside her, in her veins, behind her eyes, making her high on him.

It was shadowed where they'd landed, away from the light of the lantern, but she could see his eyes locked on hers, could see them shift to her mouth. He leaned in, his lips hovering over hers, his breath warming the breaths she pulled inside her lungs.

If she lifted her chin but an inch it would put their hungry lips in perfect alignment, and they would kiss.

And they wouldn't stop there. She wanted her hands between his legs, touching him. She wanted to rip open his jeans, shove them down just enough to free his cock. She wanted to guide him into her wet and aching pussy, wanted him to pound into her, fill her emptiness, make her come, make her feel whole. She wanted all of it, and she pushed those thoughts into him, not caring that he could hear them, not caring that it was wrong.

Her nipples were hard against his chest, her breasts tightened and rounded as if they were forming into a shape to fit his hands. The beginnings of an orgasm quivered inside her, shaking a trembling groan from her mouth. Her body shuddered, and she was unable to stop her hips from pressing up against him as he pressed down into her. She wanted this man. There was no hiding it. Even if he couldn't read her thoughts, he could read her body.

But allowing herself the gift of Ian McCanna would destroy her marriage. She didn't want to stop. She had to stop. Before she was unable to.

"*Hashkeh*, please," she pleaded, their hearts pounding louder than her shaky whisper. "Don't." She was counting on him to be her hero, to be strong, because at that moment she was anything but.

"I'm not that strong either," he said.

They stared at each other for tight, tense moments, trying to rouse the strength to separate, to not give in to what they wanted more than anything.

"Where's a video camera when you need one?" They turned at hearing Meggan's voice. She stood a few feet away, by where they'd left the cameras.

Sabrina's eyes went wide. Ian's narrowed. They both muttered "Shit."

He scrambled to his feet and helped her up. They faced Meggan, who had one of their video cameras in her hands, pointing it right at them.

"Oh, look, here's one," she said with a laugh, holding it aloft. The light was on, telling them she was recording them.

Ian walked toward her, took the camera from her, and turned it off. She didn't even put up a fight.

Sabrina turned her back to them and wrapped her arms around her waist. She was shaking from the realization of what she had almost done. She had almost cheated on her husband. With his best friend. Her stomach clenched in pain, regret, shame.

What was wrong with her? If Meggan hadn't… Ah, shit! Meggan. Why did she have to be the one to see them? At least it wasn't— Oh, God, if it had been Dominic who had seen them… She wanted to throw up, expel the self-loathing churning inside her.

"What do you want?" Ian asked Meggan, his voice tight.

"You two are just photographers, so maybe you don't know," Meggan said, ignoring his question. "But what you were doing just now? That's not the way to unearth bones. Boners, maybe. But not bones."

Snickering, she turned and headed toward camp, leaving them alone.

Sabrina and Ian stood grounded in place, their backs to each other, guilt over what they'd done rolling off them.

"She won't tell him," he said.

"Why *wouldn't* she? It would give her what she wants—for him to leave me so she can have him. I know it."

"Because then I'd tell him the thing she doesn't want him to know." He headed back to the trench, picked up his trowel, and began to scrape away dirt from the skeleton. She joined him.

"Ian."

He kept digging.

"We have to stop this. Whatever's going on between us. I love Dominic, and I know you love him, too. Here in Ireland, we watch out for those we love, do anything to protect them, keep them from getting hurt. Isn't that what you said?"

When he didn't respond, she touched his arm. "*Hashkeh*."

He stopped digging and met her eyes. She saw the same anguish in him that she felt inside. The confusion and frustration at what was happening to them. The guilt. The shame. And most of all, the burning desire.

"I don't want to hurt him," she said. "You don't either. *This* would kill him."

After a moment, he nodded. It was a fragile agreement, and she had doubts whether either of them could keep it from shattering.

"Let's call it a night," she said.

"You go on home. I'll put our stuff away." His tone left no room for argument.

She took his hand, just to get his attention, not because of the constant need she had to touch him, not to satisfy the craving to feed the fever raging across her skin. "Ian—"

"Breena." He looked at her, his eyes hard, his voice rough with frustrated desire. "Go. Now. Because if you stay, we're going to finish what Meggan interrupted."

She started to retract her hand from his, but he held

on, gripped it tightly. "Stay."

They stared at each other for a long moment, their eyes simmering over each other, and in that moment she used every bit of strength she possessed not to give in and give them both what they wanted. Unable to speak, she shook her head.

He broke their gaze, released her hand, and moved away to gather their tools. She didn't want to leave him, but she did.

Self-loathing filled her as she hurried home, thinking about what she'd done—almost done. Shit! Why couldn't she leave him alone? It was like she was addicted to him, to the feelings he stirred in her. And addictions were no easy matter to overcome.

Flashbacks of that dark time in middle school flooded in, squeezing her chest and her throat. In a cliché dick move, her physician father had run away to Belize with his nurse, and her mom spent longer and longer hours at her law firm, leaving Sabrina to deal with her shattered world alone. The need to feel good again led her to try cocaine, and she'd gotten hooked. The drug had made all her problems disappear and made her feel nothing but glowing pleasure and happiness. At least until she came down.

One of the servants had found her stash and ratted on her, and her mom had thrown her into rehab. After that, she'd stayed clean, didn't drink until college, and even then just a little. She'd had no real addictions since then, except maybe running. Until now. Until Ian.

Like the drug she'd been hooked on, Ian made her feel good, made her feel whole and happy, made all her problems go away. But when she came down, she felt like shit and as guilty as hell.

As she climbed into bed with Dominic after her shower, she silently vowed she would not give in to her craving. She would not cheat on her husband.

"Take me away from here, Dominic," she whispered into the darkness, but only her ghost heard her plea.

****

Ian watched Breena climb out of the trench and disappear into the darkness. He threw the shovel like a spear into the blackness. What the fuck was wrong with him? Why couldn't he leave her alone? He felt like an addict who was relentlessly searching for his next fix. Sabrina Sullivan was his drug of choice, and he felt like he was going to die if he didn't have her.

Dropping to the ground, he leaned back against the trench wall and propped his arms on bent knees. He stared at the stars and asked the universe for help in showing him the way out of this trap. Hurt Dom or hurt himself. Those were his options. He knew what he had to do.

He grabbed the camera with the intent to delete the video Meggan had recorded but gave in to temptation instead. He rewound it, watched it, relived every sensation that had filled his body as he lay nestled between Breena's thighs—desire, need, hunger, joy…love.

He had wanted to kiss her. Touch her. Fuck her right there in the dirt.

Her thoughts confirmed that she wanted it, too. That she wanted to rip open his pants, take his hard cock in hand, spread her legs wide, and guide him into her wet-for-him pussy.

He had wanted to take her hard and fast, make her

scream his name as her cum bathed his cock, growl out her name as his cum filled her. Then he wanted to do it all again. Slowly. Lovingly. Drawing out their pleasure and spending all night getting to know her body again.

Again? Yes. As sure as he knew his name, he was sure she had been his at some point in time. Something inside him remembered and was fighting to have her again. And she wanted him. There was no longer any doubt in his mind. Had Meggan not interrupted them, they would have fucked.

And broken Dom's heart.

He rubbed a dirty hand across his face. "Ah, hell, Breena. This is fucked. What are we going to do?"

His attention back on the video, he watched them separate when Meggan announced herself. He noticed something odd then. He rewound and watched it again. When he and Breena were together, touching body to body, there was a pale blue haze surrounding them that grew brighter and closed tighter the longer they touched. When they weren't touching, it disappeared.

He watched that section of the video a few times to make sure. His eyes could be playing tricks on him. It could be flaw in the medium or the device. It could be a trick of the light. But it was the same every viewing.

Was the haze the bubble they felt surrounding them whenever they touched? The same blue haze Ena had surrounded them in? Had she put a spell on them? They needed to find out. They couldn't go to Ena. If she had caused it, she wouldn't admit it and undo it. And he didn't know any other witches. But he knew someone who did.

He hated to do it, but desperate times and all. He pulled his phone from his backpack and dialed. "Hey, mam. How are ya? Good. I'm good, but I need a favor. And no questions."

****

"You missed it," Sabrina said when Ian passed the store and kept on toward the highway. When he didn't respond, she added, "Are we going into town?"

The store in little Anamcara carried basic camera supplies, but for anything else, they had to go into the larger town two hours away.

Ian kept his eyes on the road.

"We're not getting supplies are we?"

He glanced at her long enough to see her confusion, but he didn't respond.

"Ian, where are we going?"

"To see a woman named Fiona Wilde."

"Who is this Fiona and why are we—" She inhaled sharply. "Oh, shit! She's a witch, isn't she? You're taking me to see a witch? After what Ena did to us?"

"We need to do this, Breena."

"Take me home," she insisted. When he didn't stop, she opened the door.

"Shit!" He grabbed her arm in case she really tried to jump from the moving jeep. He steered to the side of the road and skidded to a stop. When he let her arm go to shift into neutral and set the brake, she jumped out and ran back the way they'd come.

"Goddammit!" He turned off the engine, grabbed the keys, and jumped out to run after her, chasing her through the meadow at the side of the road. He caught her, but she fought him, slashing out with her hands.

"Stop it," he growled and grabbed her wrists. With his body he pushed her back against a tree and pinned her there, holding her hands captive above her head.

215

"Listen to me."

"I'm not doing this, Ian," she said, twisting and bucking against him.

The fear and anger in her face, in her voice, slashed his heart. He knew what was going on. She didn't want to examine too closely whatever was between them. If they examined it, received confirmation that it was real, they'd have to acknowledge it. If they acknowledged it and talked about it, they might do something about it. If they did something about it, it would change their entire world, and that might be too much to handle. He'd had the same thoughts himself.

"*Hashkeh,*" he whispered at the corner of her mouth, then lifted his mouth to kiss her eyes, tasting her tears on his tongue. "If Ena put a spell on us, maybe this Fiona can break it. And if we are soulmates, maybe she can help us control what's going on between us."

"We're controlling it."

He shook his head. "One of these days, we'll do something we can't undo. You know it."

"No." She shook her head and squeezed her eyes closed. "We love Dominic too much to—"

"Look at me." He dipped his head to look into her eyes. "Twice now we've almost made love. And right this minute, we want each other so bad it hurts."

"You're wrong!"

"I'm not wrong, Goddammit," he barked, unable to keep the frustration from his voice. He released her, his hands curling into fists as he stepped back, away from her, putting some distance between them, his chest heaving to try to draw enough Sabrina-free air into his lungs.

"It's almost more than I can bear to keep my hands

off you, Breena. It hurts. Physically hurts to stop myself from making love to you. My head. My stomach. My heart. My fucking cock." He pounded his chest with his fists. "Fucking everywhere. Staying away from you hurts. Not touching you hurts. Not kissing your mouth…hurts. Don't tell me you don't feel the same way, because I read you. I feel what you feel."

He watched her juggle the lie and the truth. Then her body slumped against the tree, and she sighed, a deep release that stripped away all her pretense. "It hurts. Constantly. Except when we touch. But even that's not enough because," she closed her eyes, "I want more."

The anguish in her voice sank him. He moved back to her, put his arms around her, and pressed his body into hers, as deeply as he could, holding her tight to him, whispering sweet Irish words of love into her ear.

She gripped the back of his shirt, holding on for dear life, and they locked into each other, the desire firing between them trying to fuse them into one being. They both wanted more. So much more. But between them was their love for Dom, the only thing keeping them from doing the unthinkable.

"Do you really think seeing that witch will help?" she whispered against his mouth.

He wanted to lie and tell her yes, just to make her feel better. But he couldn't. He couldn't lie to her. So instead he forced a little grin to his face. "It couldn't hurt." Maybe.

Chapter Thirteen

Sabrina had never seen a witch's house before, so she hadn't been sure what to expect. But the little white cottage with the thatched roof, purple shutters and door, and vine-swallowed white fence Ian pulled the jeep to a stop in front of, wasn't it. It looked too normal.

She grinned at him, raised an eyebrow.

He grinned back, raising the same eyebrow. "Not what I expected either."

His hand at the small of her back, he led her through the vine-covered arched gateway and walked beside her up the flower-lined path. The thick arched wooden door had several unfamiliar symbols burned into it, but there was nothing else that definitively said "witch in residence." But what did she know? She was out of her element in this magical, mystical place.

Ian used the ornate dragon knocker to announce their arrival. She slid her hand into his, and he squeezed it reassuringly. Needing more, she gripped his bicep with her other hand and met his eyes. He leaned in and pressed a soft, lingering kiss to her forehead, another to her temple.

The door swung open, revealing a petite, forty-something woman. Her feet were bare beneath faded blue jeans, and her toenails were painted deep purple to match the tone of the long-sleeved, flowing lavender blouse she wore. Cotton-white hair was looped into a long braid that curved over one shoulder like a thick rope. The smile she gave them reached her violet eyes, giving the orbs a friendly and wise sparkle.

"Ian, Sabrina…welcome." She moved aside so they could enter, then shut the door. "Good timing. I've just wet the tea."

The backyard she led them to was a lush oasis of flowers and other growth. A canopy of climbing ivy blanketed the portico, creating a cool shaded area out of the sun.

"Be comfortable." Fiona gestured to a six-foot-long oak bench that looked like it had been carved eons ago. She studied them as they settled beside each other.

"You didn't say you were lovers," Fiona said, a smile on her face, her eyes shining.

The statement caught Sabrina off guard, and she rushed to negate it. "We're not."

"You could have sat anywhere along that bench, yet you sat right next to each other, your bodies turned into each other, touching as if you have to."

Fiona was right. Despite having six feet of bench to sit on, they had settled right next to each other at one end. Ian's arm was around her shoulders, holding her close, and she leaned into him, legs crossed toward him, her knee touching his, needing to be that much closer. Her hand had rested on his thigh until he scooped it up and linked their fingers. Fiona was right. They looked like lovers who couldn't keep their hands off each other.

"And the energy racing between you…" Fiona added with a chuckle, sounding pleased at their behavior. "This will be interesting." She headed into the house.

Sabrina started to scoot over a bit, but Ian held her close, shook his head. "We're safe here," he said. "We can be who we are. Who we want to be."

She nodded and settled against him. It was odd, but she did feel safe in this stranger's house with Fiona Wilde, their witch, protecting them.

Fiona set a tray, with a teapot and three white cups and saucers, on the table stretched out in front of the bench and poured tea. They didn't move out of their embrace until she handed a cup to Sabrina.

"I don't care for any thanks," Sabrina said.

"Please." Fiona smiled, but Sabrina got the feeling she couldn't refuse.

She took the cup and handed it to Ian, taking the next one for herself.

"I'm sorry if you use cream and sugar, but those additions would cloud the reading," Fiona said as she poured a cup for herself. "And we wouldn't want that." She sat in the padded wicker chair beside the bench, her legs curled under her. She took a sip, sighed, and smiled again. "Tea is medicine for the soul." She took another sip, watching them the whole time. "Ian, you told me you believe there's a spell on the two of you."

"Yes."

"And you, Sabrina? Do you believe this also?"

When Sabrina didn't immediately respond, Fiona spoke again. "Any treatment I prescribe won't be effective unless you both commit. Not just to the solution but to the need for it."

Sabrina looked at Ian, needing to see his eyes. If he believed there was a spell on them and that Fiona could remove it, she would believe it, too. Because she trusted him.

She turned back to Fiona. "I'm committed."

Fiona nodded and sipped her tea.

"Can you remove the spell?" Sabrina wanted to skip the tea and get to business.

Instead of answering the question, Fiona asked one of her own. "What happens when a droplet of water hits a hot skillet?"

"I don't cook much," Sabrina said, "but I suppose it sizzles and evaporates. Burns away."

Fiona nodded. "That's what happened to the spell cast on you."

"Breena and I being the hot skillet?" Ian asked.

"Your *connection* is the hot skillet. It will extinguish any spell attempted on you."

"Our connection?" he asked.

"You are soulmates."

The skin on Sabrina's skull tightened as despair gripped her. So it was true. She set her half-full cup on the table before it fell from her shaking hands. "Can you break the connection?"

Fiona's cup halted on its way to her lips. "Finding a soulmate is a joyous thing. Why would you throw away that gift?"

"It's destroying our lives."

Fiona drank deeply, studying her. "Is your husband your soulmate?"

She had pulled her ring off before leaving the jeep, and Ian hadn't mentioned she was married. Was she that transparent? Or was Fiona that good? "I thought so when I married him."

"And after finding Ian, you no longer think that?"

"No, he still is, but... I love my husband, but what I feel for Ian is..." She shook her head, not knowing how to explain her and Ian.

Fiona leaned forward and put her hand atop Sabrina's. "Tell me what's happening."

A calm spread through her at Fiona's touch, and she gathered her thoughts. "Ian and I felt an attraction to each other from the moment we met about a month ago, and that attraction grows stronger every day. The actions that could come with it will destroy my marriage."

"You want to make love to each other."

Desire fluttered in her womb, and heat filled her cheeks. "Yes."

"You touch each other. Compulsively and sometimes with no awareness that you're doing it until after you've forced yourself to stop. You call each other by terms of endearment you call no one else. Feel completely at ease with each other, like you've known each other forever. Feel physical pain when you try to stay away from each other."

"Yes," she said.

Ian nodded. "To all of it."

"Sexual spirit is the strongest type of energy flowing in humans. But in you two, it is as vibrant and vigorous as I've ever seen. It is pure desire, pure love, pure adoration that manifests as a blue aura surrounding you. I can see it from here, rising from you both like heat waves, tangling, intertwining, alive. And I smell..." She closed her eyes and inhaled. "Wildflowers basking in the sun." She opened her eyes and focused on them. "I'm astounded you haven't given in to its call. You both must love Dominic very much to endure such pain so he won't."

Had they mentioned Dominic's name?

Fiona set her cup on the table. "Soulmates enter our lives—throughout our lives—to love us, to help us learn the lessons we need to learn, to lead us to be the person we're supposed to be. We might not think of them as soulmates at the time—they often go by the name friend or teacher or boss or parent—but they are. It's very possible Dominic is a soulmate whose charge was to bring you to Ian, your original soulmate."

"I love Dominic, and I refuse to believe he had no other role in my life but to bring me to another man. I don't want to feel this way about any man but my husband. Ian doesn't want to feel this way about a woman who can't give all of herself to him. These feelings aren't just lust or a little crush. They're real, powerful, consuming, persistent. If unleashed, they'll destroy everyone we care about. You have to make them go away."

Fiona turned her gaze to Ian. "You want this also?"

When Ian didn't answer, Sabrina turned to him. His eyes were already on her, and the sadness that colored them split her open. She felt his pain.

"What I *want*," he said, setting his cup on the table beside hers, "is her."

A little moan slipped from her mouth, and she leaned into him, her lips at his ear, her hand cupping his face. *Hashkeh, I hate that I'm hurting you*, she said silently, just for him.

He turned his head and kissed her forehead. "I know, love."

"Ian?" Fiona asked, softly breaking into their cocoon.

They shifted apart.

"She belongs to my friend, and I don't want to hurt

223

him. Since I can't have her, I want the feelings to stop."

"Have you kissed her on the mouth?" Fiona asked.

"No."

"Why not?"

"You know why not," he said, anger sharpening his tone.

She nodded, studying him with her piercing violet eyes. "You two belonged to each other first, have spent several lifetimes together…but it's such a miracle when you do unite and in such a perfect match. It's a shame you're giving it up." She looked at Sabrina. "Have you thought about telling your husband what's happening? Getting his help to keep you away from Ian?"

"I can't tell him about this."

"Secrets kill marriages…and friendships."

"So would telling him I want to make love with his best friend."

"Would telling him *after* you've made love with his best friend be any easier?"

The words hung in the air, and Sabrina dodged them even as part of her embraced them.

Fiona stood, picked up the tray. "Finish your tea so we can get a clear picture of what's going on." She left the room.

They drank down all but a bit of their tea just to do it and put the cups on the table.

"Why did she ask whether we had kissed on the mouth?"

"C'mere, love." Ian pulled her across his lap and held her in his arms. "Long ago, people believed that the soul was carried on the breath, and that a kiss between true soulmates would reunite their souls and fuse them together forever in an unbreakable bond."

"That's why you never kissed me on the mouth?"

"If I kissed you on the mouth, Breena, there'd be no going back for us. You would be mine. Only mine."

The intense love in his eyes shook her, and she had to look away or risk giving in to her burning desire to test the ancient myth. Breaking their gaze, she settled her head against his shoulder, her hands on his chest at his heart. Not that she needed to test it. She knew he was right.

"How do you think Dominic would take it? If we told him about us?"

"He'd never believe it. He'd be broken."

"So, we don't tell him."

He sighed. "We don't tell him."

"We learn to stay away from each other." *And we don't kiss.*

She closed her eyes against the pain of the idea. If Fiona succeeded today, they might never enjoy this magic again, enjoy the connection that gave them everything they needed, everything they wanted, everything they had ever longed for. Wanting to enjoy it while she still could, she sank deeper into the merging, the peace, the joy of Ian's embrace.

They didn't notice Fiona's return until she cleared her throat delicately. They slowly separated. Several items sat before them on the table—a blood-red chunk of sharp smelling incense, two white candles, one yellow candle, and four black candles.

Fiona sat. "Take your cup by the handle in your left hand and quickly swirl the cup three times from left to right." After they did, she instructed, "Slowly and carefully invert your cup over your saucer and turn it three times."

At that point, she lifted Sabrina's cup and studied the pattern of the tea leaves clinging to the bottom and sides, then did the same to Ian's cup.

She reached for their right hands. "You share an ancient soul, two halves of a whole, destined to unite, again and again, through time. In your search for each other over each lifetime, you often find loving partners only to have the relationships fail when you realize they aren't your *true one*."

She peered into their eyes as if she were picking through their hearts, brains, and souls for ancient secrets buried deep. "Your souls want to be together, are constantly reaching for their other half because they were created to be together. Which is why it feels as if some force has taken over, making you behave in ways you otherwise wouldn't."

Neither Sabrina nor Ian said a word, only stared at her, soaking in the truth that they, deep down, had already known.

"It will be difficult, if not impossible, to dampen the attraction you feel, especially if you continue to live and work close together. Think of it in terms of being addicted to a drug. You try to stay away from it, but if it's there, at your fingertips, you're more likely to use. You are addicted to each other, to the feelings that being together stirs in you. No matter how hard you try, you won't be able to fight the craving forever. Unless you separate from each other and remain that way, your souls will get what they want. And what they want is to become whole."

"How do our souls become whole?" Sabrina asked.

Fiona smiled. "Don't you know, lass?"

Sabrina's gaze shifted to Ian's. Desire bloomed

inside her. Yeah, she knew. *They* knew. They'd always known. *By making love.* He nodded, took her hand, kissed her palm. She smiled.

Then she remembered why they were there. To prevent it. To end it. The peace left her heart, taking her smile with it.

She looked back at Fiona. "Is there anything that will curb the desire?" Her voice was flat. Sad.

Fiona looked disappointed in hearing the question. She held her hands out toward the items on the table. "A disenchantment ritual *might* lessen the attraction, but it will not kill it. Just as citronella," she said, cupping a delicate lavender bloom of the plant on the floor beside her, "repels mosquitoes but does not kill them."

"What do we do?" Ian shifted toward the table, forearms on his knees, his hands gripped tightly together, knuckles white and stretched. Sabrina heard irritation in his voice. Saw it on his face. Felt it rolling through him. He didn't want to do this. He was doing it for her. So she didn't lose her marriage and the man she loved. He was being her hero. Again.

"I will perform the first ritual here today," Fiona said. "Then you will do it for seven consecutive nights, always between midnight and one in the morning, always in exactly the same way, always using the elements you see here, which you will take with you."

Using a silver lighter, she lit the incense, swirled the smoke among the three of them, then lit the white candles and placed them on either side of the incense. She lit the yellow candle and put it at the center, nearest them, then placed the black candles around the yellow candle and lit them with a wooden match.

"Once the altar is set, like it is here, fix upon your situation. In other words, feel your souls coming together. Then call upon the power of the guardian of the stars to stop it by saying aloud the passage I will write down for you."

She spoke the passage, then extinguished the candles in the opposite order she'd lit them and then the incense.

"At the end of the seven times, if you've performed the spell correctly, your desire should diminish. One precaution. During the time you're performing the ritual, do not touch each other."

"And if it doesn't work?" Sabrina asked.

"You have three choices. Stay as you are, exhausting yourselves trying to fight it. Go away from each other. Or give in to it. If you stay as you are, you *will* eventually give in. If you go away from each other, far away, and stay away forever, your attraction will lessen, but you'll feel a constant longing that will taint every relationship you enter because it will never be *enough*. Not having what your soul needs will drain you of energy, of life." She gazed pointedly at them, letting them take in all she'd said.

"And if we give in?" Ian asked.

She smiled warmly. "If you give in, you will unite in body, soul, heart, and mind, something few lovers achieve, and you will know wondrous pleasure, the likes of which you have never before felt. But be warned. That consummate union comes at a cost. You will be obsessed with each other, letting other things in your life shift to the background. Becoming one will be your primary focus over other relationships, work, hobbies, everything that makes life full and satisfying."

"What if we give in, and then have to let each other go?" Sabrina asked.

"If you can't commit this life to each other, you're better off fighting the connection. Every time your soul unites, the desire to unite intensifies, becomes almost impossible to ignore. Once you've joined, it will be extremely painful to leave each other. Your craving for each other will *never* die, and you will struggle with the degenerative symptoms of addiction your entire lives." She looked at Sabrina. "Only the strongest, most loving and understanding partner will be able to bear your ever-present longing for another lover."

****

"You and Ian worked late last night," Dominic said, pulling on his jeans. "I didn't hear you come in."

Sabrina finished tying her boots to give herself time to think of a satisfactory answer. She and Ian dug until midnight, performed the ritual, and then stayed to talk. And touch. She'd gotten home around one o'clock. And had been up around five for their run.

"I showered before coming to bed. You were dead to the world when I came in."

"Is that going to be an every-night thing?"

"What? Showering before bed?" she said with a teasing grin.

"Staying out that late with Ian."

At least three more nights, she thought wryly. She stood and put her arms around his neck. "Don't tell me you're jealous."

He slid his arms around her waist and pulled her close. "Jealous that my wife is spending her days and nights with another man? Hell, yeah, I'm jealous." His face wore a serious look, not the teasing look she'd hoped to see.

She went up on her toes, kissed him, ground her pelvis against his. "You have nothing to be jealous about, *Hashkeh*. You know I can't live without you." She tried to kiss him again, but he pulled back and stared at her, his eyebrows furrowed, his mouth tight. His arms dropped from around her, and he stepped back.

At her quizzical frown, he answered. "You called me *Hashkeh*."

"So?" She snorted away her use of the term of endearment, but it shocked her she had let it slip.

She tried to put her arms around him again, but he grabbed her wrists to stop her. "Where did you learn that word?"

She and Ian had been calling each other that for a long time, but she had never asked him what it meant. She shrugged her response. "What does it mean?"

He dropped down onto the side of the bed and pulled on his boots, yanking the laces to tie them. "My treasure." He said the words like they left a bad taste in his mouth.

She was Ian's treasure? Warmth filled her heart. Yes. And he hers.

Dominic looked up at her when she didn't respond. He opened his mouth to say something, but then shut it, lips tight. He shook his head and dropped his attention to tying his boots.

She insinuated herself between his legs and put her hands on his head, caressing him. "Baby, talk to me," she said, her voice quiet, loving.

He raised his head to look at her. Sparks filled his eyes. "You come home later and later, spending most of the day and night with him. You touch each other too damn much. You smell like him. You talk like him, and he you. And he has no right to call you *Hashkeh.*"

She raised her eyebrow. "Dominic—"

"See. That right there…that eyebrow lift. That's all Ian."

She lowered the eyebrow and stared at him, trying to devise a response that was more truth than lie and that protected her and Ian's secret. "Ian and I work together. Our mannerisms are bound to rub off on each other. Just like Meggan always cocks her head up and to the left with her arms crossed, like you do when you're not buying something someone's telling you. I don't know what else to say."

After a moment, he pulled her close to him, buried his face in her breasts, and breathed her in. "I can't wait til you find that fucking skeleton and stop spending all your time with him."

Her breasts and arms cradled his head. She held him, caressed him, whispered *Baby, I love you* into his ear, kissed his face, trying everything to reassure him that her love for him was intact and exclusive.

She was Ian's *Hashkeh.* And he was hers. But she would stop it if she could. Because she was Dominic's wife.

So far Fiona's ritual wasn't working one fucking bit.

Chapter Fourteen

After weeks of steamy sun, the weather turned, and the team woke to heavy rain.

Back home in L.A. Sabrina often celebrated rainy days by staying home in bed with a good book or a good lover. She had the latter tucked around her in bed, if the feel of the morning wood against her bare ass was any indication. She turned to face her husband, a smile on her face. His eyes were opened to slits and a sleepy smile touched his lips.

"Good morning," she said, her fingers trailing down his chest, his stomach, to his erection.

"Mmm, yes it is," he mumbled.

She cupped his balls and gently tugged. "How about we make it a great morning."

"And just how would we do that?"

She took his dick in her hand and stroked it from base to tip. "Stay in bed all day, wrapped around each other, and listen to the rain."

"Wish we could," he said, the low words rumbling from his chest on a groan. "But this isn't L.A. Here in Ireland if we stop work because of the rain, we'd never get anything done."

"We can be late." She kissed her way down his body, enjoying the sleepy heat of his skin, the smell of him, the taste, the reassuring thud of his heart against her skin, the sounds of pleasure he made as her mouth made its way to his fully erect cock.

"I guess a few minutes late wouldn't hurt," he murmured and spread his legs for her.

She moved between them and took his cock just inside her mouth, her tongue slowly tracing the ridge, then the V of his head. His hands settled gently on her head, and he moaned at her tongue's exploration of the slit. His hips rose when her tongue spiraled lower, using slow, wide strokes to taste the length of him.

She wrapped her fingers around the base of his shaft and enveloped the upper half in her mouth. Keeping the pressure of her lips on him constant, she slid down him, letting more of him deep into her mouth, sucking him, licking him, stroking him, dipping down occasionally to swirl her tongue around his balls.

His breathing was shallow, and she knew he was close.

"Wait." His hands on her head stopped her, and he withdrew from her mouth. He hauled her on top of him, then rolled her onto her back.

"Why did you stop me?" she said.

"I want to take care of you first." He moved down between her legs and kissed her wet flesh, nibbling, sucking, letting his tongue taste it all. She let her legs go up and wide, and he licked her cleft thoroughly before zipping across the swollen clit then back into her core, over and over.

****

Cookie brought in Breena's favorite chocolate croissants, and Ian snagged one for her, two for him. Because of the rain, they weren't running today, but he stopped by her caravan so they could walk to their office together to continue their video editing.

Just as he raised his hand to rap on the side, by the window, he heard her moan. He peered in. Sabrina's fingers were clenched in Dominic's hair, holding his mouth tight against her pussy, and her head was back, her jaw slack, her eyes closed tight in bliss.

Ian's cock rose, hard and aching and throbbing, in his jeans. Anger, jealousy, envy, and yes, even white-hot hatred of his friend rose in his heart. Spinning away from the window, he hurried to his office, the image in his mind slicing through him. He threw the croissants into the trashcan.

****

Sabrina closed her eyes and focused on Dominic's movements, on the core of pleasure swirling between her legs, on how much she loved him. "I want you inside me."

He was climbing up to give her what she wanted when a loud, quick rap sounded on the door. "Dom, Jack's looking for you."

Shit! Meggan. "You've got to be kidding me," Sabrina muttered.

Dominic hovered over her body ready to enter her. "Why?" he called out.

"Problem with the floating device. He wants you to go for parts."

"Send Sean."

"He's working with Gabe today."

"Rusty, then."

"Jack has him and Shane on something else, and it's Angus' day off."

"Send one of the students," Sabrina whispered.

"They aren't allowed to drive company vehicles," he whispered back, then rolled off her and lay on his back, his erection half of what it was and shrinking fast. "Tell him I'm on my way," he called out to Meggan.

"My bags came in, so I'm going with."

"I can get them."

"I need to check them."

"Fifteen. Snag the—"

"Got 'em in my pocket."

Sabrina's mood had deflated as fast as Dominic's erection.

"Sorry." He kissed her. "We'll finish this tonight." He left the bed. She sat up, too pissed off to speak as she watched him wash his face, brush his teeth, comb his hair.

"Better get up," he called from the bathroom. "You'll be late."

Seconds later, he came back to the bed, pulled on his clothes, then leaned over and kissed her. "Love you, babe." At the door he pulled on his boots and called "see you later" as he headed out.

She hadn't needed her vibrator since she'd met Dominic. She pulled it out now and bedded the hunger he'd started. But it didn't bed her anger. Fuming her way through her morning routine, she washed, dressed, and grabbed breakfast to go—two coffees and the last two chocolate croissants to share with Ian—then rushed to work. Ian was chill about most everything, including being on time, but she didn't want to take advantage. Fifteen minutes was pushing it.

The rain kept the team from digging, but there was plenty of work to do indoors. For her and Ian that meant editing videos, writing scripts, finding music, and combing through the photos they'd taken and sorting them according to subject.

"Morning, *jefe*," she said as she entered their office. She pulled off her rain jacket and hung it on the coat rack and left her muckers by the door.

"You're late," Ian grumbled, his eyes never leaving the monitor in front of him.

"I brought breakfast." She set his coffee and croissant on his desk, hers on her desk, and moved behind him to see the video he was editing. It was an early one she'd taken of Dominic digging. At that particular point in time, he had been more focused on her than on work. It reminded her how much had changed between them in such a short time.

"Fine piece of work, that," she boasted.

"The shots are fine, but you need to stop the sex talk with your husband while you're filming. Besides being unprofessional, it makes the video unusable."

His intensity startled her, then pissed her off. "My work is always professional."

"Professional? You two are always acting like you're still in bed fucking."

"That's not true."

"No?" He rewound the video and let it play. "Then what's that?" He glared at the image of Dominic pulling her into his arms and kissing her. "And that?" he said after her voice came through in a whisper, saying, 'I can't wait to get you naked.' "Nobody wants to hear that shit." His eyes bore into hers like lasers, his cheeks as red as hers felt, his wide mouth pulled into a tight line. "That may be acceptable behavior in America but not here in Ireland and not on this project as long as I'm in charge of media."

She usually kept her comments professional as she was filming, but everyone joked around, and it was a given that unsavory talk would make it in. Some could be edited out or a voice or music track laid over it.

"I notice you don't yell at Sean and Kristin for kissing every five minutes or the rest of the team when they drop the F bomb every other word while I'm filming. Is this anger a special treat you saved just for me?"

"Why don't you take the whole fucking day off and spend it in bed fucking your goddamned husband. It's what you're best at."

Her hand was up and swinging toward his face before good sense demand she stop it. Her palm connected perfectly with his cheek, the sound cracking open the tension flooding the room. She stared wide-eyed at him, her palm stinging, her body shaking, her mouth dry at what she'd done, at the hateful thing he'd said to her. This wasn't like him.

She looked deeply into him, wanting to feel what he was feeling. Pain, anger, fire, jealousy twisted inside him. "Ian." She put her palm on his red cheek, wanting to soothe it and his emotions.

"Don't." He jerked away from her touch. It was the first time he'd done that. His anger or his rebuff, she wasn't sure which upset her more. Both were like razors to her soul.

"What's wrong?" she said, keeping her voice calm and soft and her hands to herself.

His answer was to turn away from her, fix his eyes on the monitor again.

"Fine. Don't tell me." She moved away from him and toward her computer.

"I need to work alone today," he said before she could sit.

The tear-ass was gone from his voice, but what replaced it was as disturbing. It felt as if his soul were encased in a dark shadow, inaccessible to her. He was locking her out. The pain and emptiness she felt inside was unbelievable.

"Don't shut me out." She waited for him to face her, tell her what was going on, yell at her some more, or whisper "just messing with you" and apologize for the joke that had gone too far. But he didn't. "Ian, please." She hated the begging tone in her voice, but it worked. He turned to face her, his mouth hard, his eyes troubled.

She moved toward him, stood between his legs. "You're hurting," she whispered. "But I don't know why. Tell me. Let me help you." Her hand went to his chest, but he caught her wrist and pulled away her hand. That was twice.

"You don't want me to touch you?"

He didn't respond.

"Just say it. So I'll know for sure."

He stood, his body so close it brushed all along hers on the way up. In the long, quiet, tight moment when their gazes locked, she could hear their hearts beating together, feel them.

He gripped her arms, tight, leaned in, his mouth at her ear. "All I want is for you to leave me the fuck alone." Then he brushed past her and walked to the cabinet.

His voice had never gone that sharp and rough, especially to her. Had she done something to piss him off?

"No problem," she growled. "I have lots of work to do." She sat in her chair and booted up her computer.

He grabbed and started unwrapping a pack of DVDs that he didn't need because a nearly full stack sat on his desk. "Today you're working in finds helping Meggan with the washing, labeling, and bagging."

"She has interns for that. Only you and I can edit videos. You need me here," she countered.

"No, I don't." His tone was dismissive and gruff, and her insides crumbled to her toes. God! The pain—in her, in him—was unbearable.

She stood and faced him. "Look at me and tell me you don't want me here."

He ignored her and walked back to his computer, not meeting her eyes. The rain pounding on the roof and their hearts pounding inside their chests made it sound like they were in the middle of a war.

His silence made it clear. He didn't want her here. "I'm not sorry I slapped you, Ian. That was a hateful thing you said to me. But you're still my *Hashkeh*."

He spun around to face her. "Don't say it if you don't fucking mean it."

His voice was sharp, angry. So hers would be soft, loving. "I mean it. Even if you never say it back."

She needed him to say it, gave him time to say it, but he didn't. Seeing him silent, angry, hurting, a million miles away from her, ripped a trench through her soul and pissed her off. If she stayed another second, she'd either pound him or start crying, neither of which would fix whatever was going on with him or between them.

"You're always my *Hashkeh*, but today you're also a fucking ass." She stormed to the coat rack, jerked on her jacket, stepped into her muckers, and without waiting for the response she knew wouldn't come, she pushed out the door, slamming it behind her.

Fuming, she headed to finds, stopped when she heard her name called behind her. Natasha, the student from Spain who was always staring at Ian, ran up to her.

"*Que tal*, Sabrina," she said and hugged her.

Sabrina forced a smile to her face. "Hey, Tasha. No day off?"

"Before Dom left, he told us Meggan needs help. So…"

She wasn't surprised that Meggan was behind as much time as she spent with Dominic instead of doing her job. Though to be fair, the washing, labeling, and bagging process was a slow one, so there was always a danger of finds getting backed up.

"Yeah, me, too," she said.

"You're, um, not working with Ian today?"

Their encounter sat heavy in her stomach. She wanted to run back to the trailer and demand he tell her what was troubling him. She wanted to caress him, kiss him, love away his bad mood. "He's editing and needs solitude."

"Oh. Are you going to the pub tonight?"

Pub Night was a tradition the Holy Hell Trinity started back when they were interns for Jack on one of his digs, and it had continued through the years. Every so often, the team went to the pub in the closest town to celebrate their accomplishments.

"You bet," she said. "I'm ready for a little fun. You?"

"Is Ian going?"

Sabrina noticed the pink on Natasha's cheeks, and that, plus her obvious interest in Ian, pissed her off, but she tried not to show it. "Would you like him to?"

"You bet. I'm ready for a little fun, too." She giggled.

"You should ask him," Sabrina said as they joined the other students at finds, hoping her friend didn't hear the jealousy in her voice.

Natasha grabbed her arm to halt her. "Would you do it? I've never actually talked to him, so it would be weird coming from me. But I'm sure he'd say yes to you."

Not wanting to explain that Ian wouldn't give her the time of day at the moment, she just said, "Sure."

The washing tub was broken, necessitating Dominic's trip into town, so six plastic dish-washing tubs had been set up on a table outside the finds trailer under a lofted tarp. Since it was raining, the drying tables had been set up inside the trailer. The worse part of the task wasn't having to stand in the drizzling cold but having to deal with Meggan's foul mood, which no doubt stemmed from whatever reason she hadn't been allowed to go into town with Dominic.

"Which brush do I use?" Natasha whispered to Sabrina in Spanish after Meggan mumbled vague instructions to the students on how to wash the bones and went back inside the office to bring out more trays of bones.

"The toothbrush," Sabrina said, also in Spanish, and gently brushed the dirt from the intact skull in her tub to show Natasha how to do it.

"Like this?" she asked, mimicking Sabrina's movements.

"Yes, but gently. Wet bones are softer than dry, so the surfaces could be damaged by hard brushing. The skull could—"

The skull in Natasha's hand came apart. She stared at it, her mouth and eyes round in shock and fear. "*Ay, mierda!*"

At the exclamation, Meggan rushed over and grabbed the pieces from Natasha's hand.

"I warned you about brushing too hard." Meggan gave the pieces to Bruce, the grad student who had worked with the team last year, and turned back to Natasha. "A tenth century treasure destroyed because of your carelessness."

"It's rare for any skull to stay intact through the entire process of washing, labeling, bagging, transport, and analysis," Sabrina said. "You know that." Dominic had taught her that.

Meggan stood stick-straight upright, feet apart, fists on her hips—a Dominic posture if she'd ever seen one—her eyes fierce and pissed as they bore into Sabrina. "You're not in charge of finds. You're not even a digger. So keep your opinions to yourself. I don't want you feeding them wrong information that could cost us valuable time and data."

She turned her glare on the students. "If you have questions, ask me or Bruce," she stabbed a finger at Sabrina, "not her. Clear?" At their quick nods, she turned back to Sabrina. "Are you clear?"

"Fine. Then you better spend more time doing your job, explaining *your* way. Because they're not getting it when you mumble unclear instructions then leave."

Meggan moved around the table, picking up and inspecting the bones in the tubs. It was clear that some of the students had either used the wrong brush or brushed too hard, and scratches marred several bones.

She turned to Bruce. "Show them how to properly wash a bone." She turned to leave.

"Where are you going?" Bruce asked, looking nervous about being left in charge.

"Dom needs my help." She glared at Sabrina, a snarky grin on her face, and left.

"Red doesn't like you," Natasha whispered in Spanish after she'd left.

"What was your first clue?"

They laughed and kept up a quiet conversation that helped pass the time. Mid-afternoon, when it was clear the rain wasn't letting up, Jack gave everyone the rest of the day off to start the festivities at the pub early.

By the time Sabrina had her turn at the showers and changed, the rain had slowed to a mist and the lazy sun was half-heartedly trying to burn a hole through the thick blanket of clouds. Everything was wet. The grass was bright green and the air smelled fresh and carried a slight nip, so she pulled on a lightweight sweater over the backless sundress she was wearing to the pub, which always felt like a sauna after a few minutes of mingling and drinking and, she hoped, dancing.

Ian wasn't in his office. Wasn't in any of the trenches. She caught a glimpse of a lone figure walking toward the river. She had watched Ian often enough to know it was him by the line of his body, his movements, the cap he wore.

By the time she had set off across the field to catch up with him and ask him about going to pub night for Natasha, he had settled under a tree. He pulled off his cap, dropped it beside him on the wet grass, and dragged his fingers through his hair, making it stand on end.

"Hey," she said softly, coming up behind him, unsure what mood she'd find him in.

He turned to her, looked her up and down then back at the river. "Hey."

At least he didn't ignore her. "Can I join you?"

"You'll get your pretty little dress wet."

She shrugged off her sweater, laid it on the grassy ground, and plopped down next to him, kicking off her flip-flops and sitting cross-legged. She picked up his cap, ran her fingers along the brim he had rounded to his taste, brought it to her nose. It smelled like him. She loved the way he smelled, like sunshine. She put his cap on and faced the river, content to just sit with him until he was ready to talk.

He tried to snatch it off her head, but she blocked him. "I picked out this cap for you. The least you can do is let me wear it sometimes."

"It's *manky*," he said and tried to get it again.

"I don't care."

"You don't care that your hair will smell like dirt and sweat instead of flowers?"

"How do you know my hair smells like flowers?"

He wouldn't look at her but picked a little blue flower from the grass and twirled it in his fingers. "I know what you smell like, Breena."

And she him. She'd be able to locate him in a pitch-black room full of people by his scent alone.

"You don't want your cap to smell like me?" she asked, teasing him.

He said nothing, so she sat quiet, watched him twirl his flower, and waited for him to say something. When he didn't, she reached over, took the flower from his fingers, and brought it to her nose. "If it's something I did, I'm sorry."

He lifted the cap from her head and set it on the other side of him. "It's not you."

She set the flower in her lap and shuffled her fingers through her hair to reverse any hat hair that had set in. "Then what?"

He took the flower from her lap and, leaning toward her, tucked her hair behind her left ear and then the flower. He kept his gaze on hers, and she could see something in the shadows of his eyes, feel it in her heart as their breath collided.

She caught his hand. There was a fever to his skin that fed the one burning across hers. "Tell me."

He linked their fingers and dropped his gaze to their hands, and she knew he wasn't going to tell her. She covered their laced hands with her other hand as a sign of surrender and felt his pulse racing at his wrist— the wrist with the pale eternity symbol on it. No one had ever noticed the symbols. They seemed to be something that only she and Ian could see, a secret gift shared between the two of them.

Sabrina traced his symbol with her thumb and felt hers pulse, reminding her that they were connected, reminding her that she shouldn't be touching him. Whenever they touched, it felt like thick, honeyed whiskey oozed through her veins, hot and strong and sweet and intoxicating enough to lower her inhibitions to heed his half of their soul's call to her. But now that they were linked and it felt so damn good, she couldn't let go.

"You know what'll make you feel better?" she said.

"Yeah. I do." He was undressing her with his eyes,

and she could feel his desire enter her.

"I meant Pub Night."

"Nah, that won't do it." He tried to pull away, but she held tight to his hand.

"Natasha will be there. You know, she's really into you."

"Are you trying to get me laid?"

Having Ian and sex sharing the same thought eased a wicked smile across her face. "Maybe it'll improve your disposition."

"About this morning... Let's just say we missed our run and it put me in a bad mood."

Her smile died. "We could say that, but it would be a lie. And we don't lie to each other."

"Let it be, Breena," he said, a hint of exasperation in his tone.

"I'll let it be if you come to the pub tonight."

"So I can watch you make out with your husband?"

Before she could respond, her cell buzzed through a text.

"That's probably him, telling you to come home for a quickie before you go to the pub," he said, his sarcasm biting.

Her eyes didn't leave his. "Promise me you'll be there."

"You better go before he comes looking for you and gets pissed 'cause you're with me."

"Promise me you'll be there."

Her cell buzzed again. She ignored it again, keeping her eyes glued to Ian's, waiting for an answer.

"Anybody ever tell you you're a pain in the ass?" he said.

She took his soft but grumbled words for his

promise. She grinned and slid her hand into his hair. "No, I'm usually the one calling someone an ass." It wasn't an outright apology for calling him a fucking ass earlier, but if he was listening to her thoughts, he heard it.

He took her hand, brought it to his mouth, and kissed her palm, their eyes connected.

When her cell rang for a third time, she knew she had to answer it or risk having Dominic come look for her. Picking it up, Sabrina stood, Ian's hand still in hers, and stepped into her flip-flips. "See you there. I expect you to save me a dance or two." She squeezed his hand then released it.

To her surprise, his hand caught the back of her thigh, underneath her dress, just below the curve of her ass. Her breath audibly left her lungs at the feel of his palm so hot on her, his fingertips lightly gripping the sensitive skin so high on her inside thigh.

For a moment she didn't know whether his hand would go up or down her leg, but then it slid down, slowly, leaving a heated trail of tingles to remind her where he had touched. His fingers grazed the skin at the back of her knee, making her shiver. Moving lower, his hand palmed over her calf, slowly, lightly, filling her head with the heady smoke of desire. It eased down to her ankle and caressed the delicate bones.

"Love...I won't be going to the pub tonight." He turned away, pulling his cap on and down to hide his eyes, but he couldn't hide the sharp and hungry and overpowering desire slamming into her like a wall of emotion.

"I hope you change your mind," she whispered and on shaky legs left him before she dropped down beside him and made him do to her every erotic, nasty thing he was thinking.

****

With a heavy heart, Ian watched Breena fly into Dom's arms. Watched her raise her head to accept his kiss. Watched her body arch into his when he pulled her close to deepen the kiss. Watched Dom's hand dip low to caress her sweet ass. Watched them head to the SUVs, wrapped around each other, to join the team at the pub. And it made his insides burn.

Dom had been one of his best friends since they were old enough to understand what it meant. They had been through everything together and had come out more like brothers. He'd never been jealous of him or what he had. Until now.

He wanted Breena. He needed her. He loved her.

He'd never admit that his bad mood today was born of raging jealousy from seeing Dom pleasure her. He'd never admit that he burned to take her from her husband, no matter the consequences. He'd never admit there were moments when he was willing to do anything—*anything*—to have her for his own.

Like when he touched her leg a moment ago. He hadn't planned to. But there his hand was, high on her thigh. And she didn't stop him. Didn't slap his face. Cuss him out. Move away. Like she should have. Just stared at him with those big blue eyes, liquid with desire. *For him.*

He had wanted to slide his hand upward until he touched between her legs, where Dom had touched her this morning. He'd wanted to push up that sexy little dress, rip off her panties, and tease and taste and fuck her pussy with *his* tongue until she came, squirming, screaming *his* name. He wanted to lay her beneath him and settle between her legs, plunge *his* cock inside her, again and again, until they exploded around each other in a noisy, scent-filled tornado of pleasure. He wanted to kiss her from the top of her head to the tip of her toes, front and back, then do it again. And again. And, oh God, again. Until they were empty of themselves and filled with each other.

That he had these thoughts, these desires, about his best friend's wife sat heavy on his conscience. He wasn't the kind of man who took his friends' women. At least he hadn't been. Until Breena came into his life and released in him an almost unmanageable desire for her. He'd have her, too. One day. As hard as they were trying to control it, still it would happen. Especially since he wasn't sure he wanted to try that hard anymore to stop it. But tonight, while he still could, he'd be honorable. He would disappoint her and not go to the pub.

His cock calling him an *eejit*, he stood with every intention to head back to his office, jerk off to the image of his tongue working over Breena's pussy, then edit videos the rest of the night.

Then he noticed her sweater on the ground.

He picked it up, held the softness to his face, and breathed in. Her scent went straight to his head, making his heart pound and his balls clench.

"Fuck it."

Her sweater gripped in his hand, he headed to his caravan. He would shower, go to the pub, take Natasha to bed if that's what Breena wanted—and any other woman who wanted it—and get to work fucking his best friend's wife out of his system.

Chapter Fifteen

The pub was packed to its grimy wood-paneled walls with students, staff, and locals. The same small band as the last time played an assortment of songs, from trad to contemporary. A bottle or glass in every hand, a smile on most faces, the team celebrated their successes and each other.

Sabrina stood at Dominic's side, his arm looped loosely around her shoulders as he talked to Jack. She inserted an occasional comment, but it was clear the two were too deep into their discussion to be enticed into a more entertaining subject.

She gazed longingly toward the dance floor, where Sean and Kristin danced, wrapped up in each other's arms like there was no one else there. That's how newlyweds were supposed to act. By Dominic's actions, one would think they'd been married a hundred years and were tired of each other's stories.

She wanted to be laughing, playing, dancing, talking of something other than output and schedules and timeframes. She wanted to be doing it with Dominic. Only he wasn't cooperating. But since they had very little time together, she would stay by his side.

The night was turning out to be a lot less fun than she had hoped.

Laughter from the table where Natasha played a drinking game with some of the students drew her attention. The blonde caught her looking and got up, picking her way through the crowd toward her. Sabrina left Dominic's embrace to turn and face her friend, who hugged her, kissed her on the cheeks.

"Come play with us." Natasha spoke in Spanish, so Sabrina did, too.

"Maybe later. Are you having fun?"

She leaned in. "Yes, but I would have more fun if Ian were here. Did you talk to him?"

Sabrina leaned in, too, even though no one else spoke Spanish and would not understand their conversation. "I did. He said no, but I have a feeling he'll show up."

"I hope so. I've wanted to talk to him for a while, but he's always with you."

The door opened, and Sabrina knew before she turned that it was Ian by the heat suddenly spiraling up her core like a column of fire.

His cap was gone and his hair was damp, sticking up. Like the other team members, he wore the shovelbum's uniform—T-shirt, jeans, and work boots—but the big difference was the pink sweater in his hand.

His eyes found her immediately, as if there were a massive blinking neon sign with his name on it over her head. He grinned that cocky little grin he did when he was unsure about something he was doing but was committed to faking it until he made it.

She smiled back, her eyes never leaving his. "Don't look, but he just walked in," she said to Natasha, who, of course, looked.

"Oh, my God, he's so hot I just came a little in my panties," she said in a breathy whisper Sabrina was sure had accompanied her eyes rolling back in her head.

Sabrina crossed the floor to him, her eyes locked on his the whole way. With no hesitation they moved into each other's arms. She clung to him, breathed him in, and her heart expanded in joy and relief that he'd come. That she was in his arms. That they were touching. Whatever had him in a mood earlier had faded. She felt it in his hug, heard it in his emotions surging against her. The cloud had lifted.

"You smell good," she whispered.

His nose nuzzled her hair, near her ear, and he breathed her in, too. "So do you."

"Thought you weren't coming?" she teased and moved back a step.

"You forgot this." He held out her sweater, the soft pink of it popping bright against the dark tan of his skin. "Thought you might need it."

"Thanks." She took it from his hands and tied it around her waist. "But I didn't forget it."

His eyes narrowed at her comment, and he shook his head, knowing he'd been tricked. "You left it on purpose."

Grinning, she took his hand and led him to Natasha. "Ian, have you met Natasha? She's from Spain. Natasha, this is Ian." Natasha gave him a flirty smile, and Sabrina knew the blonde was about to pee herself she was so excited.

"*Hola*, Ian."

He smiled back and let his gaze travel over her, from her pretty face and big boobs to curvy hips and long legs. "*Hola*, Natasha from Spain. *Hablas Español?*"

"*Si, claro*," Natasha gushed.

"I hope that means yes. Breena's always calling me names in Spanish, and since I don't know the language, it puts me at a disadvantage. Maybe you can teach me a few things."

The appreciative glances and sexy tone he lavished on Natasha jolted Sabrina like live tazer prongs to her heart.

"Maybe I can," Natasha said and took his hand in hers. "Buy me a drink and we'll start lesson one."

Before letting Natasha lead him toward a table, Ian put his other hand low on Sabrina's back and brought their bodies flush. "You're a fucking pain in the ass, too, princess," he whispered into her ear.

More surprising than his echoing her words today or his teeth nipping her lobe, was his hand slipping beneath her sweater and over her ass and cupping it when he said "ass."

He released her and followed Natasha, leaving Sabrina with chills sweeping through her body, her breath lodging in her throat, her nipples rising hard against her dress, her heart thundering, and the spot between her legs tingling with trickling moisture. Watching the two settle beside each other on the bench along the wall, smiles on their faces, it was all she could do not to yank Natasha away from Ian by her hair. On shaky legs, she headed back to her husband.

Dominic's arm around her, hers around him, she took a sip of his beer. The dark brew set her stomach churning and wishing she'd eaten something before she came. Wishing she hadn't interfered in Ian's love life. She hugged Dominic to her, needing his comfort, wishing they could go home and climb into each other, leave the outside world far behind.

He and Jack were talking about the same thing they were before she'd left to talk to Natasha, and Meggan had joined them. The dynamic was feeding a throbbing headache and souring mood.

Only half-tuned to the conversation, she stole glances at Ian. Natasha's body faced his, her hand on his knee, her head bent toward him in conversation. His arms were along the top of the booth, his body faced into the room, not toward Natasha. He caught Sabrina looking at him and winked at her. She rolled her eyes at him and grinned back.

Despite her misgivings about setting them up, she hoped they connected. Ian needed someone. By the look of them, there'd be sparks tonight. Swallowing the bitter taste of jealousy in her mouth, she turned her attention back to Dominic and tried to focus on the conversation.

Natasha brushed her hand against Sabrina's back a half hour later when she passed her on the way to the bathroom.

"Thank you!" she whispered in Spanish and hugged her after she had pulled her away from Dominic. "We're going to my trailer."

Sabrina smiled because it was expected, but her stomach flipped almost out of her mouth. As Natasha hurried on to the bathroom, Sabrina turned to look at Ian, her face burning, her fingertips ice cold, her heart banging a protest against her ribs, her stomach rolling with unexplainable anguish and anger. He tipped his head in a *come here* gesture, and she went eagerly to him, taking Natasha's spot.

"*Que has aprendido?*" she asked.

"What?" He turned his body toward her with a

sexy grin and dropped his arm around her shoulders.

The trad song the band had switched to was so boisterous they had to lean in to hear and to be heard.

"I said, 'what did you learn?'"

"I learned *cerveza*, which is actually an old Irish word, a few nasty things I can't wait to call you, and *te amo*."

Her eyebrow raised in surprise. "*Te amo?*"

"Yeah."

"Do you know what *te amo* means?" she asked.

"I love you."

Maybe he wasn't saying the words about her, but her heart fluttered as if he were. She grabbed the nearly full bottle of beer on the table next to an empty highball of melting ice.

"This yours?" When he nodded, she drank. The lager went down smooth. "So, what do you think?"

"About?"

"Natasha."

He shrugged. "She's nice."

"And hot?"

Leaning in, he reached out and tucked a thick strand of hair behind her ear, his fingers brushing the little flower he'd put there earlier. He smiled, as if it made him happy she'd kept it and hidden it away like a special secret just for them. "Love, why are you trying to hook me up?"

"She wanted to meet you. I just made the intro. If you guys hook up, that's—"

He put his hand on the beer bottle, his fingers around hers. "Breena, I'm not that kind of guy." She slid her fingers away, and he brought the bottle to his mouth and drank.

"The way I hear it, you invented the hookup. In Ireland, anyway," she teased.

"Are you questioning my morals?"

"Did I say that?"

He raised his eyebrow. "Because if there's anyone at this table whose morals are questionable, it's yours."

She raised hers. Did he mean her having feelings for him while being married to Dominic? It was the truth, but it still hurt for him to bring it up. "Excuse me?"

"You left your sweater on purpose to lure me here so Natasha could have her way with me. Know what that makes you?"

Oh. She laughed in relief. "Smart enough to know you'll play true to character."

"True to character?" His eyes sparkled as he handed her the beer.

"You like being the hero," she said into the mouth of the bottle and tipped it for a taste. The alcohol—or something else—was making her cheeks flame.

He shook his head. "Just *your* hero."

She set the beer down. "That could be a problem."

"Oh? Tell me." He leaned in, as if they were sharing secrets and he wanted to hear everything.

"Natasha thinks you're *her* hero."

"Why's that?"

"Because you're taking her to bed." Even she heard the jealousy in her tone.

He lifted his hand to the back of her head, let his fingers tangle in her hair. "Well, now, love. Isn't that what you wanted?" Dipping his head, he leaned a little closer, close enough for her to breathe in his exhalation as he spoke. "For me to fuck her?"

Up until that point, it had been mostly teasing between them. But when she felt his guttural "fuck" sink into her skin and lodge deep in her body, the mood shifted. At that moment, she was acutely, achingly aware that she didn't want him fucking Natasha. She didn't want him fucking any woman. Any woman but… No. She couldn't say it. Not even to herself.

"Do you want to?" she managed.

His eyes—lazy, hazy, and unwavering—gripped hers, holding her still. The intensity in their blue depths wouldn't let her look away or speak. She could barely breathe from the way he was looking at her. Time slowed, freezing them in place, mouths inches from each other.

"Breena." His whisper burned into her skin. "You're the only woman I want to fuck."

Her eyes opened wide. The words, the brush of his breath on her face, the weight of his hand in her hair, the feel of him so close threw off sparks all through her body, and she couldn't think. Pulling on her last sliver of sanity, she tried to ease back from him to scatter the sensations trampolining over every square inch of her feverish skin, but he held her to him, leaned in even closer like he was going to whisper his deepest, darkest secrets into her skin. His head dipped, and she trembled at the feel of his lips at her neck.

"Ian…" The word, his name, hushed out of her mouth like a plea for more.

"Ask me not to fuck her," he breathed, then kissed and nibbled all the sensitive spots of flesh— At her earlobe. Beneath her ear. Along her jaw. On her neck. Where her neck met her shoulder. His tongue pushed aside the thin strap of her dress, and his teeth nipped her shoulder, his tongue tasted her, moving, flicking, like it would over her pussy. "Ask me to fuck you."

She inhaled sharply but the scanty breath caught in her lungs was of no use. Her trembling body gave itself over to the pleasure rolling through her like the thunderstorm rolling across the sky. Her fingers gripped his thigh but only to keep her fingers from sliding up into his hair to pull his delicious mouth to her mouth, then to her breasts, then to her pussy. Her eyes fluttered closed as a soft growl escaped her parted lips. In that growl were the words "Only me."

His head rose just enough to look her in the eyes. "What did you say?"

"I…" She stared at him through heavy lids. Her face heated. Oh, God. What had she just said? What had she just admitted? Her eyes darted from his, and she shifted away from him and pulled her strap up. Her hands shaking, she grabbed a piece of gum from her pocket, unwrapped it, and held it out to him.

Grinning, pleased with her response, he lowered his mouth to the offering. Before biting off his half, his tongue dabbed out and circled her thumb, then took it into his mouth and nipped it with his teeth.

****

"I'm staying horizontal on that back section so we can—" For the third time, something had shifted Jack's attention from Dom's words. The man wasn't making eye contact, and he hadn't butted in for at least a half a second.

He clinked his beer bottle to Jack's whiskey glass. Jack's eyes came back.

"What's wrong with you?" Dom asked.

Jack jutted out his chin and shook his head.

"Nothing."

The man was lying his arse off. Dom's eyes darted to Meg, who tipped her head and darted her eyes toward a spot to the side of where he stood. His head swung toward the grouping of tables where Meg indicated and Jack seemed to be so focused on.

Sabrina sat at a table with Ian, their bodies turned into each other, a pale blue spotlight on them. His arms were around her, one hand at the back of her head, fingers gripped in her hair. His head was bent close, and he was whispering in her ear...or kissing her...it was too dark to know for sure. They were lost in each other, like there was no one else in the pub.

"Son-of-a-bitch."

Jack caught his arm. "Dom, it's not what it looks like."

Dom shrugged off Jack's hand. It was exactly what it looked like. Ian was coming on to his wife. He dragged himself to their table, feet made of lead, his heart pounding hot and loud in his ears, and pulled a chair up next to Sabrina just as she fed Ian gum.

She turned as she was putting her half of the gum into her mouth. When she saw it was him, she blinked, then put on a quick smile. "Hey, baby." Her voice was shaky as she leaned in and kissed him, letting her lips linger on his, her tongue dip into his mouth. He tasted her favorite gum and Ian's favorite beer.

He pulled back when she tried to advance the kiss. "Hey, yourself," he said, his tone flat. Her pale blue eyes were heavy, shiny, ringed in dark blue. He knew that look. His wife wasn't drunk. She was horny. With Ian by her side. With Ian's hands on her. A sick feeling spread through him and solidified into bedrock in his stomach.

He leaned forward, resting his arms on the table in front of him, and stared hard at Ian, pointing at him.

Ian shifted forward, too, and met Dom's steely gaze with one of his own.

"You're getting too friendly with my wife," Dom said, his tone, like his words, hard.

"Am I now?" A quick, icy challenge hardened Ian's voice, and his face was a mask. No emotion showed to tell Dom what was going on inside his head.

"Keep your distance, Ian."

Ian's eyebrow lifted and a cocky smirk took his lips.

Dom could have overlooked everything, but Ian's dismissive attitude pushed him over the edge. He knew Ian, knew his mannerisms, his moves, his effortless way of getting women to spread their legs, his equally effective tactics for getting rid of any challengers. That attitude, that look, meant *I'll do whatever the fuck I want and there's nothing you can do to stop me.*

Without even realizing he was going to do it, Dom lunged forward and grabbed the front of Ian's shirt. Eye-to-eye, toe-to-toe, the two surged to their feet in one swift motion, upending the table and sending it crashing into the table next to it. Bottles and glasses scattered across the room, some breaking. Alcohol splattered on the floor and walls and on anyone unlucky enough to be sitting nearby. All conversation came to an abrupt halt at the clatter. Even the band playing in the corner stilled their instruments.

"Keep your fucking hands off my wife." The low words sliced out of his mouth as cold and deadly as a knife blade in the hot, thick silence.

Sabrina had jumped up, too. Her hands were on his, trying to pull them from Ian's shirt.

"Dominic, what are you doing? Stop it!"

Her voice trembled with fear. He was sure her eyes were wide with fear, too, but he couldn't see them. His eyes were fixed on Ian's, the two of them—for the first time in their lives—a heartbeat away from using their fists on each other.

Suddenly Natasha was there beside Ian. "I'm ready to go, Ian," she said, fear in her voice, too. Ian didn't move, didn't break eye contact, didn't acknowledge her presence.

Out of the corner of his eye, he saw that Sean had joined them, too, his body tense as if he were ready to jump in if this went any further. "Dom, you don't want to do this."

Neither Dom or Ian broke their gaze, said a word, or moved.

At Sabrina's continued efforts, he finally loosened his grip, dropped his fists to his sides, and she quickly stepped between him and Ian. Facing him, her hands on his chest resting on his aching heart, she walked him back a couple of steps.

"Get him home," Sean said to Natasha, referring to Ian.

She nodded and tugged Ian's hand.

Ian's eyes left Dom's and flew to Sabrina. As if she felt the touch of his stare, she glanced over her shoulder at him. Their unblinking gaze held for several long beats. They communicated something to each other in that look. Something only the two of them heard and understood. Then, in sync, she turned back to Dom and Ian let Natasha lead him toward the door.

Sean went back to Kristin on the dance floor but watched the situation to make sure tempers wouldn't flare again.

Dom stared at Sabrina, she at him. Her eyes were troubled, filled with worry, as if the scene had shaken her, and she looked like she was going to throw up. Was she worried about him? Or about Ian? He took her hand and led her away from the mess as workers righted the tables, swept broken glass, and mopped spilled liquor. On his way to the door, he stopped at the bar and fished money from his wallet.

"Quinn, if this doesn't cover it, catch me later."

The owner/bartender nodded his thanks, and Dom and Sabrina walked out of the pub to the roar of silence.

****

Ian's jeep was speeding away when Dominic opened the door to the SUV for her. He slammed it after she got in, then climbed in on his side. He didn't start the engine, just gripped the steering wheel. The dim moonlight flowing in the window showed his jaw clenching and unclenching.

"What was that about?" she asked.

He turned to her, anger sizzling in his eyes. "Are you fucking kidding me?" The rage and anguish consuming him colored his voice.

"Tell me," she said quietly but firmly.

"He was touching you."

"We were talking."

He leaned in so that their lips were an inch from each other. "You needed to talk this fucking close?"

"It's really loud in there. We had to sit close just to hear each other."

"His fingers were in your hair." He cupped her

head with his hand and let his fingers tangle in her hair as Ian had done. "His mouth was on you." He nuzzled her neck, near her ear, like Ian had done. "Did that help you hear better, too?"

"Dominic, Ian's your best friend. He—"

His hand in her hair tightened, and he jerked her head back enough to glare into her eyes. "*You're* my best friend, Sabrina."

"And he's the closest thing you have to a brother. I don't know what you think you saw, but Ian wouldn't betray you. Neither would I."

"I know what I saw, and I know Ian well enough to know what it means."

"What you saw was us talking and laughing, enjoying ourselves, just like everyone else in the pub."

"By *my* side is where *my wife* should have been enjoying herself, not by Ian's." He roared the statement.

"So I'm not allowed to talk to anyone but you? If that's the case, then I might as well have stayed at home since you haven't talked to me all night."

"*Jaysus*, Sabrina, I don't care who you talk to. I'm not mad because you were talking to Ian. I'm mad that he was all over you, and you were enjoying it instead of stopping him. I'm embarrassed that I had to tell my wife and my friend, in front of my team, to stop touching each other. I'm sick to my soul that you looked like you were ready to fuck each other right there in the pub. Do you have any idea how seeing you two like that made me feel?"

"I have good idea, yeah." Anger painted the words crimson.

"What does that mean?"

"I've had to watch you and your *ex*-lover since we

got to the dig. The looks, the laughter, the closeness, the touches, the bent heads, talking in whispers, sharing water bottles, sharing food. How you're always together. Don't you think it hurts me seeing you two so close? I never said anything because I trust you. I know that whatever it might look like—and what it looks like is that you two want to fuck each other—I know you love me and would never cheat. Tell me if I'm wrong."

"Meg and I work together. That's it."

"You lie together in the trench as close to her as you do to me in bed, touching, close enough to kiss."

"Bollocks!"

"Oh, don't even deny it. I have pictures that prove it."

His eyes narrowed. "Pictures? For what?"

She shook her head, trying to shake away the anguish suddenly overflowing inside her. "I don't know." She swallowed back the tears and let her anger get her through the confession. "Day after day, I hear her laughing across the field, and I train my camera on her. You're *always* there with her. I zoom in tight on your face. You're so…happy. Because of her." She wiped the tears from her cheeks. "You're standing close, your hand on her shoulder or her back. Your heads are together, and she's talking to you, and you're captivated by her every word, like it's gold pouring from her mouth. The look that passes between you…" Her breath shattered, but she kept going. "It's a look that says 'we belong together.' It's certainly not a look you ever give me."

"Sabrina—"

She held up her hand to stop him and caught a shaky breath. "I never said anything, never acted like the jealous, paranoid wife. I just trusted you. Because the alternative was too much to bear. The thought that you…" The words stuck when a horrible thought rose in her mind. What if Dominic and Meggan were soulmates? She swallowed the agony of it. "That you still love her…" She couldn't even finish the thought.

He grabbed her arms. "I love *you*, Sabrina. Can you say the same thing about me?"

"Yes."

"You should tell Ian that."

"And you should tell Meggan."

He released her and pounded the steering wheel, then gripped it, pressing his forehead into his hands. She had never seen him so upset. He rarely cussed and yelled, but he'd done both more tonight than in all the time she'd known him.

"When we married, we promised each other it was forever," he said, keeping his head down. "If your feelings have changed, I deserve to know."

It crushed her that he thought otherwise, but she could see why he might. She scooted next to him and rubbed her hand across his back. "I love you, Dominic. I want our marriage. That hasn't changed for me." And she meant it. "Has it changed for you?"

He lifted his head and found her eyes. The look of heartbreak in his eyes broke her heart.

"No. I love you more now than when we married." His hand cupped the back of her neck, and he pulled her close, kissed her long and hard, a punishing, demanding kiss of possession that took her breath away.

"Just so you know," he said after ending the kiss. "If I see him touching you like that again, I won't let him walk away."

He started the engine and drove home. They resolved their argument in bed, his consuming and rough and dirty love-making leaving behind evidence she would feel and others would see the next day that she belonged only to him. Before they fell asleep in each other's arms, exhausted, he admitted he had overreacted and told her again that he loved her and wanted their marriage.

When she awoke the next morning, without him beside her, the memories of Ian's kisses and touches sneaked into bed with her, haunting her mind and heating her body. Like it or not, right or wrong, Ian was a part of her. She didn't know how to change it. But if they didn't figure it out soon, people would get hurt. Her marriage was hanging by a string.

"Dom."

Her heart fluttered at hearing Ian's voice outside the trailer. She wrapped the sheet around her naked body and rose to look out the window.

"Is he here?" he asked.

"No."

They took a long moment to just look at each other before speaking.

"I'm sorry," they said in unison.

"You first," he said.

"I behaved inappropriately last night, and I'm—"

"No, you didn't," he said, "and neither did I. We behaved how soulmates are supposed to, so don't apologize for it."

"Then what are you apologizing for?" she said.

"I caused problems for you and wasn't there to defend you. Was it rough?"

She nodded. It had been rough and raw and painful.

"But I think we're okay."

He nodded. They stared at each other for a long moment, neither saying a word. Not needing to. Their connection allowed them to feel what the other was feeling. What they were feeling now was regret. Not for what they'd done. But for what they could no longer do. They would have to be extra cautious around each other. Pay attention to how they touched, what they said, what they did, all the time, especially around others. Not let their desire spin out of control again.

"Cookie brought in chocolate croissants for breakfast yesterday," he said, breaking the silence. "I know they're your favorite, so I grabbed some for us and stopped by here to walk to work with you. I heard you cry out, and I looked in. Dom's mouth was between your legs, giving you the pleasure I want to give you. At that moment, I realized I'd never get that chance, and it pissed me off. That's why I acted like an ass. I hurt your feelings and put your marriage on shaky ground. That's what I'm sorry for."

The sadness and hopelessness in his voice stripped her raw. "I hurt you so much every day by not being able to be with you like you need and deserve," she said. She put her hand on the window screen, wanting his touch. "That's what I'm sorry for."

His hand settled against hers. Heat pulsed through the small tight spaces in the mesh and into their palms before spreading through their bodies.

"Enjoy your day off, *Hashkeh.*" With a final look, he moved away from the window, from her. "Don't miss our run in the morning," he said over his shoulder.

"Five sharp," she called out.

"Rain or shine," he responded.

"Ian," she said before he'd gone far.

He stopped and turned around, but didn't come back to the window.

"Why did you come to see Dominic?"

"I came to see you, to make sure you were okay. But I also came to make peace with my friend." He sighed deeply. "If that's even possible at this point."

****

Ian found Dom coming out of the mess tent, carrying a tray with breakfast for two. Dom eyed him as he approached, his face a mask.

"You still want to bash my skull in?" Ian asked, an apology in his teasing tone. Seeing Breena, talking to her, had lifted his mood somewhat.

Dom set the tray on a table. "I *might* have overreacted."

Ian stepped closer. "What? Dominic Sullivan admitting he was wrong? That's a first."

"Fuck you," Dom said with a grin. "If you're still looking for an arse-whipping, I could oblige."

Ian let his smile soften. "Dom...I'm sorry. I meant no disrespect, to you or your wife. She loves you. So do I."

He nodded. "I know."

"Still friends?" Ian stuck out his hand.

"Yeah." Dom took his hand, and Ian pulled him in. They hugged, a fist pound on each other's backs.

Jack approached them. "If you two are done kissing and making up, we need to talk. Effective immediately, I'm moving Sabrina to finds with Red."

Ian surged forward. "Oh, hell no! No fucking way can I get everything done on my own in our tight timeframe."

"If this is because of what happened last night," Dom chimed in, "there's no problem. I overreacted, and—"

"Glad to hear that, but I'm still moving her."

"You can't do that," Ian said.

"I can and I am. Dom, go get your wife so I can deliver the news."

Dom's eyebrows furrowed. "She's not going to be happy about it."

"This ain't Happyland, and it ain't my goddamned job to make sure the inmates are happy. Go get her."

"Jack, reconsider—" Dom began.

"Now!" Jack exploded.

Dom left to get Sabrina, leaving Ian to face off with his boss.

"Goddammit, Jack. Don't take her from me." Ian's body was rigid, his voice steely, his eyes hot on Jack's. "I need her."

"I warned you this would happen if you two didn't knock it off. Besides," Jack put his hand on Ian's shoulder, "haven't you tortured yourself enough?"

"What are you talking about?"

"You gonna make me say it?"

Heat rushed into Ian's chest, making his heart race and his skin tighten. No, he didn't want Jack to say it. He didn't want to speak of it aloud. He wanted to keep it safely tucked inside, like a gift just for him.

"*Don't.*" Ian's voice slid through his teeth.

"No, I'm gonna say it so you can face the goddamned truth." He glanced around to make sure no one was close enough to overhear, then leaned in. "For the first time in your life, you're in love. Unfortunately, it's with your *best friend's wife*, and you're one touch

269

away from having a full-blown affair with her."

Ian dropped his gaze, trying to hide the truth, but Jack already knew, had already seen the truth. Still he denied it. "You're full of shit." He shot him a hard look and stormed away.

Jack caught his arm. "It's better this way, son."

Ian spun toward him, jerking his arm away to break his hold. "Better for who? Not her. Not me. Not this project. She loves her job. She's brilliant at it. And for Christ's sake, how can you put her with Meggan? You know what a devil she is. Breena will be miserable."

"Red needs help in finds to meet schedule, but more important, Sabrina needs to get away from you so you both can remember who she's married to. The lit stick of dynamite you two are holding between you is gonna destroy her, you, Dom, a marriage, a friendship, and a team in the explosion. Are you blind to it, Ian? Or do you just not care? Is that the kind of man you are now?"

Ian wanted to pop the fucker in the mouth to stop his accusations. The only thing stopping him was Breena appearing at that moment.

As if she knew he was a breath away from blowing, she got between them, facing him, and covered his fists with her hands. "Ian, what's wrong?"

Out of need and instinct, he linked their fingers, held tight to her hands, and met her worried eyes. He wanted to draw her to him, kiss the worried look off her face. Instead he shook his head, pulled his hands from hers, and backed away.

Jack was right. The explosion would destroy them all. He just wasn't sure he could do what was required to prevent it when part of him longed for the explosion that would rip her from Dom and propel her into *his* arms. It was coming. He just didn't know when.

As he stormed toward the media office, he could feel her eyes, feel her deep emotions that were telling her to run after him, soothe him, love him, but he knew Jack would stop her. As he damn well should.

Chapter Sixteen

Sabrina used every argument in the book to change Jack's mind, even tried tears, but he held firm. Despite what he said—that Meggan needed help in finds—taking her from media, from Ian, was punishment. For what happened at the pub? Or for something else? All she knew was that his decision had sucked all the fun out of the dig.

She wasn't working with Dominic, wasn't working with Ian, wasn't working the job she knew and enjoyed, but was stuck with the bitch who was as pleasant as having a hot branding iron shoved up the ass. The only consolation was that Meggan was as unhappy about the situation as she was and was no longer allowed in the trenches with Dominic.

For the past week, Sabrina and Meggan had bagged the washed, dried, and labeled bones and prepared them for transport to the lab at HQ for more analysis than Kristin could do onsite. Today they were labeling the newest batch of washed and dried bones. Meggan had sent the students outside to wash bones, which was a good thing, considering the tension and loathing in the small finds room was so palatable and toxic it could annihilate anyone within a five-foot radius.

"You're doing it wrong," Meggan said as Sabrina labeled a femur with black ink.

"I'm doing it the way Bruce said you wanted it

done." She pointed behind her to the example written on the board that he had put up as a model to follow.

"Your writing is too fat."

"It's legible."

"You'll do it my way, or I'll tell Jack you're not doing your job."

"Your way?" Sabrina scoffed. "If your way was working, you wouldn't be so behind."

"Why don't you take a break. Ian's probably overdue for his afternoon fuck."

"Now I understand why Jack sent me here. Someone had to do your work."

"Bitch."

"*Puta.*"

"*Striapach.*"

"*Pogue mahone.*"

"You don't love Dom," Meggan shouted. "Why don't you leave him, give him a chance to be happy with someone who loves only him, someone who understands him and what's important to him."

Meggan's poison-tipped barbs had ripped open the most vulnerable part of Sabrina's fears, but she glared at her, refusing to let her see it. "Dominic and I love each other. We're committed to spending the rest of our lives together as husband and wife. Just because you don't like it doesn't mean it's not true."

"You love Ian, and he loves you. Everyone can see it. There's even a pool on how long it'll be before you two fuck each other. Personally, I think you've already done it. He's never gone this long without a woman, and I know he hasn't been with any of the students or locals lately, so my guess is he's doing you."

Sabrina was fairly certain Ian had been with

Natasha, so Meggan was wrong about that, and she hoped she was bluffing about the pool. "No matter what delusions you choose to believe or lies you make up, it won't get you Dominic. You think you'd have learned that by now, after all the times he turned you down and chose other women to be with."

Meggan grinned. "Are you so sure he turns me down? I'm sure you've seen it, how we are together. That connection. Kind of like you and Ian. Except we have history."

Sabrina and Ian had more history that Meggan could conceive of. "History. Exactly. You're a part of his past. I'm his present and his future. He fucked you a long time ago, but he married me. I'm the only woman he wants."

Meggan laughed. "Talk about delusions."

She wanted to smack the smug smile from Meggan's face with the labeled bone in her hand, but instead she set it aside and stood. "I will take that break now. I want to find my husband and tell him about our conversation. Maybe he can get you to see the truth."

Anxiety flashed across the redhead's face and she opened her mouth to say something but then clamped it shut and dropped her eyes to her work, her cheeks red, her motions jerky and unsure, reactions that suggested she didn't want Dominic to know what she'd said.

Outside, Sabrina turned her face up to the bleak sun and closed her eyes. She longed for the heat of home, where the azure skies were clear and blinding and the sun was hot enough to burn away her blues. After being shut up inside with a bitter, angry snake for so long, Sabrina felt drained.

Oh, Dominic, I need you.

She made a long, thorough scan across the field of brown. He wasn't in any of the trenches. But Ian was. He was overseeing a media student filming the other students sifting dirt for pieces of bone, sherds, and other items that might have been overlooked as the dirt was removed from the grid initially. That supervision would have been her job while he was editing. Which meant he would be behind in editing and have to work longer hours. All because she couldn't be there to help him. Because she couldn't keep her hands off him.

He focused the camera lens on her. She smiled and mouthed "Hi," knowing he'd zoomed in, but the sadness filling her quickly stripped the smile away.

She missed her job. Missed the rhythm and flow and routine of working in the trenches, talking to the team about their work, filming and photographing their digging and the finds coming out of the dirt. She missed working with Ian. He made her laugh, made her feel appreciated, made her feel like she was an important part of the project. Made her feel good. Happy. Whole. Working with Meggan made her want to break every bone in finds, including those holding up Meggan's body.

Face the truth. You miss Ian. His touch. His feelings filling your head. The blue haze wrapping the two of you together in a tight bond. The orgasmic bliss he stirs in you. Yes.

For the first time since she came to Ireland, she felt empty, lost, alone. Her heart ached like it was shriveling and dying because her two most important relationships were at risk.

The incident in the pub a week ago had altered her relationship with Dominic. He said he'd overreacted and had agreed to drop it, but he was holding back with her. Their fairy tale life in L.A. seemed far removed from their life today, like they were different people.

And she hadn't touched Ian since she'd been reassigned, even when they dug at night. She worried that Landis, the student Dominic had assigned to "help" them, would report back that they'd laughed too hard, looked too long at each other, stood too close to each other, or touched, and Dominic would make good on his promise to hurt Ian. It bothered her that Dominic hadn't just decided to join them himself, which would have been the better choice if he was still worried about her and Ian.

Ian lowered the camera from his face and stared at her across the distance, the same way she was staring at him, with deep sorrow and deeper need in his eyes. He started her way and pointed toward the media trailer.

She took a few steps that way then stopped. Everyone knew Jack had taken her off media. If they were found together, there'd be no explanation for why she was alone with Ian in the media office other than she wanted to. And she did want to. With every particle of her being she wanted to. He would comfort her, touch her, kiss her. And she would let him. Which was exactly why she had to stay away. She met his gaze, shook her head, and headed the other way.

Dominic. She needed to find Dominic. She needed his hug, his kiss, his love. Since he wasn't in the trenches, likely he was in Gabe's office, or maybe Jack's. On the way there, she saw Natasha on her way into camp.

Natasha glanced her way, then put her head down and kept walking. It wasn't the first time the blonde had avoided her in the aftermath of the pub scene, but today it pissed her off enough to find out why. She ran to her and grabbed her arm. "Why are you avoiding me?"

Natasha glared at her.

"What's wrong?" Sabrina asked her in Spanish, having a feeling this conversation needed to be in a language few, if any, at the camp site understood.

"Why didn't you tell me?" Natasha answered in Spanish, her voice sharp and biting.

"Tell you what?"

Natasha looked around to see who might overhear. "That you and Ian are lovers."

Sabrina stepped back as if she'd been slapped. "We're not." The words came out in English. Her breath caught in her throat. She swallowed and switched back to Spanish. "Who told you this lie?"

"Ian."

Sabrina's eyebrows furrowed. "He would never say something like that because it's not true. We've never—"

"After the pub that night, we went to my trailer."

"Yeah, so?" She knew he had, but it still hurt hearing it confirmed.

"He said *your* name when he came inside me."

Sabrina blinked a couple of times as her heart rose in her chest. "You must have misunderstood."

"I didn't misunderstand."

"Then it was a mistake. Ian and I aren't—"

"Oh, come on. You and I both know what it means when the man you're fucking calls out another woman's name. If you're not lovers now, you soon will be."

"I'm in love with my husband. He's the *only* man

I'm fucking. Why can't everybody believe that?"

"You may be fucking Dom, but you want to fuck Ian and he wants to fuck you. Everyone knows it."

"*Everyone* needs to mind their own business!" Sabrina said and stormed away.

"You'll never have peace until you admit what you want," Natasha called out in Spanish.

If only. Admitting it hadn't brought her peace at all. Just the opposite, she thought as she headed on, desperate to find Dominic.

Chapter Seventeen

"Hello, Ian."

Ian looked up from the camera's eyepiece. A petite woman with long white hair hanging in a braid over one slender shoulder and a soft smile lighting her violet eyes stood before him on the lip of the trench where he was taking pictures of a skeleton.

A glance at the two students in the trench behind him told him they were too into scraping out the other skeleton to pay the stranger any mind. A quick scan of the other trenches told him Meggan and Dom were nowhere to be seen. A low sigh of relief exited his pursed lips, but he knew he had to get Fiona out of sight before someone noticed her and started asking questions. Explaining her presence would be sticky, and Breena didn't need more trouble with Dom.

He climbed out of the trench. Putting his hand at her back, he led her toward the finds office. "What are you doing here?" Not wanting to be overheard, he kept his voice low.

"I felt I needed to check in on you and Sabrina," she said, her volume matching his, concern filling her eyes. "Did it work?"

Knowing she meant the ritual, he shook his head. "No."

She sighed. "I was afraid of that. Let's get Sabrina, shall we."

He led her toward the finds office. "Wait at the end of the caravan, out of sight," he said. "It would be best for her if no one in there saw you."

She moved away, and he went in through the propped-open door.

"He asked me because you didn't explain anything," Breena seethed at Meggan. "If you did your job, I wouldn't have to—" She clamped her mouth closed on the rest of the retort and swung her head toward the door, as if she could sense him there. Her gaze crashed into his, and he could feel her reach out to him.

Everyone at the table turned their gaze to him, too, including Meggan, who watched with a smirk on her face that said she couldn't wait to run tell Dom.

Breena looked tired—as tired as he felt—and like she was going to crack, and what would come out would be either flaying rage or bone-deep sorrow. Without a word between them, she left the table and joined him.

"Make it a quickie," Meggan called out as Sabrina walked out the door. "You have work to do."

He followed Breena out and, without a word or touch, led her toward the media office. He nodded his head toward Fiona, who stepped out from behind the finds trailer.

Sabrina stopped in her tracks, then flew into Fiona's open arms like a despondent child who needed her mother's comfort.

"We need to go," he said quietly, and the three of them hurried to his office. Once inside, he locked the door and turned on the fans while Breena went to shut the windows, blinds, and curtains. It made it stifling inside, but neither wanted the coming conversation overheard or seen.

"Who is that horrible red-haired woman?" Fiona asked Breena.

"My worst nightmare," she said.

"You have to get away from her," Fiona warned. "She means you harm."

"Yeah, well, I don't have a choice. The boss assigned me to work with her."

"Child," she said, "you always have a choice."

"Not if I want to stay on this project with my husband."

The hopelessness in her voice drove him to her where she stood by the window. The thin curtains strained the sunlight, and weak streaks of gold dappled the places on her face and body he wanted to kiss. The crotch of his jeans tightened. Yeah, he wanted to kiss her…as he ripped off her clothes and fucked her up against the wall, on the table, on the floor, anywhere. But mostly, he just wanted to touch her, run his hands over her body, run his mouth over hers, and feel her energy flowing into him again.

Her gaze swung toward him, sharply, as if she could hear his thoughts, smell his desire. She went into his arms so quickly and fluidly it was as if they'd choreographed the move to the nanosecond.

Tucking her head against his chest, she sighed her hopelessness through his shirt onto his skin, into his heart, and he tightened his hold on her, kissing the top of her head. Wherever his body touched, hers tingled, as if they were reabsorbing each other, replenishing each other, becoming whole again.

They hadn't spoken more than a word or two since

the pub fiasco, and it felt like a lifetime since they'd connected. His soul was ravenous for hers. To have her entire body stretched out against his, their bodies joined like this, was pure joy. Rejuvenating. Like a feast to a starving man. He drank her in. Breathed her in. Ate her up. Absorbed her. While he could.

"Ian said the ritual didn't work," Fiona said.

Breena roped her arms around Ian and eased closer to him at the interruption. "It didn't." Her muffled words hummed inside him, and he dropped a kiss on her temple.

"I miss you, *Hashkeh*," he whispered so only she could hear.

"I miss *you*. So much."

"Show me how you performed the ritual," Fiona said.

He kissed Breena's face, and they forced themselves to separate. He grabbed from the *press* the box that held the candles, incense, and written spell, then he and Breena sat on the floor opposite each other and set up the altar between them. They arranged and lit the incense and candles accordingly and clasped each other's hands. Their gaze as one, they recited the incantation they knew by heart.

"Stop," Fiona said when they were a few words in. "Is this how you performed it?"

They looked at her. "Yes."

"Every time?"

"Yes."

"Holding hands?"

They dropped hands like they were on fire.

"Yes," Breena said, sounding exasperated. "So?"

"Why did you hold hands?"

They hadn't discussed it, and he wasn't sure why they'd done it that way. It had just seemed right. "We thought we'd be stronger together than separate." He looked at Breena.

"And that the spell would be more powerful if we were," she finished.

"You are stronger together, and that's exactly why it didn't work. The power of your love for each other overpowered the ritual meant to stop it, which is why I specifically said you weren't to touch while doing it. All you did was strengthen your connection."

Breena jumped to her feet. "Then we'll do it again, for another seven nights, this time not holding hands, not touching at all."

The panic and frustration racing through Breena radiated toward him and, like hooks, drew him to her. He extinguished the candles and incense, then stood and went to her.

"That ritual is used up," Fiona explained. "It won't work."

Breena rubbed her forehead with her hand. "Then another one."

"There is no other like this one," Fiona said.

"Then how can we stop this?"

He knew what the response would be and wanted to be touching her when she heard it. He took her hand in his.

Fiona shook her head. "You can't."

"No!" Breena's eyes flew to his. He tried to hug her to him, but she shook off his grasp, wrapped her arms around her body, and kept her back to him. He placed his hands on her shoulders, but she shrugged away his touch. He stuffed his useless hands into his front pockets.

A thick silence surrounded the trio, held them in place, sinking them deep into their own thoughts of what this failed solution meant. Long minutes crawled by until Fiona's voice fractured the thickness.

"I should go," she said softly and lifted her bag onto her shoulder. Going to Breena, she took her hands and squeezed them. "It'll be all right, child. Things have a way of working out the way they're meant to."

Breena didn't speak, didn't raise her eyes from the floor to look at her, but she nodded.

"I'll walk you to your car," Ian said, moving to the door.

Surprisingly, Breena did not rush back to the finds office as he thought she would but joined him and Fiona as they walked up the hill to the gate where Fiona had parked her car. He made sure Fiona was between him and Breena so he wouldn't be tempted to touch her. Even though his touch could sooth her fragile, on-edge state of mind, she had made it clear she needed space.

"I know this situation is troubling for you two," Fiona said. "Since there's no stopping it, my best advice is to give in to it. You both look…depleted."

They were depleted. To stop cold turkey from being with each other was killing them both, but it's what Breena said she needed when she explained she had to stay away from him to save her marriage. It wasn't what he wanted, but because he loved her and wanted to do what was best for her—and because she wasn't his—he wouldn't fight her on it.

"I can't do that," Breena said.

"What's the worst thing that could happen?"

"I'll lose my husband."

"If that happened, you could be with Ian. You would be well pleased at the joy you'd find in each other. Ian could heal your wounds from losing Dominic."

"First of all, losing Dominic would kill me. And second, Ian is not a consolation prize. He deserves to be happy. He deserves to love someone who is free to love him with all her heart. He deserves to be rid of these chains binding us together so he can have a choice about who and what he wants."

"What's the best thing that could happen?"

Breena's eyes flew to his, and he responded for them both. "We could be together like we were meant to."

Tears formed in her eyes at his words, and she tore her gaze from his and stared out into nothing to gain control.

Fiona cupped her cheeks. "Sabrina, you are pretending you can still have your old life. You can't. The life you planned with Dominic is gone. The moment your soul touched Ian's, it set in motion a force that changed everything. Your love for your husband wars with every instinct inside you telling you that with Ian is where you belong. Only when you face reality will you, and the men you love, be able to find happiness. If you ignore it, hide from it, you'll all be miserable."

When she didn't respond, Fiona hugged her, then him. "If you need to talk or need a place to be together without prying eyes, you know where I live. You're always welcome." She climbed over the gate.

Ian's hands in his pockets, Breena's hands gripping tight to the top of the gate, they watched Fiona get into her car and drive away.

"Dammit!" Breena said when Fiona was gone. "All that time doing the ritual, I could have spent more time with Dominic, doing things that would strengthen my marriage. But instead I was just—"

"Wasting time with me." The fire raging inside her had sparked the one burning in him. The look on her face told him she had felt the angry bite in his voice.

"That's not what I—" she started.

"Yes, it is."

Her body went rigid, and her hands curled into fists. "I'm tired of being torn in half. I love Dominic. I don't want to love any man but him. But there you are, all the time. In my mind, my heart, my soul, behind my eyes when I close them, in the air I breathe, in my dreams. Staring at me across the field, across the mess tent, across the fire pit. Reminding me with your thoughts and your eyes that we're hopelessly chained together but unable to have each other. Do you have any idea how hard this is for me?"

"You think it's easy for me?" he seethed. "This *curse* has turned my fucking life upside down. Before you came here, I could fuck a different woman every night if I wanted, and I enjoyed the hell out of it. Now, I can't be with a woman without seeing your face, smelling your skin, calling out your name when I come inside her. I enjoyed my work, wanted to be the best at it, so one day I'd be considered for an international traveling position. The thing I want most now is to fuck you, then fuck you again and again and fucking again until I'm so lost in you I'll never get out. Every day I care a little less that it would destroy my best friend's life and condemn my half of our damned soul to hell if I took you from him. You consume me, Sabrina McCanna. Everything I am. You consume me like a voracious, unstoppable blaze. You're killing me, from the inside out, and I wish to God you'd never come here."

Pain flashed in her eyes as his words struck deep, and the color drained from her face. He wished he could take back every hurtful word.

"I wish that, too," she snarled and lunged at him, pummeling his chest, taking out her frustrations on him. "If I'd never come here, I wouldn't be losing my husband, I wouldn't want someone I can never have, I wouldn't be aching and miserable every minute of every day from wanting you, from wanting to climb inside you and never come out. I hate this fucking country, I hate this fucking dig, and most of all, I fucking hate you for making my life a living hell. And my name is Sabrina *Sullivan*, not McCanna!"

He grabbed her wrists, halting her attack, and bumped his body into hers. "You don't hate me," he said into her face, his words as sharp as knives. "You fucking love me, and you hate yourself for it."

"Yes, I do!"

She froze at her response, the truth in it, and her fire and anger evaporated, leaving her empty, cold, stripped of emotion. Misery filled her eyes, and she shook her head, letting the tears finally come. "Ian!" she sobbed. "Oh, God, Ian, I can't do this anymore."

He yanked her hard against him and wrapped his arms around her back as tight as chains, tying them together where they wanted to be, rocking them so hard they almost fell. Her arms wound around him, too, and clung to him as if he were her only chance of survival.

He kissed the top of her head and let her hair absorb the falling tears that had pooled in his eyes when she had broken apart.

They stood wrapped around each other, weeping for what they could never have, filling each other with the love they felt nevertheless.

****

Jack and Gabe went into a closed-door meeting, leaving Dom with a rare twenty-minute break, which he wanted to spend with Sabrina. In their caravan. In their bed. In her. His dick stretched his boxers at the thought. Since the pub fiasco, she had been extra attentive, their sex more loving than it had ever been, as if she wanted to ensure he knew she loved only him. And the only time she and Ian spent together was at night, digging for that skeleton. But Landis had reported that they never touched and only rarely talked.

He walked into the finds office. His wife wasn't at the table with the students where she usually sat, wasn't anywhere in the office as far as he could see.

Meg approached him, carrying a bin of bones.

"Where's Sabrina?" he asked her as she set the bin on the table.

"She left with Ian twenty minutes ago."

The words doused the desire in his body, and his shoulders sagged under the weight of the news that she was with Ian. Again. Fuck. Would this never end?

He turned and headed to the door.

"If she comes back, I'll tell her you came by," Meg said.

On his way to Ian's office, he saw her up by the gate with Ian and a white-haired woman. The woman climbed over the gate and drove away. Sabrina and Ian faced each other. Even from this distance, he could see the tension in their stances that told him they were arguing.

The closer he got, the clearer the picture became. Though he still couldn't hear them, their actions spoke volumes. She pounded Ian on the chest in fury before he grabbed her wrists to stop her. She fought to pull away, but he held her tight and said something to her, right in her face. They both cocked back as if his words had been so harsh it doused their fire. Then they rushed into each other's arms so violently they almost fell. Wrapped around each other, pressed tight against each other, then stayed that way. For the entire time it took him to reach them.

"What the hell's going on?"

Their tangled embrace splintered immediately, and a gulf several feet wide opened between them. The first thing he noticed was Sabrina's nipples poking hard against her T-shirt, and Ian's hard-on tenting his pants. The second was her wiping tears from her eyes with her fingers, and Ian swiping his hand across his eyes. Ian, who hadn't cried since he was eight years old and had lost his *daideó*, was crying. Why?

Neither spoke. Neither met his eyes.

"Who was the white-haired woman?" He still wanted an answer to his first question, but maybe they'd be more forthcoming with the less-threatening second.

Ian crossed his arms over his chest like it was aching. "A witch."

Sabrina's gaze swung to Ian, as if she were shocked by his answer, then quickly turned away.

"Why was she here?"

"To check on the *sonuachar* issue."

"Did she threaten you?"

"No."

He approached Sabrina, who had yet to speak. "Are you okay?"

"I'm fine."

Her voice was shaky, her chin trembling, and she was fighting back tears. Clearly, she was not fine. He put his hand on her shoulder, peered into the red-rimmed eyes that would not meet his. A tear rolled down her cheek, and he brushed it away with his thumb. At the tender touch, she drew in a ragged breath and closed her eyes.

"Then why are you crying?"

"Let it go, Dominic. Please." She pulled away from him and ran down the hill toward their caravan.

Ian started down the hill, too, but Dom stopped him. "What the fuck's going on, Ian? Why is she crying?"

"She's not happy here."

"So you hugged her? Bet that made her happy. I can see how happy it made you." His tone was sharper than he had intended it to be, revealing how angry he was at catching them in another intimate embrace and, he was sure, in another grid of lies.

Ian stabbed a finger at him, his eyes on fire. "If you love your wife, get her away from—from this place. Now."

The angry outburst filled Dom with rage. His chin lifted in stubborn defiance. "And if I don't get her away? What then? What'll happen?"

The two friends glared at each other across the green field.

"Believe me, brother, you don't want to find out," Ian said finally, his voice heavy and dark with mystery and doom.

Dom rushed forward and grabbed his arm, intent on making him explain his statement. Ian jerked away, his fists at the ready.

"Fuck me, but I do want to find out," Dom yelled. "I want to find out what's going on between the two of you. Why every time I turn around, my wife is in your arms and you look like you want to fuck her."

Ian's eyes blazed. "For once in your life, don't question. Don't argue. Just do what you know in your gut is right. Take her and just go, before even God himself can't stop what's about to happen."

He turned and stormed down the hill. Ignoring Dom's calls, he broke into a sprint and ran straight out and didn't stop until he got to his office. He went in and slammed the door.

Standing alone at the top of the rise, Dom took in the dig site below him laid out in a neat, orderly pattern.

He liked order. It was how he made sense of his world. This profession had always done it for him.

Until this dig.

He sighed. From almost the minute he and Sabrina had stepped foot on this plot of land, it felt as if chaos haunted them. His team believed Ena had cursed them. He wasn't ready to go there, but it did feel like they were living in a puzzle that was missing half its pieces. His brain felt scrambled, and he couldn't get a clear picture of what was what. And because of it, questions scratched his mind with razor-sharp blades, and suspicion twisted his gut.

Sabrina and Ian were hiding something. Whatever

it was, he knew he wouldn't like it. Knew it would be a stinky, fucking pile of shit to dig through. But dig he would. Until he found the truth that lay beneath. Because as Ian had intimated, that's who he was.

He headed down the hill to his caravan.

Sabrina was lying on the bed when he walked in. He sat on the edge, his back to her, and twisted his wedding ring. "What was going on between you and Ian?" He kept his voice calm so she wouldn't shut down.

"I'm having a shittier than usual day with Meggan. Then the witch showed up, and we had to deal with that. Ian sensed how upset I was, and he comforted me."

He knew there was more to it, but he was too fucking tired to drag it out of her. Ian's words came back to him.

"Are you happy here?" When she didn't respond, he turned and looked at her.

She stared into his eyes, as if she was giving herself time to come up with a story other than the truth. Then she shook her head.

"Why?" he said.

She crawled over to him and stood on her knees behind him, wrapped her arms tight around his chest. "Meggan despises me and treats me like shit, and I know it's because she thinks I stole you from her. The team thinks I'm the cause of all the problems at the dig. I'm working as an untrained shovelbum instead of a photographer. You and I are constantly fighting." She dropped her head to his shoulders. "Let's go away from here, Dominic. Now. Today."

He jerked to his feet and faced her. "I can't just

quit."

"Sure, you can. We'll just pack up and leave, go to another team or another company. Hell, another country if you want. I have plenty of money for us to live on until we find new jobs."

"What you're asking is not that easy. I can't join another team unless there's an opening. When Gabe retires next year, I get his position. If I go to another team, I'll have to start at the bottom. I don't want to do that. I've worked hard to get where I am. Besides, I can't just leave in the middle of a dig. What would that say about me, as a professional, as a man?"

She lay back on the bed and stared up at the ceiling. "You're right. It was selfish of me to ask that of you. I'm sorry."

"I'm sorry you're not happy," he said. "I'll talk to Meg about—"

"That would make things worse. Look, today was a bad day. I'll be okay tomorrow. Really." She stretched out her hand to him.

He took her hand. "What can I do to make you feel better *now*?"

"Show me and tell me I'm important to you."

He lay beside her, drew her into his arms, cupped her face in his hand, and made her look at him. "You mean more to me than anything in this world." He kissed her.

"Now show me," she whispered.

It was time for him to get back to work, and he didn't want Jack or Gabe to have to come looking for him. But his wife needed him. And he needed her.

He sat up, helped her to do the same, then grabbed the hem of her T-shirt and pulled it over her head. He flipped open the front clasp of her bra and pushed the lacy cups aside to capture her heavy breasts. While she slid the bra off her arms and tossed it onto the floor, his hands slid down her belly to undo her shorts. She lay back and arched up to allow him to tug her shorts and panties over her hips, down her legs. He undressed and lay beside her.

He kissed her mouth before softly kissing down her body, giving extra attention to her breasts and nipples, the way she liked. She slid her hands into his hair and caressed his head as he kissed and licked her. His tongue drew a wet path down to her navel before traveling over the soft curve of her lower belly. His mouth at her mound, he breathed her in, tugged at her blonde puff, then lower to her already wet pussy lips.

"Ahh, Dominic," she moaned on a ragged breath. His gaze settled on hers. She was looking at him with such love, such heat, like she used to before their life became so confused.

With sharp regret he realized how long it had been since he'd taken the time to be this thorough. Why had he waited so long? She deserved to be loved, thoroughly, every day, every night. The few times he'd made love to her in the past few weeks, he hadn't given her his best. That would change. Starting now.

He licked her pussy lips, teased them open with his tongue, and she lifted her legs to give him more room to explore. The tip of his tongue dug deeper, parting her slick flesh, tasting the red velvet sweetness between her legs. He caressed her with his mouth, again and again, with the tip of his tongue, the long flat of it, his lips, until she arched against him, pressing into his mouth.

"I want you inside me, connecting us."

He eased up her body. His cock had gone hard the second his tongue tasted her, and he was ready to be inside her. His weight on his forearms, his eyes locked on hers, his cock settled at the hot spot between her legs. She slid her hands between them and gripped him, guiding him to her opening. He pushed in slowly, just the tip of his cock. When she grabbed his ass and pressed into him, he slid in all the way.

He took all of her mouth with his mouth and all of her pussy with his dick. He kept the pace slow, wanting to make her crazy, wanting it to last, wanting her to remember this, remember what he did for her, remember how much he loved her.

Her hips thrust upward, against his, wanting, needing, desperate. She wrapped her legs around his hips, hands at his back, pulling him hard into her, fighting for her pleasure.

He couldn't hold out much longer. His eyes were already going hazy, a sign that the consuming blackness was coming to his brain, and he could barely breathe. Then he felt it. She held her breath, she tensed, she groaned, and her pussy gripped his cock in ripples of pleasure so hard he let go, too. Coarse moans of pleasure filled the room, his and hers. He sawed into her, again and again, grunting with every thrust, shooting his cum with every stroke until he lay empty on her trembling body. They lay connected, silent, just trying to breathe.

She kissed his damp forehead, caressed his head. "I wish you could read my mind and know how very much I love you," she whispered, her voice fragile.

Her choice of words surprised him. As if she knew he wasn't sure she loved him. His eyes went to hers.

She wasn't crying, but all her feelings were right at the shiny surface, ready to spill out. She loved him. He could see it. And seeing the truth of it softened his suspicious heart. "I *do* know, baby."

He wasn't lying. He knew she loved him, but… No. He wouldn't analyze the buts. Not now. Right now, all he wanted was this, to be one with his wife…while he still could.

"I love you, too," he added, so there'd be no doubt in her mind. "I'd be lost without you."

Chapter Eighteen

Knowing that the entire team thought she and Ian were lovers made her want to do everything possible to show them—and Dominic—they were mistaken, that she and Dominic were strong. The day she'd asked him to take her away from the dig, he'd been so eager to do or say anything to make her feel better that he'd agreed to spend their next day off together in town and mostly in the room she reserved at the B&B. Today was that day, and she woke feeling happier than she had in a long time.

Jack stopped them as they were climbing into the SUV.

"Gabe's wife went into labor early this morning—he left as soon as he got the call—so you're my second through the end of the project." He handed him a fat folder. "Take a minute to familiarize yourself with this, then drive to HQ for the monthly project meeting. You'll report on our progress, answer questions, then have dinner and drinks with the senior management team so take appropriate clothes. Stay the night then hot-foot it back here early the next morning." He looked at Sabrina. "Sorry about your plans." He headed to breakfast.

"Oh, my God. This is fantastic!" she gushed. "I've been dying to go back to Dublin."

"We won't get to spend any time together,"

Dominic said. "You'd be alone and bored the whole time."

"Bored in Dublin? No way! I'll get my nails done, get a massage, go shopping, buy something sexy for tonight that you can rip off me with your bare hands," she put her arms around him and kissed him, "or your teeth, whichever you prefer."

His hand rested lightly on her hip, but he didn't hug her. He just shook his head. "I'd be worried about you running around alone. I wouldn't be able to concentrate on work."

"I'm not twelve," she said, with more annoyance than she meant, so she reined it in. "I'll be fine on my own." The look on his face told her he wasn't giving in. "Baby, I really need to spend time alone with you, away from this place. Even a few hours."

"Next time."

"Give me one good reason why—"

"Sabrina." The annoyance in his tone shut her down. "As soon as this dig is over, we'll spend a week alone. In Dublin if you want. Just the two of us."

That may be too late. She stared at him, torn between going crazy on his ass and being the understanding wife. In the end, she just said, "Let's get breakfast before you go."

"I don't have time."

She forced a smile to her lips. "Then we can go with my first choice—a quickie in the backseat," she said, grasping at the last chance to get him to allow her in."

He shook his head. "If I'm to get there on time, I need to go now."

Her smile died. She was getting the message. His

work trumped their marriage. She grabbed her packed bag from the backseat. "Have a good trip."

He hooked his arm around her waist before she could walk away. "I would like a hug and a kiss goodbye."

It was the last thing she wanted to do, but she agreed, giving him what he'd asked for while trying to ignore the ball of distress lodged in her chest.

After he drove away, she headed to breakfast, her mind on their wedding day and honeymoon and how happy she'd been. Anything to remind herself that she loved him.

****

Sabrina awoke deep in the night, feeling a presence in the trailer that wasn't her ghost. When her eyes had focused in the dark, she realized it was Ian. He was standing at the edge of her bed, little more than a shadow.

"Let's go." His whispered words sounded strange, muffled, like they were coming from inside her head and not from his mouth, but nothing in her said to resist the request. She got out of bed, pulled on her robe, and stepped into her boots. She went to the door, Ian behind her, but when she had walked down the steps, the door closed and he wasn't there. She tried to go back in to find out why he hadn't come outside, but the door was locked.

"Ian," she whispered. "Open up."

With no answer from him, and no way to get in, she walked to the window, looked in. He stood by the oven, still shrouded in darkness, facing her. Chills rose on her skin, making every little hair stand up. Panic made them rise higher.

"Quit fucking around, Ian. This isn't funny."

She caught a whiff of something odd then, like wires burning. Just as she realized the odor was coming from her trailer, she heard a pop. Rushing to the far side of the trailer, she saw flames shooting from the electrical access panel near the kitchenette. She raced back to the window. Ian was still standing at the oven, not moving, just looking at her.

The curtain at the kitchen window caught fire, and the hungry flames dissolved the filmy material like a wet tongue on cotton candy. The fire crawled toward the oven, toward the propane tank connected to the oven. Shit! If it hit that tank, it would be over for both of them.

"Ian!" She ran to the door, pulled on it, but it still wouldn't open. She ran back to the window and pounded on the glass. "Ian, get out of there!" He didn't move, just stared at her. Her soul crumpled. She couldn't get to him. She was going to lose him.

"Oh, God! Ian! *Hashkeh!*" she yelled.

She had started tearing out the screen when, from behind her, a pair of strong hands gripped her arms and pulled her away from the trailer. She wrenched away, but they wrapped around her waist, lifted her, and pulled her backward. Fighting with all her strength to get away, she shouted Ian's name, again and again, frantic. She had to get to him before it was too late.

"Breena, it's me. Breena!"

At the familiar voice, she looked over her shoulder. Ian was behind her, hands gripping her, worry in his eyes. She turned back toward the trailer. Only Rusty was in there, spraying the fire with an extinguisher. Angus was spraying it outside.

She turned back to Ian and put her hands on his face. He was real, solid, no shadowy figure. Bursting into tears, she launched herself into his arms so hard he stumbled back a step but held her tight. She wrapped her leg around his, wanting to climb inside him where it was safe.

"Ian!" she cried into his neck.

"*Haskheh*," he whispered against her. "I'm here."

Sean and Kristin ran to them. "Are you okay?" Kristin asked, her hand on Sabrina's back.

Sabrina nodded, but the shock of what she'd seen brought on more tears. Ian's hold on her tightened, because he knew she needed it.

"What happened?" Sean asked.

"I heard her calling my name. When I ran out to see what was going on, the trailer was on fire and she was trying to get inside. I pulled her away."

Jack joined them. "Sabrina, what the hell happened?" Worry made his tone sharp.

She dug deeper into Ian's arms, tears flowing.

"Not now, Jack." Ian picked her up in his arms and walked toward his trailer.

"Ian. Not in your trailer."

Jack's stern voice carried a warning that stopped him and turned him around to deliver a hard stare to his boss. "*Jaysus!* Where's she going to stay? In that firetrap? With you? One of the guys? Meggan?"

"She can use Gabe's trailer," Jack replied.

"She's in no condition to be left alone." Ian started toward his trailer again.

"She can stay with us," Kristin offered.

"She's staying with me," Ian said firmly, not even turning around to deliver the decision.

"Don't do it, son," Jack called after him. "It's not right."

In a symbolic middle finger salute, Ian carried her to his trailer, up the steps, and inside. He laid her on his bed, pulled off her boots, and started back to the door.

She reached for him. "Please don't leave me."

He took her hand and kissed it. "I'm not, love. Just going to close the door."

She watched his every move as he walked to the door, closed it, locked it, then returned to the bed. He toed off his boots and crawled onto the mattress, curling his body around hers in a protective spooning position. Her body absorbed his heat, his love, like a sponge. It was just what she needed. He always knew what she needed and always gave it to her. Never had he put anything above her. Not even himself or his needs.

"You're shivering." He tried to let go of her to pull the sheet over them, but she grabbed his hand and held it to her chest.

"Oh, Ian." Tears flooded from her eyes again, and he held her tighter, comforting her, warming her, calming her.

"Shhhhh," he murmured. "It's okay. You're safe. Shhhhh." His kisses on her head and on her shoulder and his warm breath on her skin eased her fears.

When her tears had subsided, she turned in his arms to face him. His arm settled around her waist. They stared at each other deep until she had absorbed enough of his strength to speak. "You saved my life."

"I just pulled you away," he said. "Rusty and Gussy put out the fire."

She shook her head. "Your soul came to me tonight. It woke me up and got me out of the trailer so I wouldn't die in that fire. I know that sounds crazy, but that's what happened. You saved me. I don't know how, but you did."

"I believe you, love," he said quietly, his voice calming her. "Tell me what happened."

Tears wet her face as she told him everything. Seeing acceptance in his eyes, during the story and afterward, she knew everything was okay.

"You really are my hero," she concluded, sniffing.

He laughed softly. "I didn't even have to twist your arm to say it this time."

She managed a rough chuckle, but a fresh batch of tears started again when she remembered. "I thought I'd lost you."

"But you didn't," he said. "I'm right here. Right by your side." He let her go long enough to grab his T-shirt from the end of the bed and hand it to her.

She wiped her eyes and nose with the scent of him, and their arms went right back around each other. She lay in the crook of his arm, and he held her against his chest, her head tucked against his heart, her arm around him.

He tangled his legs with hers and kissed her forehead. "Get some sleep."

"I will, but don't leave me."

"I'm not leaving you."

Surrounded by his comfort and love and scent and their blue haze, she fell asleep to the soothing feel of his hand trailing up and down her back in long, slow touches. Of his skin and muscles and heat against hers. Of his heart beating against her heart. Of her first ghost-free night.

She slept for hours, not waking until his cell alarm

went off. Though his arm was probably numb, he hadn't moved from her the whole time. He had kept his promise. He hadn't left her. She could always count on him. Her hero. Her *Hashkeh*. Her soulmate. Her Ian.

He reached over her and turned it off, laid back down, and held her in her arms. "Morning, love," he said, sleep and contentment in his voice. "How do you feel?"

"Safe, cherished, like I always feel with my hero."

He smiled. "Fuckin' A, love."

She smiled back.

"I don't want to run today," he said. "Let's stay in bed. We could use the rest after last night."

She wanted to, but she there was something she needed to do. "I need to call Dominic. Tell him what happened. I don't want him to hear it from someone else."

His smile faded. "My phone's on the table when you're ready."

She nodded, then slowly pulled out of their knot to climb out of bed.

He caught her around the waist. "No, *Hashkeh*. Not yet," he whispered. "Please."

Another few minutes wouldn't matter. She sank back into his embrace. A minute turned into two, then ten, then more than an hour had passed, and the sun was well into its rise before she forced herself out of his bed. He grabbed her hand and brought it to his mouth, kissed it. Then he let her go.

Taking his phone, she stepped outside, sat on his steps, and called her husband. She told him everything, including the part about sleeping in Ian's bed.

****

"It's hard to say without more investigation, but it looks like one of the wires was exposed, which allowed the current to arc onto debris present in the panel, resulting in a fire. You'll need a new circuit breaker and wiring."

Dom was taking time he couldn't spare to deal with this problem, and the electrician's news did nothing to improve his mood. "How does a wire just get exposed?"

"Well, now, it was a clean cut."

A cut? Dom gritted his teeth. The man was saying someone intentionally cut the wire. For what purpose? To start a fire? To hurt Sabrina? Him? "How much will it cost to fix? Including installing a panel with a lock?"

"I'll work up the numbers and get back to you this afternoon."

"Sooner the better." He and Sabrina had been sleeping in Gabe's caravan the past two nights, and he was ready to get back to their own place, ready to put this latest drama behind him.

He walked the electrician to his truck as they finalized plans for making the repairs. He still had to get someone to fix the wall and inspect the appliances. Fortunately, MAC would reimburse him for the repairs, but that wasn't his primary concern. Someone had cut the wire. Who? And why?

Meg joined him as he headed back to the dig. "HQ is on the phone. They have some questions about one of the finds, and Jack sent me to find you."

"You're the finds supervisor. Why can't you answer their fucking questions?"

"Hey, don't kill the messenger."

"Sorry," he mumbled under his breath and changed

direction.

She stayed with him. "That the electrician just leaving?"

"Yeah." He kept walking, not in the mood to chat about what he'd learned.

"So, did the wiring fail?"

"Something like that."

"It should have been checked before the caravan was delivered."

"It was."

"Makes no sense that it failed."

"No."

"Sabrina's lucky to have gotten out," Meg said.

Pain stabbed his stomach at the thought of losing Sabrina. He stopped and looked at Meg. "He said the wire was cut, intentionally, which started the fire."

Her eyes widened and her face paled. "What? Is he sure?"

He nodded. "I can't believe someone on the team would do something like that. But who else could have?"

She averted her eyes from his.

"What?" he asked.

"What what?"

"You know something."

"No." She walked away, but he caught her arm.

"Say what's on your mind."

"I think Sabrina or Ian cut the wire, knowing it would cause a fire."

"Why would they?"

"Why else?" she scoffed. "To give them an excuse to sleep together all night. Like they did."

"I don't believe that."

"But you do believe that Ian's soul miraculously got her out of the caravan and saved her from a fiery death?"

"It happened just the way I said it happened, whether you have the mental capacity to understand it or not."

Sabrina's icy tone came from behind them, and they turned to face her. Her eyes bore hard into Meg, and she was tense, shaking as if she were barely controlling her desire to strangle her.

"You and Ian are the only two people who believe it," Meg said with a smirk then looked at him. There was a confidence in her gaze that said she knew he'd side with her.

Sabrina looked at him, too, her gaze less confident. He saw a mix of emotions that included rage and a plea for him to stand by her, along with the question he didn't want to answer. *Do you believe me?* When he took a little too long to refute Meg's statement, dejection and disappointment flashed in his wife's eyes before she looked away.

To convince her that he believed her, he forced himself to move to her and take her in his arms. She wrapped her arms around him and tucked herself into his embrace, clinging to him.

Meg snorted in derision and walked away.

He held his wife, not even separating when Jack joined them.

"Did Red tell you I need you to respond to some questions HQ has about the HR in T-311?"

"Yes. And I'll be right there," he said, his level of annoyance matching Jack's.

"Make it quick," Jack said, then stormed off,

mumbling "…goddamned marriage drama."

"Baby, I swear, everything I told you is true. I *slept* in Ian's bed. Nothing else."

"I believe you."

She found his eyes and held on. "It means everything to me to hear you say that."

He nodded and gave her a little smile. "Where're you headed?"

A look of nausea flashed across her face. "To down a few shots before I go to finds."

He frowned at her insinuation that she needed chemical help to get through her workday. It was time he asked Meg outright to be nice to her. His mobile rang. He ignored it, sure it was Jack again about the bloody questions.

"Sorry, baby, I really gotta go answer those questions. I'll see you tonight," he said and turned to leave her.

She caught his arm. "And I really need a kiss."

He turned back, cupped her face, and stared into her eyes. He said he believed her. He wanted to believe her. He just wasn't sure he did. It was the latest crazy thing in a long line of crazy things to happen to her. Just her. And Ian. The ghost. Ena telling them to find the soulmate. Ian's soul saving her from a fire that never should have happened. Them spending the night in his bed when she could have, should have, slept in Gabe's caravan.

He pulled her back into his arms and kissed her. Her arms slid up around his neck and held his head close, deepening the kiss, touching her tongue to his, inviting it to play. And he responded appropriately, giving her the kiss she craved.

But he felt himself holding back. Because when he closed his eyes, all he could see was her in Ian's bed. In Ian's arms. Doing things he didn't want to name. The images were eating holes in his gut. So were the thoughts of what it meant that the first woman Ian had allowed into his caravan was Sabrina. It shot a blade of steel through him, widening the already gaping wound.

"I love you, Dominic," she said, "so much."

She loved him. She wouldn't cheat on him. She wouldn't hurt him. That's what he kept telling himself. Every single day. He loved her so much, which gave her ultimate power to hurt him deep, so deep that any injuries she inflicted might never heal. But he couldn't give her up, not even to protect himself, so he'd live with his suspicions, his distress. For now.

"I love you, too."

Chapter Nineteen

Running the overall site in Gabe's absence was an exercise in constant motion. Dominic was in charge of general excavation strategy, keeping notes and records, survey work on the site, and excavation of the burials.

He went from trench to trench getting reports from each supervisor. He wrote notes about the finds and features exposed, measured positions, and drew sketch maps. He checked everyone's field notes, checked to make sure all the bags were labeled correctly, conducted training sessions, supervised the students and created their schedules, and a myriad of other never-ending duties.

He relied on Sean for help with the details and to work with Ian to get specific shots. He seemed to have adopted the stance that the less time he spent with Ian the better. In between all that, he grabbed a trowel or brush and joined the digging when he could.

While he worked late to get it all done, Sabrina and Ian—and Landis—worked late, too, trying to find the skeleton that would release her from the ghost. She and Dominic both came home later and later. Most of the time, he showered and fell asleep as soon as his head hit the pillow. He was so tired she felt bad initiating sex, so their frequency took a sharp dive, and when they did make love, the act was more about physical release than spiritual connection. The distance between them was growing, and she felt powerless to stop it.

One day dragging into the next, Sabrina worked alongside the students who had been assigned to finds. After giving the crew their orders, Meggan usually left. It was a good/bad situation. Bad because it probably meant she was with Dominic. Good because it left Bruce in charge. Funny how no one made the careless mistakes they did when Meggan was there yelling at them, ridiculing them, turning the place into hell.

Meggan disappeared every day but had never been gone this long. Was she with Dominic? Sabrina's head pounded, thinking about the possibilities. She rubbed her forehead, and it was clear she had to down some meds before the headache morphed into a migraine.

She told Bruce she was taking a quick break. On the way out, she ran into Rusty.

"Sabrina, have you seen—"

"On the table." She nodded toward the office. She had pulled Nessy from one of the wheelbarrows of dump dirt she'd been sifting earlier.

"Thanks!"

****

Dom stepped inside his caravan, Meg behind him. "You've got to step up the work," he said, continuing the conversation they'd started on the way over to see whether his mobile had finished charging. "We're behind schedule. If you need more students, I can divert a couple from the trenches your way."

"Take them from Ian. At this point, getting the finds processed is more important than filming them coming up."

"Ian only has two, and he needs them since Sabrina was reassigned."

"Too bad Jack split them up. They worked so well together."

The muscles in his neck and jaws tensed. "I'll talk to Sean to see if he can spare anyone. In the meantime, you need to spend the bulk of your time in finds."

"The students—and Sabrina—can handle the labeling and bagging." She took a step closer to him and ran her hand down his arm. "I need to be helping you. You're doing your job and Gabe's, for Christ sake."

He stepped away from her. "Your expertise is needed in finds." His voice was low, with an edge he hoped made it clear he wasn't interested in anything but her doing her job.

She advanced again, raised her hands to his chest, then raked her fingers down to his stomach and lower to cup his crotch. His whole body went rigid at her touch. He and Sabrina hadn't had sex in days, and at Meg's touch, pent-up desire unwound low in his stomach like coiled snakes coming awake. His cock knew her touch. Had in the past enjoyed it tremendously. Feeling her hands, his cock jumped in welcome. The movement encouraged her to linger, to scratch her nails over the sensitive flesh.

"Do you ever think about us?" she asked. "How we were?"

Oh, he'd thought about her all right. Too much. Of all his lovers over the years, she was the most like him, passionate about digging. One of the best times of his life was that summer they'd met. Waking up next to her, her wild curls wrapped around him, his cock finding quick release in her always-eager body. Heading out to the site to dig side-by-side all day, showering together, then sharing stories about their day around the fire. Fucking most of the night, then sleeping curled around her, his cock between her legs, his hand cupped around one of her little diddies that perfectly fit his half-closed palm. Day after day after day. It had been heaven.

Right up until the time she broke up with him.

He hadn't believed her lie, that they were getting too serious too fast. But it hurt too much to push for the truth, so he acted like it was no big deal, even told her a lie of his own, that he would have broken up with her at the end of the dig anyway. She hadn't pushed for the truth, either, just walked away, looking like her world had crashed and burned as hard as his had. It had crushed his heart, but because she'd let him go, he'd found Sabrina, the woman who'd taught him what real love was.

Thoughts of Sabrina cleared his senses, and he caught his former lover's wrists and moved her hands away from his crotch before letting her go. "Dammit, Meg. I told you I love my wife. I'm faithful to her."

"You sure she's faithful to you?"

"I'm sure."

She said nothing, but her raised eyebrow and smirk spoke volumes.

"What?" he said, the word biting out of his mouth at the look on her face. "If you have something to say, say it."

"You deserve to be loved by a woman who loves only you." She brushed the hair back from his forehead with the tips of her fingers and caressed his face with her hand.

His soul was soaking up her comfort like a desert

floor soaks up rain, but he forced himself to step away from her. He grabbed his mobile from the charger and slipped it into his pocket. "I don't doubt my wife's love and faithfulness." He moved toward the door.

"Visit her and Ian while they're digging. Then tell me you're of the same opinion."

He turned back to her. "What have you seen?"

After a long, telling moment, she answered. "Nothing. Nothing at all." Her tone suggested she had seen plenty but wasn't going to elaborate.

He closed the space between them in less than a heartbeat and gripped her arms. He stuck his face in hers, ready to demand she tell him what she knew, by God.

In a flash, Meg moved in, too, her hands going to his head and pulling his mouth against hers in a hard, wet kiss. He pushed her away quickly, but not quickly enough. Not before the door opened.

Sabrina stood in the open doorway, mouth agape, shock and hurt widening her eyes.

He couldn't hide the emotions crackling between him and Meg or the bulge in his pants or the guilty look on his face. He couldn't make her understand that it wasn't what it looked like. But he had to try. "Sabrina—"

****

The sight of her husband kissing another woman, kissing *Meg*, about blew Sabrina backward out of the trailer. Misery drowned her, head to toe, like it had been dumped from a swimming pool over her, but she held onto her emotions.

It's not what it looks like. There's a logical explanation.

But there was only one explanation for the budge in his jeans, the guilty look on his face, the hard tips of Meggan's itty-bitty-titties poking her shirt, and the smug grin on her face.

Oh, God. No.

It was all she could do to stop herself from grabbing Meggan's ponytail at its red roots, yanking her to the ground, straddling her, and pummeling her freckled face with her fists so hard she'd never look at Dominic again without flinching. It was all she could do not to dissolve into a pool of tears at Dominic's feet and beg him again to take her away from this horrible, cursed place before the wedge between them was buried so deep they'd lose each other forever.

He said her name, but she didn't let him continue. She corralled the emotions slicing her open into enough energy to walk past him to the bathroom without falling apart. Behind the closed door, she searched the medicine cabinet for what felt like an hour, the image of them in each other's arms blinding her to any image but that one. Finally finding her bottle of migraine meds, she popped one into her mouth and swallowed it back with her bottle of water, hoping she wouldn't throw it up.

It was harder to force herself to leave the bathroom than it had been to force herself to enter it. Meggan was gone, but Dominic was there, and he stepped toward her. He said her name again when she walked past him to the door, and he grabbed her arm, but she slung it off.

"Don't," she snapped, swallowing the rest of what she wanted to say.

All the way back to finds, her mind tortured her—

By showing her pictures of the two of them in the trailer, finishing what she'd interrupted.

By urging her to run to Ian for comfort, even though she knew it would create more problems.

By pummeling her with one thought. *We're not going to make it.*

Chapter Twenty

Ian turned away from his digging to switch on the lantern. The light pushed aside the darkness threatening to smother the trench.

"You mad at me, *Hashkeh*?" he asked, staring at her across the way.

"No."

"Avoiding me?"

He'd tried for an hour to engage her in conversation while they dug for the *sonuachar*, but with little luck. Truth be told, she was avoiding him. For many reasons. Because Landis had begged off for the night so he could hit the pub with some of the other students and wasn't there providing the buffer that kept them apart. Because of what everyone was saying about her and Ian. Because they were no longer allowed to work together. Because it was a constant struggle to keep her hands off him. Because she knew how she felt seeing Dominic touch another woman and knew he felt the same way seeing her touch Ian…or him her.

"Maybe I'm not in the mood to talk."

Actually, she very much wanted to talk to her *Hashkeh*, pour out her heart to him, tell him what she'd seen, and ask him what to do about it. Avoiding him exacted a high price from her. It gouged a burning pit inside her soul, and she knew of no way to remedy her malady other than to let him fill her up.

But it wasn't fair to him. Or her. Or Dominic.

"What did Dom do?"

"Forget about it."

"Talk to me."

"No."

He dropped his shovel and moved behind her, dropped his hands on her shoulders, and massaged, his fingers digging into her tense, aching muscles. She also felt him digging into her thoughts. The thoughts she had tried so hard to hide from him.

"He loves you."

At his words, his touch, his concern, she folded like a fan. "He wants to be with Meggan." And burst into tears. "I caught them in our trailer, kissing."

Ian took the shovel from her hand and tossed it beside his, then pulled her into his arms, tight against his chest. He made soft shushing noises at her ear, murmured *Hashkeh*, soothed her, comforted her, held her, let her cry. When her tears subsided, she put her hands on his chest and applied gentle pressure, knowing she shouldn't be wrapped up in him. But he didn't let her go.

"*Hashkeh*, we shouldn't…" she started.

"Yes, we should. I need you, Breena, and you need me. It's been so long since we connected, and we're both in pain. Don't deny us this moment."

Her hands relaxed on his chest. Slid up to his shoulders. Wound around his neck. Cupped his head. Her body pressed against his, and she gave him what he needed. Took what she needed.

She did need him. Being in his arms made her feel like everything would be okay. Made all her fears and insecurities disappear. Made her feel good. Really good. Too good. His kisses on her head, neck, and face, his touch, reminded her that eyes were everywhere.

She forced herself to move away from him and then grabbed her shovel and his.

"He doesn't want her." He took his shovel from her outstretched hand. "He only wants you."

"What I saw says differently."

He started to say something else to counter her statement, but she interrupted him. "Let's talk about something else."

They dug side-by-side, him doing his best to lift her spirits by keeping the talk light, entertaining her. He told her a story about his childhood. She told him about hers. They talked favorite foods and favorite songs and favorite movies. They talked about family. Both of them from somewhat dysfunctional families, they tried to outdo each other with their you-think-that's-bad sob stories that soon had them laughing.

In between the words they said, they listened to the words they didn't say. *I want to hold you again. I want to touch you again. I want to taste your lips. I want that, too. Make love to me.*

This, their latest grid, was set up a few feet from the last several dozen they'd dug. Most of the skeletons they'd turned up had been male. Four were female but were older, while one was a child under ten. Not that they had any idea of the age of the ghost's *sonuachar*, but the male skeleton had been about 25, making it likely that his love was of similar age. Unless, of course, she had outlived him by many years and died an old woman.

Just to be safe, she had touched them all, along with all the other skeletons the team had dug up, but none triggered the response she'd hoped.

God, she was tired. She hadn't had a full night's sleep, except that one night in Ian's bed, in his arms, since she'd arrived. The ghost, the night-time digging mission, working with Meggan, fighting with Dominic, and trying to stay away from Ian had depleted her. But she had to keep going. They had to find the skeleton. Once they did, she would devote her time to making sure Dominic didn't get that close with anyone but her.

A curse on her lips for her situation, she cut hard into the soil. The shovel hit resistance half a foot down, the impact shimmying up the handle. The muscles in her arms twanged, and the tool fell from her hands.

"Shit," she said, slinging her hands to work out the ache.

"You hit something?" Ian asked.

"Yeah." She dropped to the ground, grabbed her trowel, and began clearing away the dirt.

The cool breath of a presence raised the tiny hairs on her skin, and she couldn't suppress a shiver. She looked up. Her ghost hovered on the lip of the trench, staring down at the grave, a soft look to his face. Then he *stepped* into the trench and toward her.

Energy surged through her, making her dig faster. "Ian, this is her."

"What makes you think so?"

"He's back." She nodded toward the ghost, and Ian turned around and looked that way.

His lips parted, and his eyes widened as they stared into the darkness. "Holy mother."

He could see him. She smiled. "Let's dig her out."

She scraped the dirt too fast and with not enough care, but this was it. It was almost done. They were at the end of this mission that, once done, might allow her obsession with Ian to fade, might allow her to reclaim her husband's love and attention.

When Ian didn't move, she tapped his leg with her trowel. "Love, help me." He dropped down beside her.

After what seemed like hours, a patch of skull about the size of a quarter appeared in the dirt. Sabrina traded her trowel for a brush and swept the spot until it had grown to softball size. She reached out her hand, hesitantly. She didn't want to touch it, but she had to.

This will end the curse was her last rational thought before the dizziness overtook her. A spinning in her head, a blackening of her vision, a feeling like she was being sucked into nothingness. Right before she passed out, she felt Ian behind her, holding her against him, giving her a safe place to fall.

****

"Breena," Ian whispered, gently shaking her. She came to, her back against his chest, his arms around her. "Look." He pointed to the lip of the trench.

She followed his gaze to where the soulmates stood, embracing. They looked at Sabrina and Ian, smiled, nodded once as if in thanks, then kissed, merging into each other, fading ever more transparent until they were no more.

Sabrina sat between Ian's legs, his arms around her. Turning to face him, she hugged him, resting her head on his shoulder. His strong arms, his wide chest, the rhythmic beat of his heart were so comfortable, so comforting, she closed her eyes to enjoy it.

At that moment she realized how physically and emotionally exhausted she was. It was as if she had been endowed with super energy to get this job done.

Now that it was done, her energy vanished like the ghosts.

"That settles it," she whispered sleepily. "No more cheesy blanket capes for you. I'm buying you a genuine, top-of-the-line hero's cape."

He chuckled softly. "'Bout damn time."

"You deserve so much more, for everything you do for me."

"I'd do anything for you, *Hashkeh.*" He kissed her cheek.

"I know." She knew she should get up and drag her ass to bed. But exhaustion sat so heavy on her she couldn't move, couldn't keep her eyes open another moment. She knew she shouldn't be this close to Ian, lying in his arms. But she couldn't leave the pleasurable circle of his love surrounding her.

And he did love her. The strength and truth of it was as clear as the stars in the cloudless night sky sparkling down on them. As real as the cool breeze teasing her face. As heady as the scent of the blue flowers growing across the dig site. As hot as the pulse of emotions rushing back and forth between their bodies.

Ian loved her.

And she loved him.

"*Hashkeh,* I love you." She sighed the words as peace, his arms, and their bubble wrapped her in a soft blue blanket and rocked her to sleep.

****

Ian held Breena, relishing the feel of her body in his arms, the smell of her. They had kept their distance during the day since Jack separated them and put her with Meggan. He had her for a few hours at night while they dug, time while everyone was eating, or sleeping, or doing something other than watching them to see whether they'd touch or kiss or fuck. But now that they'd found the skeleton that freed the *sonuachar*, that time would be gone. So he would be a prick and take advantage of this opportunity, which could be his last.

As much as he loved her, he wasn't sure he could take much more of wanting her but not having her. It was ripping him up inside. If she wouldn't choose him, he'd leave and go far away. Even though he was pretty sure she loved him, too, he knew she'd never choose him over her husband, over her marriage.

Then she murmured their name for each other. *Hashkeh. My treasure.* Said aloud the words he'd heard only in the thoughts she allowed him to access. *I love you.*

He smiled, his heart swelling in joy as it beat in sync inside hers. His breath rose in her lungs, hers fell in his. Her soft curves cradled his hard edges. Her soul melted into his, and they fused into one, within the blue haze surrounding them. She was his, and he hers, no matter whose ring she wore. He loved this woman, his woman in blue, and *she loved him.*

"I love you, too, *Hashkeh*. With everything I am." He brushed a soft kiss across her smiling lips, inhaled her breath into his system like a drug, then lay back in the dirt with her atop him, closed his eyes, and fell into a deep sleep where it was just them.

****

Dom woke, uneasiness sitting like a boulder on his chest. Something wasn't right. He stretched out his arm and found only a cold empty space where Sabrina's warm body should have been. She often got out of bed at night so her restlessness wouldn't disturb his sleep. But she wasn't in the caravan.

He grabbed his mobile to check the time. One in the morning. She was usually home no later than nine-thirty, and that was after her shower.

Instantly awake, he jumped out of bed, pulled on boxers and boots, and went to find her. She wasn't in the bathrooms, the showers, the mess tent, or the first aid tent. He was on his way to check Ian's caravan when he noticed a faint light coming from the dig site.

Jaysus, she's still digging?

As he ran to the trench, Meg's words pricked his mind, but he dismissed them. Sabrina loved him. Would not cheat on him. Would not hurt him.

He halted at the lip of the trench. His chest broke open, and the shattered pieces of his heart tumbled out onto the rich, freshly turned dirt.

Ian lay on the ground, Sabrina sprawled against him from crotch to chest. One of her hands curled at his heart, the other held his arm, her head tucked into his shoulder. His arms were around her, one across her back, the other curved around her ass, hands holding her tight, one leg hooked possessively around her calf. Both of them were sound asleep, contentment smoothing their faces and lifting their mouths into matching smiles.

His first reaction was to kick the traitorous fucker's arse all over the camp, but instead he jumped into the trench and kicked the sole of his boot until he awoke. The son-of-a-bitch's arms tightened around Sabrina, as if he were laying claim to her, body and soul.

****

Jerked from his sweet dream, Ian woke to Dom's

scowl. In his half-drowsy state, he felt no guilt at having Dom catch him holding his wife in his arms. He even wrapped his arms tighter around her, holding on to the blessed feel of her body against his, like a sleeper who, upon awakening, tries to stay nestled in the sweet spot on the bed to delay leaving the magical dream.

But as the haze of sleep cleared from his mind and his eyes, reality flooded in. The broken look in his best friend's eyes carved out a hunk of his conscience.

Holding Breena against him, he eased himself into a sitting position, then to a kneeling to a standing position, her in his arms the whole way up.

Dom stepped up out of the trench and held out his arms. "Give her to me."

Ian didn't speak, didn't move, just settled his gaze on Breena's sleeping form in his arms. Her beautiful face was relaxed, her soft lips curled into a smile, her eyes closed, long lashes brushing her cheeks.

He had put that contented look on her face. Not Dom.

He deserved her. Not Dom, who cared more about digging up treasure than he did about the precious treasure in his arms.

But the shitty fact was, she was Dom's wife and Dom was his best friend. It was wrong to come between them, no matter how much he wanted her or deserved her.

Letting his senses inhale her one last time, he stepped forward and handed her over to her husband. It was the hardest thing he'd ever had to do. He could have easier ripped out his own heart and handed it over.

Breena secure in his arms, Dom stared down at Ian. "We've shared women before, Ian, but I won't share this one. Sabrina is *my wife*. She's *mine*. Only mine. You can't have her. And if I ever see you with her again like you were with her just now, we are not friends, we're not even enemies…we're nothing, and I *will* kick your fucking arse, with no regrets."

Dom turned away and headed toward his caravan, taking Breena from him and leaving his heart in shreds.

****

Sabrina never woke as Dom laid her on the bed, pulled off her boots, undressed her, and covered her. He stared down at her in their bed, wanting to crawl in with her, curl around her naked body, claim it, make her his again. But she smelled like another man. Like Ian. She had laid with him in the dirt, her pussy against his prick. She had let him hold her intimately and had done the same with him. What else had they done?

The thoughts shredded what was left of his heart and sent him from their home. His mind heavy, he headed away from camp and found himself at the vehicles. He hopped up on the hood of the big black SUV, leaned back on the windshield, and stared up at the inky sky pin-poked with light. Opening his heart, he let it bleed out his grief.

His wife, his beloved, was in love with Ian, and Ian, his oldest and dearest friend, was in love with her.

Where did that leave him? Where did it leave his marriage? He meant what he told Ian. He wouldn't share Sabrina. But having said that, it occurred to him that he wasn't sure which one of them would be the man out.

Movement behind him had him dragging his hand across his wet face. Meg appeared beside him. They stared at each other in the moonlight. She had been right. She had seen what he couldn't see, what he wouldn't see, what love had blinded him to.

She didn't speak but took his hand in hers, the one with his tears staining it, and brought it to her lips, kissing them away. And he let her.

****

Ian put the cameras and tools away and headed to his caravan. He would shower and catch a few hours of sleep before getting up and starting the shooting and editing all over again.

Fuck, he was *knackered*. Not just physically. Emotionally. Mentally. He needed a change. What that change was he didn't have a clue.

No, what he needed—all he needed—was Breena. The job didn't matter or the place.

On his way up, he saw Meggan walking up the hill toward the vehicles. He followed her to the black SUV where Dom sat on the hood.

Meggan took his hand, raised it to her lips and kissed it. After a moment, Dom slid off the hood and went into her arms, her hands caressing his bare back and his head, her mouth whispering in his ear, kissing his face.

His hands stayed at his sides for a time, but then they rose and settled at her hips, then wrapped around her thin waist, his head dropping onto her shoulder.

Rage filled Ian. He walked closer, stopping a few feet from them. "You fucking *gobshite*."

Dom spun toward him in surprise, breaking from Meg's arms. When Dom saw it was him, his hands clenched into angry fists, but his face wore a mask of guilt and shame.

"You have Breena in your bed, and you're

sneaking out to be with another woman," Ian scoffed, his eyes darting to Meggan and back. "Keep that shit up, and you'll lose her."

Dom took a step forward. "Is that a threat?"

"Nah, mate. It's a fact." With a last long glare, he turned and headed to his caravan, a hard scowl on his face. *And when she leaves you, she'll come to me. I'll take her from you, with no regrets.*

****

Sabrina stretched deeply and smiled, remembering last night. What she and Ian had done had worked. No tenth century warrior slashing his sword and yelling last night, no dreams or visions, just sweet sleep. She'd miss her warrior. She'd miss working with Ian even more. There'd be absolutely no excuse for them to be together now. The only upside was that she could focus all her love and attention on Dominic, get their marriage back on track. She turned and reached for him. His side was empty and cold.

As she showered, she tried to remember how she had gotten to the trailer, into bed, out of her clothes last night. On her own? Had Ian brought her home? Had Dominic come for her? It was all a black hole.

The shower curtain slid open, and she spun around to see Dominic there. His eyes glided up and down her body before meeting her eyes. He didn't look happy. She reached behind her and turned off the shower to conserve water, and so she could hear his words.

"I wasn't hugging Meg yesterday," he said. "I grabbed her in anger because of something she said."

"What did she say?"

"Not important."

It was about her and Ian or he would have said. But

it wasn't important. Now that she and Ian had found the skeleton, she'd be spending more time making sure that whatever Meggan had said would never come to be.

"And I didn't kiss her; she kissed me. I was pushing her away when you walked in."

After a moment of searching his eyes, she thought she saw the truth. "I believe you."

He nodded and shifted back to close the curtain, but she quickly stepped forward and caught his hand.

"I missed you this morning," she said.

"I was up early."

She tugged on his hand. "Join me."

"I already showered."

When he refused to be led into the shower, she stepped out and put his hand on her breast. "Then take me to bed."

"I need to get back to work." He pulled his hand away.

"Dominic." Arms around his waist, she pressed her dripping wet body against him and dropped wet kisses on his chest. "Please, baby, don't go. I need you. I need you so much."

He looked down into her face, his lips a tight line, his eyes hard.

What the hell was he so mad about? If either of them had a reason to be mad, it was her, who had caught him hugging and kissing another woman.

He reached behind him, his hands circling her wrists, and pulled her arms from around him, then shifted back to put some space between them.

"Tonight. If you're not *busy* with Ian."

"We found her," she said with a tentative smile. "The *sonuachar*. We'll lift her tonight." She put her hands on his chest. "Then my only nighttime activity will be you."

"I'll help you lift her," he said. "Then it'll be done."

He turned and left without a goodbye, without a kiss. What had he meant about *it* being done? For some reason, she didn't think he just meant digging with Ian. She finished her shower, dressed, and went to the torture chamber that was her work.

Chapter Twenty-One

"Where are you going?" Dominic asked Sabrina as they left the tent after breakfast.

It seemed like he was always asking her that question these days—where are you going—like he wanted to be able to track her down at any moment. Or trap her in a lie.

He'd never asked her about being in Ian's arms. Ian had texted her that Dominic had found them together in the trench. But a week later and they seemed to have found a fragile peace between them where they were consciously trying to spend more time together and trying to reset their marriage to what it had been before they came here.

Although it was physically and emotionally painful, she spent little time with Ian, no alone time at all. And from what she could tell, Dominic and Meggan spent less time together, too. Their marriage was far from being back on track, but she was convinced they were going to make it.

She slipped her hand into his. "*We* are going to get a wash tag." Sundays meant laundry day, but the only launderette in town didn't have enough machines for everyone to do laundry at the same time, so each person drew a tag for one of three shifts. The number one on the tag meant morning shift, which ran from eight to noon. The facility closed for lunch from noon to one. A two meant the afternoon shift from one to five. A three was evening shift from five to nine.

"Sorry, babe," he said. "I can't go."

"You promised me," she said.

"That report and presentation I told you about is due tonight, and I'm only half done."

"I was really looking forward to us going together, grabbing a pint, having some fun."

"I know. Me, too. Next time."

Next time, next time, fucking next time. That's all she heard from him. She sighed. Not wanting to break their fragile peace, she would walk away.

"Next time," she mumbled.

He caught her hand as she left him. "If you're still here at lunchtime, come get me. We'll eat in our caravan. Just the two of us."

"Sure," she said and again tried to leave.

He drew her into his arms, and his mouth captured hers, his tongue sliding between her lips. He deepened the kiss, kissing her how he used to, when all his passion was for her. He kissed her until she responded with enthusiasm, until she had wrapped her arms around his neck and arched into him, until her little moan of surrender slid from her mouth into his. Only then did he shift back from the kiss.

"We okay?" he asked, the sex in his voice making her weak in the knees. He was trying. He never before would have given her a kiss like that out in the open where everyone could see.

"Yeah," she said with a grin. "We're okay."

He kissed her one last time, then went on to work while she joined the team to draw a tag. She couldn't wait to get back to him.

****

Sabrina silently cursed the big, black three on her tag. She couldn't spend time with Dominic now because he was working, and she would still be at the launderette by the time he finished.

She went to find Rusty. He always traded for third so he could go to the pub, which didn't open until four o'clock on Sundays.

"Did you already trade?" she asked him.

"Yep."

She sighed. "You driving?"

"Yep."

"Shotgun."

Ian joined them and draped his arm around her shoulder but immediately removed it, as if he'd remembered they shouldn't touch. "What did you get?"

She and Rusty held up their tags. "You?" she asked, although by the smile he gave her, she already knew.

He held up his tag. A big three sat in the center of the white tag.

Perfect.

A perfect storm for disaster, that is.

Dominic's jealousy would rocket to the moon when he found out she and Ian had the same shift. But to tell him would make it sound like a bigger deal than it was. Like admitting they couldn't be trusted to spend a few hours in each other's company. It wasn't like they'd be alone. At least two others would be going with them, and she could hang with them. She wouldn't allow herself to hang just with Ian.

Shit. Yeah, she would.

She asked nearly everyone in camp to trade shifts

but got no takers.

When it was time to go into town, she grabbed her laundry stuff, kissed Dominic goodbye, then went to the SUV. Ian had kicked Rusty to the back and claimed the driver's seat. Sabrina climbed in front, her stomach knotting into a tangled ball of barbed wire. Meggan was in the backseat with Rusty.

Four. It was a number that added up to trouble. Rusty would go to the pub and Meggan would ignore them, leaving Sabrina and Ian to amuse themselves. But for the first time ever, she was glad Meggan was there. Her presence would keep her and Ian from getting too close because she knew Red would report to Dominic everything they said and did.

****

The smell of soap and fabric softener hung in the air like a hot, thick scent cloud as the four of them entered the empty launderette.

Rusty dumped clothes into one washer, towels and sheets together into another, shook some soap in each, shut the doors, punched in coins, and headed for the door.

"Be back at eight-thirty," Ian told him. He raised a hand and kept going.

Meggan loaded laundry into two machines, curled up in one of the plastic chairs, and pulled out her phone. She put her earbuds in and sank into whatever was on the screen.

Ian and Sabrina each filled two machines with clothes. Sheets and towels would go last. They climbed on top of the machines, facing Meggan, a human stop sign to remind them to be careful.

"Let's go grab a pint," he said, his knee touching

hers.

"Better not. I'm down to my last bra." She didn't move her knee away.

He grinned. "I've got money. You don't need to pin your bra."

Quinn's Pub had a long history of accepting women's bras in exchange for a pint. Of course, the giver had to remove her bra in full view of the bar patrons and nail it to the knockerwall.

Grinning, she nodded toward Meggan. "If we leave her here alone, it'll piss her off, and I'm afraid she'll shred my clothes."

"How about a *mineral*?" He nodded to the soda machine in the corner.

"Nah, I'm good. I have some water in my backpack. Wanna share?"

"Sure."

Scooting to the edge of the machine, she stuck out her foot and hooked it on the strap of her backpack, then lifted her leg and grabbed the pack with her hand.

"And for your next trick?" he asked.

"You're just jealous you're not that flexible and talented."

"Yeah, that's it."

She unzipped the pack, pulled out a bottle of water, and handed it to him.

"Thanks." He uncapped it and swallowed down nearly the entire bottle.

"You're not having any?" He wiped the wet clinging to his lips with the back of his hand.

"That's my only one."

"Ah, shit, love. Why didn't you tell me?" He tried to hand it back to her, a couple of inches of water left in the bottle.

She scoffed. "You think I want your nasty backwash?"

He jumped off the machine and dug his hand into his pocket for change. "I'll buy you one."

While he was counting change, she reached inside her backpack and pulled out another bottle, cracked open the lid, and sipped. "Ahh. I'll just have this one."

His eyes flashed with humor, and he grinned. "Your only one, my ass."

She grinned back and took another sip.

"You little—"

"Don't say it," she said, pointing at him.

"—shit! Way to make me feel bad."

She giggled at his reaction.

In retaliation, he reached out and squeezed her bottle, making water geyser all over her. He laughed as she shrieked when the cold water soaked through her T-shirt and hit her skin.

Jumping off the washer, she held the material away from her body. "Oh, you are so going to get it." She advanced toward him with her bottle.

He backed up, laughing, trying to get out of range of her retaliation.

She rushed after him, slinging water at him. A long finger of water slashed on the front of his body, from neck to crotch.

"Shit, that's cold," he said, laughing.

"No shit," she said and shot after him as he zagged to get away from her.

She had him cornered, her hand on the bottle, ready to douse him, when he launched himself at her, put his hands around hers on the bottle, and squeezed. As the water shot out, she charged into him, knocking him back against the wall, water flowing over both of them. They fought for the bottle, both squeezing it until all but a few drops of water was gone, but still they held the bottle between them, laughing, struggling for it, wet bodies pressed together.

He won the battle and roared around the room in victory, pumping the bottle in his hand like a trophy, while she giggled at his antics and enjoyed the view of the wet and clinging T-shirt outlining his chest and stomach.

Shit! Was her shirt as revealing? His gaze dropped to her breasts, giving her the answer. The twin points of her nipples poked against the material outlining her breasts and the indention of her belly button.

Her body heated as his gaze caressed her. He tossed the bottle into the trashcan and stepped closer to her. She didn't step back. About a foot separated them and still he moved closer, his hands reaching for hers, hers for his. Finding them, they linked fingers, moved closer.

"Too bad there's no wet T-shirt contests going on," Meggan said. "You two would win the couples category."

Their hands unlinked as their heads whipped toward her. They had been so involved in each other, she had slipped into their blind spot. They certainly hadn't noticed the phone in her hand recording them.

Panic filled Sabrina. She knew what Meggan would do with that video. Knew she would twist it to make sure Dominic saw their actions as something other than harmless play.

Her hand touched Ian's, and in that one touch,

without a single word passing between them, she asked him to be her hero, again. And he accepted.

He walked to where Meggan sat smirking and recording and held out his hand.

She snatched the phone to her chest. "Get the feck away from me with that boner."

"Hand it over."

Ian's face and voice were hard, cold, deadly serious. Sabrina had never seen him that intense. He was going against his nature for her so that Meggan couldn't start more trouble.

Still Meggan resisted, her hands wrapped tight around the phone.

Ian moved closer. His body pressed deep into her space. Sabrina could see Meggan's unease and feel Ian's power. Ian would never hurt any woman, but he was a formidable man. Tall, muscular, strong, confident, her fierce and angry protector had a presence that couldn't be overlooked or ignored, even by a woman as tall and tough as Meggan. He would not accept any action from her but to hand over the phone.

"Ian, listen. If Dom sees the video, he'll dump her and you can have her," she whispered.

"Last chance," Ian said.

"You're a stupid, stupid fuck!" She slapped the phone into his hand.

He walked to the other side of the room with it. Sabrina didn't have to be beside him to know what he was doing. He would find the video, watch it to make sure it was the one, then delete it. Thorough man he was, he would scroll through her phone for any other incriminating photos or videos of the two of them.

Minutes later, he slipped the phone into his pocket.

"Give it back," Meggan said.

"When we get back to camp."

When she opened her mouth to say something in protest, he jumped off the machine. "If you ever record or photograph Breena or me again, I'll file a grievance against you for harassment, for creating a hostile work environment, and for unlawful recording. You'll be out on your ass with no job, and no one will lift a finger to save you this time. I'll make sure of it."

"And you know what I'll do if you do that," she said, her voice less confident than Ian's.

"And you know what I'll do. Don't test me, Meggan." He turned away from her and sat on the machine where his darks were washing.

Meggan was quiet after that, and Sabrina stayed in the chair on the other side from where Ian sat until the washers with their lights in them stopped. Her body felt like a lump of clay, but she stood and made herself move to her machine, which was right next to Ian's.

"Thank you," she whispered to him, keeping her eyes on the washer and not on him. He didn't look at her either. Didn't speak. But out of the corner of her eye, she saw him nod.

She pulled out the wet clothes and put them into the dryer. Ian did the same with his. A long, tense few minutes later, the washers with their darks stopped, too, and they put their loads in a dryer, then started their sheets and towels.

While Meggan was turned away from them, occupied with her clothes, Ian pulled the keys to the SUV out of his pocket, took Sabrina's hand, put the keys on her palm, and closed her fingers over them, keeping his hands on hers, keeping his eyes on hers.

"Go with me."

He meant to the pub, and for half a beat she considered it. Getting away from Meggan and spending time with him would be heaven. But Dominic would flip.

"It's not a good idea." She pulled her hand from his and stuffed the keys into her pocket.

Rusty walked in, a loud burp rolling from his mouth, and headed straight for his washers. He dumped his loads into the dryers, punched in some coin, and headed back out.

"Rusty, wait up. I'm going with you," Ian said.

Rusty stopped at the door, turned toward him, and waited.

Ian tucked her hair behind her ear and let his hand linger at her cheek. "I'll be back by eight."

"You better be, 'cause I'm *not* folding your laundry."

"Shrew."

"Brat."

His thumb brushed her lower lip. Shivers ran up her thighs at the soft touch and at the hungry look in his eyes. She wanted to pull him in so his mouth could brush her lower lip, too.

"C'mon, Ian, piss or get off the pot," an irritated Rusty called out, holding open the door. "I got a pint waiting for me."

Ian's hand left her face and grabbed her hand. "The lad's got a pint waiting," he said with a little grin.

"You best get off the pot then," she teased back, linking their fingers.

"Last chance."

She shook her head.

He looked at her as if he were reconsidering leaving her but then squeezed her hand, let it go, and left with Rusty.

She sat on the washer Ian had vacated, hoping it would help fill the void of his leaving. She pulled out her cell to text Dominic and to keep herself entertained, but it was dead and she hadn't brought the charger.

Meggan sat in the chair on the opposite side of the room, also without a phone. They didn't talk, but the periodic stab of Meggan's glare reminded Sabrina how much the woman despised her.

An hour later when the lights had dried, she folded hers and Ian's, putting his in the bag he'd brought for that reason. When the darks were dry, she folded hers and Ian's and put them away. When their sheets and towels were washed and dried, she folded hers and his and packed them. She restarted Rusty's dryer when one cycle didn't dry his clothes and towels. Meggan folded and packed her laundry. And the two sat. And waited. Growing angrier by the second.

The attendant came out of the back and told them he was closing and they had to leave. Sabrina stuffed Rusty's laundry into his bag, and she and Meggan loaded everything into the back of the SUV and stood beside it for ten minutes, waiting and fuming.

"Let's go," Sabrina said.

"Finally! The long walk home'll teach their sorry arses to be on time."

"We're not leaving their sorry arses. We're going to get them."

Chapter Twenty-Two

The sounds of music, laughter, and conversation and the smells of smoke, alcohol, and sweat plowed into her when they entered the pub. As her eyes adjusted to the dimness, she walked deeper into the room, Meggan at her side, and scanned the shadowed faces, looking for Ian and Rusty.

Sabrina knew the moment they'd been spied. Conversations stuttered away to nothing. Heads, one after the other, turned in their direction. Leering grins lit bloated, red faces. She had a bad feeling about this. Maybe Meggan had been right. Maybe they should have gone home without them.

"Ian McCanna," Sabrina called out soundly in the thick quiet, trying to infuse her voice with bravado she didn't possess to let the men know she was here for someone, not anyone.

A chorus of oohs and laughter rang out, as if everyone there knew Ian was in trouble.

"Yer Betties are here for yer sorry arse, McCanna." The bartender/owner she recognized as Quinn yelled before laughing along with the rest of the Sunday night patrons.

****

Ian pushed back from the bar and stared in the direction Quinn pointed. Breena and Meggan stood side by side, twin masks of fury on their faces. He grinned at the men chuckling around him and switched to full Irish. "I'm about to be fucked, lads, and not in a good way."

They roared, and a group of them nudged him forward to face the women.

His eyes feasted on his soulmate, and his breath caught fire in his lungs. Her nipples pressed against her T-shirt, bead-hard, begging him to suck them, to twirl his tongue around them. And those lips of hers. Fuck. He wanted them pressed against his mouth, then wrapped around his cock.

A sloppy smile lifted his lips, and his gaze pushed its way back to her flushed face. Her blue eyes were on fire with ire—and lust—as if she'd read his thoughts.

"Hello, *Hashkeh*." He slurred the syllables dribbling out of his mouth. "Have you come for me?"

"Meggan and I are leaving. If you and Rusty want to *ride* home rather than *walk* it, you'll get your asses in the SUV right now." The bite to her voice said she was not happy, and it prompted another round of oohs from the crowd.

"Pure fire, that one is," Quinn commented in Irish, a leering grin on his pocked, ruddy face.

Ian's eyes slid up and down her body again, and his hand shifted to his swelling cock, adjusting it. "Aye, that she is."

Breena rushed toward him with angry strides, likely to take his hand and drag him out the door. Before she could reach him, Tom O'Malley, a tall, burly farmer with a pint of stout in his hand, bumped into her. She jumped back before all of the dark brew spilled on her, but enough of it sloshed out, once again turning the front of her shirt into a wet, clinging, second skin.

"Son-of-a-bitch," she growled, and the crowd cackled.

"O'Malley. 'Ere's a towel fer the lass." Quinn tossed him a rag.

The farmer caught it one-handed and ambled forward, grinning, and eyeing her breasts. "Sorry, lass. Lemma hep ya dray awff."

She shoved him hard, away from her. "Touch me, and I'll choke you with that damn towel."

The crowd roared again at the little bit of woman giving what for to a giant. Still grinning, Tom retreated slowly, tossing the towel over his shoulder to the bar.

At that moment, Rusty stumbled next to Ian, swaying on his feet. "Nice jugs, Sabrina," he said and burped loudly.

Even in his inebriated state, Ian noticed the air had risen several degrees in heat and intensity. The odor of lust mingled with sweat, stale beer, and cheap whiskey and bloomed into a steamy, enveloping vapor that gave him a bad feeling.

"Let's go, Rusty. Now," Ian said, sure a couple dozen pairs of eyes were beaded on Breena's *nice jugs*.

Fortunately, Rusty didn't argue. He downed the beer in his glass, set it on the bar, and wobbled toward the door.

Ian took a hesitant step forward, relieved he could actually move. He hooked Breena around the waist and turned her toward the door, tucking her close to his side to show possession. He did the same with Meggan, surprised but relieved she didn't protest.

He guided them to the door as fast as he could, hoping he wouldn't trip and fall on his face, hoping someone didn't suddenly decide it was too early for the women—the only ones in the pub—to leave. Fuck-faced drunk and not at all sure he could win in a fight for their honor at the moment, he was regretting every sip he'd taken tonight. How could he protect Breena if he was twisted out of his fucking mind?

He ignored the salty advice from the men in the pub, spoken in Irish, about what he should do to the women once he got them outside, and he didn't start to feel a measure of safety until they reached the SUV.

Breena unlocked the doors with the fob and rushed to the driver's side as he climbed in on the other side, and Rusty and Meggan got in the back. Rusty passed out before closing his door, his legs hanging half out the door.

"Dammit, Rusty!" Breena jumped out, shoved in Rusty's monster feet and tree-trunks for legs, and slammed the door. Before she could climb back in, O'Malley, the farmer who had spilled his beer on her, pulled her backward, and pushed her against the rear side of the SUV.

Ian blinked a few times and tried to concentrate on what he needed to do. Only one thought filled his mind as he staggered out of the vehicle: Breena needed him.

****

"Don't leave so soon, lass. We could have some fun, me and you." The man's breath could stop a truck, and his meaty hands were quick for a drunk guy.

"Get your hands off me." Sabrina thrust her knee hard into his groin. He blocked the blow, and her knee dug into his thigh.

"McCanna's right, ye're a fiery—" Before he could finish the sentence, he was jerked away from her by the back straps of his overalls and flung to the ground.

Ian stood over the fallen man in a wicked but wobbly warrior's stance, ready to do serious injury. "Touch my woman again, and I'll fuckin' kill ya." The warning sliced out of his mouth in a deadly tone.

O'Malley, who was a good three inches taller than Ian and outweighed him by at least fifty pounds, clambered to his knees, then to his feet. He took a swing at Ian, who dodged the man's fist and came back quick and strong to land a solid jab to his nose. The big man stumbled back, dropped again, and sat there for a stunned moment, shaking his head slowly, blood flowing.

"Feck, McCanna, she not even yers to fight fer," he said and managed to stand. After taking a moment to steady himself, he staggered back toward the bar.

Ian turned to Sabrina, emotion still running high in his eyes, his body. He pulled her tight against him, buried his face in her hair, and inhaled her scent. "You okay?"

"Yes." She tried to push away from him, but he held on.

"If anything happened to you, I'd…." He raised his head, looked at her through a haze of blue, then leaned in to kiss her. She turned her head so his lips only grazed her cheek. Undeterred by her dodge, he moved those lips to her neck, ravaging her.

She tried again to push him away, but he wasn't budging. "Get in, Ian—in the back. I need Meggan up front to help me watch for the turnoff." She kept her voice low.

"*Hashkeh*, don't push me away. I need you."

She could feel his heart pounding inside hers. Feel

his head swimming. Feel the storm raging in his stomach. She knew he needed her, and she needed him, but she was too pissed to give him even a small amount of comfort. Because of him and Rusty, they wouldn't be home until after ten, and Dominic would be pissed again. Just when they'd found an easy peace between them. Shit! Shit! Shit!

"And I need to go home to Dominic," she whispered.

"No. You need to fucking come home to me," he said in a harsh whisper, his hands gripping her ass as he pressed himself into her, grinding against her. "You need me to fuck you, long, hard, and often..." He grabbed her hand and pressed it to his crotch. "With this cock." He cupped his hand over hers, squeezed her hand around him, and rubbed her hand along his rigid length. She gasped at the feel of his erection straining against his fly. It grew longer and harder as he ground himself into her hand, against her body.

Then his hand left hers and cupped her mound, his fingers finding her throbbing clit behind her jeans. "And I need to bury my face in your pussy so I can smell you in my nose and taste you in my mouth all day long."

Her heart thundered in every cell of her body at his words and his touch, silencing the voice of her conscience telling her to move away from him and cementing her in place. She wanted what he wanted...his face, his tongue, in her pussy.

"I know you want it, too. If I slid my fingers up inside your sweet pussy, you'd be wet and ready for me. You wanna fuck me as much as I wanna fuck you."

Wet? Ready? Hell, her panties were soaked with

her juices from being past ready for his cock. And she did want him, a hungry, hot, nasty wanting that obliterated every bit of common sense and decency she possessed.

Her breath hitched. Her nipples punched hard against his chest. Her pussy contracted as if it were squeezing and stroking his cock like her hand was doing. Her body trembled. Every cell in her body was focused on him and the spots where they touched. He would make her come. Again and again, until she had nothing left. And it would be the most glorious thing she'd ever felt.

"Fuck, yeah, I'll make you come. With my fingers, my tongue, my cock, until the only word you can say is my name. I'll make you feel so fucking good you won't wanna live without my cock inside you."

Both of them were breathing hard, rubbing and grinding against each other hard, their sensuous, erotic dance erecting her orgasm with every urgent scrape of his cock against her pussy, every touch of his lips against her neck, every squeeze of his hands on her ass, every ragged breath in her ear whispering her name, whispering what he wanted to do to her. If he were to touch her clit with his finger, she'd go off like a fireworks display.

At that silent admission, Ian's hands flew to the waistband of her jeans, unbuttoning them, unzipping them, and she couldn't stop him, couldn't stop that familiar, welcome blue light pulsing and swelling, not just around her but inside her. She wanted it too much. She needed it. Needed him. Ian. Ian.

His fingers were sliding inside her panties, sliding over her mound, into her hair—

The SUV horn sounded, loud in the carnal-filled air. "Let's go!" Meggan called out.

Oh, God! What the hell was she doing? Shaking with desire and shame, she shoved Ian away, the action diffusing their blue haze like a fan on smoke. Breaths rapid and short, chests heaving, they stared at each other, buzzing from head to toe with aching desire.

"Get in the back." The words stuttered from her dry mouth, and her inability to catch a full breath in her lungs made it clear she was more turned on than angry.

He blinked and swallowed, then none too steadily walked around the SUV, leaving her to button and zip her jeans with trembling hands. He was telling Meggan to get in front as Sabrina none too steadily climbed behind the wheel.

She gripped the wheel hard, trying to will her body down from the high. Releasing a deep breath, she started the vehicle and drove home, the only sounds in the vehicle Rusty's snoring and her heart pounding with shame. What would Dominic say about her dragging in late, smelling like beer, smoke, sex, and Ian? What had Meggan seen, and what would she tell him? How were they going to survive the ravages of this insane craving?

It was after ten when they arrived at camp. Before she even had the engine off, her door flew open. Dominic towered there, as volatile as a volcano.

"Where the hell have you been?" he snarled, the sharpness of his tone saying he was furious, suspicious, and scared. He grabbed her arm and hauled her out of the vehicle.

She jerked her arm from his grip. "You know perfectly well where I was."

He sniffed her. "Smells like you were at the pub."

"I was doing *our* laundry."

"It doesn't take all fucking night to do a couple loads."

Rusty was still passed out, but Ian and Meggan had climbed out and were watching the heated exchange. Sabrina wished they'd go off to their trailers and not hang around to see her and Dominic argue. Meggan would get pleasure from it. Ian would want to protect her from it.

Right on cue, Ian pushed forward, his gait still a bit wobbly but his stance steady. "Don't talk to her that way."

Dominic pointed at him. "This is between me and my wife. Stay out of it."

Her warrior charged closer, chest puffed, hands fisted, but Sabrina held out her arm to stop him. "Dominic, I know you were worried because we were late, but you're overreact—"

"When you crawl into camp this late and smelling like the pub, you don't get to say how I should react. I've been ringing you all night and couldn't get an answer from any of you. I was out of my mind thinking something had happened and was on my way into town to find you."

"My cell's dead or I would've called, but—"

"And you were having too much fun to think about finding another way to ring me?"

She glared a *fuck you* at him. "When you're ready to listen to me instead of attacking me, I'll be glad to restart this conversation." She pushed past him, marched to the back of the SUV, and opened it.

"I've been ringing all of you all night," he yelled at

Ian and Meggan. "Were your mobiles dead, too?"

"I don't owe you an explanation about why I don't answer my own fucking phone," Ian said then joined Sabrina at the back. He touched her arm, and the apology in his eyes was sincere, but it didn't help the situation.

Tearing her gaze from his, she slipped her backpack over her shoulder and pulled her laundry basket toward her. All she wanted was to shower off Ian's touch, her shame, and Dominic's angry accusations, fall into bed, and forget this entire night. She knew, however, that Dominic would not let it go once they got home. He would want a blow-by-blow report on what happened and would twist it to fit his already-decided-on scenario. God! She wasn't sure she could take another month of this.

Ian lifted her basket, intending to carry it home for her.

"Back off, Ian." Dominic stood behind them, glaring at them. "If my wife needs help, I'll give it to her."

"Do you want me to back off?" Ian asked her, his hands on the basket, his eyes on hers.

Out of spite she wanted to accept his offer of help and go with him to her trailer, giving Dominic something real to be pissed about. But that would only make things worse. "I got it. Thanks."

After a few beats of hesitation, he let go.

Dominic pushed past him to grab the basket, but she blocked him so he couldn't take it. "I got it." She handed the keys to the SUV to Ian, then turned and headed toward her trailer.

The last thing she heard was Ian's angry, "What

the fuck's the matter with you, treating her like that?"

And Dominic's equally angry, "Who the fuck said you could take *my* wife to the pub?"

She kept walking, wanting nothing more than to escape the firestorm raging at the SUV.

****

Dom couldn't remember a time he'd been this mad, this scared. When he couldn't reach Sabrina or any of the others and she wasn't home when she was supposed to be, he'd been out of his mind with worry that something bad had happened. To learn that she'd been with Ian, that she hadn't told him they'd be doing wash together, that she'd gone to the pub with him, that she hadn't called him to tell him she would be late, made him want to punch something. Ian's face for starters.

He controlled his fists but not his mouth. "Who the fuck said you could take *my* wife to the pub?"

"She didn't go to the pub," Ian said. "She stayed at the launderette with Meggan."

"She reeks of beer and smoke. The launderette serving pints and fags now?"

"The only reason I'm willing to explain anything is to help Breena, otherwise I'd just kick your ass and be done with this fucking conversation. Rusty and I went to the pub. We lost track of time. Breena and Meggan came to get us. O'Malley spilt his beer on her. I kicked his fucking ass, and we left. You want someone to blame for Breena being home late, blame me. But you owe her an apology."

He looked at Meg. "Is that what happened?"

"What the fuck?" Ian raged. "Asking *her* if I'm telling the truth? Some trust, brother."

"I used to trust you with my life. *Brother*. But since

I got here with Sabrina, you're not the friend I knew and counted on. You're not the Ian McCanna I grew up with." Dom could see Ian's shock and disappointment at the harsh, life-changing words.

"Who am I now?" he said finally, in a thick, dull tone void of emotion.

"A threat to my marriage."

Ian shook his head and scoffed. "You're the biggest threat to your marriage, you fuck. Her, too," he said, nodding toward Meg. "Don't forget I saw the two of you."

The urge to use his fists on Ian's smug face had never been so strong, but Dom kept them at his sides. "And don't you forget that I watched you practically make love to my wife in the pub," he growled. "Or that I found her on top of you in the trench. Or that you took her to your bed when I was in Dublin. You're the fucking problem in our relationship, not Meg."

"If you think that, maybe you should work harder to be a better husband. You remember what I taught you about why a woman turns to another man?"

Dom's mind called up that particular lesson: *The woman who feels underloved in the bedroom and underappreciated outside it is a sure thing. Give her the attention she's craving and her legs will open like magic.*

He grabbed Ian's T-shirt at the neck and stuck his face close to his. "Is that what you're doing? Taking advantage of mine and Sabrina's problems so you can fuck her?"

Ian grabbed Dom's wrists and yanked his hands from his shirt, then shoved him back. "That's twice." He glared at him in the darkness, eyes narrowed to glints of icy steel, his demeanor cold, deadly. "Next time you put your fucking hands on me, be prepared to go all the way."

"If you weren't drunk, I'd kick your fucking arse now," Dom said.

"Another time then." Ian grabbed his bag of laundry from the SUV and headed toward his caravan.

Dom watched him go, knowing with certainty they would have their fight, sooner or later. He turned toward Meg. "What happened tonight?"

"Help me get my laundry home, and I'll tell you."

He grabbed her bag, tossed it over his shoulder, and slammed the back of the SUV. As they headed toward her caravan, she slipped her hand into his. Something in his gut told him to let go. But he didn't. He held on. Tight. Like a lifeline.

There was no place to sit in Meg's caravan except the bed, so he sat on the edge, anxiety spiking over his skin, telling him he shouldn't be here. But he would ignore the warning because he needed to calm the hell down before he did something that destroyed his marriage.

Meg set down her laundry and went to the refrigerator and put ice cubes in two plastic cups. Then she poured a healthy amount of what smelled like whiskey into them and handed him one.

"Just water for me," he said.

"Water won't calm you down. This will."

He took it.

She smiled and touched her cup to his. "*Slainte.*" She drank deep.

He brought his cup to his lips and sipped. The amber liquid burned down his throat, leaving a familiar trail of heat he knew would soon soothe his nerves. He took another sip, a bigger sip, then curled his hands around the cup, hands between his knees, to keep from guzzling the whole thing. "So, what happened tonight?"

She sat next to him on the bed and scooted back until her back met the wall, legs crossed. "Pretty much what Ian said. He and Rusty didn't come back from the pub when they said they would. Sabrina insisted on going to get them. Some farmer named O'Malley spilt his beer on her. When we left, O'Malley followed us outside, tried to get Sabrina to hang around awhile. Ian punched him. We drove home."

"Why wasn't anyone answering their mobiles?" He settled back against the wall, too, so his back wouldn't be to her, and took another drink.

"Ian and Rusty probably couldn't hear theirs. You know how loud the pub is."

"And yours?" One more sip to bank the warmth rushing through his body, then that was it.

"Um, Ian had it."

"Why?"

"Ask Ian."

"I'm asking you." When she remained quiet, he knew he wasn't going to like what she had to say. "Tell me."

"He and Sabrina were messing around. I recorded them. He went all mental, took my mobile, deleted the video, and kept it."

He looked into his cup. Somehow he'd downed all of his drink and was feeling loose from head to toe. "Messing around how?"

"Water fight, chasing each other, laughing, touching."

Touching. He worked his mouth around the full meaning of the word. "Did she go with him to the pub?"

"No."

On its face, Meg's explanation sounded like typical Sabrina and Ian antics—playing, laughing, touching. But there was more to it this time. He felt it. His eyes rose to hers. "What is it that you want to tell me?"

She got up and grabbed the bottle. "After O'Malley left, Ian and Sabrina stayed by the side of the SUV for a long time." She refilled his cup nearly to the top. "It looked like they were…" She set the bottle back on the table. "There was moaning and grinding and kissing."

Dom's heart stopped and fell to his stomach, and he felt like he'd been kicked in the balls. Fuck. It was worse than he'd thought. Aching all over, he tossed back nearly half of the liquid fire in one gulp, needing to ease the pain running wild inside him before it ate him alive.

Finishing a third cup of whiskey would do the trick, but the aftereffects would be worse than the agony that needed healing. Ditto for going after Ian and having their fight. And he wasn't ready to go home and have it out with Sabrina. He'd end up saying something he regretted or hearing something that would make him feel a million times worse.

His gaze rose to Meg's. She could talk him out of this pit. She always calmed him. Helped him see the way forward. And afterward, he always felt better. Tonight, she'd be his cure. He'd talk it out, calm down, then go home and settle things with his wife.

"I don't know what to do, Meg," he said. "I can't lose her. I love her." Unable to stop himself, he downed the rest of his drink.

Meg took the cup from his hand and set it, and hers, next to the bottle. She sat next to him, reached out and brushed the hair from his forehead, cupped the back of his head. "I know."

Tears gathered in his eyes at the care in her touch and voice and eyes. She drew him into her arms, hugging him, holding him tight, her protective embrace soothing him.

"I'm sorry you're hurting," she whispered in his ear.

Hurting? That didn't cover it. What was the appropriate word to describe the soul-gutting feeling that resulted from his best friend trying to steal his wife, his other best friend being too wrapped up in his own new marriage to care about anything else, and his wife… He didn't know what the hell his wife was doing. Cheating on him? If not physically, then emotionally? Definitely lying about something. She loved him. He knew it. But he'd seen too much not to believe something was going on, and it had cracked open a wide gulf between them.

All he had was work. And Meg. Meg who had always been there for him, through good and bad, never asking anything of him, just giving…loyal friendship and an occasional fuck.

His stomach rolled, and his head spun with thoughts of betrayal. The whiskey wasn't helping it, but it was numbing a little of the pain in his chest. And so was Meg. Her arms warm around him. Her soothing, supportive words in his ear. Her kisses…on his head, his forehead, his cheek, his eyes. He pulled her to him, tight against him, needing comfort as his world fell apart.

Lifting his head from her shoulder, he looked into her soft hazelnut eyes to tell her how much her friendship meant to him. Before he could open his mouth to tell her, her lips touched his. That one little kiss, more a brush of an open mouth against open mouth, set afire the whiskey racing through his veins.

Heat flooded his body, and he couldn't breathe, couldn't think from the smoke in his lungs, his head, his eyes.

Those sweet lips seared to his again, and he couldn't move away, even to take in a deeper breath that might clear the haze filling his head. The familiar feel and taste of his Meggie rushed through his system, numbing his pain, replacing it with red hot need.

He was only vaguely aware that her hands had left his back and were at his crotch until he felt her unzipping and unbuttoning his jeans.

"I can make you feel good, Dom," she whispered.

Yes, she could. She always could. But…

"We shouldn't," he mumbled, the voice in the back of his brain screaming at him to stop her. But his body either hadn't heard the three-alarm warning or was simply unable to comply with it because stopping meant leaving this bubble in time where the stinging misery didn't exist.

"Everything will be okay. I promise," she continued, her voice low and comforting as her hands stroked his dick to life.

Her touch, her kisses, and the whiskey made his head spin faster. And it was so good. So soothing. He needed this. He deserved this. Deserved to crawl inside this tight, warm, safe place where anger, pain, and suspicion didn't exist. Deserved someone who wanted only him.

Rational thought left him and was replaced with the single need to grab all he could of what was being offered. He dove deep into the pool of building pleasure, his cock a penetrating, pounding, punishing tool. The only thing that mattered was getting to nirvana and stopping the pain. And he was almost there. He quickened the pace, driving harder, deeper, rougher, focusing on reaching goddamn oblivion.

The explosive detonation ripped everything from him, shattered him into a million pieces, each piece filled only with life-saving, mind-numbing pleasure.

But it faded too quickly, and he came back to himself hovering over Meg, his pants shoved to his hips. Meg still wore her shirt, and one leg was still in her shorts, the other leg bare and clenched around his back. Trickling wetness pulled his gaze to a spot between his legs, between *her* legs, to his cock, inside her, still twitching.

Ah, fuck. No! What had he done? He jerked his gaze to Meg's. Her eyes as hazy as his, breath as ragged, she grinned. Oh, God. He scrambled off her and out of bed, stuffing his wet cock into his boxers, yanking up his jeans, and fastening them with shaking hands.

Without a word, he stumbled to the door and ran out, not even bothering to close it. He raced to the showers, tore off his clothes, and stood in the cold water, trying to wash away his sin. But when he tried to dress, in the clothes that still smelled like Meg, the weight of his sin had tripled, crushing his soul.

He dropped his clothes on the bench and plunked

down beside them, the weight of his actions crashing down on him. He'd betrayed his wife. No matter what Sabrina might have done with Ian, he'd made promises, vows that were supposed to last a lifetime. And he'd broken them in a matter of seconds.

His chest burned with shame and regret. Anguish backed up in his throat, choking him. His eyes filled with tears. He'd fucked up and in the worst possible way. Oh, God, she was going to leave him.

A sob broke free, and his shoulders shook as he doubled over, hands covering his face. How the hell was he going to fix this? Why hadn't he listened when she pleaded for him to take her away? If he had, none of this would have happened. She wouldn't have done whatever she'd done with Ian, and he wouldn't have fucked Meggan.

He prayed as he sobbed, asking for a solution to save his marriage and for the strength to do it.

The solution came several long, tormented minutes later.

Confess your sins, and you will be forgiven.

That's what he'd been taught in school, that's what the Father promised in Mass. So that's what he'd do. Confess. But not to God. He didn't need God's forgiveness. He needed Sabrina's.

He dressed and stumbled home, the weight of his mistake making every step more difficult, slower, the fear that she wouldn't, couldn't, forgive him. But telling her was the only way. How could he not? And then, if she forgave him—*God, please let her forgive me*—he'd take her the hell away from this place.

Chapter Twenty-Three

Sabrina had just put the last of the laundry away when Ian whispered her name at the window. She flipped off the light, climbed on the bed, and looked out.

"You shouldn't be here, Ian."

"I crossed the line tonight, talking to you the way I did, touching you. I was drunk." He rubbed his hands over his face and into his hair. "Still fuckin' drunk," he mumbled. "That's no excuse, but…. Love, I'm sorry."

"I could have tried harder to push away from you. I…I should have. I'm sorry, too."

"Breena…" Her name slid out of his mouth on a sigh. "I may be drunk off my ass, but I remember everything I said. And I meant it. Every word. I want you. I need you."

"I want you, too. Which is why I'm telling Dominic tonight. About us. Our connection."

He stepped closer to the window, face inches from hers, and put his hands on the screen. "No. He'll take you away from me."

She put her hands on his, feeling his heat, his love, seep into her body at her fingertips, her palms, wherever their hands touched. "I have to. Tonight was the closest we've come to…" She bit her lip. "Had Meggan not honked the horn, I'd be telling Dominic I cheated on him."

"I can't be without you." He shook his head. "I can't." The end of his sentences rose in a lilt that made the words sound even more heartbreaking.

"Oh, Ian." Her heart *was* breaking. She dropped her forehead to the screen and closed her eyes when she felt his head touch hers. They remained connected for a long moment before she moved away from the window and slumped down onto the bed. "I'm sorry."

Only after he walked away did she head to the bathroom to rinse the night from her body. When she finished her shower, Dominic still wasn't home, so she answered a few emails. Checked her social media accounts for updates from friends. Scanned a few U.S. news reports. Read a few paragraphs of the latest Scarlet Cox novel. Her mind was too occupied with her coming talk with Dominic to focus on anything.

He still wasn't home when she turned everything off and crawled into bed. She lay awake in the dark, praying he wasn't with Meggan or fighting with Ian.

Minutes later, when he finally did come in, he didn't say a word. He didn't turn on the light. He didn't get undressed. He didn't get in bed. He just stood at the foot of the bed looking at her. The depth of his anger was deeper than she'd thought.

"Baby, I should have called you when I realized we were going to be so late." Her voice sounded like a thunderclap in the quiet. "I'm sorry for worrying you. If I were in your place, I'd have felt the same way. Please forgive me."

He said nothing.

"I know you're mad but don't ignore me. Let's talk this out. Settle it."

His continued silence scared her.

"Dominic?"

Needing to see his face, she sat up in bed and turned the lamp on low.

His face was awash in misery, as if he'd just learned that someone he loved had died. Unshed tears sparkled in his red eyes. He'd been crying.

She crawled across the bed to him, rose to her knees, and put her hands on his shoulders. Parts of his clothes were wet. And his hair.

"What's wrong," she demanded, her voice panicked.

"Sabrina," he managed in a broken voice. "I love you so much."

A sudden rush of fear filled her chest, and she hugged him to her, her arms around his head, and held him close, like it was her last chance. "I know."

He pulled back from her and swiped his hand across his eyes. "I'm so sorry. I didn't—"

"No, baby, I'm sorry. Sorry I worried you. I promise you, Ian and I didn't plan to do laundry together. I tried to switch with someone because I knew our being there together would make you uncomfortable. I asked everyone. No one wanted the late shift. From now on I'll—"

"Sabrina—"

"—stay away from him completely because it upsets you, and—"

"Sabrina—"

"—I want our marriage to work. I love—"

He grabbed her arms and held her away from him, making her look into his face. "Sabrina, stop! Just... Stop."

"Dominic, you're scaring me."

"I… Baby, I…"

"What? Just say it!"

He closed his eyes for a few beats before opening them on hers. "I fucked Meg."

The words that choked out of his mouth split open her chest. Her eyes and mouth flew open wide as the air in her lungs left her body. Her stomach slammed into her heart. A loud pounding beat in her ears. She felt her face go slack as blood drained from it. Inside her, a firestorm spread, scorching her. On the outside, a sheet of ice encased her, numbing her.

She hadn't heard him right.

She had misunderstood.

He hadn't just said… He didn't actually…

But the despair in his eyes said… Oh, God! He did. He fucked another woman.

"No!" The word ripped from the ball of agony swirling in her soul. "Oh, God. Dominic, no. No!"

She fell back onto the bed, hands over her eyes, tears flowing. Her body was so numb she barely felt him beside her, pulling her into his arms, curling his body around hers, holding her tight. She heard him talking but couldn't understand a single muffled word.

Then, as if her ears had popped, sounds of him pleading, of her sobbing, broke through the numbness, and she felt and saw and heard everything, the pain of it rushing at her like fists to the stomach, the chest. His touch made her want to scratch his eyes out. His scent, mixed with Meggan's, made her want to vomit.

Sabrina pushed and twisted away from him. When he wouldn't let her go, she slapped his face. Stunned, he released her, and she scrambled into the corner of the bed, back to the wall, knees to her chest, arms around her legs. She pulled herself into a tight ball.

His eyes pleading, he reached out his hand but didn't touch her. "It didn't mean a thing, and it'll never happen again. I swear it."

"Why did it happen at all?" she yelled, her heart a solid shard of ice in her chest, her voice trembling as violently as her body.

"She told me you and Ian were kissing in the pub lot. The thought of it broke me open, Sabrina." He shook his head, as if trying to clear out the visions swirling there. "She was comforting me. I just needed—she kissed me… And I…" He ran his knuckle hard over his lips.

"How could you just take *her* word for it? The woman who's been trying to come between us since we got here? Your ex-lover, who still loves you?"

"Because I know you fucking want him," he growled, his eyes wild with pain, his hands in fists in his hair. "And he wants you. I see it in the way you look at each other, touch each other, and talk to each other. It rips my fucking spine out, Sabrina."

She heard the pain in his voice, and she couldn't even comfort him by denying his accusations, but she could defend herself. "And I knew you wanted her. I just never thought you'd actually…" Her voice broke, and she covered her face with her hands. "Oh, Dominic."

"Baby, I swear if I could take it back, I would. I'd give up years of my life just to take it back."

She lowered her hands and glared at him. "But you can't. And now I can't be with you." She squeezed her eyes shut, and her head fell back, letting out another wail. "You ruined our life."

With that she scrambled up out of bed. He got up, too, and tried to pull her into his arms, but she shoved him away.

"Don't touch me. Not when your hands have been all over her. It makes me sick."

Ignoring her command, he yanked her into his arms. "I made a mistake, the worst of my life, and I'll regret it forever, but our love is strong enough to get us past this. Forgive me."

Through his entire speech, she fought to get free of his grip and finally succeeded in shoving him away. "I'll never forgive you for this." She grabbed her robe. "We're done."

The wedding ring on her left hand, the one binding the two of them together forever, caught on the sleeve of her robe as she pulled it on. It suddenly felt heavy and tight on her finger, like it no longer fit, like it didn't belong to her. Something broke inside her as she slid it off and heard the finality of the metallic clink as she set it on the table.

He caught her ringless hand as she headed to the door. "Don't go, Sabrina. I can't live without you."

"You should have thought about that before you *fucked her!*" She yelled the last two words at the top of her lungs.

She opened the door and charged down the steps. The wind bells sang a friendly greeting in the light breeze that was in complete contrast to the gazes of the teammates she smacked into. Sean and Kristin stood together, arms around each other, Kristin crying softly. Rusty looked like he'd been punched. Angus looked like he wanted to punch something. Jack looked like he'd lost his best friend. She didn't see Meggan but knew she was out there, in the dark, watching, gloating at the destruction she had caused. Others stood on the fringes, watching with similar looks of shock and sadness on their faces.

And Ian, her *Hashkeh*, her soulmate, waited at the end of the steps, waited for her. A wave of sorrow, anger, and love rushed from him to her as she met his eyes.

He stepped forward and held out his hand.

She stepped forward and took it.

Dominic caught her other hand. "Sabrina, don't go to him. It'll destroy us."

Seeing the pain in his eyes sliced her open. Leaving him would hurt him even more. But she *would* leave him because she couldn't be with a man who cheated so easily.

"You already did that." She pulled her hand away and went into Ian's embrace. His arm around her, they walked to his trailer. Halfway there her knees buckled, and he caught her up in his arms and carried her the rest of the way. He climbed the steps and went inside, closing the door on Dominic's roar.

****

Ian laid her in his bed and climbed in with her. He pulled her into his arms and scooted close, their bodies pressed tight together. "*Hashkeh,*" he whispered. "What do you need?"

Pain filled every cell in her body, even with Ian's soul mingling with hers. Even with his hands caressing her. Even with his body surrounding hers with love. What did she need? She needed Dominic not to have fucked Meggan. She needed her marriage to be strong and perfect like it was before they'd come to this cursed place. She needed to be loving Dominic in their bed, wrapped up in him, feeling his love surrounding her, filling her.

But she couldn't have any of that. Not after what he'd done.

What did she need that she could actually have?

Ian.

He could obliterate her pain. For a little while at least.

"I need you to make love to me," she said, her hand going to his boxers and rubbing his cock. "Like you said you wanted."

His hand on hers halted her caresses. "Breena, I've wanted you since the day I met you and I want you now, but tonight isn't the right time. You're hurting. If you let sorrow make this decision, you'll regret it. Tomorrow, when you go back to him, you'll be glad you didn't do what he did."

"I won't go back to him."

"Yeah, you will. Because you love him. Despite what he's done."

Tears blurred her eyes. "How could he do this, Ian?"

"He made a bad choice, but it's not the end of your marriage. Unless you want it to be."

Ian held her all night, whispering to her, caressing her, making her feel safe and comforted. As she drifted into sleep in his arms, she knew she was going to give Dominic another chance because, as Ian said, she loved him, despite what he'd done.

****

Meggan stood in the dark, watching the shocked members of her team trickle away to their caravans.

The spell she'd paid Ena to cast on Sabrina and Ian was worth every euro. Who did that bitch think she was fooling with that melodramatic scene? She'd wanted to fuck Ian from the moment she arrived. It was so obvious. How dare she try to make Dom look like the bad guy? And crush him in the process?

Earlier, when Dom had raced out of her caravan, Meggan thought that was the end for them. He was clearly guilt-stricken over what he'd done, which in itself wasn't surprising. Loyalty was his driving force, and he didn't tolerate the lack of it in anyone, but especially in himself.

What was surprising was the degree to which he was devastated by Sabrina's disloyalty and his own, his desire to go back to her despite what she and Ian had done, and the depth and strength of his love for his new wife. It had become all too clear as he'd broken down in her arms before they'd made love.

But hopefully his wife leaving him for his best friend was the last straw for Dom. No way in hell would he take her back after she fucked Ian all night long in his caravan.

That knowledge assuaged the guilt that had flooded her system for taking advantage of Dom's grief. Even though he didn't belong with Sabrina, he loved the blonde, big-boobed slut. And because he did, Meggan could almost feel the level of torture gripping him.

She could help him get over Sabrina. Her love could heal his heart and open his eyes to the fact that they were soulmates. And thanks to Sabrina and Ian's whoring ways—and Ena's spell—she had another chance, maybe her final chance, to prove it.

When the last teammate had drifted away, she

slipped into Dom's caravan. The love of her life lay on the bed, naked, one hand thrown over his eyes, the other holding a plastic cup full of—judging by the bottle on the table—whiskey. He was in a bad way if he was drinking more of the hard stuff. She could soothe the aches the whiskey couldn't reach.

He didn't speak, but his eyes held hers.

She walked toward him, slowly, stared at the man she had wanted at first sight and had wanted with a never-ending fury in the years following. Her heart sped up as a bolt of lightning shimmied up her pussy, and she about creamed her panties at the thought of what was going to happen again.

Her eyes traced a long line down his body, from his face to his feet and back up, slowly, so he could see she appreciated what she was seeing. Her gaze stilled on his cock. Even flaccid it was magnificent. Long, thick. Her pussy contracted, as if it remembered his hardness and was eager for it to fill her again.

He sat up slowly, pulled himself to his feet, and walked to the table. Grabbing the bottle of whiskey, he splashed some into his cup, swirled it over the ice, and took a deep drink.

"What do you want?" His voice was low and flat, as if saying those few words took too much effort.

She moved toward him, stopped in front of him, right against him, toe to toe, almost eye-to-eye. Just two inches shorter than Dom's six foot, Meggan always thought she fit him better than any other woman he'd been with over the years. They stood so close his cock rested on her mound. Fucking perfect.

She put her hands on his face. "Let me show you." She pulled him toward her and kissed him, her tongue slicing into his mouth, claiming him, the taste of whiskey on his tongue igniting her passion further.

He snapped his head back, away from her kiss, and dropped the drink in his hand to grab her wrists to stop her. Whiskey and ice splashed on their legs and feet. For one panicked moment, she thought he was going to kick her out. But then, the flare in his eyes shifted, and he forced her against the wall of his caravan.

They landed hard against it, making the whole tin can shake, making her teeth rattle. She forgot all about the pain when he pinned her arms above her head and rammed his dick between her legs.

"No," he said, just short of a growl. "You need to *tell* me what the fuck you want."

****

He was being too rough, and he could see the shock in her eyes—maybe even fear—but Dom didn't give a fuck about either.

"What I've always wanted," she said, her light brown eyes firmly on his despite the fear in her voice. "I want you. I want you to fuck me."

Earlier when he'd fucked her, the mistake that destroyed his life, he didn't remember much of it, but he knew he'd just taken her, fucked her hard and fast, needing a release from the torture crippling him. Having her close and eager, with him feeling so lost and alone—and in more pain than he could imagine—was a bad idea.

He looked down at her perky little breasts barely pushing out her thin tank top. So different from Sabrina's ripe fullness. The smell of Meg's musky pussy, so different from Sabrina's sweet perfume, rose up like a cloud, and he pulled the scent of her deep into his nose. He could smell her juices, which told him she was ready for him. And he could smell his cum on her, reminding him what he'd done.

"You want me to fuck you?" he asked, his voice low, mocking.

"Yes." Her eyes and smile didn't waver, and her voice was strong.

Her steadfast certainty was a godsend. She wanted him. Sabrina wanted Ian. He wanted pain relief.

Don't do this. Send her away.

Dom tried to obey the voice of reason in his head, but images that had played over and over in his mind since Sabrina disappeared behind the door of Ian's caravan wouldn't let him. Images of the two of them, naked, in bed, bodies writhing, limbs entwined, hips pumping, her calling out Ian's name as she came.

She hadn't forgiven him. He'd told her the truth, owned up to his mistake, and she'd turned against him. As if she were blameless. If she really wanted their marriage to work, she would have stayed. Fought for it. She didn't love him, or she wouldn't have gone to Ian. It's what she wanted all along. To be with Ian. She was probably fucking him right now.

Something inside him broke. Red-hot flames of rage consumed his soul, leaving him with a single desire to destroy, to punish, to hurt.

He smashed his mouth down onto Meg's. His scruff probably stung her face, his teeth hurt her lips, but he let the punishing kiss go on until he felt her struggle for air. He claimed her eyes then, stared at her so fiercely she couldn't even blink. His face was in hers. Tight. It was critical that she hear and understand what he had to say.

"I'll fuck you. All fucking day and night, if you can bear it. But get this straight: The *only* thing I want from you, the *only* thing you'll get from me, is sex. If you can't deal with that, then you need to leave."

Her eyes grew hard, but her chin lifted slightly.

When he looked into Sabrina's pale blue eyes, he saw love. His future. The world and all its possibilities waiting for him to take. The woman in front of him had only lust in her eyes. At the moment, that worked for him because it was all he had left. Sabrina didn't want him.

His stomach rolled, and he forced himself to stay upright and not collapse under the despair.

"I can deal," Meg said. "Now, shut up and fuck me."

Why the fuck not?

In one rough yank, Dominic ripped Meg's tank top from her lean body. He sucked one of her breasts completely into his mouth, using his tongue to spiral at the nipple to make it stand up in his mouth. He tasted her sweat on his tongue. While he brushed his face across her skin on the way to its twin and sucked it into his mouth, his hands fell to her shorts. Unbuttoned and unzipped, they fell to the floor. He thrust one hand into her panties and slid two fingers inside the slick heat of her pussy, biting her nipple simultaneously.

She yelped and pushed him away. Part of him hoped his roughness would scare her away, make this decision easier. But in one quick motion, she pulled her panties off and dropped to her knees. Grabbing his flaccid cock, she sucked it like he'd sucked her tits.

One hand braced on the wall to steady himself, he put the other to the back of her head, gripped her hair, and held her sucking, stroking mouth to his growing cock. He kept his eyes open and on her mouth so he wouldn't see Sabrina's face. He shoved his hips toward that mouth, fucked her hard, her lips tight on him, taking him deep, wrapping around him like her pussy lips had earlier. He thought about blowing his cum down her throat, making her swallow him. But if this act was going to settle his despair, it had to last longer than that.

He pulled his rigid dick from her mouth with a slurping pop, yanked her to her feet, and drove her back onto the bed. He spread her legs and used his arms to open her wide as he fell upon her, his mouth feasting on her pussy.

Her groan was a mix of surprise, pain, and pleasure, but she held his head tight between her legs, fingers clenched in his hair, keeping his mouth against her pulsing center, squirming with the need raging inside her body.

His tongue delved deep inside her pussy, then rolled over her hard clit. Her body arched against his mouth, wanting, needing him to make her come, which he hadn't done earlier.

With every rough scrape of his beard, every flick of his tongue, every nip of his teeth on her sensitive flesh, he was sending her higher, where she would find her pleasure. She was close already. He could feel it, smell it. He had fucked her enough to read her signals, her smells, her moves, her sounds that told him so.

"Dom!" she ground out, her hands pressing his mouth so close to her pussy he thought he was going to pass out from lack of oxygen. Her hips arched hard and high, and she tensed and released a groan the whole camp likely heard. He tasted her pleasure in his mouth, and he drank her until she calmed, her tremors rolling one into another.

He rose from between her legs, his mouth and chin wet with her cum. He grabbed a condom from the bedside table, ripped it open, and rolled it on. Climbing on top of her, he centered his cock over her dripping and still throbbing cunt and plunged into her, full hilt. She was tight but slick and deep.

She cried out, low and long as his cock entered her. With one hand, he grabbed a handful of her hair and gripped it as he thrust in and out, fast and hard. She bucked against his assault, digging her nails into his arse so hard he was sure they'd leave bloody tracks.

"You like me fucking your pussy?"

She groaned.

"Tell me, bitch. Tell me how much you want my cock."

"I want you, Dom. I've always… Ah…I'm coming again!"

And come she did, her gripping pussy milking him, pulling his cum up from his rock-solid balls until he could hold back no longer. Grunting like an animal, he jammed his cock all the way in and exploded at the top of her clenching sheath, enjoying a temporary release from his shit life.

He closed his eyes and forgot everything but the sensations gripping his body. The whispered name on his lips wasn't Meggan's. The face floating before his closed eyes wasn't hers. But when he opened his eyes, it was her body his was connected to.

His dick spent, he pulled out of her, stumbled into the bathroom, and threw the condom into the trash.

"Oh, God," she said, still reveling in her orgasms, gasping to catch her breath. "No one's better than you."

He said nothing as she rambled on about his ability. He was too caught up in a trap in his mind to feel pride about his performance.

Twice he'd had sex with a woman who wasn't his beloved wife. And he felt like the biggest asshole ever born and allowed to live.

He'd taken out his grief and anger on Meg, his friend. He'd simply fucked her tonight, hard and rough, had been crude and nasty, which was in complete opposition to the caring sex they'd enjoyed in the past. She hadn't complained or stopped him and had obviously enjoyed it.

But the act provided a hollow release for him. It had done nothing to erase the pain tormenting him, like he'd hoped it would.

Fuck, he needed another drink. The numbing layer of alcohol haze was growing thin and lacy, allowing memories to seep through, allowing guilt to claw at him, opening the fresh wound in his heart Sabrina had inflicted when she left him. He loved his wife. He wanted only her. How could he be with another woman? Especially Meggan. Sabrina despised her.

Sabrina left you for Ian.

He tossed back another tumbler full of whiskey.

To fuck Ian.

He was in his caravan, his cock in Sabrina's pussy. She was screaming Ian's name when he made her come.

Dom fisted his cock in his hand at the vision.

Why shouldn't you enjoy Meg's cunt? Your wife doesn't want you. She's fucking your best friend. She's gone. Not coming back. Are you supposed to live like a monk for the rest of your life? What's stopping you from fucking every woman who asks for it? She's…goddammit, she's fucking Ian.

Anger shoved aside his thoughts of Sabrina. Most of them anyway. He rolled on another condom, flipped Meg over, yanked her ass into the air, and found a wet place to dock his cock.

They tried every position he knew—thanks to Ian's and Sabrina's teachings there were quite a few—until the wee hours of the morning. When she moaned that she had nothing left and begged for sleep, he left her alone.

And there, on the bed he'd christened and shared so many sacred moments with the woman he loved more than life, he slept the sleep of the damned with another woman.

****

Ian's phone alarm went off at four-fifty a.m. for their five a.m. run. He reached over to shut it off, then settled back around Sabrina and kissed her shoulder.

His embrace through the night had kept her together, kept her from shattering. But in the harsh light of the morning after, she wasn't sure anything could keep her together if Dominic wouldn't take her back.

"Ian…if Dominic doesn't want me back—"

"He wants you."

"He might not, because I went with you…"

"Go to him, and take my duffle with you. If you don't like what he has to say, pack your stuff and come home to me."

A half an hour later, wearing the robe she'd slept in, she rushed to Dominic's trailer, Ian's duffle in her hand, a thin smile on her face, her plan set firmly in her mind. She'd slip off her robe and crawl into bed with her husband, and they'd hold each other, cry together, talk it out, fight it out, make love, then take the first of many steps that would get them past their many mistakes.

One of those steps would be to leave this place. Today. Even if it cost them their jobs. Better their jobs than their marriage. It would be devastating to leave Ian, but it was the only way to save her marriage.

She opened the door to a chorus of grunting and panting and squeaking. Dominic and skank were in bed, him on top, his weight on his straight arms, furiously pounding his cock into her pussy. The musky smell of cum hung thick in the air, like they'd had an all-night marathon.

Tears flooded her eyes, and her trembling hand flew to her mouth to stop from crying out loud at the pain. It was last night all over again but even more heartbreaking, seeing them in the act, hearing the sounds of their fucking, the sounds she knew so well coming from him while he was inside someone else.

Jealousy fired through her. For the first time in her life, she fully understood crimes of passion. She wanted to skewer both of them to the bed.

Was he enjoying Meggan's cunt? It sounded like it. Sounded like he was close to coming. His grunts were sharp and close together, and his thrusts were, too. They weren't kissing. He wasn't caressing her. He wasn't looking *her* in the eyes like he'd always done with her. He was fucking. And enjoying the hell out of it.

The bitch beneath him had her legs spread wide, knees up, almost around his shoulders, giving him all of her, her eyes closed tight in concentration. Her fingers gripped his back, and she was making little squeaky noises that said she wasn't getting enough air. Breathless. Yes. That's how he'd always made her feel, too.

Sabrina almost turned around and left but decided the hell with that. She needed her things, and she wasn't going to wait another second to get them and get out for good, so she'd never have to step foot in this trailer again. Going to the dresser, she one by one pulled out the drawers and stuffed her clothes into Ian's duffle.

Dominic's head snapped toward her, and he choked out her name. He quickly rolled off Meggan, sat up in bed, and pulled the sheet over them.

Meggan squeaked a rough "no!" that suggested she had just missed her climax.

Ah. Too fucking bad, bitch.

No one spoke, the only sound their breathing and the opening and closing of the drawers.

Without a glance, she rushed past them to the bathroom, duffle in hand, and packed her toiletries, then went to the bedside table, where her laptop, cell, personal papers, and wallet were, and added them to the duffle. She hadn't planned to say anything, but she couldn't help herself.

She stopped in front of Dominic, close enough to smell the cum clinging to his skin. His and Meggan's. The stale odor of whiskey oozing from their pores. Meggan's sex sweat on his slick skin. She set the duffle down.

He met her eyes. How did he feel staring into the eyes of his heartbroken wife as his well-fucked lover lay beside him on their bed?

She took hold of the sheet and yanked it off them. Meggan squawked and hugged Sabrina's pillow to her body to cover herself. Dominic didn't bother covering himself, his half-stiff cock still encased in the condom. Her eyes rose from it to lock on his eyes again.

"You said fucking her was the biggest mistake of your life, that it meant nothing, that you'd never do it again."

His cheeks flushed. "Sabrina..." Her name slid from his mouth on a breath.

"I believed you, Dominic. I believed, despite your *mistake*, that we could get past it because we love each other. I came here this morning to work things out so we could hold on to our marriage."

He dropped his head into his hands, and a soft fuck rolled from his lips.

"Look at me," she demanded.

His red-eyed gaze crawled to her face, his tongue snaking across his lips.

"Ian and I didn't fuck last night. We won't make that mistake tonight."

Wide-eyed, he blinked a few times, processing her meaning, his lips parting in pained surprise. The last bit of light in his eyes died, and a strangled groan caught in his throat. She could almost hear his heart thud to a stop.

Stone-faced, heart pounding, she grabbed the duffle and on shaky legs left the trailer. Her last action was to unhook her wind bells from her old home and take them to her new one.

Ian was outside, affixing a hook to his trailer for her wind bells. Like he knew. He took them from her and hung them up, then pulled her into his arms. "Go get changed for our run."

She nodded numbly but couldn't make her legs move. Her hero swung her up in his arms, carried her into her new life, and shut the door on her old one.

Chapter Twenty-Four

All through their run, her mind replayed the scenes from the night before and that morning. Of Dominic telling her he'd fucked Meggan. Of him begging her forgiveness. Of him fucking Meggan in his bed.

How could they come back from this? They couldn't. Their marriage was over. Well and truly over. Dominic wasn't hers anymore. The thoughts, like a witch's brew of poison, seized her mind, her heart, her lungs, her stomach, her soul, then her body. She dropped out of her run and bent over, hands on her thighs, trying to breathe through the pain gripping her.

Ian stopped when she did and was at her side, hand at her back. "*Hashkeh.*"

Tears rolling unchecked down her face, she dropped to her knees. He dropped to his and pulled her into his arms. She clutched him to her and clung to him. He lay back in the field of blue flowers, her on top of him, and held her tight, absorbed her tears, kissed her face, calmed her with soothing love sounds at her ear until she was cried out.

"She was in there, Ian," she said after a long moment, her voice amazingly calm to her ears. "He was fucking her in our bed."

He caught her hand in his and kissed it.

"He said it was the worst mistake of his life and would never happen again, but I was barely out the door before he moved her in. I never thought he'd do this to me. To us."

"I know you don't want to hear this, but it was just sex. It doesn't mean he doesn't love you. I'm sure he thought you and I were doing the same thing. People do stupid things when they're hurting."

"There were times I wanted to rip your clothes off and fuck you in the dirt just to stop hurting, but I didn't because of Dominic. All it took for him to fuck her was her telling him you and I were kissing. Without even checking with me to see if it was true or asking what happened, he fucked her, just to make himself feel better."

He grinned.

"What's so damn funny?" she asked, shooting him a look and scrambling to her feet.

He rose, too. "You wanted to fuck me in the dirt?"

"Asshole," she muttered, looking away so he couldn't see her hot face.

He caught her by the chin and turned her face to his, then dipped his head so she would meet his eyes. "I wanted the same thing."

She dropped the top of her head against his chest. He put his arms around her, and she sank into his embrace. "Last chance, McCanna."

He caressed her head, then kissed it. "For?"

She lifted her head to look at him. "To kick me out of your trailer and your life and save yourself from the shitty mess that's about to hit the fan."

"Kick you out? Now that wouldn't be very heroic."

Wrapping her arms around his waist, she smiled. "Always my hero."

"Fuckin' A, love."

****

Back at camp, they grabbed their toiletries and went to the showers. As she washed, she pictured the water flowing down Ian's body in the stall next to her, and her body began to buzz with the message that she was in the wrong place.

She rinsed and turned off her shower. Grabbing her stuff, she went into his stall and set her stuff down on the little bench outside it. She thought about pulling back the curtain and just going in, surprising him, but didn't want to catch him in the middle of anything.

"Ian?"

The shower curtain opened, and he looked out. His eyes lit up as they flit across her body.

Can I join you? Please don't say no.

She hadn't spoken aloud. But she didn't need to. He'd heard her request. He slid the curtain back all the way, welcoming her into the shower and into his life.

Her heart raced. His body was magnificent. Better than she'd even imagined. And now she could have him, like she'd always wanted. But first she had to take that first step—that step into the shower. Once she crossed that line, she couldn't go back, wouldn't go back. Was she ready for what that would mean? Was she sure Dominic was no longer hers?

Images of him fucking Meggan pushed her forward. She needed Ian's comfort now, more than ever before. But it wasn't only his comfort she was after. She also wanted to test the theory that making love to him would unite their souls.

Holding his eyes with hers, she stepped into the shower and closed the curtain. Slowly, she stepped into him and ran her hands up his chest as his hands took her low on her hips.

She cupped his face and went up on her toes. This was the thing she'd wanted since they'd met—his mouth on hers. Without another thought, she moved closer and touched her lips to his.

At the first tingling touch, they both jerked a breath into their lungs, their eyes flying open, like it was the very first kiss of their lives—shocking, delicious, orgasmic, filled with the heart-pounding excitement of all daredevil actions. She thought back to what he'd said about the ancients believing that the spirit was carried on the breath and that a kiss between soulmates was enough to reunite their souls forever. Sabrina believed it now.

Everything inside them saying *this is right*, they merged into each other. Mouth feasted on mouth, tongue swirled with tongue, breaths and moans were swallowed whole. Their first mouth-to-mouth kiss caused something inside her to unfurl and expand, to open up to him more than she'd ever done. His soul entered her and filled all her empty, hurting spaces. It was good, but not enough. Would never be enough until he was locked inside her.

Their bodies were ready, his already hard cock jutting at her pussy, begging to come home. They were so ready for each other, had wanted this for so long. They'd come after a few lightning quick thrusts. But she didn't want to rush. This was a precious moment that deserved the time and attention to make it last.

They stood together, embracing, clinging, trying to breathe. Then she left his arms, grabbed his soap, handed him hers, and silently they washed each other, slowly, thoroughly, touching, caressing, getting to know every inch of each other's bodies. She soaped up his arms and his chest, her hands gliding across skin, muscles, a sprinkling of hair. He soaped her arms and breasts, making her nipples hard with the pleasure of his touch. She soaped his stomach and the thin line of hair that trailed downward from his belly button.

He soaped down, then up her legs. She soaped his back, his ass, and he did the same for her. She soaped the long and throbbing cock that jutted from between his legs, the tight balls that tucked close to his body. He soaped the heat between her legs, from her mound to her ass.

Her heart was racing, his thundering alongside hers. The feel of his hands on her had stolen all ability for her to do much else but breathe. And that was labored.

Their bodies thoroughly washed and rinsed, he gripped her ass with one hand, her head with the other, and held her tight to him as his mouth got to know her mouth, her face, her neck, her shoulders, her chest, slowly, relishing every taste. He kissed her breasts and licked her nipples, twirling his tongue around them, sucking them, making them harder with every wet movement, making her moan.

Before she could fathom what he was doing, he knelt before her, his lips never leaving her body, and kissed and licked down her stomach, teased the tip of his tongue in her belly button until she shivered in pleasure. Encouraged, he ran his tongue lower, tasting her clean, wet skin, going lower until his hot mouth had made its way to the top of her mound. There he breathed into her blonde puff.

Her body electrified at the touch of his mouth, his

tongue, on her, at what she knew he had in mind to do with that mouth and tongue. Powerless to stop him—not wanting to stop him—her hands went to his head, her fingers in his hair, not to hold him back, but to hold him closer, to give him her silent permission. God, she wanted his lips and tongue on her pussy, licking it, tasting it, kissing it, sucking it.

He groaned, pressed his mouth into her wetness, and her breath shuddered out of her mouth, erratic and shallow, at the feelings he was bringing to life. Her head fell back on a gasp as she held on to him for dear life.

He lifted her leg, setting it over his shoulder, the stance opening her wide to his feasting mouth, and his lips and tongue moved over her turgid flesh in a mind-blowing pattern. He sucked her into his mouth, first her slick lips, then her clit. He licked the entrance of her wet cunt and back to her clit, taking time to flick the stem of nerves until it stood in a tight erection before circling it in the infinity pattern she loved. Then he jabbed his tongue deep inside her again, stroking her, lapping her juices and creating more. And he repeated the move, over and over, again and again, until she was as high as she could go without breathing.

She held his head close, her pussy against his mouth, feeling every bit of him pulsing at that spot between her legs. Her whole body tensed, and she came hard, releasing a long, low groan, his name riding the breaths that squeezed from her tight throat.

Still coming, still moaning, she gulped breaths of air as he helped her ride out the pleasure. His hands gripping her ass firmly was the only thing holding her upright. She loosened her hands fisted in his hair, leaned over him, shuddering, and wrapped her arms around his head, kissing it.

When she could stand without falling, she lowered her leg from his shoulder. He stood, too, and her sleepy eyes went to his. She kissed him, tasting herself, her cum, the pleasure he'd given her. She would give him the same.

Ian couldn't believe he was naked with Breena in the shower, with her hands on him, with the feel of her kisses on his lips, the taste of her cum in his mouth, with the knowledge they were about to get a lot more intimate. It was almost enough to make him come right then.

To make sure this wasn't a dream, he kept his eyes on her. She was so fucking sexy and beautiful it took his breath away. The hot water beat down over the strong, toned, curvy body he'd seen every night in his dreams, the steam turning her cheeks pink, making her lips and nipples wet and plump. The sight of her, the scent of her, the feel of her sent a strong thrust of desire and possession plowing through him, but he kept his hands lightly at her hips, letting her drive this. He didn't want to scare her away from this perfect moment by chasing his own urgency.

She kissed his mouth, bit his lips, sucked his tongue deep into her mouth, showing him how she would suck other parts of him.

He closed his eyes in ecstasy when she kissed down his neck, his chest, his nipples, his stomach, then popped them open again to see what she would do with the hard, wet cock twitching in her face. His legs went weak when she dropped to her knees in front of him, her hands gripping his ass like he'd done hers. She kissed up his inner thighs, took time to gently and thoroughly lick and suck his balls, then she buried her face in his crotch and breathed him in. Pulling back slightly, her mouth poised at the head of his cock, she looked up at him and smiled.

Fuck! She was really going to—

And then she did.

Pleasure rifled through him, and he groaned and shuddered her name when she licked the head of his cock, swirled her tongue around it, getting to know the taste of him. Suddenly, as if the one taste had ramped up her hunger, she enveloped him in her sweet, red mouth. Her lips tightened around his swollen flesh and alternately pulled back and slid forward, sucking, her tongue licking around and around his head and up and down his shaft, again and again, until he gulped air into his lungs, growled low, and tried not to pump his hips against her.

Her sexy blue eyes looked up at him, wanting to see the affect her loving had on him. Seeing her desire for him in those eyes, he almost lost it. He shifted back, out of her mouth, tried to drag her up to him, but she pulled him back to her. Into her hungry mouth. God, she wanted him. Wanted to taste him, eat him, swallow him. As much as he wanted her. And it was the hottest fucking thing he'd ever experienced.

His hands went to her head, and he caressed her, held her hair back in one hand so he could watch her mouth on him. As much as he wanted to come with her lips around him, feel her swallowing him whole, he wanted to be touching her, making her cum, even more.

He pulled out of her mouth again and quickly lifted her to her feet. Holding her to him, he kissed her deep and eased two fingers inside her slick, tight channel, using his thumb to rub her clit into a tight peak of pleasure. Their lips locked, she clung to him with one leg up around him, one arm around his neck, her hand rhythmically stroking his throbbing cock.

Her pussy tightened around his fingers, clenched them as her muscles seized and she came, harder than before. She called out his name in a low shuddering moan that set off a series of quakes inside him until he came, too, shooting ropes of hot cum across her stomach, her breasts.

He gave her all of him in that moment—his cum, his last breath, his love—and took all of her. Pressing their still-shaking bodies tight, trying to breathe, they lost themselves in the steamy cloud of peace swirling around them.

He loved this woman with everything he was. Holding her, skin to skin, heart to heart, mouth to mouth, soul to soul was a treasure he'd never felt with anyone. At this second, this was the best moment of his life, his one perfect moment. But he knew that would change. Because as soon as he could breathe, and walk, he'd take her to his bed and show her so much love she'd never want to leave him.

****

They rushed to their trailer and into bed. They lay on their sides, facing each other, legs entwined, touching, kissing.

"I've dreamed of this," he whispered, brushing his mouth against hers.

"Then we've been having the same dream," she said.

Desire swelled inside her as he kissed her, and she

shivered at the exquisite power of it. Colors and lights and feelings burst inside her body as her hands slid over his hard body, wanting—needing—to touch him, all of him, everywhere, again and again. She had wanted this for so long. His heat singed the skin of her fingertips as she caressed him. She took his cock in her hands, stroked it, pinched the head, swirled her thumb around the wet slit.

"I want you, Ian. All of you. In every way possible."

They kissed, hard and wet, deep and slow, with open mouths, hands exploring, caressing, pleasing. His tongue probed and twined with hers. Their mouths fused together into one soul-sharing breath. Showers of pleasure rained down on her as his lips moved to her breast and sucked her nipple into his mouth, rolling his tongue over it, then moved to the other.

They murmured their pleasure but didn't talk. They didn't need words in their world, where it was just the two of them, where they knew what the other was thinking and feeling and wanting, where they talked in touches, listened in looks. Ian, her soulmate, her *Hashkeh*, knew what she wanted, body and soul, and was the only one who could give it to her with such ease and precision.

She let him go when he kissed down her stomach, and she laid back and luxuriated in the joy of his attention. He tongued her bellybutton, kissed across the curve of her lower stomach, nuzzled the soft puff at her mound, licked the juice wetting her swollen outer lips. She opened her legs wider to him, wanting to give him all of her, wanting to take all of him.

He teased between her folds with his tongue, then

parted them gently with his fingers to expose the tiny extended head. His tongue circled her clit in an infinity shape that felt so familiar and so right, making it harder, sucking on it.

She cried out at the blinding pleasure, her hands going to his head and holding him there, her fingers clenched in his wet hair. He was good with his mouth. So good.

His top lip feasted on her clit and his tongue loved her deep, pulling the climax from her body in a few short minutes. She arched into his mouth and cried out, the breath hitching out of her lungs as she came, his tongue lapping her juice. Soon his lips softened against her, her body shaking to the core from the pleasure throbbing through her.

Kissing and licking his way back up to her breasts, one hand riding her mound, he plunged a finger inside her still-throbbing pussy and rocked it in and out of her wetness, the tip of his thumb brushing across her sensitive clit in a steady pattern. He sucked her nipples, first one then the other, licking them, nipping them. His mouth devoured hers until she was flying high again, the need building faster. So quickly.

She grabbed his cock and stroked it, imagining it was inside her, filling her, instead of his finger. She pressed up against his hand as the wave hit again, sweeping her so far away she couldn't even groan her pleasure, only tremble and jerk. She wanted more. Wanted him. And he knew it.

He rose over her. Keeping her gaze locked on his, she guided his cock into place at her slick entrance, and he slid into her body for the first time.

"*Aaaahhhashkeh.*" The words combined as one

long sound, she sighed it deep in her throat, almost in shock at the pleasure of their full joining, her breath rising up out of her, her hips rising against him, her hands clenching his flesh, wanting to feel it all. Her eyes rolled back in her head at the fit they'd found with each other. She smiled, knowing she'd been here before with him, knowing how good it was going to be.

"Look at me, Breena."

Her eyes opened a crack, met his, and in that moment, she understood. The blue haze connecting them was their love for each other, the substance that allowed their souls to twine in love. She had never felt so connected to another person. Never felt so swaddled in love and pleasure. She never wanted it to end. Never wanted to come down from this exquisite high.

"I want you to see the face of the man who's making love to you, who's making you come."

"I see *you*, Ian. I feel *you*. I want *you*."

He rocked into her, slowly, fully, stimulating every nerve inside her. When the head of his cock reached the depth of her, he pushed a little farther, making her bow up, making her legs go wider, her hips rise higher, to meet his thrust, then he dragged out slowly. Then he did it all again, in ecstatic slowness that drove her mad. Mini orgasms rocked her body, but the one building between them made her hang on to him with everything she had. It would blow them both away when they came.

He raised one of her legs and put it over his shoulder, opening space for him to plunge deeper and to tease her clit with his fingers at the same time. His thrusts became faster, and she felt his cock swelling.

They stared at each other through their simmering

blue haze, their labored breaths passing like sparks between their all-but-joined lips.

The blue light at the center of the coming climax pulsed as it came closer, Ian's thick rod hitting it every stroke, making it flash and expand. His last stroke broke through it, and it exploded like a star inside her, making her insides seize and quake and heat with pleasure.

Her head dropped back, her mouth open, her throat arched in a silent cry before a wild groan broke through, followed by his name, again and again, turning into a long, low moan. This was the first orgasm that had left her shattered and struggling to pull the scattered pieces of her soul back together.

At the height of her release, Ian found his. His groan joining hers, he clenched her tighter, thrust harder, pulling more from her than she thought she had in her to give.

"Ah, *Hashkeh*. I love you," he said in a long, low growl as he bathed her pussy with his hot, healing love.

After one last deep push, he stilled, his breath ragged in his heaving chest, his body trembling with the power of their union. He kissed her mouth tenderly, lovingly. Kissed her eyes. Her forehead. Her mouth again. It was such a sweet moment between them. He had taken her to the stars, where she felt nothing but pleasure.

They had breathed life into the thing they had inched and scratched toward from the second they laid eyes on each other. It was more than she had thought it would be. More pleasurable, more healing, more right, giving her the full, intimate connection she'd always wanted and needed with a lover. For the first time in her life, the emptiness inside her was filled. With the other half of her soul. With Ian.

They stared into each other's eyes, neither speaking, not wanting to scatter the euphoric haze surrounding them. Wrapped fully in the warmth of each other's bodies, they melted into each other, all but absorbed each other, reveling in and shaken by the miracle that for the first time in this life, they were whole.

They spent hours trying positions she'd never tried before. He touched her in places she'd never been touched before, and she touched him in ways she'd never touched anyone. There wasn't a spot on his body she hadn't touched or kissed or licked, and he hers. He made her come, again and again, more than she thought her body knew how. Hours passed before they fell into a light sleep, exhausted, in each other's arms.

****

"Kelly, I assigned you to Rusty's trench," Sean said to the student shooting video in Angus' trench. She left the camera running and turned to face him.

"Well, I was, but…" She glanced at Angus, who pulled himself up from a kneeling position in the three-foot-deep trench.

"I needed a media person here," he said. "I've got sherds and stycas coming up."

Sean nodded. "Ian was going to cover it."

"Yeah, well, I haven't seen him all fucking morning." Angus went back to work.

"So, what do you want me to do?" Kelly asked.

His eyes scanned the dig site. The other media student, Dylan, was in T520. Without Ian on media, they needed at least two other students. "Stay here for now."

He left the trench and went to finds, his mind worrying over why Ian hadn't shown up for work or called. It wasn't like him. Likely Sabrina could shed some light on his odd behavior. He'd ask her to take on some media tasks in Ian's absence.

He poked his head into the doorway of finds and looked around for Sabrina. She wasn't there. Meggan saw him, and he motioned her over. She joined him outside, away from the ears of the students labeling the bones.

"Where's Sabrina?" he asked.

"She didn't show up."

"Ian didn't either."

"Check his caravan," she snarked.

"I need two of your students to act as media until I can find Ian."

"I need all my students, Sean."

He was in no mood to argue. "Send one to Rusty with a videocam, and the other with a camera to Angus."

"Fine," she said and stormed back inside.

He headed to Ian's caravan, somehow knowing he was there with Sabrina. He knocked on the door. Receiving no response, he knocked again and called out Ian's name. Two unanswered knocks and calls later, he opened the door.

"I'm coming in," he warned and stepped inside.

It smelled like the sun had leached the scent from a field of flowers and the wind had blown it into Ian's caravan for safekeeping.

Sabrina and Ian were in bed, naked and sweaty and tangled, enclosed in a shimmering blue haze. She was sprawled on top of him, arms around him, head on his chest, her sex against his. His arms were around her, one hand slowly brushing along the curve of her ass, one at her head, fingers lazily teasing her wet, messy hair. It almost looked like they had melted into each other.

So they had done it. Made love. He was surprised. Though Dom had cheated on Sabrina, he never thought Ian would take Dom's wife, no matter his feelings for her. There might be no coming back from this betrayal.

"Ian, you're needed at the dig," he said.

Ian didn't move, didn't turn his head to look at him, didn't open his eyes. Neither did Sabrina. If his hands weren't moving, he'd think they were dead.

"Ian." He reached out to shake Ian out of whatever euphoric stupor he was in, but the second his finger penetrated the blue fog, a low-volt of electricity shimmied up his hand to his arm. He jerked back his hand.

"We're taking a day off," Ian murmured, his voice calm, peaceful, low, as if he were riding a solid buzz. He spoke as if it were a chore and the words were getting caught on his tongue.

If he didn't know Ian as well as he did, he'd swear he was high. Maybe he was. High on Sabrina. Or maybe that odd blue fog surrounding them had fried his brain.

Taking a final look at the tangled couple, he left the caravan and headed back to the field. He'd tell Kristin about the blue fog tonight, have her ask her mother to dig into her little bag of magic and figure out what it was and how to combat it.

Until then, he would be extra careful not to allow

whatever curse was happening at this dig to touch his and Kristin's marriage. He'd pack them up and leave before he let their marriage be put at risk.

These last few weeks were going to be painful and drastically life-changing.

****

The tension in the mess tent at dinner that night when Ian and Sabrina entered was palpable and painful. The eyes staring at them were sharp. It was so quiet it was spooky.

Dominic and Meggan sat alone at a table, her rubbing his back, him glaring at Ian and Sabrina, murder in his eyes. Jack sat alone, head in his hand, staring at his plate. Rusty, Angus, and Shane sat together, eating but not joking with each other like they usually did. The students sat here and there, saying little. Sean and Kristin sat alone, too, misery in Sean's features no doubt from the blow that had fractured the Trinity.

It was like there'd been a death. In a way, there had been. Dominic and Sabrina, the loving newlywed couple. Dom and Ian, the best friends. The solid, cohesive, harmonious, well-run team. They were no more. The choices made weren't just affecting her and Dominic. They were affecting everyone.

She and Ian got their food and sat at a table far from everyone. Seeing Dominic with Meggan and knowing he was no longer hers twisted her stomach into knots. She was with Ian and was glad they'd found each other, but she still loved her husband. It was one of the hardest things in the world to see someone she loved loving someone else. She put her fork down.

"You okay?" Ian asked.

She shook her head and found his eyes. "I didn't realize it would hurt this much to see him with her."

He put his hand at the back of her head, caressing her, then leaned in and kissed her lips. He stood, took her hand, and helped her up. Every eye in the tent followed them as they left, her body curled into his.

They went into town for dinner, and when they got back, she went to see Jack. She wanted the work situation clear before morning.

Chapter Twenty-Five

Sabrina knocked on Sean and Kristin's door. Kristin answered in her robe.

"Hey, Kristin. Sorry to drop by so late."

"No, it's okay. How are you?" Kristin asked, welcoming her in with a hug.

"Um…" She couldn't get the words out, so she just moved on to why she had come. "I need to talk to Sean about work," she said, surprised by the shakiness in her voice.

"He's finishing up some paperwork." Kristin walked over to the bed, Sabrina behind her.

Sean was sitting up in bed, in just in his boxers, reading over what looked like the schedule. She remembered Dominic doing the same thing at night.

"Hey, Sabrina. Grab a chair," he said.

"I'm going to check on Ian," Kristin said, then looked at Sabrina. "Is he at home?"

Sabrina nodded and sat in the chair she'd pulled up.

Kristin kissed Sean. "I'll be right back."

As Kristin left, he put the schedule into a folder and sat up on the edge of the bed, arms resting on his knees, hands gripped between his legs. "What's on your mind?"

Sabrina started in on her rehearsed speech. "I went to Jack, but he was on a conference call, and I can't talk about this with Dominic. You're next in the chain of command, so…. Jack moved me to finds to keep Ian and me away from each other to protect my marriage. The reason to separate us no longer exists. So, I'll be working with Ian, only Ian, for the rest of the dig. Give the media students to finds if you want—Ian and I will work extra hours to get everything done."

"Sabrina—"

"I'm not asking you, Sean. This is how it has to be."

"I was going to say how sorry I am about how things turned out for you and Dom," he said. "I never thought he'd do something like that. That's not who he is." He looked at her, sadness in his eyes. "He's sick about it, would take it back in a second if he could."

"But he can't."

"Give him another chance. He's still the man you loved enough to marry. He's just a little more human now. All humans fall eventually. It's the good ones that seem to fall the hardest."

"Would you forgive Kristin if she slept with her ex-lover?"

He didn't even pause before responding. "As much as I love her… Yeah, I would."

She scoffed, suddenly outraged by his staunch support of Dominic. "I hope you're going to be as supportive of Ian, your *other* best friend, through all this, because he's the innocent party."

"Dominic is one of my best friends, but Ian is closer to me than my own brother. He lived with me and my family for years. I'll love him and support him no matter what he does, even if what he does is wrong."

"You think he's wrong for being with me?"

"You're married, and to his best friend. He should be helping Dom get you back, where you belong, not keeping you for himself."

She jumped to her feet, her heart on fire. "First of all, Ian didn't take me from Dominic, and he's not keeping me from Dominic. I went to him when Dominic cheated on me."

"I know, but—"

"And second, with Ian *is* where I belong. Where I've *always* belonged." Tears burned her eyes at hearing the trembling words leave her mouth. "From the beginning of time."

Eyes wide with surprise, Sean's lips moved like there were words rolling around in his mouth that he wasn't sure he should speak, but then he did. "Did he tell you about the woman in blue?"

Sabrina licked her lips. "I'm her. That's why he…why we…" Tears clogging her throat, she pushed out the door and raced back to Ian.

****

Ian ignored the knock on the door. He didn't want to talk to anyone. All he wanted was to be wrapped around Breena in their bed. He plopped down onto the mattress, his fingertips resting on his heart.

The knock sounded again. "Ian, it's Kristin. Can I come in?"

Shit. He thought about continuing to ignore it. Had it been anyone else, he would have. He got up and walked to the door and opened it, allowing her inside.

"I'm surprised you're talking to me." He closed the door. "I'm like the plague victim no one wants to be around."

She hugged him to prove that wasn't the case, and

he let her. Even hugged her back.

"Can we sit?" she asked.

He pulled a chair next to the bed for her and took the edge of the bed for himself, arms propped on his knees.

She sat facing him, her hand on his. "How are you?"

"That's a hard one to answer," he said finally.

"Give it a try."

"I feel like shit because I've ripped the heart out of one of my best friends and disappointed the one who's like my brother. At the same time, I feel happier than I've ever been because I'm with the woman who has been my soulmate since the beginning of time."

Kristin's eyes flickered with surprise. "How do you know Sabrina's your soulmate?"

"Ena told us, and so did the witch we met with to try to end our connection. And I feel it."

"I'm guessing you don't mean just a normal 'hey, we get each other' connection."

He shook his head. "It's like nothing either of us has felt before. When we're together, we're whole. We have everything we want, everything we need, all wrapped up in each other. Shit. I don't expect you to understand."

She smiled. "The second I met Sean, I knew he was the one. I couldn't explain it, couldn't even admit it. But I could feel it. He told me fate had brought us together. I knew it, too, but it scared the crap out of me. He was the one who made me believe when I was afraid to. So, yeah, I get it."

"You understand, but you don't approve."

"Sabrina and Dom loved each other enough to

commit to each other in marriage. That means something. That love isn't gone, for either of them, and they deserve a chance to keep that love, that relationship, and make it work."

Ian dropped his gaze to the floor. It pissed him off that she made sense. Before he and Breena had made love, she had gone back to Dom to tell him she forgave him and wanted to try again. If Meggan hadn't been in their bed, Breena would have stayed with him, made their marriage work, because she wanted her marriage. She wanted Dom.

Was Kristin right? Should he give her up and let her work things out with her husband? It was the moral thing to do. But, dammit, it wasn't the right thing to do. He didn't want to give her up. Even to salvage his oldest and dearest friendships.

His gaze rose to hers. "Would you go back to Sean if he fucked another woman?"

She didn't even blink. "As much as I love him...I would. I'd do anything to make it work between us."

"And that would be your choice to make. Who Breena decides to be with is *her* choice. Not mine. Not Dom's. Not yours and Sean's. *Hers*. Right now, she's chosen me. So unless *she* tells me she's choosing him, I'm not letting her go."

"Ian, if you let her go, maybe it will help heal things. All sides can agree that mistakes were made, agree to forgive, and agree to start over with a promise it won't happen again."

"He doesn't deserve her. She's a precious treasure, and he just threw her away." He shook his head. "I'll love her and cherish her the way she deserves, for the rest of my life."

"Are you sure that's what she wants?"

He wanted to yell out an emphatic *yes, goddammit*, but the truth was, she still loved Dom. How their story played out would come down to who she loved more. Or what her conscience told her to do. He said nothing.

"I'm sorry you're going through this." Kristin put her hand on his arm. "I want you to know that Sean loves and supports you and Dom, and it's killing him that you both are hurting."

"I appreciate that. And I want you to know that even if it costs me my job, my family, every fucking friend I have, I won't give her up," he said, his voice growing louder as he spoke. "She and I are *not* a mistake to apologize for. We're a fucking miracle. We're meant to be."

The door opened and Breena walked in. Her gaze meshed with his, and it was clear she'd heard his words. She rushed to him, and he pulled her into his arms, kissing her as he took her onto the bed, her arms and legs tangling around his, their bodies connecting, needing to restore the energy lost from being apart, and knowing that being wrapped around each other was the only way to do it.

****

Kristin watched in awkward silence as Ian and Sabrina locked into each other, as though trying to absorb each other.

Sabrina's shorts and panties had somehow found their way off her body and onto the floor. A second later, Ian's boxers were scrunching down his hips, then his ass. They were a breath away from full-out sex, and she didn't want to be there when it happened.

But before she could get up and walk out,

something that felt like static electricity surged from the two lovers. A blue cloud rose from their bodies and surrounded them like a sheer blanket as they rocked against each other. The edges of it pulsed into the room, toward her, and slid along her skin like tentacles. The shock of it made her gasp and made her heart pound in her skull.

Swallowing back fear, Kristin jumped to her feet, desperate to get away. A rush of vertigo and nausea swept over her, making her sway on her feet. She grabbed the chairback to steady herself and breathed deeply to fight back the urge to vomit. When the rush eased a little and the black dots floating in front of her eyes faded, she made her way to the door on shaky legs.

By the time she'd made it home, the nausea had hit full force. She ran straight to their bathroom and emptied her stomach into the toilet.

"Darlin', you okay?" Sean came into the bathroom as she rinsed her mouth.

"Yeah," she said weakly.

His arms slid around her waist. Worry filled his eyes as he looked at her in the mirror.

She would tell him about the blue haze, but she wanted to think about it first, try to understand what it was she thought she saw. "I'm fine. Just something I ate, or the bad vibes going on here."

"Come to bed. Let me take care of you."

They had made love just before Sabrina showed up, but she was ready for him again. She gave him a soft smile. "I'll brush my teeth and be right there."

He kissed her head and went back to bed.

As she brushed, she felt better. That thing in Sabrina and Ian's trailer had been weird. Some kind of force? Or spell? Had it been the cause of her sickness? She would call her mom in the morning and ask about a protective spell for her and Sean. Whatever craziness had taken over this dig, she did not want it to touch her marriage.

After gargling with mouthwash, she stripped down to nothing. She stood in front of the mirror, cupped her breasts. They felt heavy tonight, her nipples swollen and rosy. She ran her hands over her stomach and down between her legs. Her body felt lush and ripe, signs that usually accompanied the arrival of her period, but she was weeks away from that visitor. A slight pink flush tinted her cheeks, and an internal heat simmered inside her. An urgent desire for Sean filled her.

She flipped off the light and crawled into bed. Sean held her tight, dropping a kiss on her head, and she tucked into his side, her arm around his waist.

"Ian and Sabrina are soulmates," she said. "They have to be together."

He sighed. "I know."

"This last month here is going to be hell."

"Yep," he said.

"I'm so glad we have each other." She rolled onto him, feeling The Legend ready and hard.

"Me, too, darlin'. Me too," he said as she took him inside her.

Chapter Twenty-Six

The whiskey Dom had consumed steadily since the night Sabrina left him burned hotter in his gut, in his chest, and in his head as he watched Sabrina and Ian together. Ian put his hands on her. She leaned into him and kissed him. The scum bastard's hands curved around her sweet little ass and pulled her against his cock.

The son-of-a-bitch. He should break Ian's fucking hands for touching his wife like that. Hack off his cock for daring to use it on her. The fucker had it coming. He'd had his sights on Sabrina from the day she arrived. He should have kicked his arse then, made it clear who she belonged to. He just never thought his best friend would betray him.

Sabrina kissed Ian again and with a loving smile walked away to another trench. Dom stumbled over to the trench where Ian stood taking pictures and jumped in, barely catching himself before he fell on his arse.

"Leave my wife alone, you fucker," he shouted, stabbing a finger at him.

Ian turned, looked at him, shook his head, pity on his face.

Dom didn't want Ian's fucking pity. He wanted his blood. He took a wobbly step toward him, then stopped to gain his footing. "My marriage fell apart 'cause of you. 'Cause you couldn't keep your fucking hands off her."

"Your marriage fell apart because you fucked Meggan," Ian said.

"Sabrina's still my wife."

"Not for long."

"You can't have her, you fucking son-of-a-bitch." His head was on fire, his hands ready and eager to rip Ian open.

"She's already mine," Ian shouted back.

Their argument was loud enough to draw a crowd, but he barely noticed. All he saw was red and Ian's lying, cheating face. "I'll kill you before I let you have her."

"Same here, you stupid fuck," Ian said, his brittle tone and hard expression a warning to back off, but Dom took it as a battle cry.

Fists hard as steel, driven by rage and pain, intent on doing damage, Dom charged at Ian, swinging at his face, his fist catching him solidly in the jaw. Ian stumbled back a few steps, then rounded his fist toward Dom's face, his knuckles connecting with a solid hit. Bells rang in Dom's head. Colors flashed behind his eyes. Pain radiated from his face throughout his body and racked him backward, where he fell hard in the dirt. He clambered to his feet just as Ian attacked again.

****

A raucous drew Sabrina's attention, and she ran to the circle of spectators in the area where she'd left Ian. Dominic and Ian were in the middle of it, beating the shit out of each other. Fists pounded and pummeled each other. Arms strangled each other. Loud grunts and dull groans filled the air. Blood and sweat flecked off both.

She rushed to Sean. "You have to stop them. They're going to kill each other."

"This fight's been brewing between them a long time. They need to get it out of their systems. Get it done. Before they do kill each other."

Not liking his answer, she moved toward them with the intent of getting between them, but he grabbed her arms and pulled her back. "You'll just get hurt."

Blood flowed from Ian's mouth and from Dom's nose and a cut above his right eye. Both men bore injuries she couldn't see, to ribs, to knuckles, to red, battered flesh that would soon turn the purple, yellow, and green of bruises. Worst of all was the injury to the solid bond that had been forged in childhood. Seeing the two men she loved beating each other was too much to take. Her stomach rolling, she broke out of Sean's hold and left the circle, headed to her trailer.

"Are you happy?" Meggan said behind Sabrina, distress in her voice saying she couldn't stand to witness the fight either. "Does it get you off that they're fighting over you?"

Sabrina rounded on her. "This is *your* fault, bitch. You did everything you could to come between Dominic and me. You fucked my husband. You're the reason we're not together. You're the reason he's drinking. You're the reason he's fighting with his best friend. If they get hurt, it's on *you*."

Meggan's eyes narrowed in anger. "All this trouble is because of you, because you whored after Ian even though you're married."

Without giving it a second thought—or much of a first one, for that matter—Sabrina pulled back her arm and propelled her fist forward from the shoulder, punching Meggan solid in the face. Meggan fell backward onto the ground with a startled yelp, and Sabrina jumped on her, straddling her. The two hit and scratched blindly at each other, yanking fistfuls of hair.

"You can't have my husband, you fucking bitch," Sabrina yelled, all her rage at the situation congealing into a tight ball of fury consuming the tight, thin space between her and Meggan.

"He's not yours anymore," Meggan yelled back.

With her head down, Sabrina couldn't see where she was hitting, but she felt her hands connecting with solid flesh, and that's all that mattered.

Suddenly, she was being lifted off Meggan, and Dominic was helping Meggan up, putting her behind him for protection. It hurt to see him being so protective of his lover. It hurt worse to see his bloody face. She wanted to run into his arms, comfort and kiss his battered body, clean and bandage his wounds. She even took a step toward him until she remembered he had Meggan for that.

And she had Ian, who needed her to comfort him, clean his wounds. She turned to her lover and went into his arms. He had been the one who had pulled her off Meggan, the one who had protected her.

"Are you okay?" she whispered, caressing his face.

He nodded, the whole time glaring at Dominic.

"She's my wife," Dominic yelled, spitting blood between them. "She doesn't fucking belong with you."

Ian jerked forward to punch him again, but Sabrina blocked him with her body and held onto him. "Ian," she whispered. "Please, no more."

"She's always belonged with me," he yelled back.

Dominic eyes darted between her and Ian in

411

confusion. "What do you mean, always?"

Jack stepped between the two couples before Ian could respond. "You four go home. Clean up. Cool down. The rest of you, back to work."

Ian and Dominic stayed put, both rigid with anger, ready to go again.

"That wasn't a fucking request," Jack growled.

"Come on, love." She tried to turn Ian toward home. "Let's go home."

Finally, he put his arm around her shoulders, and they headed to their trailer. She didn't watch to see what Dominic and Meggan did, but she felt their stares piercing her back.

Inside their trailer, she and Ian kicked off their boots, pulled off socks, and stood together, stared at each other, saying nothing for a moment. Then a little grin lifted one corner of his bloody lip. "We're quite a pair, you and me. If photography doesn't pan out, we've got a future in tag-team events."

She went into his arms. He groaned at her touch, and she eased back, helped him off with his bloody shirt, feeling his pain when he flinched.

"Oh, love. Look at you." Red blotches covered his ribs, chest, stomach, and back where Dominic's fists had pummeled him. Tears stung her eyes at the fury and violence that had caused this damage. Had Dominic fared as badly?

She kissed every spot that was red or bruising, and a few that weren't, then ran her fingers along his ribs, feeling for any breaks. "Anything feel broken?"

He clenched and unclenched his scraped and bloody knuckles and gingerly rolled his shoulders to test his ribs. "Nah, just sore as shit. How're you, scrapper?"

"Embarrassed. Not my finest moment."

"Don't be embarrassed, love. Cat fights are fucking hot." He cupped his cock. "Made me hard."

How he could be turned on after that fight she'd never know, but sure enough, a bulge pushed out the front of his jeans. She chuckled and rolled her eyes. "I prefer the less violent methods of getting you hard."

He stepped closer, slid his arms around her, gripped her ass, and rubbed his bulge against her. "Everything you do gets me hard." He lowered his head and kissed her neck. "Moving..." His touch and his voice sent chills thundering over her abused body. He kissed the other side of her neck, and a second battalion joined the first. "Sleeping..." He kissed her mouth. "Breathing..." With a grin and a promise, he moved his hand to her shorts and undid the button.

Smiling, she stepped back and rebuttoned her shorts. "Let me clean your battle wounds first, my warrior lover, before you sheathe your sword in my scabbard." She took his hand and led him to the bathroom.

"I love your scabbard."

"I know."

He sat on the toilet while she grabbed a few washcloths from the shelf and wet one. Standing between his legs, his hands lightly at the backs of her thighs, she gently cleaned the blood from his face so she could see the damage. The intimacy of the moment, of the tight space, his touch, dissolved the remaining rage and adrenalin flowing through her.

"What started it?" she asked, her voice quiet in the small space.

"Seems he doesn't like me fucking his wife."

His flippant words sent an agonizing shock through her. The thought that sex and possession, not love, had prompted the fight... Well, it hurt. Worse than the blows Meggan had landed on her body. Not responding, she rinsed and wrung the cloth, then used it to clean his nose that was still bleeding. He winced, and she did, too, feeling his pain.

"It's your love we were fighting for, *Hashkeh*," he added quietly. He'd heard her thoughts, of course, and was trying to ease her feelings. "We both want it more than we want to breathe."

Fighting for love. It had always seemed like such an odd concept to her, until today, when she found herself rolling in the dirt, pummeling Meggan for stealing Dominic.

"Pinch your nostrils together to help stop the blood," she said softly, then turned away to wet another cloth. She held it to his split lip and met his eyes. "There's no need to fight for my love. You already have it. You have me."

He caught her wrist. "Weren't you and Meggan fighting for the same thing? For Dom's love?" He pasted kisses along the scratch that ran from her wrist to her elbow, leaving partial bloody lip prints.

The feel of his lips on her raw, sensitive flesh made her shiver. "I've fought for him, for his love, for our marriage, since we got here, and I still lost him. No point in fighting for something I've already lost." She thought about how Dom was with Meggan. *Maybe I never really had it.* She removed her hand from Ian's and turned to the sink to wet the last cloth. "I'm ashamed to say it, but I just wanted to hurt her for all

414

the trouble she's caused."

She lifted his hand to dab the blood from his battered knuckles, but he waved her off and stood. She turned to stare into the mirror to clean her own face and was shocked at the reflection. Her hair had come half out of its ponytail from when Red had yanked on it, and it was sticking up on one side. Her lip was bleeding and suddenly hurt like the devil. Scratches crisscrossed her chest and neck, some leaving dotted bloody trails.

"Shit, I hope she looks worse than I do," she said, cleaning her wounds.

"She does. Your fist had a good talk with her eye." Behind her, he eased the elastic from her hair, letting his fingers thread through the strands, gently untangling them. Then he took the cloth from her hand. "Let me do that."

"I got it." She took the cloth back and dabbed her lip.

He put his arms around her waist, and his hands slowly slid up and covered her breasts. "Then let me do this."

The cloth halted in her hand, and her gaze in the mirror went to his hands squeezing and massaging her breasts, leaving bloody fingerprints, then rose to his eyes.

"Definitely yes." She dropped the cloth into the sink with the others as Ian tweaked her nipples hard as pebbles.

"Raise your arms," he said.

She did, and he lifted off her shirt. His hands skimmed up her skin to her breasts that were more than ready for his touch. She rarely wore a bra anymore. Ian liked having easy, quick access to her, and she liked knowing he could have his hands on her in an instant.

His hips pressed into her, and she pressed back, loving the feel of his cock ridged against her ass. Their eyes locked in the mirror. Watching him touch her like this was a first for them, and it accelerated her desire. Wetness slicked between her legs, her pussy swelling with the moisture. She wanted their clothes off and him inside her. And she wanted it now.

One of his scraped hands stayed at her breasts, and the other went to her shorts. His talented fingers lowered the zipper, then flicked open the button, and his hand slid into the open space, cupping her pussy, squeezing it, rubbing it, his middle finger finding her clit.

Her eyes on his in the reflection, she dropped her head back on his chest. "I love it when you touch me."

His hands went to her shorts and shoved them down. He ripped one of the slim straps of her thong and shoved down the scrap of material. "I know." He thrust a finger into her wetness.

She growled at the feeling of him inside her. It was just what she wanted. He always knew. Watching the joy flush her face as he pleasured her rocketed her desire, and she put her hand on his, pressing into it, rolling her hips against it, wanting more.

She found his eyes again. "Fuck me, Ian."

"I'm gonna fuck you." His hands left her body and moved to his jeans. "Right now."

Almost panting, she tried to turn around to help him, but he kept her faced toward the mirror. She gripped the sink and watched him in the mirror as his long fingers unbuckled his belt. The thick black leather strap that had to come undone before she got to have his cock. God, she loved unbuckling it, sliding it out of his belt loops, dropping it to the floor, stripping the clothes from his body. It was those intimate actions that told her he was hers, his body was hers.

"And you're going to scream *my* name when I make you come."

His fingers flipped the stud open at the band of his faded jeans, and she felt the rasp of his lowering zipper down her spine, making her tremble with the need of him. He was opening his jeans so she could have his cock, and she was out of her mind with the idea of it.

"Because you're *mine*." He shoved down his jeans and boxers, and his cock sprang out, long, hard, thick, and just for her. Her breath hitched audibly in a whimper as he fisted himself at the base, showing her what she was getting. "Say it."

Her tongue snaked across her dry lips. "I'm yours." She wanted him inside her. Pounding. Driving out thoughts of Dominic and Meggan and her failed marriage.

He moved in behind her, pressed his cock against her. "After we fuck standing up, we're gonna fuck again, in our bed, with you riding this cock. If you can still move and breathe after that, I know other ways to make you scream."

With a groan, she leaned over the sink, pushing her wet pussy against him, circling her hips against him, begging him to take her. "Yes. Oh, God, Ian, I want it. I want you."

"Show me where you want it."

She spread her legs and arched her ass up. "In my pussy." She was ready, wet, hot, and throbbing for him. "Fuck my pussy."

He kneed her legs farther open, then slid his cock between them, letting her feel it from her ass to her clit. She moaned and went up higher on her toes, arching back so that her pussy opened more for him.

He took a handful of her hair and pulled, exaggerating her arch. His other hand splayed low on her stomach, fingers digging in. He bent his knees and rammed his cock toward the general vicinity of her soaking pussy. Luck was with him on the first try, and he thrust hard up into her. All the way. Easily. Like her body was made just for his.

"Ian!" Her face twisted in passion at the hardness filling her, his hand gripping her hair, his body cemented to hers.

"Look at us," he growled at her ear. "Watch us fuck."

She watched, mesmerized by their naked, raw rutting, by their animalistic grunting urging them on, by the hunger of their constant and blinding need to be one. Fuck. Fuck. Fuck. The erotic vulgarity of the word roared through her veins. They were one, in body and soul. This was their true state. Connected. In lust, in passion, in love. How they were meant to be. How they were created to be. How they *had* to be.

"Touch my ass," she begged.

He released his hold on her hair, and his thumb went to her tight star, circling it, stroking, pushing inside.

Giving her no time to adjust to being so filled, he fucked her, hard, fast, his pounding cock slapping her pussy, his thumb fucking her rosebud, keeping up a rhythm that was barreling them to the cosmos.

"Touch your clit," he demanded, and her hand

moved there and circled the slick, sensitive network of nerves.

The sounds of their slapping flesh, the feel of him so full inside her, the sight of her touching herself, the smell of them, their sex, their grunts, her low moans of "fuck me Ian," watching them fuck in the mirror... It rushed her to climax like a bullet shot from a gun.

Almost in tears from the pleasure, she cried out, again and again, his name wrapped in nonsensical sounds of lustful, loving, joyful fucking as she came, as he thrust into her, harder, deeper, faster, taking her body for his own, giving her all of his.

"I want your cum, Ian. Come in me." She growled the command deep in her throat, and he let go, roaring like a bloodied and victorious warrior at battle's end, shooting his cum deep inside her in triumph, giving her the most precious treasure his body could give—his very essence.

Empty of cum, of breath, of energy, he slumped over her body, the edge of the sink digging into her flesh until she could find the strength to use her arms to ease back a bit. His open mouth gasping for breath, his teeth grazed the damp and scraped skin of her shoulder. She was gasping, too, flushed with exertion, her ass, her pussy, her clit throbbing, her entire body pulsing with pleasure.

His arms circled her, at her waist and chest, and he brought her upright, her back against his front, his cock still inside her, still connecting them. He cradled her, his head on her shoulder, her hand on his, the other up and caressing his head. Love coursed through them, and she could smell their sunshine/flower scent, feel their entwined souls slowly separating, like a pulling of their inner-most muscles, until he slid out of her.

In the struggle to catch their breath, a sudden chill swept over her. It came from Ian. She went inside him. A bitter cloud of dark feelings from guilt to self-hatred eased out his euphoria. Her eyes jumped to his face in the mirror, her thoughts questioning, asking *what's wrong*.

He lifted his head from her shoulder, found her eyes in the mirror. "I beat up my best friend today."

Her stomach clenched at the anguish in his voice and his eyes.

"I never thought there'd be anything on this earth that would make us fight like that." He dropped his head back down to her shoulder and tightened his arms around her, almost clinging, like she was the last thing he had left.

She was the *anything* that had sent Ian and Dominic to war with each other. Her eyes opened, her mind cleared, reality came into sharp focus as she looked at herself in the mirror, seeing her real self. Hair disheveled. Blood and dirt on her face. Scratches on her neck, chest, arms. Standing naked and fucked with her husband's best friend in his tiny bathroom, his spent cock sliding out of her, his cum running down her legs. While her husband, the man she also loved, was hurt, broken, bleeding, and having to turn to another woman to heal his wounds, the wounds she and Ian—two of the most important people in his life—had inflicted.

It turned her insides to ice. She was to blame. For everything. Her failed marriage. Dominic's drinking. The fight. The destruction of his and Ian's friendship. She was the curse on this dig that had seen problem after problem from the start.

What the hell was she doing? What had she become? Self-loathing wound inside her like the prickly blackthorn bushes consuming this part of Ireland. *Dominic. Ian. I'm sorry. I'm sorry.*

She started to leave Ian's arms, but he wouldn't let her. He turned her to him. "Look at me, love."

Not wanting to look and let him see the monster she was, she hid her face in his chest.

He put his hand to her chin, lifted her face, but her eyes didn't rise. "Breena." His whispering voice was cajoling but commanding, and she could deny him nothing.

Her eyes rose to his, saw only love, and she melted. Her eyes burned, her nose burned, her throat and jaw tightened. The tears were coming. Nothing could stop them.

He hugged her to him. "This isn't your fault."

"Yes, it is. I'm such a horrible person," she sobbed and broke apart in his arms.

"No, you're not." He picked her up and carried her out of the bathroom and to their bed. He laid her down, lay beside her, held her, comforted her, his touches and kisses loving her.

"I destroyed everything." She ran her hand across her face and into her hair. "I should have told him about us, asked for his help."

"Since we found each other, I've never felt more whole or happy or loved," Ian said, his hand stroking her skin. "I wouldn't have chosen to love you, because you're Dom's wife, but I *do* love you, with everything I am. I can't help it. I can't stop it. I don't want to stop it. Our love isn't wrong."

He rolled on top of her. "*Ahoshle muh kree*, the

truth is, no two people are more right for each other than you and me. Our souls made love long before our bodies did. We were meant to be."

Yes, they were the pulse that kept the other alive. Yes, they were perfect for each other. Maybe it wasn't right, but it wasn't wrong.

"God help me, Ian, I love you, too. Right or wrong, I do."

Then his swollen mouth was on hers, and she felt no pain, only the pulse leaping hot and wild inside her, inside him. She felt his cock pulsing at her center, and she spread her legs, took him inside her again, wrapped her thighs tightly around his waist, let him fill her up.

"Love me to the stars again," she said. "This time, let's get lost there. And never come down. So we can stay as happy and whole and alive as we are right this minute."

He took her there, but they came down, her remorse for all the heartache she'd caused waiting there to slice into her again.

****

Dom stood in the shower, letting the icy water dampen the fire inside him. His heart hammered in his chest, against his battered ribs, and he wanted to pluck out the abused organ and crush it to put it out of its misery. Anything to not feel the pain of knowing Sabrina was with Ian.

"God...help me," he mumbled. Eyes closed, he leaned against the wall of the shower and raised his battered face into the spray, saying her name, over and over, as if the repetition of it would bring her back. But he knew it would take more than prayer. It would take a miracle.

After showering he went to the first-aid tent and got bandages and salve for his wounds. When he got to his caravan, Meg was sitting in his bed. She hastily wiped her wet face when he came in. Her eye was already bruising from the punch Sabrina had landed on it. Her nose was no longer bleeding but was swelling. And her lip was puffy. Assorted scratches crisscrossed her face, neck, chest, and arms.

Sabrina had fought like a wildcat. Was it because she loved him? Or because she hated Meg?

Meg jumped from the bed, rushed to him, and hugged him. "Are you okay?"

Stepping out of her arms, he kicked off his boots, then pulled off his T-shirt and unbuttoned his jeans, letting them smack to the floor in a wet slap before moving to the dresser and pulling out dry clothes.

He had felt no pain during the fight—his first with Ian—but now every muscle in his body hurt. It hurt to raise his arms to put them into the sleeves of his T-shirt. It hurt to bend over to pull up his boxers. The skin across his first two knuckles was broken where it had connected with Ian's face or teeth—he didn't know which. His lip was split and swelling. The gash on his right eyebrow oozed. His nose was tender and red, and he'd have one hell of a black eye. He felt along each of his ribs, gingerly, confident they weren't broken, just sore as shit.

As bad as his body hurt, it didn't come close to the agony spearing his heart.

He went into the bathroom to apply salve and bandages to his external wounds. The internal wounds would take longer to heal. No salve or bandage would hasten the process.

"Let me do that for you," Meg said behind him and tried to squeeze in and take the salve from him.

"No room. It's a one-butter."

"One butter? What's that?"

Dom grinned, chuckled, laughed out loud. Then the laughter broke apart in his throat and turned to choking tears. Roaring, he banged his wounded fist against the wall over and over.

"Oh, Dom," Meg started, her voice cracking. She touched his back.

"Leave me alone," he said, the low words gurgling from his throat.

"Let me help you."

He spun around, his cold, wet, angry eyes on her. "I said no!"

She scuttled backward. Hurt rippled in her eyes, and her chin quivered as she fought back tears. She had never been one for showing her deepest emotions, but today he saw straight through her barriers to the emotions wailing inside her. It was hard to care about her pain, though, when his own was screaming so loud in his body he couldn't think...and when she was partly at fault for it. Just looking at her reminded him what a fuckup he was. Reminded him of what he had lost.

A weaker woman would have run from his growls in fear or collapsed in tears at his feet. Meg swallowed her tears, stood a fraction taller, then took his hand, pulled him from the bathroom and laid him down on the bed. She crawled in with him and curled around his backside, holding him, letting her body be his salve. He hurt too much to send her away.

Despite her comfort, all he could think about was how fucked up his life was. A few months ago he had the job of his dreams, the woman of his dreams, and two best friends who were more like brothers at his side.

Now he was failing at his job, and rattling around in his body was a broken spirit and shattered heart because two of the people who meant the most to him were no longer his. Even the woman in his bed, her hands ever so gently caressing him, had once betrayed him after claiming she loved him.

His life was dissolving and slipping through his fingers like sand. And when it was gone, would he have anything left worth living for?

Chapter Twenty-Seven

"Goddammit, Sullivan!"

At Jack's furious exclamation, Ian rushed to the trench to investigate the problem. His boss' face was redder than usual and looked like his head was about to pop off his neck. Dom was on the ground, on top of a ready-to-be-lifted skeleton, drunkenly trying to roll off of it, blood flowing from the gash in his head.

Jack pulled him to his feet, then checked the damage, cussing again. The skeleton was broken in several places. "Son, if you can't get your fucking shit together, I'm going to can your ass. Go get a shower, then go to bed and sleep it off. Don't come out until you're sober. And if you ever come to work drunk again, you're gone. You understand me?"

Dom mumbled something that sounded like a yeah and stumbled toward his caravan. Ian watched him go, a bone-deep sadness gripping him. His friend's hair was a mass of tangles, his face haggard, pale, and unshaven. The smell of whiskey oozed from his pores, and he was still drunk. He didn't know that person.

It was Dom's first week without Sabrina, days after their big fight, and it was clear his life was rolling downhill fast, sending him ever closer toward the edge of a deep, dark, beckoning abyss. Normally, he'd be the one at Dom's side, telling him to get his shit together, helping him through this dark time. Instead, he was the cause of it.

"Fuck! Red…salvage this mess," Jack yelled. "McCanna, where is she?"

"Who?" he asked, though he already knew.

"Who the fuck do you think? The only person who can fix that goddamn mess."

****

Sabrina looked up as Jack climbed into Rusty's trench where she was taking photos.

"Rusty, take a break," he said.

Rusty stuffed Nessy into his back pocket and climbed out, but one step from the trench and the wayward trowel fell out onto the ground.

Shaking her head, Sabrina picked it up and set it where he'd see it when he came back, then turned to face her boss, letting the camera hang by its strap around her neck.

"You and Ian can't see past each other so you may not have noticed, but your husband's falling apart. He's drinking the hard stuff. Comes to work hung over or still drunk. He doesn't shower, comb his hair, eat."

"Of course, we've noticed." Dominic was just this side of a neat freak, so not paying attention to his hygiene was way outside the norm for him. He'd never had more than two beers at a time—and never any hard liquor—the whole time she'd known him. And for him to go to work drunk? It said a lot about where his head was and added up to serious problems.

"Just now he was still so drunk he fell on one of the skeletons we were lifting. Broke the skull, the back, the arms, the pelvis, and the right leg. Reopened the gash in his own fool head. I sent him to his trailer to have a shower and sleep it off."

"Why are you telling me this?"

"You need to talk to him, shove some sense into that thick skull of his."

She grabbed her camera and turned back to the skeleton. "Ask his lover."

"You're his wife. The woman he loves. The reason he's in this fucked-up condition."

Anger spun her back to face him. "He chose to break our marriage vows. He chose her over me. He chose to drink to excess. Don't pin the cause or solution of his problems on me."

He pointed one stubby finger at her. "This goddamned well is your fault, as much as it is his. Maybe you and Ian weren't fucking before, but it was clear as glass you wanted to, and that tore at Dom so much he made a bad choice to deal with the pain of it."

"Yeah, it was a bad choice. But it was *his* choice. It's not my place to fix his mistakes."

"We've all been fixing his mistakes lately, because we care about him, because he's not himself, because he's as low as we've ever seen him, but that comes to a halt starting right now. He's got to get himself together or firing him will be my only option. He's putting the team and the project in jeopardy, and I can't let it continue. No matter my personal feelings for him."

She rubbed the spot at her temple where a stabbing icepick ache had set in. Dominic had lost her and Ian. Losing his job, which meant everything to him, might send him over the edge into the darkness pulling at him with greedy hands.

"Don't fire him, Jack. He can't lose one more thing."

"Do you love him?" he asked.

After a short pause, she responded. "Yes."

"Then act like it. Save your husband's life." He climbed out of the trench and looked back at her. "You're the only one who can."

He left before she could come up with another excuse as to why she couldn't help her husband and talk him off the ledge.

****

It took Dominic so long to answer the door that next morning she thought he wasn't going to. She had turned to leave when he finally did. Her heart stopped.

He looked bad. His hair was full of tangles and sticking up. Beneath the bruises and more than a week of beard growth, his face was pallid. He was stark naked, and the absence of clothes showed he'd lost weight. He looked older than his twenty-five years.

Damn it, Dominic. What are you doing to yourself?

Leaving the door open, he stumbled back to the bed and sat on the edge.

Shock momentarily paralyzed her when she stepped inside the trailer that had once been her home. The place smelled like something had crawled in and died, and it looked like a dump, with clothes strewn everywhere, empty whiskey bottles on the floor, old food containers piled on the table. The windows and curtains were closed, blocking out the fresh air, trapping the sour stench of sex, despair, hopelessness, and grief until it felt like a fixture in the trailer.

Meggan was asleep, also naked, the comforter and sheet in a tangled heap on the floor.

"Is this a bad time?" Sabrina asked.

He rubbed his hands over his face. "What do you want?"

"I, um…" She looked around and spied one of the chairs covered by a pile of what looked like more dirty clothes. Tilting the chair to drop the pile to the floor, she pulled it over in front of him so she could face him, eye to eye, and sat. "I wanted to talk to you about—"

He grabbed a half-empty bottle of whiskey from the floor, uncapped it, and drank deep.

She wanted to rip the fucking bottle from his hands and throw it against the wall. "Dominic, we're all worried about you—Jack, Sean, Ian, the team…me."

"That's a lot of worry. Why?"

"Your drinking, your inattention on the job, your disconnection with the team. You're not yourself."

"This is who I am now, so everybody might as fucking well get used to it." He tipped the bottle to his mouth and drank again, trickles of amber liquid spilling from his mouth and trickling down his neck and chest. He barely winced at the biting liquid going down.

She was shocked by his vehemence. "I don't believe that for a second."

"Believe it."

"I know you're hurting. But don't let it drag you down into that dark place. You're stronger than that. You're better than that." He said nothing, so she continued. "I don't think you realize what a huge hole you've left in the team because you're not…you. They need you."

He scoffed. "Yeah, well, if they need somebody to fuck things up, I'm their man."

She chuckled softly, and his eyes darted to hers.

"What's so fucking funny?"

"I can't believe you fell on the HR and broke it in five places."

"Six."

"Excuse me," she said lightly, grinning. "Six. If Rusty or Angus or anyone else had done that, you'd have strung him up by his balls. You'd have outright castrated him for coming to work drunk."

A rough chuckle scraped past his throat. "Yeah. I would have." He dropped his eyes to the floor. "The old me anyway."

"Your team misses the old you. They're falling apart because you're not there to guide them. They want their friend and their leader back, and they're worried he's gone."

He shrugged. "He is."

Seeing him like this scared the hell of her. He was one foot in the dead zone, and nothing she'd said was getting through. He brought the bottle to his mouth again. She reached out and put her hand on his, halting the bottle's journey to his mouth. With her other hand, she took the bottle away and set it on the floor beside her, then held his hand in hers. His gaze went to the spot where they were connected.

"Baby, you have so much to offer," she said. "Don't deprive everyone of your brilliance. The world would be a sadder, darker place without you in it."

"Careful, wife. I might think you still care about me."

"Of course, I care about you."

He dropped his head, shook it as if he didn't believe her, then let it slowly rise, his hazy, bloodshot eyes finding hers. "Then come back to me."

His voice was fragile, like delicate glass. So was his spirit. What could she say to his request? What could she say that wouldn't derail everything she'd just said? What could she say that wouldn't give him false hope? Or totally break him? Before she could come up with something, he pulled her hand between both of his and held it, his thumb brushing the back of it.

She'd forgotten how big his hands were, how small they made hers look, how skilled they were at so many things, from loving to digging. They could deliver the gentlest caress and stroke the hottest fire on her body, his calluses providing just enough roughness on her skin to electrify every nerve ending to send her body into orgasmic oblivion. The touch of his hand was one of the many, many things she missed about him.

Loss and longing swept over her as she watched his hands caress hers. She had loved this man more than anyone she'd ever known. And now he was gone to her. He was with another woman, the woman asleep and naked in his bed. Now he caressed *her* body with these talented hands. Kissed *her* lips with that delicious mouth. Made love to *her*.

And she was with another man—her husband's best friend—who caressed, kissed, and loved her. It sometimes felt like they'd all awakened in an alternate universe.

"Say you still love me, Sabrina," he whispered and brought her hand to his face, closing his eyes as he rubbed his stubbled cheek against her palm then kissed the center of it. "Even if it's a lie." He looked up into her eyes. "Give me a reason to save myself."

Deep in his amber eyes was a glimpse of the husband, the man she loved. Maybe she couldn't go back to him, but she could be honest with him. She swallowed the ball of tears in her throat so she could speak. "I still love you."

Four syllables. Four words. One truth. Packed with powerful magic, like a spell incanted to break a curse. She felt it the second it left her mouth. He felt it, too. His eyes, wet with unshed tears, opened a bit more, lit up, just a spark, like the real him had in that moment found a way out of his prison.

She had to get out of here before she…what? What did she want to do? Hold him? Comfort him? Kiss him? Yes. Yes. Yes. She slowly pulled her hand from his and stood. "Take care of yourself."

Before she could move away, he grabbed her, pulled her between his legs, and hugged her, arms around her waist, his head at her breasts. After a moment, she cradled his head in her arms.

"Love me, Sabrina," he whispered through quiet tears.

"Baby, I do love you," she whispered into the crown of his head as her own tears fell. "I do. I do."

Together, they mourned their loss for long, bittersweet minutes. When his back had stopped shaking and his breathing returned to normal, she left his arms, left his trailer, and ran down to the river to cry great wracking sobs that left her body in misery.

Ian found her there and held her until she could breathe. Then he took her home and loved away her tears.

****

Dom sat where Sabrina left him, his eyes wet, his swollen head buried in his hands. When he'd settled his stomach enough to breathe straight, he stood. Still unsteady on his feet, he knocked over the bottle of whiskey she'd taken from him.

He picked it up, stumbled into the bathroom,

emptied it into the toilet, and peed on it, then placed the bottle atop the heap in the overflowing trashcan. Then he washed his hands and face, rinsed his mouth, and crawled into bed, his back to Meg.

When Sabrina had packed her clothes, she'd inadvertently left a T-shirt behind. He'd found it and kept it in his pillowcase ever since. He pulled the shirt out and held it to his nose, inhaled her scent, attempted a smile.

She still loves me.

Sabrina's shirt against his chest, he buried his nose in it as a reminder, a talisman of sorts, to keep him on track for getting himself back, then getting her back. As long as she loved him, he had a chance. A smile on his face, his arms around her soft shirt, he drifted to sleep, his wife on his mind, her words in his ears. *Baby, I do love you.*

He woke before dawn the next morning, alone, and showered in the one-butt shower, scrubbing his body and his mouth clean of whiskey, hopelessness…and Meg, who had left him sometime while he was sleeping.

Had she overheard his conversation with Sabrina? He felt bad about hurting her, but for a chance to get Sabrina back, he'd do anything, no matter who got hurt.

The face in the mirror staring back at him as he scraped away weeks-old beard growth was a pitiful, broken stranger he wanted to turn away from in disgust, but he didn't give in to it. He didn't like himself very much, had been to the edge and nearly jumped, but because of Sabrina's visit, because she still loved him, he could survive. He would survive. She had given him something to live for.

Pulling out his electric shaver, he buzzed off his hair. As every tangled knot fell, it seemed to lift the mistakes, the bad choices from his soul, and he felt almost like himself again, the man he was before he fucked up his life.

Now that he smelled better, he realized how bad the caravan smelled. He opened the curtains and windows, letting the bit of morning breeze begin to clear the stench. He popped four pain relievers, chasing them down with a bottle of water, then went around the caravan, picking up the empty bottles, food trays, and other trash and putting them into a large garbage bag. He changed the sheets on the bed, adding the dirty ones to the bag. He straightened up the caravan, washed the few dishes, wiped away a layer of dust and grime from the furniture, swept and mopped the filthy floor, and piled the scattered dirty clothes into the already full basket. With disgust, he realized that every bit of clothing he owned was dirty. He'd go into town tonight to do a few loads, he decided as he pulled on his cleanest dirty clothes.

The sun was creeping over the horizon, streaking the sky pink, yellow, and purple when he went outside to face the world and reclaim his place in it. Other than Sabrina's face the day before, it was the most beautiful thing he'd seen in a long time.

The smell of *rashers* sizzling permeated the morning air, and his stomach growled angrily as if he hadn't eaten in months. Cookie had set up for breakfast, and a few teammates were already in line to fill their plates. He dumped his bag of trash into the bin, then stepped in line next to Jack, Rusty, and Angus. They eyed him warily, which told him he had some apologies to make, fences to mend, trust to rebuild.

"Sorry, boss," he said to Jack and held out his hand, a sheepish grin on his face.

Jack took his hand and shook it. "Good to see you can still stand upright."

"What the hell did Red do to your hair?" Rusty asked.

Dom ran his scraped and bandaged hand over his buzzed and bandaged head and couldn't stop the grin taking over his face. "Wasn't her. My wife talked some sense into my thick skull. This is a reminder that she still loves me."

Angus patted his back. "Well, feck. We can't call you Samson anymore."

"Nobody called me Samson," he said authoritatively.

"Not to your face." His mates laughed heartily, as if they were glad to have him back.

Dom laughed with them, but their ribbing was like a sword in his side. His favorite parable in school had been the one about Samson, a good, strong man who used his God-given powers to perform heroic deeds. But his vulnerabilities—which included his hair and his attraction to untrustworthy women—led to his downfall. The parallelism to his own life wasn't lost on him. He hadn't had a lot of luck in the faithful woman department either, and now he'd cut his hair. Was his complete downfall behind him? Or ahead?

Dom's gaze snagged on Meg, several people ahead of them in line, as she moved away after filling her plate.

"Grab some grub, slim," Angus said patting his flat stomach. "You need it."

"Save me some," he said good-naturedly and stepped away to head toward where Meg sat.

As he cleaned his caravan, he had carefully gathered the words he'd say to his long-time teammate/friend/lover. Even though she had come to him of her own free will, he'd used her to salve his pain. And now he was dumping her. She would hurt, no matter what, but he'd deliver the news as gently as he could. He sat beside her.

Her gaze wouldn't settle on his, as if she knew what he'd come to say.

"I owe you an apology," he started. "I'm ashamed of myself for putting you in the middle of my marriage problems." He stared out the mesh window at the brightening sky, seeing Sabrina's face. "I love my wife, and I'm going to get her back." His eyes came back to her. "You understand what I'm saying?"

"We can't be lovers anymore."

"Yes, but I also think it's best if we don't work together anymore."

Her watery gaze flew to his, her trembling chin showing her fragility. She swallowed. "If that's what you need." Her voice was rough, thick with tears.

"It is. We worked well together for a long time. I'll miss it."

"Me, too," she choked out.

They stared at each other, wordlessly saying bye, until his growling stomach broke the connection. "Don't sit alone," he said. "Come join your team."

He stood. So did she. He had taken one step when she grabbed his arm to stop him. She angled close to him so only he could hear what she had to say.

"She's not your soulmate, Dom. She's Ian's. Even

437

if she comes back to you, a part of her will always belong to him. Don't settle for less than you deserve." She punctuated her sentence with a warm, deep kiss, her wet lips on his making his heart flip in his chest. Then she turned away, leaving her full plate of untouched food on the table, and headed out of the tent, her back rod straight.

He watched her go, remembering what she'd done for him. She'd kept him alive when he wanted to die after Sabrina left him for Ian. No doubt about it, he would miss her. A lot, he suddenly realized, his chest heavy and tight like a bag of boulders was sitting on it, a strange aching emptiness inside his gut that wasn't about the need for food.

Chapter Twenty-Eight

"Hello, Sabrina." Dominic set his tray of food on the table where she and Ian sat eating lunch and took the chair beside her. "How's your day?" He dug into his food.

An angry bruise rimmed one eye and several dotted his face, but he looked and smelled clean, had shaved, and his cropped hair was clean. The result of their talk? She smiled. "Good. Yours?"

He smiled that smile he used when he was pulling her into bed for a long session of loving. "It's grand, now, talking to you."

"I'm glad you're feeling better."

His eyes danced over her. "You're wearing the shirt I picked out for you on our honeymoon."

Her nipples hardened at the mention of their honeymoon, as if they were responding to the memory of the love he'd showered on them.

"You look as beautiful in it today as you did the first time you wore it." He chuckled. "*Tried* to wear it. Remember?"

She remembered. Every detail. In vivid color. Her body heated at the memories of how he'd taken it off her the morning she'd first put it on, how they'd never made it out of their hotel bed. The smile on his face and the long, sizzling stare told her he was remembering it, too.

"Don't you have your planning meeting?" Ian said, his words like blockades interrupting their stroll down memory lane.

"Yeah, but I'd rather spend this time talking to my beautiful wife," Dominic said.

"Since when?" Ian asked.

"Now, that's not really your business, is it? It's between me and my wife."

"Breena is my business."

"Not for long."

"That's up to her. Not you."

"Or you."

"She's with me, by choice. Accept it," Ian said.

"I won't accept anything but having my wife back with me where she belongs."

"She is where she belongs. Where she's *always* belonged. With me."

Their voices were getting louder and louder as they talked, and a quick glance around the tent confirmed that everyone was watching them, listening. Ian looked ready to let Dominic have it—the truth, that is—and she knew she had to end this before it escalated into another fist fight.

"Ian," Sabrina said and stood.

He looked at her. "Breena, it's time."

"But it's not the place." She put her hand on his neck and slid it up into his hair. "Our lunch break is almost over," she said, her voice soft. "Let's go to our trailer."

He stood, put his arm around her, his stare firmly on Dominic's. "I won't give her up." He and Sabrina walked toward the door.

"Neither will I. And I'm up for the fight," Dominic

called out.

****

Inside their trailer, her hands immediately went to his shirt and yanked it off before moving on to his belt. "I've wanted you all morning," she said, unfastening his belt and jeans and sliding her hand in, stroking his cock. But the only emotion strumming through his veins was anger.

His hands halted her touch, and his eyes roamed over her shirt. "Did you wear that for him?"

"You know I didn't." The truth was, she had worn it because it was one of her only clean shirts. They hadn't done laundry in over a week, choosing instead to spend every free moment in bed.

"I want to rip that fucking shirt off you," he said, his voice steeped with jealous emotion.

She put his hands at the low-V neckline of the shirt. "Then do it. Your feelings mean more to me than any shirt, more to me than anything."

He gripped the material tight, then let go. "Destroying the shirt won't destroy your memories or your feelings for him."

She took his hands again, brought them to her mouth and kissed them, sucked his fingers, nipped them. "Focus on me, love, on us, on building *our* memories, on my feelings for you." She raised her arms. "Take it off me."

He lifted the shirt off her and flung it across the room. His actions were calmer, but anger still pulsed from him. Action would quell that anger.

"Now my shorts," she said as she fondled her heavy breasts.

He unzipped her shorts, unsnapped them, and

pushed them down. Before they had settled around her feet, he hooked his fingers at the waistband of her panties and pulled them down her legs. His gaze strolled across her naked body, desire flaring in his eyes.

"I want your hands on me." She took his hands and placed them on her breasts, squeezing her hands over his. "I want my hands on you." She pushed down his jeans and boxers and stroked his cock. "I want my mouth on you."

She started to drop to her knees, but he stopped her, threw his arms around her and held her close, tight, like he was afraid she'd leave at any moment. She hugged him just as tight to show him she wasn't going anywhere.

"*Muy kwid den tay ol, ma gra,*" she whispered in his ear to further convince him.

"And you're mine," he responded in the same tone. He picked her up and laid her on their bed. She opened her legs, and he settled his body between her thighs. He entered her, connecting them, but he didn't move. He just stared into her eyes.

"Love," she said, slowly rotating her hips against his, squeezing her pussy around his prick, arching up into him. "This will feel even better if you move, too."

He didn't return her smile. "I meant what I said. I won't give you up."

She cupped his face with her hands. "Or me you."

He began to move.

****

A shadow passed over Sabrina's logbook, blocking the late morning sun as she sat at the trench lip noting the pictures she'd taken of one of the last skeletons they'd see at the dig. When the shadow stayed put, she turned and looked up. Dominic towered over her, sparks of red and gold shining in his cropped hair, love shining in his eyes, a smile lighting his handsome face. He was more like his old self every day, and it eased her mind and soul.

"Hello, wife," he said.

"Hi," she said.

"How are you?"

"Good. You?"

He held his arms out to the side. "More like the old me every day, thanks to you."

"I'm glad. But I can't take credit. I didn't tell you anything you didn't already know."

"You're the only one who could get me to see it."

"You here to check the logbook?" She held it out, really wanting to change the subject.

"I'm here to check on you."

"Why?"

"I've been thinking about you all morning, and I wanted you to know it."

The loving look in his eye made her heart flutter. "I'd have given anything to hear you say that a month ago."

"But not now?"

"We're not together now."

He moved closer to her and held her with his intense eyes. "We're still married."

A shiver climbed her spine. Yes, they were still husband and wife. Legally, but not emotionally. Those ties were well severed. She turned her back to him and walked toward the skeleton to take a photo, but when he stepped closer, right behind her, and she felt his heat and his breath, she couldn't remember how to focus the damn camera.

"Does it bother him that you're still in love with me?"

Yes. It bothered Ian. But she wasn't going to have that conversation with Dominic.

"Do you see my face when you're making love?" His hand caressed her hair. "Do you call out my name when you come?"

His voice licked slow through her like the flames from a low fire, reminding her that it had been so long since she'd felt his touch. She missed his arms around her. Missed his smell. The taste of his kisses. The feel of his cock that fit her so well. Tingling from head to toe, she spun to face him. "Don't do this."

"Don't do what? Remind you how great we are together?"

"Oh, God, Dominic. We *were* great together. But that stopped right around the time you stopped wanting to be with me. Somewhere around week four I think."

"No, Sabrina, I always wanted to be with you."

"No, you wanted to work. And you wanted *her*."

"I always wanted to be with *you*," he repeated and caught her hand, "even if I didn't always show it."

It was on the tip of her tongue to come back with "Ian shows me and tells me every day that he loves me," but she swallowed it. She didn't want to hurt him any more than she already had. And telling him that Ian loved her better than he did would hurt him.

Tears burned her nose and eyes. It was so hard to stand so close to him and not hug him, touch him, kiss him. She loved him. He loved her. He had been hers, and she his. And now it was over. Gone.

"We still love each other, Sabrina. Fate, in her infinite wisdom, brought us together and wants us to stay that way."

"Fate?" she scoffed. She pulled her hand away. "I'm surprised you believe in something as inexplicable as fate. That's right up there with ghosts and witches and magic spells. You don't believe anything you can't see, right?"

He lifted his hand to her face and dragged the tip of his thumb across her mouth. "I believe in love. Our love."

Goosebumps sheeted her skin as memories of the two of them locked in love flooded in. Her breath stopped. Her knees went weak. So did the rest of her body. She couldn't even move to shift away when he eased her into his embrace. Oh, it felt good. Comfortable.

But it was wrong. He had cheated, and she was Ian's. She started to move away, but he held her tighter, trying to cement their bond.

"Something—call it fate, or destiny, or divine intervention—*something* knew we belonged together, knew we needed each other, and made it happen," he said.

Her eyes rose to his. "Then something tore us apart and sent us into the arms of other people." Remembering what he'd done with Meggan gave her strength to leave his arms.

He caught her hand. "Our world won't be right until we're back together. You know it. You feel it." He squeezed her hand. "I love you, wife." He brought her hand to his mouth and kissed her palm. "See you at dinner."

As she watched him walk away toward Angus' trench, part of her wanted to call him back, tell him to convince her he was the one she should choose. Considering all the many things that had to happen, not happen, align perfectly to ensure they met, fell in love, married, was he right? Or had they come together, like Fiona said, only so he could bring her to Ian?

She loved Ian, needed their connection, but if she'd never met him, she'd have been content to live out this life with the man who had just left, his heart on his sleeve, his love bright and warm in his eyes for her to see and feel. Knowing it made the coming decision all that more difficult.

****

Sabrina stopped at the bathroom before going to join Ian for dinner in the mess tent that night, and when she got close to the tent, she heard yelling coming from inside. Even before entering she knew it was Dominic and Ian. The two of them stood across the table from each other, arguing.

"Bullshit!" Ian said with an angry scoff as he glared at Dominic. "Don't think you can suddenly pay attention to her and she'll forgive you and go back to you."

"She's coming back to me because she loves me," Dominic said, his eyes raging. "She told me so when she came to our caravan to save my life."

Ian's pain filled her head. He knew she still loved Dominic, and that she'd told him so when she visited his trailer that day, but the way Dominic phrased it made it sound like she had told him she was coming back to him, which she hadn't.

Ian turned sorrow-filled eyes on her, silently asking

whether it was true. As if he thought he'd read a yes in her jumbled thoughts, he stormed from the table.

"Ian—" She caught his hand.

"Tell him, Sabrina. Now."

At her silence, he pulled his hand away. "Fuck this shit," he growled and stormed toward the door.

She spun around to face her husband. "Leave him alone." She turned to go after Ian, but Dominic caught her hand.

"I'm walking around with my chest ripped open from what he's done to us, our marriage, our life, and you're worried about *his* feelings? What about *my* feelings?"

"Ian is the reason I can still breathe. He's the reason my heart still beats. He's the reason I didn't just curl up in a ball and die after you cheated on me. It's your fault our marriage is broken, not his. Don't punish him for your mistakes or your pain."

"You're my wife, and he took you from me. It's his fault we're—"

"No! Let me make this really clear—Ian did *not* take me. I went to him, *willingly,* when you fucked Meggan. Take responsibility for your part in this."

"I did." His cheeks flushed. "I do. I made a mistake. I've admitted it, apologized for it. But as my best friend, Ian should have protected my marriage not contributed to its destruction."

Every word tightened the knot in her stomach. She dug her nails into her palms to stop herself from lashing out physically at him, but she couldn't temper her tongue. "He tried. Oh, God, you won't believe how he tried to save our marriage. You're the one who destroyed it. You and Meggan."

"When you told me you still love me, did you mean it? Or was it a lie just to get me off the bottle? To get me to back to work? To ease your conscience?"

"Of course I meant it. You think I can just stop loving you?"

"How can you love me and go to his bed every night?" he asked.

"How could you love me and fuck her in our bed?" The thought, the image of the two of them in bed was seared into her mind forever. It brought tears to her eyes every time.

"Sabrina," he said, his voice soft, his gaze soft on hers. He took her hand in his. "Baby, you gotta forgive me so we can get past this."

She pulled her hand away. "I'll forgive on my timescale, not yours."

"Look, I understand you need time to think, to sort out your feelings. But for Christ's sake, move out of Ian's caravan while you're doing it."

"Ian is the only thing in this godforsaken place that makes me happy. He's precious to me. Why would I leave him?"

Dominic's face clouded over in fury, and he drew himself up tall, hands in fists. "Because you're my wife and you shouldn't be living with another man, sleeping in his bed. If you love me, if you want to save our marriage, you'll move out. Today."

"After what you did, you're in no position to give me ultimatums."

Desperate to find Ian and ease the damage to his bruised heart, she turned from Dominic. Her *Hashkeh* stood by the door, watching, listening to the passionate exchange. Their eyes met. Love flared inside her like it always did whenever he looked at her.

I love you, Ian. So much.

She flew into his arms, clutching him. "I didn't tell him I was going back to him," she whispered.

"You didn't tell him you're not," he whispered at her ear.

"Take me home," she said. "Please."

They left the tent to the sound of Dominic flipping the table and flinging curses.

****

The alarm went off at four-fifty a.m. for their run, and as usual Ian rolled onto Sabrina and gave her her first kiss of the morning.

She spread her legs, and he settled between them, rotating his hips against her, pressing his hard cock against her opening.

"Mmm. If you keep that up, we're going to miss our run," she murmured, stroking the curve of his ass and breathing in the sleepy scent of his skin.

"No run today," he said, leaving a trail of kisses down her neck.

"Oh? What are we doing instead? If it's having sex all morning, I'm down for it."

"Is that all you think about?" he teased, his mouth awakening the nipple at her breast.

She chuckled. "Well, excuse me. I'll dial it down a notch."

"Sorry, I can't allow that." He slid his rod into her slick heat.

Eyes closed in ecstasy, she arched into him. "Don't worry. I was lying. So why are we missing our run?"

****

They arrived at MAC HQ in Dublin shortly before

lunch and carried in the boxes that contained their DVDs, which would be archived.

They were leaving when the CEO's assistant stopped them. "Mr. MacDougal would like to speak with you." She led them to a conference room. "I'll let him know you've arrived."

"Wow. What a view." Sabrina stood at the wall of windows looking out on the River Liffey as it flowed under the O'Connell Bridge.

Ian joined her, slid his arm around her waist, brushed aside her hair, and nuzzled her neck. "Yeah, but that view comes with a high price tag."

"What's that?" she asked, dropping her head back so he could have more of her flesh.

"Being caged inside a glass and steel building all day, every day."

"So, you never want a job where you're not at the mercy of the elements?"

"Temperature-controlled environments are overrated." He kissed her, left her side, and walked to the heavy wooden table occupying the center of the room, running his hand along the intricate carvings and the smooth, polished surface. "I would like to have this in our office, though, for the times we have to be inside."

She left the view, joined him, and hopped up on the table. "It would take up the whole trailer."

He settled between her legs and wrapped his arms around her. "Yeah, but it's a multipurpose piece. Think about all we could do on it," he said, lowering her backward onto the table and bending over her.

She grinned and wrapped her legs around him. "Like what?"

"Like this." He yanked open her thin denim shirt, the little pearl snaps releasing with a racy pop, pop, pop, exposing her white cami, her nipples rising in anticipation of his touch.

"And this." He kissed her lips.

"And this." He grabbed her wrists and slid her hands over her head, making her breasts thrust upward.

"And this." He kissed down her neck and across her chest. His grin hovered at her nipple. "And this."

"Ian," she said, panting. "Someone might—"

She lost her objection and her breath when his mouth came down on her hard nipple, sucked it through the thin material. She whimpered when he did the same to the other one, wrapping her legs tighter around his waist, pulling him closer to her core, her hips arching up into his, his pressing into hers.

"Anything else?" Her words came out in a rough whisper.

"Fucking," he whispered. "Lots and lots of nasty fucking."

Before she could respond, he kissed her, his tongue thrusting in her mouth the way she wanted his cock to be thrusting into her pussy.

"Most people who come into this room are enthralled by the view, not the table."

Ian's mouth left hers, and they both looked up. Eric MacDougal, the owner of MAC, their boss, stood at the head of the table, watching them make out on his very expensive antique.

Ian rose and helped her up. "Most people don't come in here with her." He put his arm around her as she quickly snapped her shirt and tried to cool the heat in her face.

MacDougal's eyes roamed over her for several thorough seconds. "Fair enough," he said and stepped forward to greet her.

With a smile she stepped forward to introduce herself, holding out her hand to him. "Hi, Mr. MacDougal, I'm Sabrina—"

"Ah, the Yank." With a warm smile, he took her outstretched hand and held it like it was a delicate orchid.

"Yes," she said, surprised he knew of her.

"I was told you were married, but I had no idea it was to this scoundrel." He nodded toward Ian and winked. "I didn't think there was a woman alive who could tame him. Congratulations."

Despite the shame steaming her face, she looked him straight in the eyes. "I'm not married to Ian."

"Yet," Ian tacked on as he joined her and roped an arm around her.

Surprise ripped the smile from Mac's face, and he shot Ian, then her, a sharp look. "Ah. Well. Pleasure to meet you Sabrina…"

"Sullivan."

"Sullivan." He nodded, as if he had placed her husband. "Dominic." At the mention of her husband's name, the truth of what she was doing to him slapped her. Mac's gaze cut to Ian, displeasure flaring in his eyes as they shook hands. She looked at Ian, to see his response. Ian met the boss' eyes unashamedly, his unflinching stare saying, "You got a problem with it? Suck it!"

By the time they'd settled into the large leather chairs at the table, Mac seemed to have tucked away his judgment and was all business. "I wanted to tell you in person how pleased the client is with the media coming out of your dig. Which pleases me. And because of that," his gaze went to Ian, "and your stellar work over the years you've been with MAC, I have a proposition for you."

"Oh?" Ian asked.

"A Media Director-International position just came open, and I want you to take it. You'd work some of the world's most significant digs, either as the only media onsite or part of an international group, representing MAC and Ireland. We'd pay your travel and living expenses, of course, and give you a month of paid time off between the longer digs, along with a generous salary, enhanced benefits package, and, when applicable, hazard pay."

Sabrina looked at Ian. His eyes darted to hers, then back to Mac. In that brief glance, she knew. Despite his poker face, he wanted the job, no matter the pay or the risks. It's what he had always wanted. And closer in line to what she had always wanted. She couldn't hold back a smile, but Ian wasn't giving away anything.

"You have the option of choosing your own assistant media director. I was going to suggest Sabrina," his gaze brushed hers, "if she was interested. You two make a brilliant team. But I can't imagine her husband approving of that."

"Sabrina and I will check out the specifics and discuss it," Ian said.

Mac's darting gaze between her and Ian seemed to say he'd expected more of a reaction. "The job's yours for the taking, but you have to apply and the deadline's in two weeks. The first dig is in Italy and starts in July." He stood, so they did.

"'Preciate the offer, Mac." Ian held out his hand.

"You've earned it." He shook his hand, then turned to her. "Good to meet you, Sabrina." They, too, shook hands, and he headed to the door. Halfway there, he stopped and turned back. "Oh, and if I catch you two fucking on my eighteenth century table again, I'll fire you both." He opened the door and walked out, leaving it wide open.

They held their excitement until they'd left the building and were headed down the sidewalk. He stopped. She stopped. He laughed. She laughed. He picked her up and spun her around.

"So, love, you ready to wear out the soles of your boots, traveling the world with me?"

This was his dream job, but it was hers, too—traveling the world, capturing important happenings with her camera. "This job…*agra*, it's what you've always wanted," she said, holding his gaze, caressing his face. "I'm so happy for you. So proud of you."

"No." He shook his head. "*You're* what I've always wanted. Without you, the job's just a job. With you by my side, it's a dream come true."

Holding her hands, he dropped to one knee, looked up at her, his face and his soul as sincere and loving and open as she'd ever seen it. "Go with me, love. Be with me forever. I promise you, you won't regret one minute of our life together."

No, she wouldn't regret a single moment with him. But the matter of her husband still needed to be decided. Did she reach across the chasm of mistakes they'd both made to hold on to the man she loved enough to marry, still loved, or forge a new life with the man she loved and who had been hers in spirit forever?

Dropping to her knees, she gave him the only answer she had at the moment. "I love you, Ian McCanna."

His mouth slid possessively and hot over hers. Just like she needed.

Chapter Twenty-Nine

Dom sat on his steps, staring across at the caravan where his wife lived with his former best friend. Knowing that she made love to Ian in there every day, every night, was like being castrated, again and again, with a dull trowel.

All his apologies and promises and efforts to get her back had changed nothing. She was still with Ian. The dig was almost over. If he didn't figure out the magic formula for getting her back soon, he would lose her.

Their door opened. Ian left the caravan and was a few feet away when Sabrina came out, stood on the steps. The T-shirt she wore—one of Ian's—hit just inches below her ass, and her hair was wet, like his, as if they'd just had a shower. Together probably. She wasn't wearing a bra, hadn't worn one much since she'd gone to Ian. It was like she was a different person.

She called to Ian, and he stopped and turned back, a satisfied grin on his face. She held up his keys. He held up his hands, as if to say, "Toss 'em."

She jingled them next to her breasts, as if to say, "Come get 'em." He eagerly jogged back to her, reached for the keys, but she pulled them away. He tried again, but she lifted them out of reach, so he grabbed her and dipped her, kissing her face, tickling her, making her squirm and giggle.

Her movements made the shirt rise, and Dom saw a flash of her bare ass. Then her arms wound around Ian's neck, her mouth was on his, and they shared a deep, passionate kiss. It shocked him that it was such an intimate kiss, like they'd been lovers forever instead of barely three weeks.

After a long moment, the kiss ended, but their arms stayed around each other. She slid the keys into his pocket, letting her hand go deep. His hands slid up under the back edge of her shirt, gripping her bare ass, holding her as close as possible to the bulge in his jeans. He said something to her, and she laughed, nodded. She put her hands on his face and kissed him again, then left his arms and climbed the steps. He grabbed her hand, kissed it, then headed off again. She watched him for a long time before turning to go inside, like she couldn't take her eyes off him.

She must have seen Dom sitting there out of the corner of her eye as she turned because she stopped, looked toward him, her smile dying. Did she feel guilty that he'd witnessed her interlude with Ian? Their eyes met. Held. He raised his hand in a small wave. She smiled and raised her hand, too, then went inside.

Dom's eyes returned to Ian just as he entered the media office. He pushed himself off his steps and headed that way. It was time he had a talk with his old friend.

At hearing the door open, Ian looked up from his packing, and Dom stared into the face of the man he'd once called best friend. He seemed like a stranger now.

"If someone had told me three months ago that Ian McCanna, my best friend, would steal my wife, I'd have shut his mouth permanently. But I guess I should have known, the kind of man you are, that eventually you'd do to me what you do to every poor sap whose woman you want."

Ian set aside the box he had been packing. "First of all, in all the years we've known each other, I never went after your women. Never. Not even when some of them came after me." He stabbed a finger at him. "And you know that. Second, I never *stole* any women. They came to me freely. Every one of them. And third, your wife left you because you cheated on her."

"The Ian I grew up with would have kicked my arse for being an idiot and then done everything in his power to help me get her back. He wouldn't have taken her to his bed and kept her for his own."

"The night Breena left you, I could have made love to her, but I didn't. I encouraged her to go to you, to work things out, because I knew that despite what you did, you loved her and she loved you. I had no idea you'd be fucking Meggan in Breena's bed. Once is a mistake, Dom. Twice is a choice. It's why she won't go back to you, and why I won't let her go."

Dom's stomach churned poison into his body at his mistakes. One after another. Ian might be right. But it wasn't going to stop him from trying to get Sabrina back.

"Ian, I'm asking you, as a friend…back off. Let us work things out."

"As your friend, I wish I could. But I can't. I won't."

"Our marriage is a sacred bond that should not be broken."

"The sacred bond she and I have *can't* be broken."

458

"What bond?" he scoffed. "You barely know each other."

"What she and I have goes deeper than every relationship either of us has had. She's everything to me. She's the one I never thought I'd find."

The one I never thought I'd find. Dom knew it meant the woman in blue Ian's *daideó's* ghost told him to be with. More magic shit. Somehow, it always came down to that with them. But he couldn't afford to be sentimental and understanding. He was fighting for his wife.

"She's everything to me, too," he said. "I need her and love her even more than you do, no matter what magical connection you think you share."

"You don't deserve her, and I won't step aside and let you hurt her again."

"Maybe I don't deserve her after what I did, but I love her and she still loves me. She told me so. And I know she still wants our marriage."

Anger reddened Ian's cheeks and sparked his eyes. "She loves me, too. She tells me and shows me every day. I love her the way she deserves to be loved. I put her needs, her happiness above mine, above everything in my life. Something you *never* did. She belongs to me, and I belong to her. Then. Now. Forever."

The thought that Sabrina loved Ian as much as he loved her shredded his heart. Seeing how they were together, Dom couldn't deny that it looked like love. She looked happy. Ian looked happier and more at peace than he'd ever seen him. He'd never given a woman this kind of power over him before. Obviously, he'd found his one.

Did he even have a chance to win back his wife? It

would come down to who she loved more, unless he could get Ian to back off willingly.

"If there's any love left in your heart for me, brother, any part inside you that knows what you're doing is wrong, do the right thing and let her go."

"I love her too much to let her go."

"I'm warning you, McCanna. Make damn sure it's worth it before you keep going down this path. It won't end well for you. You'll lose me, you'll lose Sean and his family, you'll lose other friends when they find out what you've done, maybe even your job. Can you give it all up?"

"I'd give up anything if it meant I could be with her," Ian said.

They stared at each other for long, tight moments, Ian looking at him with such disgust it made him cringe, but he wasn't going to back down.

"I won't leave here without her." Dom's voice sliced through the tension.

Ian's response was just as lethal. "Neither will I."

Dom stormed out of the office and headed to the dig site before he gave into the temptation to kick Ian's arse again. Although, the last thing he was in the mood for right now was work. His head and heart were filled with a storm of fury, and there was nothing he could do about it but live with it, let it take its course. Had this been a normal day, he could have talked through this confusion with Sabrina, or Ian, or Sean, or Meg. But his days weren't filled with normal now.

Now, he had no one.

Sean was too busy with Kristin to remember he had other important relationships to tend to. Sabrina and Ian had betrayed him and were the cause of his fury. And

Meg...

He'd put Meg off limits in order to get Sabrina back. It was the right thing to do. But he missed her. Missed their easy companionship, their friendship, their private jokes, their quiet talks, the way she laughed, the way she smelled, the way she could calm him and make him see that things weren't as dire as he'd imagined them.

His mind so focused on the memories playing in his head, he was taken aback by the woman herself coming out of her caravan. It stopped him short. Her hair was down, not yet contained in its usual high ponytail. The bright morning sun turned her curls into a blaze of fire and light. It reminded him of that pivotal day during the summer they'd first met when they had sneaked off and made love behind the old church ruins while everyone was at lunch.

Along with pulling off every stitch of clothing she wore, he had also pulled her hair from its ponytail. The sun was hot that day, too, and it had set her hair ablaze like now. The way her curls had fanned around her head like a halo had made him feel as if he had joined with an angel. It was that day that he knew she was more than a friend.

Meg stopped, too, her eyes linking with his. That familiar feeling passed between them then, the feeling of warmth, connection, and understanding that had always been there. Today, it also hummed with the feeling of loss and regret that their friendship was forever changed. His instinct was to go to her, hold her, talk to her, and the shine in her eyes said she wanted it, too. It made him sad to know he couldn't.

He missed her. But if giving her up was the only

way to get Sabrina back, he'd do it. No matter how much it hurt. He forced himself to break their gaze and continue on to the dig site.

****

Ian lay awake long after Breena had drifted to sleep that night, replaying his morning conversation with Dom and aching with the uncertainties gnawing at him. She loved him. He knew it. He felt it.

But she loved Dom, too. As long as love existed between them, did their relationship deserve the chance to survive? Had their marriage only been strained because of his and Breena's connection? Or did hers and Dom's divergent personalities and unfaithful and turbulent marriage prove they weren't right for each other and should move on?

Breena and Ian fit together. They were the same. She was his other half, he hers. It couldn't get any more right and perfect than them, physically, emotionally, mentally, spiritually, every way possible. They had true love. Were true soulmates. *Bunaidh. Sonuachar.* They deserved a chance, too. Despite the love between them, he couldn't ignore the feeling that in the end he'd be the one left standing alone, burning in his skin, when she went back to her husband.

Kissing her forehead, he eased out of her arms and their bed, gently so as to not wake her, and moved to the door. No breeze pushed through the screen—the air was too heavy and humid. Not bothering to get dressed, he slid the door open and sat on the middle step. Staring out into the dark night, he went over in his head, again, all the possible things he could say and do to convince her to stay with him.

He felt her presence, smelled her scent, even before he heard her come up behind him. Euphoria flooded his system. This is what she did to him. Drugged him at just the thought of her, the scent of her.

She sat behind him, her bare breasts against his back, her arms around his neck, her thighs hugging him. He felt her nipples poking into his skin, the heat of her pussy at his back. His heart pounded against his back ribs, searching for hers. Desire gathered inside him and funneled to his cock, making it swell between his legs. God. He wanted her. All the fucking time.

Fiona had been right. They were obsessed with each other. They made love morning, noon, and night, and still they wanted more. But their connection went beyond the physical act. He loved her. Her love was alive inside him, ran through him like liquid lightning, made his heart beat, his lungs inflate, his blood flow. And it was the same for her. He felt it.

"I woke up and you were gone," she whispered, her breath teasing his neck.

He covered her hands with his. "You needed sleep."

He felt her mouth on him, slowly dotting his shoulders with soft kisses, bites, and licks from her wet tongue, and his eyes closed in ecstasy.

"You know I sleep better with you next to me," she murmured.

The love in her voice wrapped around his heart. "When I'm next to you," he said, caressing her, "I want to touch you. When I touch you, I want to kiss you." He kissed her hand. "When I kiss you, I want to make love to you. When I make love to you, you're not sleeping."

"No, I sleep through most of it."

"Smartass." He laughed at her teasing and reached back to tickle her stomach as punishment. She giggled and grabbed his hand. She slid both arms around him again, then moved her hands between his legs to his cock, stroking him. Heat swept through him at her touch.

"Actually," she said, "I hate to waste even a second of time on stupid things like sleeping and eating and working when I could be making love with you."

He cupped his hand over hers as she caressed him. "I feel the same way."

"Then why are you out here instead of in our bed making love to me with this fine hard-on?"

He took her hand from his fully erect cock and turned to look at her.

"C'mere, love. Come into my arms." Her skin glowed like the moon as he guided her down the steps and into his arms, settling her across his lap. He stared deep into her eyes. "Do you love me?"

Her feelings were written all over her face, riding her touches, her thoughts, but he needed to hear her say the words aloud.

She traced his lips with a finger, then kissed them, softly, fully. "I love you, Ian. But only forever," she whispered through a smile. "Do you love me?"

He caught her hand and held it to his mouth, kissed her palm, her fingers. Then he cracked opened his heart, showed her the depth and breadth of his love.

"*Hashkeh*, I want to marry you. I want to put my babies inside you. I want to live my whole life wrapped around you. I want to go with you into the dark at the end, and then start all over again with you. I want to do it all, again and again, with just you, until time itself runs out. That's how much I love you."

Tears and love shone in her eyes, and her teeth bit the soft smile that had taken over her lips. Her hands went to his head and caressed him. "You want to have a baby with me?"

He grinned. "Out of all the things I said, that's the one you latched on to?" Her chuckle caressed his heart.

"You said you weren't the marrying kind, and by extension, the baby-making kind."

"I wasn't. Until I found you."

She cupped his face. "I want to have your baby, Ian McCanna," she whispered. "I want to be your wife. I want an eternity with you, whether in body or spirit."

There was something in her voice that told him there was a part two. "But…"

Her gaze slid from his, rested on her husband's trailer across the way, and it gouged trenches through his gut.

A deep, shaky sigh raised and lowered his chest. "Then why are you with me?"

Her gaze flew back to his, and he could feel the panic running through her.

"Do you regret us, Ian? Our being together?"

"I regret that when this dig is over, you'll go with him and leave me half alive without you beside me. I regret that to protect your marriage after you leave, we'll never be together again like we are right this minute. I regret that you don't love me enough to choose us."

"I haven't said I'm going back to him."

"You haven't said you're staying with me."

They breathed each other in the moonlight, emotions swirling like a tornado around them.

"When I left him that night, I absolutely believed that was it for us. I was so broken, I didn't think I could be with him after what he'd done."

"What's changed?"

"He gave her up, even though I haven't given you up. He admitted his mistakes, apologized, and asked for another chance, even though I haven't apologized for what I did. He tells me every day that he loves me and wants our marriage even though I keep telling him I'm with you and happy. He shows me how he feels. He gives me the attention I needed him to give me. He's doing everything he knows to do to get me back. He loves me so much."

"What do you have to apologize for?"

"For the part I played in the breakup of our marriage."

"He cheated on you. That's the only part you played."

"I cheated on him."

He shook his head. "No, we didn't."

"*Hashkeh*, I wanted to make love with you from the minute I met you. As hard as I tried to hide it from him, he knew. And it tore him up inside. By wanting you, by giving you my time and attention and thoughts and touch and love, I was unfaithful to him. *I* broke our marriage vows. *I* sent him to her bed."

"Wanting to make love is not doing. Besides, your problems are about more than just his infidelity. How many times did he choose work over you? How many times did you go to sleep unsatisfied because he was mad or too tired to love you? How many times have I let you go to sleep unsatisfied or not been there for you?"

"You've never left me wanting for anything, and I love you deeply. You know that."

"But you're going back to him."

"He's my husband. Despite what he did, I love him. But I love you, too, and I don't want to live without you."

"You can't have both of us. You have to choose."

A feeble breeze stirred, kissing their fevered skin and stirring the wind bells hanging above them as they stared at each other.

She left his lap, and for a brief, terrifying moment, he thought she was leaving him, but she only turned to straddle his waist and wrap her legs and arms around him. Her hands slid into his hair, and she kissed him, her lips soft, wet, hungry on his. Giving in to her taste, her feel, her love, he gathered her in and kissed her deep and long, the way she wanted and needed.

"Make love to me, *Hashkeh*." Her whispered words brushed his mouth, further stirring his desire. "Here. On our steps. In our moonlight. In our bubble. Our wind bells singing to us, reminding us of our connection."

The panic thinning her soft voice told him she knew they had a limited amount of time left between them. Instead of insisting she face reality, he glided into her as she slid onto him, a smile of bliss on her face, a broken sigh on her lips, at being connected with him again. Every time they connected was better and stronger than the time before, and he couldn't say no to the drug that would send him straight to nirvana.

His hands cupped her ass as the two of them rocked slowly against each other, as their souls joined, as their blue haze swallowed them. She leaned back, and he twirled his tongue on her nipples like they were a fine delicacy, sucked them into his mouth. Her head fell back on a groan at the pleasure of it. He drew her back to him to kiss her lips, taking her tongue inside his mouth, getting high on the taste of her. He held her tight and plunged deeper into her body, giving her more, more of his cock, more of his love, more of him, more of everything she needed. She met every slow thrust, giving him what he needed. The feel of being inside her wiped out everything but this moment.

She shuddered his name as she found her pleasure, the sound coming from deep inside where her love for him had been born and now thrived. His pleasure flooded with hers, the surge of their union tossing them high into the sea of stars overhead, where they were held aloft for one supreme frozen moment as a single entity before slowly floating back down.

They clung together, a Celtic love knot of flesh and spirit, trembling from shared passion, weeping from the reality facing them. He kissed her wet eyes, cheeks, chin, lips, wanting to entice her soul back with his and keep it there so she couldn't leave him.

Her loving gaze, kisses, and touch said she wanted him, loved him, but Dom was always in her thoughts, sparring with her thoughts of him. Because he loved her, because what he wanted more than anything was her happiness, he would do what she couldn't. He would choose. He would sacrifice his happiness for hers. Because he meant what he'd said to Dom. Her happiness and needs came first. But for now, while he could, he'd accept what she could give and give her his all.

They sat joined, connected in body, heart, mind, and soul, and watched the sun rise, then went inside, back to bed, skipping their run for more time in each other's arms.

A knock at the door an hour later woke them. It was Dom, wanting to come in and talk. Breena sat up, intending to leave their bed and put her robe on, but Ian held her in place and shook his head.

"He needs to see us so he can remember how much it hurts." He put his arm around her, and she lay back down, her head on his chest, her arm around him, the sheet skimming their hips. "Come in," he called out.

Chapter Thirty

Seeing Sabrina in bed with Ian, naked, their bodies wrapped around each other, was a jackhammer assault to his pride and to his heart, but Dom forced himself to take a good look so he could remember this moment, this heartache. If he got her back, he'd never do anything that would make her want another man.

He grabbed a chair and sat facing them, his eyes trained on her. "Baby, I love you, and you said you love me. But you're still with Ian. I've apologized for what I did, and I thought by now you'd have forgiven me and come back to me. But you're still with Ian. I'm doing everything I know to show you that I want you and our marriage. But you're still…"

He lowered his head and twisted his wedding ring to give him time to corral his emotions. Hearing the mattress shift, he lifted his head. She had sat up in bed, the sheet pulled up to hide her breasts...the breasts Ian had touched and sucked. Goddammit.

"Do you want me, our marriage?" he said. "Or have you chosen Ian? I can't stand the not knowing any longer."

They stared at each other across the quiet space and tears pooled in her eyes. She was his wife and Ian his friend, and he felt like an outsider in their presence, an interloper. There was a connection between them, had been even before the sex began, and it had grown stronger in the short time they'd been together. But until he heard the words from her mouth that she no longer wanted to be married to him, he wouldn't believe the worst. And he wouldn't leave until he had an answer, as painful as it might be on all of them.

"Dominic, I want—" The meat of her sentence caught in her throat, and her gaze rushed to Ian, her entire being begging for his help, like she wanted him to speak for her.

Ian's eyes were already on her, had been on her through Dom's speech, as if he were listening to everything she wasn't saying. At her silent plea, he sat up, slid next to her. His hand cupped the back of her head, she grabbed his other hand and held it to her chest. He eased closer and kissed her eyes, dislodging the tears there. He touched his lips to hers, in more of a caress than a kiss. It was like they were talking in touches, in looks.

Dom had never seen Ian be as tender with a woman as he was with Sabrina. Love lived between them, connected them. He could see it, feel it. It made his heart crumble to ash that she might choose Ian. But it looked that way.

Feeling sick to the marrow of his bones, he was preparing himself to stand and walk out when Ian turned and glared at him, fire in his eyes.

"She'll come back to you at the end of the dig," Ian said, his voice low, gritty, stretched with what sounded like anger and agony.

A strangled little moan came from Sabrina, and she blinked, mouth open, eyes wide as she stared at Ian. The look told him Ian's comments had taken her by surprise, too. But he would grab any chance offered.

"Until then, she stays with me," Ian added, pinning Dom with his eyes. "And you'll leave us the fuck alone." Ian's gaze returned to Sabrina, who was crying. He lowered her to the bed, onto her back, and lay on top of her. Whispering against her mouth, he caressed her face, brushing away her tears. Then his lips took hers in a passionate, consuming kiss, and he drew the sheet over them, shutting out the world.

Shutting out him.

A blue haze rose from their bodies and wrapped around them, and energy surged from it. The edges of it pulsed along Dom's skin like a static shock. He jumped up, away from it, and with a final look left the caravan, his fury at Ian making love to his wife, right in front of him, overwhelming his curiosity about what the haze and energy meant.

He had come for an answer and he had one, but it hadn't made him feel better. She might be coming back to him, but she was in there now, fucking Ian, and there she would stay until the dig was done.

Before he could step away from their caravan and head on to work, he heard Sabrina say, her voice sharp, "Why did you do that…just hand me over like you're fucking done with me?"

"Because it's fucking what you want," Ian said in the same tortured tone.

Dom shifted to their window to listen.

"Ian," she said, her voice fragile and trembling. "*Hashkeh*—"

"*Hashkeh*," he interrupted, his voice soft, loving. "You love him and would be with him if not for me. This way is easier on both of us. You never have to say, and I never have to hear you say, that you're choosing him instead of me."

Ian's voice broke at the end of his sentence. He was giving her up even though it hurt him deeply, because it's what he believed she wanted. He was putting her needs before his because he loved her. Ian McCanna was actually in love.

"Love, I'm so sorry," Sabrina said, her words heavy with tears.

"I know," Ian responded. "Me, too."

The sounds of the bed creaking in a slow, steady rhythm, low moans of pleasure, and the blue haze glowing bright from the windows shifted Dom away from the caravan.

Despite what Ian said, it didn't sound like she wanted to come back to her marriage. But if she did come back, he'd make sure she never regretted it.

****

The team's last night at the dig was going full steam at the pit, with food on the grill, kegs of beer, and music by the band that played at the pub. Everyone gathered around their final fire to make some final memories.

Knowing this was their last night together, Sabrina and Ian didn't join the party but stayed in their trailer. In a few hours, they'd have to give up each other. For the rest of this life.

But for now, they wrapped around each other, arms clinging, legs entwining, lips merging. He kissed her hair, her eyes, her chin, her neck, her lips, urgently, tenderly. She kissed his eyes, the eyebrow that liked to raise, his nose, his lips, his neck, everywhere, trying to embed the feel and taste and smell of him inside her.

He whispered sweet, loving words against her lips,

letting his mouth brush across hers, breathing her. They stayed wrapped around each other, emerged in each other, enjoying the comfort of their blue glow swirling around them. Felt it strong and tight on them, like a blanket wrapped around them, linking them in that ethereal slim space of true intimacy that few lovers ever pierce, binding them one to the other, husband and wife, forever lovers. She was the woman in blue his *daideó* had told him to be with, and he was her soul's desire that she had searched for most of her life.

The rasp of his scruff on her skin, the softness of his lips on hers, the caress of his tongue against hers, the movement of his hands across her body buried their love and desire deep inside her, like precious treasure they would unearth and enjoy together when the time was right. She swallowed the blue haze surrounding them, breathed it into her lungs, pulled it inside her, wanting to bind herself with him tighter and from the inside out before they had to say goodbye for what could be a very long time.

Their alarm went off at four-fifty as usual, but this time they wouldn't start their day making love to say hello. They would be making love to say goodbye. Knowing that their time was up made her hold tighter to him, trying to absorb him into her body. Agony gripped her, like her insides being ripped apart. It wasn't just her pain she felt, but Ian's, too, and it was the deepest, sharpest soul-twisting sorrow she had ever felt.

"Sabrina McCanna. You're my heart, my soul, my love, my wife forever, whether we're together or apart." Even though he whispered the sweet declaration, his voice quiet and clear, she heard and felt the sentiment with every cell of her body.

"Ian McCanna. You're my heart, my soul, my love, my husband forever, whether we're together or apart."

He had given her his name. Called her his for eternity. Pledged his eternal love and commitment. And she had to refuse it. Because she was already bound to Dominic.

He claimed her lips, his mouth and tongue and touch expressing the power of his love that mere words could never do. Then with a shattered sob, she left their bed and dressed. She grabbed her packed suitcases and the box with her wind bells inside. Seeing him take it off his trailer had crushed her. She opened the door.

"Breena," he called out. She stopped and took a final look back at him, her view obscured by her tears.

His eyes communicated the love, passion, longing, and belonging that went soul deep. But then he spoke, adding to it.

"I want you to remember that I'm always with you, because our love lives all around you. In the notes of the music you hear. In the flashes of color you see. On the wind and rain and sun that touch your face. In the shimmer of the stars and moon in your hair. In every beat of your heart. The breath in your lungs. The blood through your veins. Our love is eternal."

She closed her teary eyes and nodded, feeling the love in his words, believing them but gaining little comfort from them as she pushed out the door.

****

A pale light shone from the window of the trailer she had once shared with her husband. Likely he was doing a last-minute check on his packing.

She set her luggage by the steps, took a deep breath, wiped the tears from her eyes and face, and knocked on the door.

Dominic answered in his boxers and a smile. "Hi, baby."

"Did I wake you?" she said.

"No. I was double-checking my packing. Come in."

Her stomach clenching, her heart pounding, her legs shaking, she climbed the steps and went inside. She hadn't been here since talking him off the bottle, when she'd told him she still loved him. Tonight there were no musky sex smells. No whiskey smells. No smells of Meggan. No offensive odors at all, except the regret and grief oozing from her pores.

He closed the door and immediately drew her into his arms and hugged her tight. "Welcome home, wife. I've missed you."

Dozens of responses swirled in her head, but none of them felt right, so she said nothing.

He lifted his head enough to look at her, his eyes silently begging her to say something. When she didn't, he lowered his head and touched his lips to hers in a sweet, soft kiss, almost instinctively knowing that anything more wouldn't fit the moment.

He took her hand and led her to the already stripped bed. Memories flooded her as she stared at that bed. Memories of them making love there. Memories of seeing him there with Meggan, fucking their marriage vows. No way in hell would she sit on that bed.

He sat, but she grabbed one of the chairs, moved it close to him and sat. They faced each other, the only sound their soft breathing. It felt strange being here with him in this place that had once been home. It no longer felt like home. She still loved Dominic, but already she felt like they'd been apart for so long that they were different people, like their relationship was little more than a fond memory.

"Where are your things?" he asked, scattering her thoughts.

"Outside." She looked around the trailer, then at her hands, then the floor. Anywhere but at him.

When the uncomfortable silence started to spread over them, his voice again held it back. "Hey, did I tell you that the next dig is near the coast?"

She shook her head.

"Yeah. Not sure how good the waves are, but maybe you can try to teach me to surf again."

This is wrong. You don't belong here.

A deep sense of panic gripped her at her thoughts, and she couldn't breathe even though her lungs were pulling hard on the suddenly limited amount of air in the room. Her heart felt like it was going to explode from overexertion. Her body had gone cold, and nausea churned in her stomach. Feeling trapped in a windowless, airless box, all she wanted to do was jump up from her chair and run out the door for some relief.

"Sabrina, are you okay?" His hand gripped hers tightly, and she felt his eyes on hers, heard the concern in his voice.

She lifted her gaze to his. The love shining in his eyes calmed her. She loved him. And because she loved him, she would do what was right.

Swallowing back the panic, she gripped his hand just as tight. "Before we can move forward, there are some things I need to tell you. About Ian and me."

"We'll have a whole week to ourselves before the next dig starts to talk about…things. Right now, I'd rather talk about us and our future. I booked us a hotel room in Dublin. I know you've been wanting to go back there."

"Baby, we need to talk about things now."

Tension hardened his face, as if he was not happy to have to talk about her and Ian, especially when she'd just come back to him. "Okay. If that's what you need."

"Before I met you, I didn't think I could ever love someone so much. I didn't realize it was possible to be so happy. You changed my life for the better in so many ways."

He squeezed her hand. "I feel the same about you." His calm voice carried a slight edge, like he sensed that the next few moments were going to be life changing and painful.

Her thumb and finger caressed his wedding ring, twisting it. They had sealed their vows with this ring and with the matching one that used to sit on her left hand. She brought his hand to her mouth and kissed the ring. The day she'd slid it onto his finger had been the happiest of her life. Until the day she had found Ian.

"I love you, Dominic Sullivan," she whispered against his band, like a vow.

Her shoulders sagging under the weight of all that had to be said, she pulled in a deep breath, released it slowly, and again found his eyes. "Ian and I are soulmates."

She hated to be so blunt, but no matter how she said it, it wouldn't be easy to hear. Even in the dim light, she saw his face pale a shade or two, then disbelief narrowed his eyes, his mouth.

He pulled his hand from hers. "What?"

"Ena Flanagan told us, and another witch

confirmed it."

"Witches," he spat, shaking his head. "How could they possibly know something like that?"

His scoffing tone hit her in the gut. "There are things in this world that defy explanation. You believe or you don't. My connection with Ian is one of those things. It's real. We're true soulmates. We share one soul."

He said nothing, but his jaw worked like he was thinking plenty, biting back his words until he could examine them. She took advantage of his silence to forge ahead while she still had the courage to do it.

"From the moment Ian touched my hand that first day, he was inside me—my skin, my body, my bones, my head, my heart, my blood, everywhere—like a living entity I could feel and hear and smell and taste. And I was inside him, too, the same way. We didn't know what it was, why it was happening, or how to stop it. We only knew that we wanted each other, with a desire so strong it was painful. Being together, touching, was the only thing that eased that pain. We tried to stop the feelings, tried to stay away from each other, but nothing worked."

His eyes stared into nothingness, his face showing that he was in the midst of a silent meltdown. Or maybe he was just flipping through images of the times he'd found them touching, their heads and bodies close together, his fingers in her hair, his arms pulling her close, her letting him. Their touching might have relieved their suffering, but she knew it had increased his.

"I wanted to tell you, to ask you to help me stay away from him, but—"

"But you didn't. You just allowed yourself to get closer and closer to him."

"I knew it would hurt you and might ruin our marriage and your friendship with Ian."

"And because you didn't want to stop."

She wanted to see his eyes, hold his hand, judge how he was doing. But he wouldn't look at her, and she wouldn't ask anything of him other than to hear her out. "I didn't want to lose you."

"Why tell me now?" he said.

"Because you deserve the truth. Because I should have told you from the beginning. Because I want you to understand why Ian and I did what we did."

His eyes finally came back to hers, giving her a good look at the pain inside him. "What's to understand? You're soulmates. What else could you do?"

The sarcasm in his tone carried a healthy bite, and it was struggle to keep the teeth out of her own response. "You're being facetious, but you're actually right on. The two halves of our soul are constantly pulling us together, demanding that we unite. It's a force that's impossible to ignore."

"How does your soul unite?"

"It starts to unite when we hug. It fully unites when we make love. I'm sure you've seen that blue light that surrounds us when we're together?" At his small nod, she added, "That's our soul uniting."

"I see it shining from the windows of his caravan at night. I saw it surrounding you two at the pub. When you were lying on top of him in the trench. When you were in bed with him."

The anguish in his voice as he clicked back through

his memories, looking for sight of that blue haze, sliced her open. From here on out, it was going to get worse, not better. More painful, not less. Harder, not easier.

"Our soul uniting is a feeling of indescribable joy and pleasure because at that moment we're whole, complete. At the beginning of time, our soul was whole, but for some reason, it was split in two. Our two halves spend every lifetime trying to find each other so they can reconnect.

"As you can imagine, it doesn't happen often. That it did this time is miraculous. I mean, everything that had to fall into place for it to happen…it's incredible. The second Ian and I touched that first day, our souls knew, and it's like they took over, pulling us together so we could unite. We fought it because we love you and didn't want to hurt you. But the harder we fought it, the more painful it became. Staying away from each other hurts, physically and emotionally, like we're being ripped apart from the inside out. But we were willing to go through the torture so you wouldn't. We didn't give in until you and Meggan—"

He held out his hand to stop her as if her explanation was ripping him apart from the inside out. "Okay, I get it. I understand. But I hope *you* understand that when we leave here in a few hours, we'll never see him again. I'll do everything I can to make you happy, but I won't share you with him."

Never see Ian again? At that moment, the cost of giving up her soulmate hit her full force, suctioning away nearly every molecule of energy from her. Never see him again. Never hear his voice or his laugh. Never feel his touch, his kisses, or his emotions. Never get lost in their blue bubble of pleasure. Never make love with him.

She loved Dominic, but Ian was her everything. Without him, her life would have no meaning, no joy. She needed him like she needed to breathe.

She couldn't live without him.

She wouldn't.

Her mouth was dry, all the moisture in her body being used to create tears she so did not want to shed. She bit her bottom lip to keep them at bay as her heart crafted the best way to relay the painful but necessary truth to her husband.

"I love you, Dominic. But I can't leave Ian now that I've found him. I need him too much."

"What are you saying?" Dominic's rough voice told her he already knew the answer.

Her response was stuck behind a ball of tears and was struggling to find its way out. They sat in the thick silence, both knowing their world was about to crack open.

She grabbed his hand, clung to it, and her heart clenched in readiness for the pain that would follow. "Baby, I'm leaving here with Ian."

A distressed sound choked from his throat before he could swallow it back, and he squeezed his eyes shut tight. He pulled away from her and dropped his head into his palms.

She left her chair and sat next to him, putting her hand on his head, her other on his thigh. "I'm so sorry. I know this hurts you, and God, believe me, that's something I never wanted to do."

He sat upright, flinging away her hands with the motion. "I knew it," he said, his voice sharp. "I fucking knew it. I knew Ian wouldn't give you up. The lying piece of shit."

"He would have. For me. Because he thought that's what I wanted. I'm the one who can't give him up."

The fire and anguish in his face revealed what her truth was doing to him. "But you can give *me* up? Our *marriage*?"

"You left our marriage when you slept with Meggan."

"And you left it when you allowed another man into your mind and heart."

"What does that say about us, our marriage, that less than six months into it, we're breaking our vows?"

"It says we're human, and we have some things to work out. But our love is strong enough to overcome anything. When we get away from Ian and Meg, things will go back to how they were before. It'll be even better than before. This was a hard but important lesson for both of us."

She said nothing, just shook her head. He didn't get it. What other words could she use to explain? "It says we're not right for each other. That we belong with other people."

"Did you ever love me? Or was I just all part of the universe's magical plan to get you to Ian?"

"I loved you. I wanted to spend my life with you," she said, her voice breaking with swallowed tears. "I love you still."

"You love me," he scoffed and swiped his hand across his face, as if he was angry at feeling tears there. "Just not enough to be with me, to be my wife."

What he'd said was true, but agreeing with it, out loud, seemed hurtful and unnecessary. She stayed quiet for a long moment, letting him adjust to his new reality, let it settle in around him and come into shocking, aching, focus.

"This is about my cheating, isn't it? You just can't forgive me."

"I have forgiven you—and myself."

"Yourself? You told me you and Ian didn't—"

She shook her head. "We didn't. We didn't even kiss until I moved in with him, after I found you and Meggan in our bed. But I wanted him from the minute I met him. You sensed it, and it hurt you. It's part of the reason you turned to Meggan. Your cheating was as much my fault as it was yours. So, no, it wasn't because you cheated."

"Is it because I didn't do a good job showing you how much I love you? Didn't spend as much time with you as you needed?" His grasping made it clear he still didn't believe her soulmate explanation.

"We had some issues in that area, but I knew you loved me. I felt it. My choice has to do with being where I'm supposed to be, with the man who has been my soulmate from the beginning of time. It also has to do with getting you to where you're supposed to be."

"With my wife, the woman I love, is where I'm supposed to be," he growled.

"Yes," she said with a small nod. "But baby, I'm not her. I'm not the wife you need or the woman you really love."

"No?"

"No. But there is someone here who is."

"If you mean Meg…" He half-heartedly shook his head. "We tried it. She dumped me, too."

"Have you ever asked her why?"

"I know why."

She shook her head. "No, you don't. Go ask her for the truth and don't leave until you have it."

"Not sure the truth matters now."

"The truth always matters. Your truth is, you love her. I saw it every day as you worked together. She wants what you want. She understands what you need, in a way I never could. She's perfect for you, she loves you, and you shouldn't let her get away again."

"Like Ian's perfect for you."

She couldn't stop a small smile from taking over her mouth at her truth. She nodded. After a long moment, he tore his gaze from hers, and they sat together, still, quiet. The thick, prickly tension that slashed them earlier had receded.

"I don't know if you remember," she said finally, "but my mom's a lawyer. I'll have her draw up the divorce papers. If you want to have the marriage annulled so you can still be part of the church and be allowed to marry again, I'll ask her to handle that as well."

Her comment drew his eyes to her. "We had a marriage, Sabrina. It was short but very real and precious to me. I won't diminish it by pretending it never existed."

She nodded, feeling the same way about it. "Thank you for everything, Dominic. You've given me a priceless gift."

"You mean Ian?"

Dominic had given her Ian. Yes. She'd never looked at it that way, but it was the truth. He'd brought her to Ireland where Ian waited for her, and he was letting her go so she could be with him. The debt she owed him could never be fully repaid, but showing him his way back to his true soulmate was a start.

Sabrina rose to stand between his legs and cupped his face in her hands. He flinched at her touch, but she didn't step back.

"Not just Ian." She leaned down and kissed his eyes. "Your love."

****

Dom watched his wife leave, then fell back across the bed, vacillating between his anger and his grief, white-hot tears flooding the eyes she had kissed. He'd lost her. And it had been so fucking easy. It was like Ian had just swooped in and taken her when his back was turned. Their marriage hadn't even lasted six months.

God, he loved her. She was the first woman he'd given his whole heart to. Well. No. That wasn't exactly right. There had been another. The first. And she'd crushed his heart, too.

He thought back to all Sabrina had said, picked it apart, sentence by sentence, word by word. And after a slow thorough review, he saw glimpses of the truth in her explanation.

She and Ian were the same. Both were wild, passionate, and impetuous, wanting adventure, excitement, something new, in all aspects of their lives.

Dom was the opposite in every way, and so was Meg. They were methodical and work-focused, liked the long, steady, routine nature of things, hated change and uncertainty.

It was obvious to anyone with eyes how in sync Sabrina and Ian were, physically, emotionally, sexually. Especially sexually if that blue light surging from their windows day and night was any indication.

He'd loved making love with Sabrina. It was

exciting, off-the-charts passionate, and incredibly pleasurable, but it was also exhausting. He felt constant pressure to come up with new ways to please her in bed. Ian knew all the tricks and could keep her happy for years.

Dom and Meg had great sex, too, but without the need for the dirty talk and kink Sabrina and Ian seemed to thrive on.

And there were more differences.

Every time there was an opening on the traveling international team, Ian had applied. Even though he'd been passed over every time for an older, more experienced digger or photographer, he kept trying because he wanted that life. Sabrina had given up a job offer to be a traveling photojournalist to marry him and was constantly checking the job boards for archaeologist jobs that required traveling, and dropping hints that they should look into them.

He'd be content if he never left Ireland again, if he could work on digs for the rest of his career. Meg wanted that, too. He'd known that about her since he met her. At that first dig. When he'd given her his heart. They were the same, him and Meg. She wanted what he wanted.

A slow easy flush burned through him at the thought. Did Meg still love him, like Sabrina claimed? Seven years ago when she broke up with him, he thought she had only pretended to love him. Maybe he'd been wrong.

He needed answers. And he needed them now.

****

Sabrina dropped her bags outside her home and walked in. The rosy predawn light streaming the new day through the trailer window revealed her lover sitting at the side of the bed as naked and aching as she'd left him.

His gaze, shiny and wet, jumped to hers like he was surprised to see her. Had her indecision about which man to choose blocked his ability to read her decision, or had the sting of his own suffering prevented it?

She smiled, sending him all her love. "When I was eight years old, just after I got trapped in that mansion, my nanny, Claire, took me to her psychic, the kind who uses a crystal ball. She told me my soulmate was in Ireland. For a brief moment, the crystal ball showed us a boy with dark hair. Just as he turned around, pale blue smoke billowed up, obscuring his face. The crystal ball actually turned from clear to blue in seconds.

"When I met Dominic, he and I clicked immediately, so I thought he was the one the psychic had foretold, even though his hair wasn't dark. I took him to meet Claire, happy to show her proof that the prediction had come true. Before we left, she pulled me aside and told me he was a very good man, but he wasn't my soulmate and I'd never be happy with him because I was meant for another, and so was he. She was right."

He stood. "What are you saying?"

"I said goodbye to my husband."

"Goodbye?"

"I told him everything." She undid her shorts. "That you're my soulmate." She pushed them and her panties down and stepped out of them. "That I can't live without you." She lifted her shirt over her head and dropped it to the floor, then unhooked and pulled off her bra. "That I'm leaving here with you."

Ian said nothing, but she could feel happiness pulsing inside him. She stood before him, for the first time ready and able to give all of herself to him. "If you want me."

He lunged forward and drew her body into his, held her tight, like he never wanted to let her go. "I'll always want you. Only you. Forever."

He scooped her up in his arms and laid her on the bed, and they wrapped around each other as their blue smoke wrapped around them, joining them, making them whole, for the first time in their new life together.

****

Dom knocked on Meg's door.

"We need to talk," he said when she opened it.

She stepped back so he could enter. "Is everything okay?"

He closed the door. "That summer we met, why did you break up with me?"

Her gaze, which had been on him, darted away, and she turned from him. "I told you. I thought we were getting too serious."

He caught her arm and made her look at him. "That was bollocks then, and it's bollocks now. Tell me the truth."

"It doesn't matter," she said with a shrug. "You're married."

The force of Sabrina's words swept through him, and he knew she had been right. "The truth always matters."

Meg's face went pink with whatever was going on inside her. "The second Jack introduced you that first day, I fell in love with you. I know that sounds ridiculous, but I remember my heart was pounding so hard I thought everyone around me could hear it. I'd never been with a guy before, and I knew in that moment you'd be the one. And I wasn't afraid, because it was the most right thing I'd ever do."

"I was your first? You should have told me."

"Why? So you could have gone with a more experienced girl?"

"No," he said, remembering that night, remembering that he'd taken her like a rutting bull that first time because he'd been so desperate to be inside her. Oh, he hadn't been a total dick. He'd gotten her off with his mouth and fingers first, but when he'd slid his rock-hard cock into her tight wet pussy, he'd shot his wad almost instantly, breaking Ian's first cardinal rule—the woman always comes first. "So I could have been gentler with you. Made it special."

"It was special because it was with you. After we made love that first time, I vowed I'd do whatever it took to stay with you."

"Uh-huh. And just how did breaking up with me play into that vow?"

"It's a long story, Dom. And you're not going to like it."

"Tell me anyway."

"I'd only had enough money to stay three weeks at the dig. I begged Jack to let me stay on for the full summer so I could be with you. I told him I'd do extra work, do anything to get to stay. He said no. 'Rules are rules,' he said. But I convinced him."

Jack was a stickler for rules. He didn't cave for just anything, especially to teenaged girls' matters of the heart. "How?"

"I had sex with him."

Dom closed his eyes on the hot emotions surging through him—anger for Jack, sorrow for Meg. He felt like he'd been kicked in the balls. "Ah, Meggie," he said and drew her in his arms, cradling her. "You were seventeen. You should have reported the son-of-a-bitch for rape."

"His wife had just left him, and he was twisted out of his mind. I used his grief to get what I wanted."

"It was still wrong."

"It was right because it got me what I wanted. You."

"But you didn't have me," he said, easing out of their embrace. "You broke up with me."

"Yeah, well that was Ian's doing."

The only two women he'd loved and Ian had torn both of them from him. How many more times had his *best friend* fucked up his life? "What did he do?"

"He walked in on Jack and me. He pulled him off me, punched him in the face, and cussed him out. Then he told me I had two choices. I could tell you I'd cheated, or I could break up with you. If I did neither, he'd tell you what I did, knowing you'd break up with me. Either way, I was going to lose you. So I broke up because I thought it was my best chance of getting you back eventually. I told Jack I'd ruin him unless he got me on whatever dig you were assigned to from that point on. He agreed. Which is how I ended up on your team."

Dom was quiet, digesting everything she'd said, putting together pieces that hadn't made sense before. "If only you'd told me the truth back then, about wanting to stay with me."

"Would it have made a difference?"

"Despite what I told you when you broke up with me, I didn't want us to end after the dig was over. I was wracking my brain, trying to come up with a way we could stay together. I was going to tell Jack to keep my pay and let you stay on. You should have been honest with me, trusted me. I would have found a way for us."

Joy radiated from her teary eyes. "I didn't know you felt that way."

"That was the best summer of my life. We had something special. I loved you, Meg. I thought you loved me. When you dumped me out of the blue like that, it crushed me."

"I did love you, so much. The last thing I wanted to do was dump you, but I thought you'd dump me for fucking another man, especially your mentor, even if it was for what I considered the right reason." When he didn't respond, she continued. "Why are you asking about this now, after all these years?"

"Something Sabrina said to me earlier. About you."

"What did she say?" she scoffed, as if saying she was sure it was bad.

"That you and I want the same things. That we're perfect for each other. That I'd be a fool to let you go again."

Her wide eyes blinked in shock. "Sabrina said that?"

He nodded and put his hands to her face. "Do you agree with her?"

"Absolutely."

He kissed her, but when she wrapped her arms around him and kissed him deeper, he slowly drew back and looked at her.

"Sabrina is…" He took a deep breath and released it. "She's leaving me for Ian." God, it was like a knife in his chest to say it aloud. He swallowed back the fire threatening to spew from the torment swirling in his gut. "I can't make a commitment to you right now, other than I think we should try again."

"I'm interested," she said with no hesitation.

"Wait. I need you to know where my head is before you agree. I still love her, and if she walked through that door now and said she'd changed her mind and wanted me back, I'd go."

She took a couple of steps back, out of his arms, and had put on that stone-face mask she adopted whenever her emotions were about to spill. Clearly, his confession had hurt her. He wouldn't blame her if she kicked his arse out. He deserved it.

"I'm interested," she said, her voice strong and sure, "but first…I have a few other confessions to make. If you still want to try after hearing them, I'll be with you. However you want. For as long as you want."

The weight of unloaded secrets already sat heavy on his shoulders. He wasn't sure he could carry many more. But he'd come here for the truth, and he was going to get it. He had to know. Everything. "Tell me."

"Ena Flanagan? Leader of *Choisant*? She's my cousin. And a witch. The main reason she was here at the dig was because I paid her to put a spell on Sabrina and Ian so they'd fall in love and you'd leave her or she'd leave you."

His hands clenched into fists as fire raced through him. "You intentionally set out to destroy my marriage?"

"This was my last chance to get you back."

493

"So all this fucking turmoil was because of you?"

She shook her head. "No. The spell didn't work."

"The hell it didn't. That spell made them think they're soulmates. It's why she's leaving me." He grabbed her arm. "Let's go." He pulled her toward the door.

"Where?"

"To Ian's. You're going to tell them what you did so I can get my fucking life back."

A look of hurt washed across her face, and the look pierced his heart, but he ignored it, pulling her forward.

She yanked her arm away. "The spell didn't work because they *are* soulmates. They're the real thing—two bodies, one soul."

"Tell me how you know that."

"I called Ena to tell her the spell worked perfectly. She laughed at me, said it hadn't worked because their soulmate connection *extinguished the spell.* Her words."

He hadn't totally believed the soulmate connection story when Sabrina confessed it, but with Meg corroborating it, the ramifications hit him solidly in the chest. Sabrina was Ian's woman in blue. The woman he was supposed to be with. His soulmate. And he was hers.

"And you believe her?" he asked, still hoping against hope.

"Yes. She could have lied, taken credit for their obvious attraction, but she didn't. She wouldn't lie to me."

He dropped down onto the edge of her bed, suddenly spent, fully defeated. He sighed. "What else do you have to confess?"

"I, uh…" She rubbed her forehead. "I'm the one who cut the wire in your caravan that caused the fire."

"Jaysus, Meg!" He gritted his teeth, fighting back the anger flaring inside him. "You could have killed Sabrina, or someone else."

"I only meant to cut the power so she'd be without a fan, the fridge, the lights. I had a feeling she'd go to Ian...and she did. But when I cut the wire, I got shocked. It scared me, and I didn't try again. I swear, I never meant to hurt her. I didn't realize the danger it would put her in, and I deeply regret it."

He shook his head and ground his teeth, too furious to speak.

"Luckily, Ian was there to save her," she added. "It's like he always knows when she needs him and is there. Like her own personal superhero."

Meg sat beside him, and he could feel her eyes on him even though he was staring at the floor.

"I told you I didn't believe Sabrina's story about Ian's soul coming to save her, but I lied," she said. "I saw her that night. She was outside the caravan, trying to get in, begging him to come out of there. She was scared to death he was going to burn up. She was tearing out the screens, would have climbed back in had he not come out of his caravan and pulled her away when he did.

"She thought he was in there. She *saw* him in there, Dom, even though it was impossible because he was behind her, holding on to her. It wasn't until she realized he *was* holding her that she knew he wasn't in there. And then she fell apart in relief, sobbing in his arms.

"There was no reason for her to come out of the

caravan on her own will that night. She was asleep. She probably wouldn't have smelled the smoke or seen the fire. Ian's soul, or whatever the hell you want to call it, got her out."

Her voice was shaky as she spoke, and he felt her tremble beside him.

"It's so fucking freaky, it still gives me night terrors." She put her hand on his, squeezed her fingers around him, and clung to him, as if she needed his touch, his comfort. "Dom, Ian's soul saved Sabrina. I don't know how. I just know it did. They're connected in some magical way that's real and miraculous."

Hearing the story from Meg's point of view supported Sabrina's telling of that night's events. Maybe it had been short-sighted of him to doubt her and the possibility of supernatural goings-on around them. Had he been more open-minded to the possibilities, he might have gotten Sabrina away from Ian before they solidified their bond.

"I'm almost afraid to ask, but anything else?"

She linked her fingers with his. "Every crazy thing I did, I did because I love you. Always have, always will. If you give me a chance to be your only, I'll never cheat on you, and I'll never leave you for another man because you're the only man I want, the only man I've ever wanted. You're *my* soulmate Dominic Sullivan, and I don't need a witch to tell me so."

He didn't know how to respond to her soulmate claim, but he knew that had she not dumped him that summer, they might still be together. That was how close they'd been, how much he'd loved her. Back then, it had felt like he had found his *one*. Like she'd been made for him. Right up to the time she broke him in half.

Could he trust her again, after everything she'd done? Could he open a space in his heart for her that wasn't already filled with Sabrina?

"I'm sorry I hurt you," she said. "I know it'll be hard for you to trust me, but I swear, everything I did was because I couldn't stand the thought of living my life without you in it. Give me a chance to remind you that you love me."

Chapter Thirty-One

When the sun rose, the sleepy and hung-over team gathered at the remains of the fire pit. One by one, they said their goodbyes and left the site. The team would take two weeks off before gathering at the next dig, but management would have to be onsite in a week to set up.

Soon, only Ian and Sabrina, Dominic and Meggan, and Sean and Kristin remained.

"This has to be the strangest dig we've ever worked," Sean said, seeing Sabrina in Ian's arms and Meggan and Dominic standing together.

"I told you that witch put a spell on our camp," Kristin said, hugging Sean to her. "Aren't you glad I threw a protective shield over us?"

"I am," he said through a smile, drew her closer, and kissed her forehead. His gaze cut to Dominic then to Ian. "You four working the same dig together is a disaster waiting to happen. You know that."

A proud little grin spread across Ian's face. "Breena and I aren't going to the new dig."

"Oh? Where are you going?" Sean asked.

"Italy."

Sean's eyes lit up, and he gave a tentative smile. "You got the job?"

Ian nodded and licked his lips. "You're looking at the new Media Director-International and his lovely and talented Assistant Media Director."

Sean and Kristin both stepped forward and hugged Ian, then Sabrina. Dominic and Meggan stayed put.

"Congratulations mate," Sean said, shaking Ian's hand. "It's what you've always wanted."

"Thanks. It's what we both want." Ian smiled at Sabrina and kissed her. "I officially resign my position in The Trinity. It's up to you and Dom to carry on as a Duo."

Sean and Kristin exchanged a knowing look.

Ian caught it and chuckled. "What did you do?"

"We've both taken jobs at HQ."

"What?" The question exploded from Dominic's mouth. "You're giving up digging?" At Sean's nod, he asked, "Why?"

Sean's face flushed, and his smile about floated off his face. "We don't want to raise our child on a dig site."

Shocked silence gave way to more laughter, hugs, and congratulations. Through it all, Sabrina watched Dominic. Although he congratulated Sean and Kristin and tried to look happy for them as they shared details of their upcoming new life, she knew he was miserable.

Life as he knew it was unraveling, and there was nothing he could do to stop it or reverse it. It left him feeling out of control, like he was dangling by a thread, and he resented and was frightened by it. She could see it, feel it. His lips remained pressed into a rigid seam. His eyes were hard and glassy. His body was tense, drawing every bit of strength he possessed to hold his emotions in check.

Then his hand took Meggan's and held it in a tight grip, like it was his only lifeline and he was drowning.

An agonizing new reality had been dumped on him with no warning, giving him no time to prepare. His two best friends would no longer be at the site with him. His wife of six months had left him and would be divorcing him. He'd been betrayed by a man, who, for twenty years, he'd called brother. Two of his team's most knowledgeable senior members had abandoned him, leaving him short-handed. All he had was Meggan and the other teammates.

Sabrina had foolishly once said she didn't believe in regrets, but she suddenly felt the weight of the regret that she'd hurt him so profoundly and couldn't be there to help him through this rough time. She hoped she was right about the depth of Meggan's love for him. He was going to need her. The thought that Red might not be there for him the way he needed shredded the already frayed ends of her emotions. Feeling Ian's arm tighten around her didn't ease her concerns but knowing he understood and felt the same regret helped her feel better about her decision.

The friends talked a few minutes more, all of them soaking in the fact that this would be the last time they'd see each other for a while, and that the next time they came together, everything would be different. They weren't just saying goodbye for now, they were saying goodbye to a bond that had connected them since they were toddlers. They were saying goodbye to the Holy Hell Trinity as it had existed. It had split into three, leaving each man to go off and bond with a woman who made him whole. The necessary but painful evolution was sad and joyous at the same time.

Sean and Kristin were the first to leave, and then it was time for the most painful part of this goodbye.

Dominic and Ian faced each other in buzzing silence.

"If you fuck her over," Dominic said, "like you've done every woman you've ever known, I swear I'll kill you."

"You think I'd do that to her?"

"You don't know how to do anything different."

Dominic's comments fisted Ian's hands at his sides, but he held his anger in check. She knew he didn't want his last words with his long-time friend to be bitter ones. "I love her, Dom. She comes first in my life. For the rest of my life."

"I hope you mean that. For her sake."

"I do." Ian held out his right hand, palm open, in an ancient gesture denoting trust, honesty, and respect. "I give you my word on it, and I've never lied to you, brother."

Dominic hesitated, but he took Ian's hand.

The cold, restrained handshake was so unlike the warm, from-the-heart embrace they'd given each other when she'd first arrived at the dig. They'd never get that closeness back. It had been too damaged. But she hoped their relationship would not be this strained forever.

"I hope we can find our way back to being friends again," Ian said, mirroring her thought. "I'll miss not having you in my life."

Dominic pulled his hand away. "Some hurts go too deep to be forgiven. This might be one of them."

Ian nodded briefly, and she felt the stinging wounds Dominic's words inflicted. She took some comfort in knowing that he hadn't outright said no way.

Dominic's emotion-filled gaze shifted to her. "I

need a minute with my wife." Without waiting for an answer, he took her hand in his. Together they walked up the hill to Ian's packed-up jeep.

"We've said everything there is to say," he said. "I just wanted a last moment alone with you."

She had wanted that, too, but didn't feel entitled to ask anything of him. "Stupid question, I know, but how are you?" It felt like forever ago that she'd told him she was leaving him.

"I feel like I've been ripped open and the buzzards are enjoying what's left of me. I'm pissed—the American pissed, not the Irish. But at the same time... I'm awed by the miracle of you and Ian, that you found each other. I want the best for you, you know. I want you to be happy."

"I want that for you, too. Even if it means giving you back to Meggan. You have no idea how much that pisses me off," she said with a rough laugh. "Very much the American pissed."

He grinned. "You never got to see her good side."

"No, I didn't," she said. "But *you* did, and that's all that matters."

They reached Ian's jeep, and he let go of her hand. He looked at her with such love, but his grin was gone. "You and I still love each other, but we're ending our marriage. It's like the doctor cutting out a healthy organ and throwing it in the garbage. It feels wrong."

"You're right. It does."

"Then change your mind."

As she stared into his eyes, all the love she had for him welled up, front and center, letting her feel it. It had been an agony-filled decision to leave him. But she wouldn't have made it if she weren't sure. Her gaze dropped to the ground as she gave him her silent no by way of a small head shake.

He dug into his pocket, pulled out her ring, then took her left hand and slid it into place. "I want you to keep it as a reminder of what we once meant to each other."

Too big, the band no longer fit, as if the person she had been and the person she was now were two different people. She'd take it off and put it away later, but for now, it would stay on her hand where he had put it, as a last gift to the husband she loved.

She met his eyes. "Will you keep your ring, too? You know, to remember me?"

He nodded. "I will, though I won't need it to remember you. Even when I'm an old man, my mind as full of holes as my *mamo's* Irish lace doilies, I'll remember you. Your face, your voice, your smell, your taste, the touch of your hand, the feel of your mouth. I'll remember how I had everything I ever wanted when we made love. I'll remember how much I loved you."

"Aw, baby," she said in a strangled whisper and brought her hand to her mouth. Tears blurring her vision, she moved into his body, dropping her head against his chest and wrapping her arms around him.

He held her close, tight, full well knowing that it was for the last time, that the moment he stepped away she'd no longer be his, or he hers. This moment was the divorce, not the legal paperwork that would come later.

"I'll always love you, Sabrina Sullivan," he said in a harsh whisper against her trembling mouth and kissed in the words, sealing them inside her. Then he spun away and charged down the hill like it was impossible for him to stay even a second longer.

****

"You were wrong," Ian said to Meggan, who stood with him watching the loves of their lives walk up the hill to his packed jeep.

"About?"

He felt her eyes on him, so he turned to face her. "You said you and I would end up broken and bleeding at the end of this one. You were wrong."

"Makes you feel good to say that, doesn't it?"

"Fuck, yeah," he said with a grin.

"That's okay, because I'm pretty happy to be wrong," she said grinning back.

"There's something else I need to tell you," he said, "and since I may not get another chance…"

"Nothing you say can ruin my good mood, so do your worst."

"On the first day of each of the summer field schools, Dom, Sean, and I would name all the girls who were there. We were crude and horny twenty-four/seven back then, so the names usually centered on their physical attributes or what we wanted to do to them."

"No! I'm shocked," Meggan mocked.

"Hold your shock and awe til the end," Ian teased. "When I saw you, I told them, 'I'm calling the redhead *Apricunt* because I bet her cunt tastes just like a sweet, juicy apricot.'"

A pink stain swept across her freckle-dusted cheeks at his words, making her look soft and pretty, like the first time he met her. "They laughed," he continued, "then Dom said, 'I'll let you know.' That was his way of calling firsts on you. It bugged me I wasn't getting you first—I'd named you so it was my right—but I backed off, knowing I'd get my turn."

"Your turn? Why did you think you'd get a turn?"

He grinned. "That's the way it worked in the Trinity, love. We shared."

She rolled her eyes, shook her head, trying to hide a grin. "Why are you telling me this?"

"Dom never did let us know, and we never got a turn, because he fell for you. And when Dom fell for a girl, he didn't share—her or his private moments with her. He loved you, Meg."

She blinked her eyes and quickly lowered her head, but before she did, he swore those were tears in her eyes, something he'd thought her incapable of.

"The name I gave you wasn't meant as an insult until you hurt my friend. And you hurt him bad. I'm sorry I said it in front of the team at the pub. I was out of my mind about Breena, and it just came out. The minute you left the table, Jack cut into us, threatened our jobs if we used the word again, so you won't have to fight that battle on the next dig. Not that Dom would let anyone get away with it. Because he still loves you. In fact, I don't think he ever stopped loving you."

She swiped her eyes with her fingers and met his gaze. "I never stopped loving him."

"I know." He sighed. "I have no room to talk…" His eyes darted up the hill to where Dom and Breena were hugging—and fuck, kissing—then back to her, "But I'm begging you….don't hurt him again."

"I won't." She lifted her chin slightly in defense, as if she were insulted he'd said it. "I have him, and that's all I ever wanted."

He nodded, and seeing Dom coming down the hill, he hugged Meggan, and she actually hugged him back.

Odd how things worked out. He had been as close to Dom as brothers, and now their relationship was strained. His relationship with Meggan had been strained since she hurt Dom, and now it was slightly less so. Such was life.

"Be happy, *frotch*," he said.

"You, too, *heartthrob*."

Ian let her go when Dom joined them, and he caught Dom's gaze and held it in a silent farewell. He wanted to thank him for bringing Breena to him, but he didn't see it going over well. He would thank him by keeping his word to put her and her happiness first in his life, he decided as he ran up the hill to his soulmate.

His *Hashkeh* jumped into his arms, and he swung her around, kissing her, eliminating her husband's last kiss from her mouth, both of them laughing like joy-filled kids on summer vacation. In that moment, he knew. Loving Breena, keeping her happy, would be the most fulfilling thing he'd ever done.

****

Dom watched his ex-wife drive away with his ex-best friend. He understood their connection, was awed by it, but it didn't mean it was easy to watch her leave with him. It didn't mean he didn't carry hard feelings toward both of them. Everything in him had wanted to handcuff her to him, carry her away to his SUV, speed away, and never let her go. But such extremes wouldn't have saved their marriage. Wouldn't have made her stop loving Ian. And as much as he loved her, he didn't want to be with a woman who couldn't give him all her love. She had spared him that by leaving him.

He'd read somewhere that grief changes shape but never ends. He hoped that was wrong. Hoped that one day he'd be able to forgive their betrayal, like Sabrina had forgiven him for his. Hoped that one day he'd be on the other side of this labyrinth of sorrow and brokenness he was in and on his way back to whole and happy.

He felt Meg's arms slide around his waist, felt her body curl warm into his side. Maybe he could with her help.

His arm went around her and held her tight as his eyes followed the jeep barreling down the road out of sight. He felt her warmth, inhaled her scent, and absorbed her into his body, feeling peace slowly settle over his ragged nerves, like a warm blanket over a shivering body on a cold rainy night settled the chills. A sense of déjà vu hit him. He'd been here with her before, and it had meant everything to him. Maybe it could again, in time.

They both had changed in the passing years, of course, but the core of who they were remained and still dovetailed nicely with the other. He felt it as they worked alongside each other nearly every day for the past seven years. During their fun and crazy times. During their occasional bouts of sex.

He felt comfortable with her, the kind of comfort that comes from having lived and worked with someone for a long time. He didn't have to explain himself to her. She knew what he was about, what was important to him, what he needed, what he liked, what he wanted. They had history, him and Meg, friendship, companionship. It would be a good base on which to build something more.

And with Sean and Ian gone, she was all he had left.

"So," she said, "we have a week 'til we have to ready the dig. What do you want to do?"

She was smiling, a light flaring in her eyes that sparked one in his. She had always been eager in the sack, responsive, giving. Remembering their deep, easy way stirred his dick. A week of raw sex would start the healing process, start working the feelings of hurt and anger out of his system, start reconnecting the two of them. She'd said she was game, despite the vague commitment he could offer. He'd test that vow.

"I heard the B&B in town is nice," he said.

"I heard the same thing. But don't get the idea we'll be sleeping much."

"Oh?" An easy grin slid across his face. "What will we be doing?"

"I'm going to make you fall in love with me again, and you're going to lie back and enjoy every second of it."

At hearing her bold words, the truth hit him square in the gut. He wasn't so sure he'd ever fallen out of love with her. "Do what you want with me. I won't stop you. Just no…"

His grin faded, and his gaze cut from hers to the direction Sabrina had gone. Pain squeezed every inch of his body at the memory of what he and his wife had done in another B&B room not so long ago.

"No what?" Meg asked softly when he didn't finish his statement.

His gaze returned to hers. "No scarves, handcuffs, blindfolds, or sex toys."

Humor and fire lit her eyes, and the throaty sound of her laughter, the promises buried in it, wrapped around his fractured heart. "We never needed them before. We won't need them now."

It wouldn't be easy getting over Sabrina, but having Meg by his side, in his bed, might first numb his pain, then eventually, hopefully, erase it. It would take a hell of a lot of sex to get to that point. Need gripped his body in a hot, tight fist, turning his cock into a steel rod just thinking about it.

As they walked up the hill to the SUV packed with their commingled possessions, he realized he wasn't waiting until they got to the B&B to have his tasty little Apricunt again. The hood would do just fine.

Epilogue

About a year and a half later

The windows were open to take advantage of the cool breeze off the raindrops. Of the lulling beat of the fragrant rain pinging the ground, the thick foliage, and the roof of the tiny trailer. Of the comforting tinkling of their dancing wind bells. The sounds and smells and the feel of the warm and familiar naked body against hers in their bed filled Breena with a contentment and satisfaction she'd never known with anyone but her soulmate. Her everything.

In a while, they'd have to get up and edit the videos they'd taken before the Peruvian rain had called a halt to the digging and therefore the photographing. But for now, she'd enjoy the gift of time with her husband in their bed. The beat of his heart, the easy rise and fall of his breathing, filled her with peace, and she sighed.

Their lives had changed dramatically since they'd met. Fiona had performed a handfast ceremony the day they left that first dig, and they made the marriage legal when her divorce from Dominic was finalized some months later.

Their new job had taken them to five countries so far and given them the chance to spend every day, every night together, living the life of adventure they'd always wanted. They were closer and happier than they'd ever been. Everything was perfect. But everything was about to change. He just didn't know it yet.

She sighed again, smiling into his chest. She would tell him. Today. Now.

"What's all that sighing about?" he asked.

Hearing Ian's voice rumble through his chest brought her out of her carefully hidden thoughts. "Oh, the usual. About how happy I am you're my husband. How happy I am you're in my life. How happy I am about…everything. Blah, blah, blah. Stuff you've heard a million times." *You're my life, Ian. My everything.*

"Are you?" he asked.

"Am I what?"

"Happy?"

The question shocked her. She looked into his eyes, and the emotion she felt sent a chill shimmying up her spine. Oh, God, he was serious. The man who could read her thoughts and emotions as easily as a book was asking her whether she was happy.

"Why would you ask me that?" She tried to hide the panic in her voice with a little chuckle. "I tell you all the time and show you all the time. You read my every thought."

"See, that's the thing, love. I haven't been able to read you, not well, anyway, for about a month. You're like cell reception through a tunnel." His phone rang, and he grumbled at the interruption. "I know you're keeping something from me." He grabbed the device and looked at it. "It's Sean," he said, then answered. "Hey, mate. That son of yours arrive yet?"

After a pause to listen to Sean's response, he laughed. "Congratulations! Give me the highlights."

This was the second child for Sean and Kristin, who also had daughter Tara, and three months ago Dominic and Meggan had a daughter they'd named Olivia, making Ian the only one of the Holy Hell Trinity who didn't have kids. She knew he longed to join his friends in their new trinity—fatherhood.

The two friends talked for a few minutes, then Ian wrapped up with a, "Yeah, you, too. Take care, man."

He was still smiling when he hung up. "They named him Merrick. Eight pounds, two ounces, twenty-two inches long. Big healthy lad, wild mop of blond curls like his da. Krissy's exhausted but happy. They'll send photos."

"Wow, two kids in two years. They're not wasting time."

"Yeah," he said, his voice wistful, far away, the emotions oozing from his thoughts all about how it would feel to hold his own child and be calling his friends with the happy news.

She settled her head back on his chest and wrapped her arm around him, hoping to coax him out of his thoughts.

He absently caressed her hair with his fingers. "You once told me you wanted to have my baby," he said finally. "If you've changed your mind, at least tell me why." His voice was resolved, as if he believed she had.

"What makes you think I've changed my mind?"

"Whenever I bring it up, you say the timing's not right."

"We move every few months and live in a tent or, if we're lucky, a tiny trailer," she said lightly so he'd know her words weren't a criticism of their chosen lifestyle. "Our work is demanding and can be dangerous. Remember Turkey? I love our life, but it's not really conducive to starting a family. A baby would change everything. Are you ready for that?"

"It won't change everything."

"Just how we live, how we work, what we—"

"We'd bring a baby into our life as it exists," he interrupted and held her tighter. "Kids need love, food, and someplace out of the heat and cold to be happy, not a big house in the burbs with a white picket fence surrounding it and a minivan in the parkway. Look, we don't have to have all the particulars figured out today. Let's just decide whether we want kids."

"Sounds like a definite yes from you."

"I want a baby with you, Breena." He kissed her, as if he wanted to make sure she felt the truth of his words. "Our love is a miracle. A child created in that love, born of that love, is a miracle on its own. A piece of you and me combined into one entity that will live on when we're gone. It's walking, talking proof."

"Proof of what?" she asked.

"Of our love, our connection, our commitment. Of the incredible gift we've been given."

The love and joy radiating from his eyes, his face, his body was palpable. She half expected to hear a hallelujah chorus rising up any second.

"You're not worried about what Fiona told us?" she asked. "That we'll always put our relationship ahead of everything in our life? You know we still struggle with that, even after nearly two years."

"We would never neglect our child. He's you. He's me. He's us."

She rose, straddled his hips, and lay atop his chest,

staring into his eyes, trying to hold her *serious* face in place. "*Hashkeh*, I'm sorry, but…" Her hesitation stripped the baby-glow from his face, and he swallowed back a lump of disappointment. She felt like shit for torturing him. "I am keeping something from you."

His eyebrow lifted, and his hazy eyes became clear and focused on hers. "What?"

"I'm not working the next dig with you."

"Why?"

The warm glow filling her womb spread throughout her body and lifted a smile onto her face she couldn't stop. "I'll be way too pregnant to crawl around in the dirt taking pictures."

His eyes rounded and blinked a few times. A sappy sweet, loving little grin grew on his face. "Breena…" he whispered, his voice a bit shaky. He rolled her over, onto her back, and lay at her side. He put his hand low on her flat belly. "*Hashkeh*. You're…. We're…"

She'd never known him to be at a loss for words. "You're going to be a da," she said, joy and love softening her voice.

The smile took over his face, and he laughed, then threw his head back and yelled up to the sky, "I fucking love you, Sabrina McCanna."

Thunder boomed overhead at his dramatic declaration, like a sonic fist bump. He laughed again, and she laughed with him as he wrapped around her and dotted kisses her all over her face, then down her body. When his head was at her stomach, he kissed the spot where his baby was growing and ran his lips over it in a loving caress.

"How far?" He ran his palm over it, as if trying to feel it.

Her hand settled on his head in a soft caress. "About two months, I think. I haven't been to the doctor to know for sure. Are you happy?"

He kissed the spot again, then found her eyes. "I'm the happiest man on Earth. Not just because of the baby. Because of you. Because you chose a life with me."

"Best decision I ever made," she said, unlocking her thoughts so he could read them all.

He kissed back up her body, and when he reached her lips, he gave her the most tender and loving kiss he'd ever given her. She hadn't believed it possible, but it felt like the baby, or simply news of it, had propelled them into a higher circle of love, one even more euphoric than the one that came before it, one saved for lovers who had created life from their love.

"You're happy you're having my baby," he said through the smile that hadn't left his face since she'd told him the news. He'd been in her head to confirm that her emotions and thoughts matched her words. "You love him already."

She nodded. "I love him because he's ours. I love him even more because he's yours…because you know how I feel about you."

He captured her face with his hand, traced her lips with his thumb. "You love me."

"Yes." She smiled. "But only forever."

As long as she was with Ian, their love alive inside them like an eternal flame, it didn't matter where they lived, what they did, how many kids they had. They would be happy. Always.

"Fuckin' A, love," he growled as he eased into her welcoming warmth.

Their blue haze surrounding them, growing stronger, tightening on them, binding them one to the other, they danced among the stars again, their son bathed in that light and cradled in their love.

About the Author

By day, I'm a writer and editor for a professional association. By night, I'm an author of erotic romance. In between, I fulfill myriad other roles.

I write the kind of books I like to read—stories where sexual heat sizzles off the page and the characters fall hard into lust and soft into love. When I'm not writing about passion, I'm indulging in it— yoga, hiking, laughing with friends over hot *chile* and cold beer, and being lazy and crazy with family.

Learn more about Sophia at
http://sophiaryan.webs.com

To chat with Sophia Ryan and other Wild Rose Press authors of erotic romance, join us at www.groups.yahoo.com/group/thewilderroses.

Also Available

Sin City Alibi
by Sophia Ryan

http://amzn.com/B014JLZ11I

Jumping libido-first into a cliché Vegas fling is the last thing on Dani Parker's mind when she flies to Sin City for some R&R after her lover/boss, Elliott, dumps her. But an innocent night of flirty fun with a sexy hunk she knows only as Matt whirlwinds into a sinfully hot weekend. Back home, she discovers her boss has been murdered, her Vegas fling is heading the investigation into financial irregularities for the company she works for, and she's smack-dab in the middle of both.

Matt Collins has filled his life with work and no-strings sex since the day his heart went on lock-down. No woman ever cracked that lock. Until Dani. Now all he wants is her in his bed and in his life, but the odds for success are stacked against him. She can't accept his conditions for love, there's evidence suggesting she and her former lover embezzled from the company, and the cops arrest her for Elliott's murder. His gut tells him she's innocent and he wasn't just an alibi, but his heart remembers the brutal past that still haunts him.

When everything Matt and Dani hold dear is on the line, they'll learn that sometimes risking everything leads to the most satisfying payouts.

Also Read

To-Do Him List
Lipstick Diaries

by

Denise Marie

http://amzn.com/B0100NNM6K

With her life expectancy most likely measured in weeks, Isabelle Chambers jettisons her risk-free, missionary-position life for a to-do list that is short on dull and long on passion.

Cole Davies may be living his dream as lead singer for Scandals complete with fame, fortune, and unlimited female attention, but life still feels incomplete. So when Isabelle takes her list viral on Twitter he can't resist her appeal.

From flying to bondage and touring with the band to getting it on in public, Isabelle's To-Do Him List turns them both inside out. Then things get hotter than either planned and they both need to decide what they'll risk for love.

Thank you for purchasing this
publication of The Wild Rose Press, Inc.
If you enjoyed the story, we would appreciate
your letting others know by leaving a review.
For other wonderful stories, please visit our
on-line bookstore at www.wilderroses.com.

For questions or more
information contact us at
info@thewildrosepress.com.

The Wild Rose Press, Inc.
www.thewilderroses.com

Stay current with The Wild Rose Press, Inc.
Like us on Facebook
https://www.facebook.com/TheWildRosePress
And Follow us on Twitter
https://twitter.com/WildRosePress

www.ingramcontent.com/pod-product-compliance
Lightning Source LLC
Chambersburg PA
CBHW052348020726
47503CB00001B/155